THE LOST RELIC

Scott Mariani grew up in the historic town of St Andrews, Scotland and now lives in the wilds of Wales. *The Lost Relic* is the sixth book in *The Sunday Times* bestselling series featuring ex-SAS hero and former theology scholar Ben Hope, translated into over twenty languages worldwide. Scott is also the author of the Vampire Federation series, which started with the novel *Uprising* (Avon, June 2010). A sequel, *The Cross*, is due to be published during autumn 2011. For further information please visit: www.scottmariani.com

By the same author

SCOTT MARIANI

The Lost Relic

AVON

AVON

A division of HarperCollins*Publishers*
77–85 Fulham Palace Road,
London W6 8JB

www.harpercollins.co.uk

A Paperback Original 2011
1

A catalogue record for this book is
available from the British Library

ISBN-13: 978-1-84756-197-8

Set in Minion by Palimpsest Book Production Limited,
Falkirk, Stirlingshire

Printed and bound in Great Britain by
Clays Ltd, St Ives plc

Mixed Sources
Product group from well-managed
forests and other controlled sources
www.fsc.org Cert no. SW-COC-001806
© 1996 Forest Stewardship Council
FSC

FSC is a non-profit international organisation established
to promote the responsible management of the world's forests.
Products carrying the FSC label are independently certified
to assure consumers that they come from forests that are managed
to meet the social, economic and ecological needs
of present and future generations.

Find out more about HarperCollins and the environment at
www.harpercollins.co.uk/green

Acknowledgements

For much of the historical background to this novel I am heavily indebted to my late and sadly-missed friend Contessa M. Manzini, whose spellbinding recollections about her life in 1920s Italy partly inspired me to write *The Lost Relic*. Thanks also to Tim Boswell for invaluable insider knowledge on SOCA and special police operations; as well as to all those others whose efforts, great or small, have contributed to the creation of this book.

To Noah Lukeman

Prologue

Italy
October 1986

The old woman was alone that night, just as she had lived alone in her rambling country house near Cesena for many years. She'd spent the evening in her studio, as she did most evenings, surrounded by her precious paintings and her beautiful things, putting the final touches to a piece of artwork she believed to be the finest she had produced in a long while.

The work that was to be her last.

It was just after ten, and the old woman was thinking about going to bed, when she heard the crash of breaking glass and the six armed men stormed into her home. They grabbed her roughly, forced her down into a chair, held guns to her head. Their leader was a big, burly man with a nose that had been broken more than once. He wore a suit and his greying hair was cropped like a brush.

The last time she had heard an accent like his had been a lifetime ago. She'd been young and beautiful then.

'Where is it?' he shouted at her, over and over, with his face so close to hers she could feel the heat of his fury when she said she didn't know, that she didn't have it. She'd never had it, never even laid eyes on it.

1

They let her go then, and she collapsed gasping to the floor. As she lay there shuddering with terror and clutching her racing heart, the six men tore apart her home with a violence she hadn't seen in all her seventy-eight years.

By the time the men had realised they wouldn't find what they'd come so far to obtain, the old woman's heart had given out and she was dead.

What they found instead was a cracked old diary that she had kept close to her for over six decades. The leader of the men flipped hungrily through its pages, running his eye down the faded lines of the old woman's elegant handwriting.

His long search was only just beginning.

Chapter One

Western Georgia
250 kilometres from the Russian border
The present day

A warm September breeze rippled softly through the conifers in the mountain ravine. The air was sweet with the scent of pine, and the late morning sunlight twinkled off the faraway snowy peaks. The mother lynx had come padding down from the forest to quench her thirst from a stream, keeping a watchful eye on her cubs as they played and wrestled in the long grass by the bank.

As she bent to lap at the cool water, her body went suddenly rigid, her acute senses alerting her to an alien presence. Her tufted ears pricked up at the unrecognisable sound that was coming out of nowhere and rising alarmingly fast. She quickly drew away from the water's edge while her cubs, sensing their mother's apprehension, grouped together and scampered behind her.

The terrifying noise was on them in moments, blasting, roaring, filling their ears. The cats bolted for the safety of the forest as two huge black shapes streaked violently overhead, shattering the tranquillity of the ravine. Then, as suddenly as they'd come hurtling over, the monsters were gone.

More dangerous predators than big cats were out hunting today.

Four kilometres across the forest, standing alone on a rocky knoll, was a craggy old stone shack. A century ago, maybe two, it might have been the humble home of a peasant farmer or shepherd. But those days were history, and nobody had lived there for a long time. It had been years since anyone had even set foot in there, until that morning.

It was cool and shady inside the windowless building. The only furnishings within its walls, spaced out in a row and crudely but securely nailed down to the floorboards, were three wooden chairs. The three occupants of the chairs sat quietly, breathing softly, tuned into their shared silence. They knew each other well, but it was some time since they'd all run out of things to say – and in any case there seemed little point in conversation. Even if they'd been able to free themselves from the ropes that bound each of them tightly to his seat, and remove the hoods that their captors had placed over their heads, they knew that the door was heavily chained. Nobody was going anywhere.

So they just waited, each of them alone with his thoughts, in the stillness that comes with true resignation to an irreversible fate. The same kinds of thoughts were running through each of their minds. Wistful thoughts of wives and girlfriends they wouldn't be seeing again. Memories of good times. Each of them knew that he'd had a good run. It tasted bittersweet now, in retrospect, but they'd all known this time would come round eventually, one way or another. They'd all known who they were dealing with. In the world they'd long ago chosen for themselves, it was just the way things were.

As long as it was over quickly. That was all they could ask for now.

The pair of identical Kamov Ka-50 Black Shark combat helicopters were closing rapidly in on their target. Behind their mirrored visors, the pilots calmly checked their readouts and readied the weapons systems that bristled across the undersides of their aircraft. Two kilometres away, their automatic laser-guided target tracking systems locked in, and a sharp image of the shack appeared simultaneously on the monitors inside each cockpit, enlarged enough to count the links in the chain that was padlocked to the door. The pilots armed their missiles and prepared to fire.

There had been no word from base. That meant the operation was a go.

The pilots hit their triggers, and felt the recoil judder their aircraft as their weapons launched simultaneously. Just under three metres long and weighing forty-five kilos each, the Vikhr anti-tank missiles could travel at six hundred metres a second. The pilots watched them go, hunting down their target with deadly accuracy. Three long seconds as the four white vapour trails snaked and twisted through the blue sky, lancing down towards the trees. They hit in rapid succession, with blinding white flashes as the fragmentation warheads detonated on impact. The shack was instantly blown into pieces of whirling debris.

The pilots closed in on the smashed target and activated their side-mounted 30mm cannons. It was complete overkill, but this was a demonstration and the boss was watching. The boss wanted it to look good, and if the boss said he wanted a show of firepower, he'd get a show. The machine cannons raked and strafed the ground with hammering shellfire. Billowing clouds of dust were churned into whirling spirals by the downdraft of the rotors as the choppers roared over the devastated scene. As the clouds slowly settled, the plot that the shack had once stood on now looked like a ploughed field.

Whatever remained of the three men, come nightfall the wild animals would soon claim it.

Chapter Two

The man watching from behind the black-tinted, bulletproof windows of his Humvee lowered his binoculars and smiled in satisfaction at the climbing wisp of smoke across the valley. His eyes narrowed against the sun, following the line of the choppers as they banked round to head back to their secret base. Back to where they'd be well hidden from their original owners.

The man's name was Grigori Shikov. They called him 'the Tsar'. He was seventy-four years old, grizzled and tough. For half a century his business ethos had been based on practicality. He liked things kept simple, and he liked loose ends to be tied up. Three of them had just been tied up permanently. That was what happened to men who tried to conflict with Grigori Shikov's interests.

Shikov twisted his bulk around to stare at the camcorder operator in the back seat. 'Did you get that?'

'Got the whole thing, boss.'

Shikov nodded. His clients were people you didn't want to disappoint – but not even they could fail to be impressed. He was sure they'd find their own uses for their new toys, once the deal was wrapped and the goods changed hands. The negotiations were in the closing stages. Everything was looking good.

'OK, let's go,' Shikov muttered to his driver. At that moment his phone buzzed in his pocket, and he reached for it. He insisted on having a new phone every few days, but disliked this latest piece of tin. It was too small for his fist and his fingers were clumsy on the tiny keys. He answered the call with a grunt. He rarely spoke on phones: people told him what he needed to hear and he listened. His unnerving way of remaining silent was one of the things he was known for. Like never sleeping. Never blinking. Never hesitating. No regrets and no apologies, never once, in a lifetime spent climbing to the top of the hardest business on the planet, and staying there. Challenged, yes, many times. But never defeated and never caught.

Shikov had been expecting a different call and he was about to hang up impatiently, but he didn't. The caller was a man named Yuri Maisky, and he was one of Shikov's closest aides. He also happened to be his nephew, and Shikov kept his family close – or what remained of it since the death of his wife three years earlier.

So he listened to what Maisky had to say, and he felt his heartbeat lurch up a gear as the importance of what he was hearing sank in.

'You're sure?' he rumbled.

It was not a casual question. Maisky knew all too well that the boss didn't waste words on idle chat. There was a tinge of a quaver in his voice as he replied, 'Quite sure. Our contact says it will be there, no question. It is definitely the one.'

The old man was silent for several seconds, holding the phone away from his ear as he digested this unexpected news.

It had turned up at last. After all these years waiting, just like that.

Then he spoke again, quietly and calmly. 'Where is my son?'

'I don't know,' Maisky said after a beat. The truthful answer was that Anatoly's whereabouts could be narrowed down fairly accurately to any one of three places: he'd either be lounging drunk on the deck of his yacht, gambling away more of his father's fortune in the casino, or making a pig of himself in the bed of some ambitious hottie somewhere. It was wiser to lie.

Shikov said, 'Find him. Tell him I have a job for him.'

Chapter Three

Italy
Six days later

Ben Hope glanced at the roughly drawn map clipped to the dashboard and steered the four-wheel-drive in through the gate. The track ahead traced a winding path through the sun-bleached valley. He couldn't see the house but guessed it must be beyond the rise about a kilometre away.

He'd had a feeling that old Boonzie McCulloch could be trusted to pick a spot that was fairly inaccessible, and was glad he'd had the instinct to hire the sturdy Mitsubishi Shogun for the drive out here. Mid-afternoon, and it was hot enough to need all the windows wound down, even up here in the hill country near Campo Basso. Ben gazed around him at the scenery as the car lurched along the rutted, rocky track.

Beyond a stand of trees, the little farmhouse came into view. It was pretty much exactly what he'd expected, a simple and neat whitewashed block with shutters and a wooden veranda, red terracotta tiles on the roof. Behind the house stood a cluster of well-kept outbuildings, and beyond those was a sweep of fields. Sunlight glittered off a long row of greenhouses in the distance.

Ben pulled up, killed the engine and stepped down from the dusty Shogun. The chickens scratching about the yard parted hurriedly as a Doberman came trotting over to investigate the visitor. From somewhere round the back, Ben heard a woman's voice call the dog's name. It paused a second to eye him up, then seemed to decide he wasn't a threat and went bounding back towards the house.

The front door opened, and a tall man in jeans and a loose-fitting khaki shirt stepped out onto the veranda. His gaze landed on Ben and the moustached face cracked into a grin.

'Hello, Boonzie,' Ben said, and he was transported back nearly seventeen years to the day they'd first met. The day a young soldier had turned up at Hereford with over a hundred other hopefuls dreaming of wearing the coveted winged dagger badge of the most elite outfit in the British army. The wiry Glaswegian sergeant had been one of the stern, grim-faced officers whose job it was to put the fledglings through unimaginable hell. By the time the selection process had done its worst and Ben had been one of just eight tired, bruised survivors, his gruff, granite-faced tormentor had become his mentor, and a friend for life. The Scotsman had been there, grinning like a proud father, when Ben had been awarded his badge. And he'd been there, calm and steady and dependable, when Ben had experienced his first serious battle.

They'd served together in the field for three years, before Boonzie had moved on to training recruits full-time. Ben had sorely missed him.

It had been four years after that, Ben now an SAS major stationed in Afghanistan, when he'd heard the unlikely rumours: that mad Scots bastard McCulloch had cracked. Gone soft in the head, found love, quit the army and set up home in the south of Italy, milking goats and growing crops. It had seemed bizarre.

But now, looking around him and seeing his old friend walking down the steps of the house with a warm grin and the sun on his tanned, creased face, Ben understood perfectly what had drawn Boonzie here.

The man hadn't changed a great deal physically over the years. He had to be fifty-eight or fifty-nine now, a little more grizzled but still as lean and wiry as a junkyard hound, with the same work-toughened look of a man who'd spent most of his life doing things the hard way. Something inside had softened, though. Those hard grey eyes had a diamond twinkle to them now.

'It's grand to see ye again, Ben.' Boonzie was one of those Scots who could go the rest of his life without ever returning to the old country but would go on wearing his accent proudly like a flag until the day he died.

'You look good, Boonzie. I can see you're happy here.'

'You wouldn't have believed this dour auld fucker could find true bliss, would you?'

'When did I ever call you a dour old fucker?'

Boonzie's grin widened an inch. 'What brings you all the way out here, Ben? You didn't say much on the phone. Just that you wanted to talk to me about something.'

Ben nodded. He'd wanted this to be face to face.

'Here, come in out of the sun.'

The house was as simple inside as it was out, but it was homely and inviting. As Boonzie ushered him through to a sitting room, a door opened and Ben turned to see a deeply tanned Italian woman walking into the room. She stood only chest-high to Boonzie, who put his hand on her shoulder and squeezed her affectionately to his side. The smile she flashed at Ben was broad and generous, like her figure. A mass of curly black hair with just a few silver strands tumbled down onto the shoulders of her blouse.

'This is my wife Mirella,' Boonzie said, gazing lovingly down at her.

Ben put out his hand. '*Piacere, Signora.*'

'I am pleased to meet you too,' Mirella replied in hesitant English. 'Please call me Mirella. And I must practise my English, as Archibald only speaks Italian to me now that he has learned.'

Archibald! In all the years in the army together, Ben had never asked what his real name was. Ben shot a glance at Boonzie, who was staring in horror at his wife, and couldn't resist breaking out into a grin that quickly threatened to spill over into a laugh. 'You and Archibald have a beautiful home,' he said.

Boonzie soon got over it. While Mirella returned to the kitchen, strictly forbidding any male to enter until dinner was prepared, Ben had a cold bottle of Peroni beer pressed into his hand and was given the tour of the smallholding.

'Nine acres,' Boonzie said grandly, sweeping an arm across his land. 'Place was just a rocky wasteland when I found it. Not what you'd call a farm, but it keeps us going. The green-houses are for basil, the rest of it is my tomato crop.'

Ben was no farmer. He shrugged and looked blank. 'Just basil and tomato?'

'That's our wee business,' Boonzie explained. 'Mirella's one hell of a cook. Her secret recipes for basil pesto and tomato sauce are like you wouldn't believe, old son. I grow the stuff, she cooks it all up and we bottle it. Once a week I go out in the van and do the rounds of the local restaurant trade. Campo Basso, the whole area. It'll never make us millionaires, but look at this place. It's heaven, man.'

Ben gazed around him and found it hard to disagree.

Running his eye across the neat rows of greenhouses, he noticed a gap between them that was just a rectangle of freshly-dug earth marked out with string. A shovel stood propped against a wheelbarrow, beside it a pile of aluminium framing and glass panels wrapped in plastic, some bags of ready-mix cement and a mixer.

'New greenhouse,' Boonzie explained, slurping beer. 'Can't build enough of the damn things. Need to finish putting it up.'

'How about I give you a hand right now?'

It took a lot of persuading, but Boonzie finally relented and ran back to the house to fetch another shovel and more beer to keep them cool while they worked. Ben didn't wait for him. He rolled up his sleeves, grabbed the shovel and dug in.

As the sun rolled by overhead, the greenhouse gradually took shape and Boonzie reminisced about the old days. 'Remember that time Cole almost shat himself in the boat?' he smiled as he bolted together a section of frame.

The legendary episode, retold countless times since, had happened during winter training up in Scotland, not long after Ben had joined 22 SAS. He, Boonzie, and two other guys named Cole and Rowson had found themselves stranded in the middle of a misty Highland loch when the outboard motor on their dinghy had cut out. Drifting through impenetrable curtains of fog, Boonzie in his mischievous way had begun working on unnerving the lads with ripping yarns of the strange, terrible creatures that lurked in the depths. As Cole bent over the motor trying to get it started and muttering irritably at Boonzie to shut up, a black shape had suddenly exploded out of the water right in his face, sending Cole into a screaming panic that almost made him fall overboard. The 'monster' had turned out to be a seal.

Ben, Boonzie and Rowson, SAS hard guys draped in weapons, trained to kill, had been so weak with laughter that they'd hardly been able to paddle the damn dinghy back to shore.

Those were the stories you carried in your heart. Not like the darker memories, the tales of dead friends, ravaged battle zones, the horror and futility of war. The things nobody reminisced over.

'So what was it you wanted to talk to me about?' Boonzie asked as Ben poured a fresh load of cement into the barrow. 'You didn't come all the way here to shovel shite.'

'Mirella seems like a lovely lady,' Ben replied, avoiding the question.

'Love at first sight, Ben, if ye could believe in such a thing. There I was in Naples. It was only meant to be a weekend away from getting soaked to the bollocks on some fucking God-forsaken hillside somewhere training a bunch of ignorant squaddies. I'm sitting in this wee restaurant sucking up spaghetti like there's no tomorrow and wondering how the fuck I'd got by on pot noodles and ketchup for all those years, when I hear screams from the kitchen and this guy comes running out like the hounds of hell're tearing at his arse. Then next thing a saucepan flies out the door after him and almost takes my ear off.'

'You're kidding me,' Ben chuckled.

'I look up,' Boonzie went on tenderly, 'and there's this fuckin' apparition standing there in the kitchen doorway, still in her apron. Never seen a woman so wild. And I thought, Boonzie, *that's* the one you've been looking for. Three days later, we were engaged and I'd put in my resignation. Hitched by the end of the month. I haven't been back to Blighty since. And I dinnae miss it, either.'

'I can see that. You picked a perfect spot, Boonzie.'

'Isn't it?'

'How did Mirella take to country life after Naples? She doesn't feel too isolated out here?'

Boonzie used the back of his shovel to spread wet cement over the footings of the greenhouse. 'When she first saw the place she was a wee bit worried about intruders and the like. Some friends of hers got burgled down in Ríccia.' He grinned up at Ben, and his eye sparkled. 'But she's got no worries with me, Ben. I have my peace of mind, if you know what I mean.'

Ben did. He didn't need to ask.

'What about you?' Boonzie said.

'Me?'

'Aye, did you ever settle down?'

'I lived in Ireland for a while. Live in France now.'

'What about a woman?'

Ben hesitated. The face that instantly flashed up in his mind's eye belonged to a woman called Brooke. He held the image there for a long moment, seeing her warm smile, the auburn curls falling across her eyes as she laughed. He could almost smell her perfume, almost feel his hands stroking her skin. 'Yeah, there's someone,' he said, and then went quiet.

Silence for a beat, and then Boonzie asked, 'So are you going to tell me what you've come all this way for?'

'It's not important now.'

'Ben, you're like a son to me. Don't force me to beat it out of you with this shovel.'

Ben gave a shrug. 'OK. I came here to offer you a job.'

16

Chapter Four

Georgia

Grigori Shikov's private study was a place few people were allowed to visit. For some it was a privilege; for others a summons to the luxurious boathouse in the villa's sprawling grounds, escorted by silent men in dark suits, spelled doom.

The dark-panelled room was filled with the treasures Shikov had assiduously collected over forty or more years. The vast antique sideboard behind him was dominated by a magnificent lapis lazuli bust of Frederick the Great. On an eighteenth-century gilt-bronze rococo commode by André-Charles Boulle stood a globe that had once belonged to Adolf Hitler; but it was the extensive collection of artefacts from Imperial Russia, dating between 1721 and 1917, reflecting Shikov's lifelong passion for what he proudly regarded as his homeland's golden era, that had earned him the nickname 'the Tsar'. And it fitted him perfectly.

Of all the historic objects in Shikov's study, the most physically impressive and intimidating was the immaculate 1910 Maxim water-cooled heavy machine gun, complete with its original wheeled carriage. It occupied the corner of the room, its snout aimed directly towards whomever might be sitting across from him at his massive desk. Between the fixed stare of the machine gun muzzle and the hard glower of the grizzled old mob boss, nobody could fail to be shrivelled to a pulp.

Nobody except Anatoly, Shikov's only son, who at this moment was lounging in the plush chair as the old man leaned heavily on his desk and outlined the job he wanted done for him.

The third man present at the meeting was Yuri Maisky, Shikov's nephew. He stood by the desk with his hands clasped behind his back, keeping quiet as his uncle did the talking. Forty-seven years old, small and wiry, Maisky secretly attributed his thinning hair and the deep worry lines on his brow to the strain of working for Shikov's organisation for most of his adult life. He loved his uncle, but he also feared him.

There weren't many men whom Maisky feared more than his boss. One was the boss's son. When the old man looked at Anatoly all he saw was his beloved only child, his pride and joy; Maisky saw a thirty-four-year-old psychopath with a blond ponytail. The face was long and lean and chiselled, the eyes were quick and dangerous. Maisky's belief that Anatoly Shikov was clinically insane was one he kept closely to himself.

Shikov could sense the tension emanating from his nephew. He knew that most of his associates and employees lived in dread and loathing of Anatoly. That just made him prouder of his only child, although he would never have shown it. Outwardly, he acted gruff and commanding.

'Are you paying attention?' Shikov snapped at Anatoly, interrupting himself.

'Sure.'

'Have you been drinking?'

'Of course not,' Anatoly lied. The Tsar abhorred alcohol. Anatoly did not. He shifted in the chair and glanced down to admire the hand-tooled perfection of his latest purchase, the alligator-skin boots he'd been trying to show off all day by turning up the legs of his Armani jeans. But not even Anatoly would have dared to put his feet up on the old man's desk. 'I'm listening. Go on.'

Anatoly had done plenty of jobs for his father, and it was something he enjoyed being called upon to do. Most guys he'd known who had worked for their dads had to go to the office, wear a suit and tie, attend meetings and conferences, sell shit of one kind or another. Not him. He felt highly privileged to be a valued member of the family firm. He and his old buddy Spartak Gourko had once kept a snitch alive for seventeen days under hard torture to extract a list of names of traitors in their organisation. Another time, Anatoly had spread-eagled a man between four posts in the ground, chains around his wrists and ankles, and lit a cigarette as Gourko drove a pickaxe through the guy's sternum. When old Spartak got going, he was something to behold.

Anatoly enjoyed his work. He never asked questions about his father's business, partly because you just didn't ask the Tsar questions about his business, and partly because Anatoly didn't really give a damn why things got done the way they did. The only questions he generally asked in life were *'Can I own it?'*; *'Can I fuck it?'*; *'Can I kill it?'*. If the answer to any of the above was negative, he quickly lost interest.

This new job sounded like fun, though.

'Our sources tell us that the piece of artwork in question will definitely be part of the exhibition,' Maisky said.

'And I want it,' Shikov finished in his gravel voice. 'I *will* have it.'

The sheaf of papers spread out across the desk was the report on the gallery's security system, put together by one of the many experts on Shikov's payroll, a usefully corruptible Moscow security tech engineer who had leaned on contacts in Milan to get the information they needed. The seventeen-page document contained the technical data on the bespoke alarm system recently installed into the gallery building whose photographs, taken with a powerful telephoto lens from a variety of angles just days before, were clipped together in a file next to the report.

Anatoly hadn't heard the old man doing this much talking in years. Half-listening as his father went on, he flicked through the series of photos. The location in Italy was printed at the bottom. He could see that the gallery was an extension of a much older building. The kind of new-fangled architecture that appealed to arty types. It had only just been built; in the pictures that showed the rear of the gallery, he could see that the groundworks weren't fully finished, with patches of freshly-dug earth and a half-built ornamental fountain. There was a works van present in two of the pictures, a slightly battered Mercedes with the company name SERVIZI GIARDINIERI ROSSI just about visible on the side.

Italy, Anatoly thought. That was cool. He'd never been there before, but currently had two Ferraris, one red, one white, and most of his wardrobe came from there as well. He even spoke a bit of the language, mostly aped from the *Godfather* movies. Girls loved it. Yes, Italy was fine by him. Anatoly could appreciate art, too, as long as it involved depictions of naked female flesh.

Sadly, the item his father seemed so desperate to acquire depicted nothing of the sort. Anatoly glanced at the glossy blow-up taken from the exhibition brochure. Just some colourless drawing of a guy on his knees praying. Who would desire such a thing? Obviously it was worth some serious cash, strange though that might seem.

'You're not listening to me, boy.'

'You were saying the alarm system's a bastard.'

Maisky cleared his throat and cut in politely. 'That's putting it mildly. The perimeter protection system is state of the art. If you can get through it, the building is filled with cameras watching from every possible vantage point. The inside of the gallery itself is scanned constantly by photo-infrared motion sensors that could pick up a cockroach. The whole thing is automated, and the only way to override it is to enter a set of passcodes that are kept under lock and key in three separate locations. You need all three to disable the system. Furthermore, the passcodes are randomly regenerated each day by computer, in staggered intervals so that the combination's constantly changing. Any breach of the system will trigger the alarms as well as sending an instant signal to the police.'

'Seems impossible,' Anatoly ventured.

'Nothing is impossible, boy.' Shikov snatched a printed sheet from his desk and flipped it over.

Anatoly picked it up. There were three names on the sheet, all Italian, all unknown to him. De Crescenzo, Corsini, Silvestri. Beside each name was an address and a thumbnail picture. De Crescenzo was a gaunt-looking man with thinning black hair. Corsini was round and fat. Silvestri looked like a preening popinjay, a man in love with himself even when he didn't know his picture was being taken. 'Who are they?'

'The three men who hold the passcodes,' Maisky told him.

'Now here's the plan,' Shikov said. 'Tomorrow evening is the inaugural opening of the gallery. Invitation only, some local VIPs and art critics, people like that, about thirty-five in all. All three passcode holders will be present. Your team will be waiting as they leave, and follow them home. At 3 a.m., you'll snatch them simultaneously from their homes, bring them back to the gallery and make them enter the codes. How you do it is up to you, but you keep them alive.'

'Right. And then we go in and grab what we came for.'

Maisky had been waiting for the first sign that the hotheaded young punk was going to handle this in his usual reckless way. *Here we go*, he thought.

'It's not that simple,' he said. 'Because the only time the owners might have to override the alarm system would be an emergency situation such as a fire, earthquake or other potential threat to the valuable contents of the gallery, the system's designers built in a function that will send an automatic alert to the police should the override codes be entered. That function is hard-wired into the system and can't be disabled remotely in any way. It uses a broadband frequency via the optic fibre landline, with cellular backup in the event that the main lines are down. So it's essential that before you go in, you ensure that the landline is chopped. And that you use this.' He pointed at a device sitting on a side table. Anatoly had been eyeing it, wondering what it was. A plain black box, about twelve inches long, wired up to four patch antennas.

'It's an 18-watt ultra-high power digital cellphone jammer,' Maisky explained. 'It will work in all countries and block the signal from any type of phone, including 3G, over a radius of 120 metres. With this in place, the police won't have a clue what's going on.'

'And if any of the owners decides to get smart and punch in a duress signal that could trip the silent alarm, they're wasting their time,' Shikov added.

'So then I can pop them.'

'Not until you have the item safely in your possession,' Maisky said as patiently as he could. 'Once you're in, you have to take care of the secondary system as well. Each painting is rigged so that any attempt to remove it from the wall will set off a separate alarm.'

'So what? If the phones are down—'

'It also fires the automatic shutter system. A sensitive electronic trigger is hooked up to a hydraulic ram system that will slam shutters down to protect the artwork. The shutters will resist attack from bullets, blowtorches, and cutting blades. They will also automatically block every possible exit and imprison the intruder like a trapped rat until the police come and take them away. And there's no override code for that. It can't be reversed.'

'Are you following all of this, Anatoly?' Shikov said, watching his son closely from across the desk.

Anatoly shrugged, as if to say all this kind of stuff was child's play to him.

'Good. Go and assemble four of your best men. I'm thinking of Turchin, Rykov, Petrovich—'

'And Gourko,' Anatoly cut in.

Oh no, Maisky thought, his heart going icy. *Not Gourko.* Anatoly's closest crony, the scarred bastard who'd been dishonourably drummed out of the Russian army's Spetsnaz GRU Special Forces unit for beating one of his officers half to death with a rifle butt. The kind of gangster who gave gangsters a bad name, and one of the few other people who frightened Maisky even more than his boss.

'You have two hours,' Shikov said. 'And then you're on your way to Italy. You'll rendezvous with our friends on the ground.'

'How many in the team?'

'Ten. Eight men inside, two on the outside.'

Anatoly nodded. 'Hardware?'

'Everything you need.'

23

Anatoly smiled. He could trust his father to be thorough on that score.

When Anatoly had left the room a few minutes afterwards, Shikov gathered up the scattered paperwork and slid it into a drawer. It would be burned later. Maisky circled the desk, frowning. His head was full of things he wanted to say. Things like, 'Are you so sure you can trust Anatoly with this? He's wild and irresponsible and his friends are all maniacs, especially Spartak Gourko. How can you be so blind, uncle?' But he had the good sense to say nothing at all.

Yuri Maisky wasn't the only one keeping his thoughts to himself. As Anatoly walked away from the boathouse, flipping his Ferrari keys in his hand, he was already thinking about how overcomplicated and boring his father's plan was.

He had other ideas.

Yup, this *was* going to be fun.

Chapter Five

'A *job*?' Boonzie said, raising his eyebrows.

The sun was beginning to dip over the hills, throwing a wash of dramatic reds and purples across the skyline. Ben nodded. Crouching on the ground beside the new greenhouse foundations, he fished out his Zippo lighter and a pack of the same Gauloises cigarettes he always smoked.

'Those fuckers'll kill you,' Boonzie muttered.

'If something else doesn't beat them to it. Want one?'

'Aye, why not. Chuck them across.' Boonzie kicked over the empty barrow and used it as a seat while he lit up.

'At the place where I live in France, I run a business,' Ben explained. 'We're out in the countryside; not so different from this place in a lot of ways. But we don't make pesto sauce. We do K and R training work.'

Boonzie didn't need Ben to spell out that K and R stood for kidnap and ransom. Ben went on talking, and Boonzie listened carefully.

In the seven years since Ben had quit the army, locating and extracting victims of kidnapping, often children, had become his speciality. He'd called himself a *Crisis Response Consultant* – a deliberately vague euphemism for someone who went out and solved problems that lay way beyond the reach of normal law enforcement agencies. His work had taken him into a lot of dark corners. His methods hadn't always been gentle, but he'd got results that few other people in his line of work could have achieved.

The bottom line, always, was helping those in need. After many successes and a few too many scrapes, he'd left the dangers of active field work behind to focus on passing on the skills and knowledge he'd acquired – still helping the innocent victims of ruthless criminals across the globe, but now doing it from behind a desk instead of from behind a gun.

The facility he'd set up, nestled in the Normandy country-side, was called Le Val. It had been growing busier by the month. Police and military units, hostage negotiation specialists, kidnap insurance execs, close-protection services personnel, had all flocked to attend the courses he ran there with his assistant, ex-SBS officer Jeff Dekker, and a couple of other ex-military guys. Dr Brooke Marcel, half French, half English, an expert psychologist based in London, had been his consultant and regular visiting lecturer in hostage psychology until – three months or so ago – their stumbling relationship had developed into something deeper.

In terms of the success of the business, Ben couldn't have asked for more. Le Val was lucrative, it was filling a very real need, and it was safe.

But there was a problem. It had started as just a grain of discomfort, like a tiny niggling itch he couldn't scratch. Through the long, hot summer, it had grown until it followed him like a shadow and he couldn't sleep at night for thinking of it.

Why he felt this way, where the demons that were driving him so crazy with restlessness had come from, he had no idea. All he knew, with a certainty that frightened him, was that the life he'd created in France was one he no longer wanted.

Boonzie McCulloch was the first person he'd chosen to confess his secret to, and even after thinking about little else for days it wasn't easy to do. When he'd finished outlining the work he and his team did at Le Val, he took a deep breath and came right out with it.

'Thing is, I'm giving serious thought to leaving it all behind,' he admitted with a frown. 'I don't mean I want to sell up. Just walk away, leave it in Jeff's hands. He can run the place, no problem, with a little help from the other guys, and Brooke. And you, if you're interested.'

Boonzie took a draw on his cigarette, said nothing. His eyes were narrowed to slits against the falling sun.

'You were the best instructor I ever knew,' Ben said. 'I can't think of anyone I'd rather have come and take over the number two position.'

'What about you?' Boonzie asked. 'Where are you going?'

Ben was quiet for a moment. 'I don't know,' he said. 'I'm not sure what I want. Maybe I need some time to figure that out.'

'Every man has to settle down sometime, Ben. It comes to us all.'

'I don't know if I'm the settling kind. God knows I've tried. Just doesn't seem to work for me.'

'You never were happy unless your arse was on fire,' Boonzie chuckled, and then looked serious. 'What about this Brooke lassie? Sounds like you and she have something going.'

Ben glanced down at his feet. 'That's what I thought, too,' he muttered. 'Sometimes I'm not so sure. For a while she's been acting—' His voice trailed off. He bit his lip.

'What?'

Ben let out a long sigh. 'Listen, I don't want to lay my personal problems on you. What do you think about my offer? Is it something you'd ever consider?'

Boonzie didn't reply. He thoughtfully stubbed out the butt of his cigarette on the belly of the upturned barrow.

Ben already knew the answer. He'd known it the moment he'd got here, and it had been so obvious and predictable that he almost hadn't asked the question. So he wasn't very surprised when after a few more moments' deliberation, looking genuinely pained, Boonzie shook his head.

'Flattered you should ask me . . .'

'But no?'

'That's the way it has to be. I'm sorry, Ben.'

'Say no more, old friend.'

'Would *you* leave this?'

'Not in my right mind, I wouldn't.' Ben stood up and dusted himself off.

'No hard feelings, then?' Boonzie said, concern in his eyes.

'Don't be daft. I'm happy for you.'

'You'll stay for dinner, though, aye? Be our guest for the night?'

'Of course.'

Boonzie had been right about Mirella's cooking. Dinner was a simple dish of tagliatelle mixed with a basil pesto sauce of the most vivid green, topped with grated parmesan and accompanied by a local wine. It was as far from fancy cuisine as you could get, but just about the best thing Ben had ever tasted and he ate a mound of it with relish under the chef's approving gaze. As they sat up until late around the plain oak table in the small dining room, he almost managed to forget all the troubling thoughts that had been on his mind lately. Boonzie told stories, more wine was poured, the fresh night air breezed in through the open windows and the cicadas chirped outside. It was after one when Ben insisted on helping the couple clear up the dishes, and Mirella showed him up to the guest bedroom.

He was awake long before dawn, edgy and feeling the need to go for a run. He slipped out quietly and spent an hour jogging in the open countryside, pausing a while to watch the sunrise before returning to the house to shower and put on clean jeans and a light denim shirt over a navy T-shirt that said 'TYRELL Genetic Replicants – More Human than Human'. A present from Brooke. She was a big *Blade Runner* fan. Ben hadn't seen the movie.

Breakfast was in the kitchen, eggs laid that morning scrambled with butter and toast as Mirella fussed and Ben kept protesting that he'd had enough delicious food to last him a week.

'No hard feelings,' Boonzie said again, frowning at him over a steaming cup of espresso. 'About what we discussed?'

'None whatsoever, Archibald,' Ben said.

'Piss off. So where's next? S'pose you'll be heading back to France?'

Ben shook his head. 'I have a flight booked from Rome to London tomorrow afternoon.'

'Business trip?'

'It's a long story.'

Boonzie and Mirella waved as Ben climbed into the Shogun. He waved back, took a last glance at the tranquil haven they'd made their home and then drove off down the bumpy track towards the road.

29

Chapter Six

Ben headed roughly south-southwest with the rising sun behind him, aiming more or less in the direction of Naples with the intention of veering slowly towards Italy's west coast. From there, he'd follow the coastal road through a hundred seaside towns and villages until eventually he reached Rome.

For a man who'd been running this way and that for most of his life, always with a precisely calculated plan in mind, always battling the clock, it felt strange to be at something of a loose end. Strange, yet welcome too – because, for the first time, he wasn't looking forward to his trip to visit Brooke in London. A month earlier, he'd have been racing to get there.

What had changed? That was the question in his mind as he drove. For the hundredth time he raked back in his mind through all their conversations, things he might have said to upset her, anything he might have done wrong. He couldn't think of a single reason. There'd been no arguments between them. No falling out, nothing to explain why things should be less than deliriously perfect. Almost three months of what he'd thought was a happy, loving, warm relationship.

So what had gone wrong? What had been eating her lately?

She'd seemed to withdraw from him, obviously preoccupied but refusing to talk about what was on her mind. Not so long ago, they'd taken every opportunity to be together, whether it was him travelling to London or her coming down to see him at Le Val. But suddenly she'd seemed less interested in leaving her place in Richmond, even cancelling the last couple of lectures in hostage psychology she'd been due to give for his clients. All of a sudden she was hard to get on the phone, and when he did manage to get through to her, he was sure he could detect a tone in her voice that hadn't been there before. Nothing had been said. It was as though she was hiding something from him.

What exactly he thought he was going to achieve by springing this surprise visit on her in London, he wasn't quite sure. Did he mean to have it out with her? Challenge her? Level with her about how much he cared for her and ask her to be straight with him in return?

Maybe the problem wasn't with her, he thought as he drove on. Maybe it was with him. Wasn't he the one who'd come to Italy looking for ways to get out of his situation at Le Val? Wasn't he the one who wanted to walk away from the stability he'd worked so hard to build? Maybe Brooke had sensed something in him, some change in him, or a lack of commitment. That thought hurt him, and he asked himself over and over again whether there was any truth in it. Was there? He didn't think so, but maybe there was.

A Paris cop called Luc Simon had once said something to Ben that had stayed with him ever since:

'Men like us are bad news for women. We're lone wolves. We want to love them, but we only hurt them. And so they walk away . . .'

Ben stayed on the minor roads, trying to hold himself down to a steady pace but finding the car's speed constantly

31

creeping up on him. After a while he just settled back and let it go as fast as it wanted. The blast from the open windows tore at his hair, and he found a radio station that was playing live jazz – hard-driving, frenetic, with shrieking saxes and thunderous drums that suited his mood.

In the few hours it took him to reach the west coast, passing through the sun-soaked hills of the rich Campania region, he'd managed to mellow somewhat. It was early afternoon when he caught his first glimpse of the blue Tyrrhenian Sea, boats and yachts dotted white on the glittering waters. He meandered on for a few more kilometres and then found an ancient fishing village just a little to the north of Mondragone, unspoilt by the tourists, where he pulled over. He checked his phone for any messages from Brooke. There were none.

After a few minutes of wandering the crumbling streets he found a restaurant that overlooked the beach – a quiet family-run place with small tables, chequered tablecloths and a homely menu that almost compared with the delights of *Casa McCulloch*. The wine tempted him but he drank less than a full glass before moving on.

Chapter Seven

Normally, nobody would have known or cared where the van was going. It was an ordinary Mercedes commercial vehicle, dirty white, battered and rattly with SERVIZI GIARDINIERI ROSSI in faded letters on its flanks. One of a million vans that came and went every day and attracted no attention. There was nothing remarkable or unusual about the driver and the two guys sitting up front with him in the cab, either. Their names were Beppe, Mauro and Carmine and they all worked for the small firm based outside Ánzio that sold garden supplies and landscaping materials. Their last job today was hauling a load of ornamental slabs and edging stones to the Academia Giordani, the art school place out in the sticks where they'd been delivering a lot of stuff lately.

At just after four in the afternoon they were heading down a narrow country road that was deserted apart from a black Audi Q7 behind them. It had been sticking with them for a few kilometres, and every so often Beppe glanced in his wing mirror and scowled at the way the big SUV was hanging so close up his arse. Mauro was smoking a cigarette and content-edly enjoying the peace before he'd have to pull on his work gloves and get down to unloading the heavy stuff in the back. In the window seat, Carmine was brooding as usual.

Without warning, a pickup truck lurched out of a side road thirty metres ahead and Beppe's attention was snatched away from the irritating Audi behind them. He braked sharply. Mauro was caught unawares and spilled forwards in his seat, his cigarette falling into his lap.

'Son of a—'

The pickup rolled out across the road and then, inexplicably, it stopped. There was no way to drive around it. It was a chunky four-wheel-drive Nissan Warrior, five guys inside. Beppe honked his horn angrily for them to get out of the way, but the only response was a flat stare from the driver. His window was rolled down and a forearm thicker than a baseball bat was draped casually along the sill. This was a guy with at least a decade of serious toil invested in the weights room. The width of his jaw hinted at steroid use. His eyes were hidden behind mirrored wraparound shades, but he appeared to be gazing calmly right at the van.

'What the fuck are they doing?' Mauro said.

'Out the way, moron!' Beppe shook his fist, fired some abuse out of the open window, and when that didn't elicit any further response he threw open his door and jumped down from the cab. Carmine and Mauro exchanged glances and then got out and followed. The pickup truck doors opened slowly and the two guys in front stepped out and began to walk over. The driver towered head and shoulders over his passenger. Mauro swallowed as they got closer.

'Hey, fuckhead. Can't you see you're blocking the road?' Beppe shouted at them. Carmine and Mauro prepared to back him up as the pickup guys kept on approaching. Road rage, Italian style. This wasn't the first time for them. But it wasn't just the size of the big guy that was unsettling. It was the way all the pickup guys looked so completely calm. The three still inside the vehicle hadn't moved a muscle, seemingly unperturbed by what was happening. Beppe's stride faltered just a little as he drew closer. 'So you going to move that truck out the way or what?' Maybe negotiation was better than outright aggression.

The big guy just smiled, and then quite casually came out with a string of obscenities so appalling and confrontational that Beppe reeled as if he'd been slapped. That was when the argument kicked off in earnest, insults flying back and forth as Beppe and his companions squared up to the pickup guys, toe to toe in the middle of the road.

The three were so taken up with yelling and threatening, prodding and shoving that they'd forgotten all about the black Audi Q7 that had been following them. Too preoccupied to notice that, like the Nissan pickup, it had two men up front and three sitting calmly in the back. And none of them noticed when the Audi's front doors opened quietly.

The driver of the Audi was Spartak Gourko. Sitting next to him in the passenger seat was Anatoly Shikov. Gourko's hair was freshly razed to his scalp in a severe buzz-cut. While Anatoly liked to look stylish, Gourko didn't make the effort. There was little point, not with the disfigurement of the mass of scar tissue that extended down the left side of his face from temple to jaw. An old fragmentation grenade wound from the first Chechen War, it twisted his mouth and brow into a permanent scowl that made him look even more pissed off than he nearly always was.

Anatoly was pleased with his little scheme so far. It was a lot more inventive than his father's. The idea of getting one of their Italian associates to call up pretending to order more materials for the art gallery grounds had occurred to him on the flight. Naturally, the Italians were under the impression that the whole thing was his father's idea, so nobody questioned anything.

And this way was going to be so much more fun.

OK, so the old man might be a little pissed off at him for altering one or two minor details of the plan – but as long as he got what he wanted in the end, what did it really matter? Ends and means, and all that. Wasn't like his father hadn't done some crazy shit himself, back in the day when he was coming up. Anatoly was well versed in the legend of the hardest son of a bitch who'd ever walked the earth. He only wanted to measure up, that was all. And have fun doing it.

Anatoly smiled quietly to himself as he climbed out of the car and he and Gourko walked unnoticed up behind the arguing Italians. He nodded to the pickup driver. The big guy's name was Rocco Massi, and he was one of their main contacts over here. Anatoly wasn't exactly sure, but he thought Massi's boss was a friend of his old man's. The rest of the Italian crew were called Bellomo, Garrone, Scagnetti and Caracciolo. Anatoly couldn't remember which was which. He trusted them well enough, though not as much as his own guys. Gourko of course, then Rykov, Petrovich, Turchin. Only Petrovich knew much Italian. Rykov seemed not to speak anything at all. But Anatoly hadn't picked them for their communication skills. They were the hardest, meanest, nastiest bunch of motherfuckers you could find anywhere in Russia. Apart from the old man, naturally.

Anatoly's hand darted inside his jacket and came out with an automatic pistol fitted with a long sound suppressor. Without pausing a beat, he raised the gun at arm's length and blew off the back of Beppe's head at point-blank range.

In the open air, the sound of the silenced gunshot was like a muffled handclap.

Beppe went straight down on his face.

Before Mauro and Carmine could react, Spartak Gourko had reached for the pistol holstered under his jacket and

Rocco Massi had produced an identical weapon from behind the hip of his jeans. Gourko's bullet took Carmine between the eyes; Mauro got one in the chest. Carmine was dead instantly and his body slumped across Beppe's, their blood intermingling on the road.

Mauro didn't die right away. Groaning in agony, he tried to crawl back towards the Mercedes, as if somehow there was some hope of getting in and escaping. Rocco Massi was about to finish off Mauro with another bullet when Anatoly shook his head and made a sharp gesture. 'I do it.' His Italian was primitive, but the warning tone in his voice was clear.

He stepped over to the dying man. Flipped him over with the toe of his expensive alligator boot and stared down at him for a moment as he lay there helplessly on his back, gasping, blood welling from the bullet hole in his chest. Then Anatoly raised his right foot, smiled and stamped the heel down on Mauro's throat. It crushed his trachea as if squashing a roach. Mauro gurgled up gouts of blood, then his eyes rolled back in their sockets and he was dead.

The road was still deserted. The three passengers from each ambush vehicle got out and quickly cleaned up the scene. Few words were exchanged between the Italians and the Russians, but they worked together quickly and efficiently. The bodies were dragged over to the pickup, where zip-up coroner's bodybags were waiting for them. Earth was sprinkled over the blood pools on the road. In less than two minutes, every last trace of the killings was erased.

Four bulging holdalls were transferred from the Audi to the van. Anatoly and Gourko clambered into the back of the Mercedes together with Rykov, Turchin and Scagnetti. Rocco Massi switched over to take the van's wheel and was joined up front by Bellomo and Garrone. Carraciolo and Petrovich took their places in the Nissan and the Audi. Doors slammed in the still, hot air. The convoy took off.

Exactly seven minutes after the van had been intercepted, it was back en route to its destination. They'd stop on the way for their final briefing, to make sure everyone knew exactly what they were doing, and to wait until the time was right.

Then it was game on.

Chapter Eight

Ben Hope loved beaches. Not the heaving nightmare of scorched flab and sun tan lotion it was so hard to avoid all up and down the coasts of Europe from May through September, but the secluded kind of place where you could sit and watch the tide hiss in over the sand and be alone with your thoughts for a while. After his lunch he'd taken a long stroll down by the shore, carrying his shoes in his hand and letting the cool water wash over his bare feet. Shielding his eyes from the sun, he'd looked out across the Gulf of Gaeta. Due west, the nearest land was Sardinia.

Then he'd retraced his steps back to the car, wiped the sand from his feet and started making his way further up the coastal road.

It was getting on for six in the afternoon, and the sun was beginning to dip lower in the sky by the time he entered a colourful-looking village a few kilometres from the town of Aprilia. He felt tired of driving. Maybe it was time to think about stopping, parking up somewhere and exploring the place for a nice, quiet hotel. It felt a little decadent to be taking things this easy, but the last thing he wanted was to hit Rome too early and have to deal with the oppressive heat and noise of the place with nothing else to do but sit around waiting for his flight tomorrow afternoon, fretting

39

about Brooke and what the hell he wanted to do with his life.

Those were the thoughts in Ben's mind when a black cat suddenly streaked out of a concealed entrance behind a hedge and darted across the road in front of him.

Followed closely by a running child.

Ben slammed his foot urgently on the brake pedal. He felt the percussive kickback of the ABS system against the sole of his shoe as the Shogun's tyres bit hard into the dusty tarmac and brought the car to a skidding halt barely a couple of metres from the kid.

The young boy was maybe nine or ten years old. He stood rooted in the middle of the road, staring wide-eyed with shock at the big square front of the Mitsubishi. Ben flung open the car door, jumped out and stormed up to him.

On the other side of the road, the black cat paused to stare a moment, then slunk away into the bushes.

'Didn't your mother teach you to look where you're going?' Ben raged at the kid in Italian. 'You could have got yourself killed.'

The boy hung his head and stared down at his feet. His hair was longish and sandy, his eyes blue and his face a lot paler than it had been just a moment ago. He looked genuinely sorry, and more than a little shaken. Softening, Ben crouched down in front of him so that he wouldn't seem like a huge big angry adult towering over him. 'What's your name?' he said in a gentler tone.

The kid didn't reply for a moment, then glanced up nervously from his feet and muttered, 'Gianni.'

'Was that your pet cat you were chasing after, Gianni?'

A shake of the head.

'Do you live around here?' He was too neatly dressed to

40

have come far, and Ben could see he wasn't some kind of street urchin running wild about the place.

Gianni pointed through the trees at the side of the road. 'Are your parents at home?'

Gianni didn't reply. He could obviously see where this was leading, and was scared of getting into trouble. His eyes began to mist up, and he sniffed, and then again. There was a trace of a quiver in his lower lip.

'Nobody's going to yell at you,' Ben said. 'I promise.' He stood up and looked around him. There was no sign of anyone around. They were on the village outskirts. The kid's home must be the other side of the woods. 'I think we need to find your mother,' he said, guiding the boy to the verge. 'Now stay there and don't move.' He quickly jumped back into the car and pulled it into the side of the road. It was too warm to wear his leather jacket. He left it on the passenger seat. 'Let's go,' he said, taking the kid's arm gently but firmly, bleeping the car locks as they set off on foot.

It wasn't until they'd walked down the side of the road for some hundred metres that Ben spotted the large, imposing mansion through the trees in the distance, nestled within what looked like its own piece of parkland behind a stone wall. Jutting out from behind the old part of the building was an ultra-modern extension, an enormous steel and glass construction that looked as if it had only recently been completed, judging by the unfinished grounds.

There were no other homes in sight.

'Is that your house?' Ben said to Gianni.

No reply.

'You don't say a lot, do you?' Ben asked, and when there was still no response he smiled and added, 'That's OK. You don't have to.'

41

They walked on, and a few metres further down the road came to a bend and then a gap in the wall. The iron gates were open and a winding private lane led up through the trees towards the isolated house.

From the number of cars parked outside the building, and the two guys in suits hanging around near the trimmed hedge who seemed to be there in some kind of official capacity, Ben realised it wasn't a residential property. It looked as if some kind of function or gathering was happening inside.

'Are we in the right place?' he asked the boy. Gianni gave a slight nod, resigned by now to the terrible punishment that was in store for him.

Ben led the boy towards the building. As they approached, he could see people milling around inside the main entrance, smiling, greeting one another, hands being shaken and a great deal of excited chatter. There were no signs anywhere, nothing to indicate what the event was. Ben was nearing the door, still holding Gianni's arm, when one of the official-looking guys in suits peeled himself away from the hedge and stepped up. Close-cropped hair, crocodile features, expressionless button eyes, arms crossed over his belly, the suit cheap and wrinkled: typical security goon. Ben had dealt with a million of them.

'May I see your invitation, sir?'

'I don't have an invitation,' Ben said, meeting his stony gaze. 'I found this boy out on the road and I think his family are inside.'

'This is a private exhibition, not open to the public. Nobody can enter without an invitation,' the guy replied as if programmed.

'I'm not interested in the exhibition.' Ben didn't try to hide the irritation in his voice. 'Didn't you hear what I just said? I need to return this boy to his parents, and I'm not leaving until I do. So either let me in or go find them. I don't care which.'

The security guard's moustached colleague walked over. 'Can I be of assistance?'

Ben glanced him up and down. He didn't seem quite as much of a specimen as the other, but Ben figured he could do better than this. 'Who's the manager here?'

'Signor Corsini.'

'Then I'd like to speak with Signor Corsini, please.'

'He's inside. He's busy.'

Ben was ready with a tough reply when a female voice cried out through the buzz of chatter inside the building. The crowd parted and a woman squeezed through in a hurry. She was maybe twenty-nine, thirty, dressed in a bright yellow frock, a fashionable handbag on a gold strap across her shoulder. Ben saw the resemblance to Gianni right away, the same blue eyes and sandy hair worn in a bob. She came running out, arms wide. 'I was so worried! Where did you disappear off to?' Her gaze switched across to Ben. 'Signore, did you find him?'

'Yes, and if I'd found him half a second later he'd have been plastered across the front of my car,' Ben said.

She glared at her son, hands on hips. 'Gianni, is this true?'

'Yes, Mama.'

'What did I tell you about crossing the road?'

'I know, Mama.'

'Wait till I tell your father,' she scolded, and the boy's shoulders sagged further as though his worst fears had been confirmed. He was for it. But Ben could see from the light in the young mother's eyes that she was more relieved than angry. She turned to him, overflowing with gratitude, pleading that he absolutely must come inside for a glass of wine. 'I beg you, it's the least I can do.'

43

Ben thanked her, made eye contact with the first security goon who was still standing there and said pointedly, 'It seems I don't have an invitation.'

'Nonsense,' she protested. Turning to the security guys, she took a slip of paper from her handbag and thrust it at them. 'My husband's invitation. He's allowed two guests. I'm one, and this gentleman is the other.'

Ben hesitated for a moment, then shrugged. *What the hell*, he thought. *It's not like I have anywhere else to go right now*. Plus, a glass of wine sounded like a decent idea at this moment. It wasn't every day he almost flattened a kid, and the after-effects of the shock were still jangling through his system.

'Well, if you insist,' he said with a smile, and shouldered past the goons as she led him inside.

Chapter Nine

Richmond, London

The grass prickled Brooke's knees as she leaned over her flower bed, reached out with the can and sprinkled water on the amaranthus, careful not to drown it. She loved the cascading red flowers of the plant she'd nurtured from a seedling, but it needed a lot of care and wasn't completely suited to the soil of her tiny garden in Richmond.

Saturday, even a beautiful early autumn afternoon like this one, wasn't normally a day of leisure for Brooke. She had a thousand other things to attend to that she knew she was neglecting, including repainting the kitchen of her ground-floor apartment in the converted Victorian red-brick house – but spending time in the garden relaxed her and that was something she needed badly right now.

As she stood up, brushing bits of grass from her bare knees and gazing at the colourful borders, she couldn't help but let her mind drift back, as it had been doing obsessively of late, to the event a month earlier that was the cause of all her troubles.

Phoebe's invitation to the fifth wedding anniversary party had seemed a wonderful opportunity to catch up with the sister Brooke was so close to but didn't get to see often enough. Their schedules seldom allowed it: Brooke was either too busy with her London clients or off in France; or else Phoebe and her husband Marshall were away on one of the frequent exotic vacations with which an investment banker and a Pilates instructor to the celebs could indulge themselves. Skiing in Aspen, snorkelling off Bermuda, high-rolling in whichever of the world's best hotels and restaurants were currently fashionable with the Serious Money Club. The couple had only recently moved into their latest acquisition, an insanely expensive eight-bedroom mock-Tudor house in Hampstead that Brooke hadn't seen until the night of the party.

And what a party. The huge house was milling. A trad jazz band were playing in the corner of one palatial room, people were dancing, champagne was flowing. If anyone there hadn't been a stockbroker or a top barrister, a billionaire banker or a PR guru, Brooke must have missed it. All she'd really wanted was to get some time alone with her sister, but Phoebe was taken up with playing the hostess and they'd barely been able to snatch more than a few words by the time the champagne was going to Brooke's head and she'd headed for the kitchen to get herself a drink of water.

Not surprisingly, the kitchen was gigantic. Miles of exotic hardwood worktop and every conceivable cooking gadget known to man – despite the fact that Phoebe and Marshall ate out almost every night – but finding something as simple as a water glass wasn't so easy. As Brooke was searching yet another cupboard, she heard the kitchen door open and turned to see Marshall come into the room, smiling at her. He clicked the door shut behind him, closing out the noise of the band and the party buzz. He'd walked up to her and leaned against the worktop, watching her. Standing a little close, she'd thought – but made nothing of it at the time.

'I was just looking for a glass.'

He pointed. 'In there. Oh, there's Evian in the fridge,' he added as she picked out a tumbler and went to fill it at the sink.

'Great party,' she'd said, opening the fridge and helping herself to the chilled water. She took a sip, and when she looked back at Marshall he'd moved a little closer. Was that a little odd, or was she just imagining things?

'I'm so glad you were able to make it,' he said. 'It seems so long since we last saw you, Brooke. Keeping busy? Still going over to France to teach at that place – what's it called?'

'Le Val.' She nodded. 'More often than ever.'

Marshall's smile had wavered a little then. 'I suppose you're still seeing that soldier fellow?'

'Ben's not exactly a soldier.'

'Anyway, it's good to see you again, Brooke,' he'd said. 'Tonight wouldn't have been the same without you.'

'Don't be silly. Tonight is all about you and Phoebe. I'm really happy for you both.'

'No, I mean it.'

'Well, it's sweet of you to say.'

They'd gone on chatting for a few moments. Brooke had noticed that Marshall was a little red in the face. Must be the champagne, she thought – until suddenly he pulled a serious frown, cleared his throat and interrupted their small talk by blurting out, 'I really did mean it, you know. I've been looking forward to seeing you again, a lot. In fact, I've been having trouble thinking about anything else the last few weeks. Or any*one* else,' he added meaningfully.

'Marshall, are you drunk? You shouldn't be talking that way.'

'I married the wrong sister,' he stammered. 'I realise that now.'

'You've had too much to drink. Let me make you a coffee.'

'I'm not drunk,' he'd protested, moving even closer and making her back away. 'I think about you all the time. I can't concentrate at work. I can't sleep at night. I'm in love with you, Brooke.'

His earnestness was shocking. She'd been opening her mouth to yell at him to stop it and back off when the door had opened again and Phoebe had walked into the kitchen. Marshall wheeled abruptly away from Brooke and planted himself against the edge of the kitchen table, trying to act normal.

Phoebe didn't appear to notice anything was wrong. 'There you are,' she'd said brightly. 'I was wondering where the two of you had vanished off to.'

'I just came in for a glass of water,' Brooke explained, heart fluttering, holding up her glass as if somehow she needed to provide evidence. Why the hell did she feel she had to justify herself? She was furious with herself, and even angrier with Marshall for putting her in this situation. The fact that she'd hidden it perfectly only made her feel more absurdly complicit.

Exit Marshall, in a hurry, suddenly in urgent need to attend to the guests. Brooke had swallowed hard and spent a while catching up on things with her sister as though nothing had happened. Twenty minutes later, she'd made her excuses and gone home, upset and confused.

One morning a week after the party, Brooke had been driving to work when Phoebe had called her sounding emotional and asking if they could have coffee that day. They'd met at Richoux in Piccadilly, and taken a small table in the corner of the tearoom. Brooke had known right away that something was up. Her sister looked suddenly much older than her thirty-eight years, gaunt and strung out. Over far more than her usual share of cream scones, she'd come out with it:

'Marshall's having an affair.'

'*What?*'

'I'm sure of it.'

'How do you know?'

'I just do. He's stopped paying me any attention. He comes home late. He's irritable and restless.'

Jesus. Under the table, Brooke's toes had been curling. 'He has a stressful job, Phoebe. It could be work related. Problems at the office. It doesn't have to mean—'

'There's more,' Phoebe cut in. 'He bought jewellery. I found a receipt in his pocket. Tiffany's. Three grand. Who's that for, eh?'

'Maybe he wants to surprise you.'

'A week after our anniversary? Christmas is miles away and my birthday's not for another seven months. It isn't for me, Brooke. I know it.' Phoebe had burst into tears at that point. 'I couldn't bear it if he left me. I'd die.'

Brooke had done her best to reassure her sister that nothing was wrong. Everything would soon go back to normal.

She could have murdered Marshall.

Then, two nights after that, the first of the phone calls.

'It's me. Are you alone?'

'Of course I'm alone. I live alone. It's three in the morning, Marshall. Go to sleep.'

'I can't sleep.'

'Good bye.'

Eleven, twelve, thirteen more times he'd tried to call that night, keeping her from sleep until dawn. The next evening had come the knock on the door that she'd been dreading. Marshall had looked wrecked there on the doorstep, demanding to know why she wouldn't answer the phone. Worried he was going to make a scene, she'd let him come inside the flat.

Big mistake.

'The way you talk to me. The way you look at me, the way you laugh when I tell a story. I know you like me. Admit it. You have feelings for me.' She could smell the alcohol on his breath.

'You're crossing the line, Marshall,' she shouted. 'I'm not going to let you hurt Phoebe like this.'

'Not going to *let* me? This is all your fault!' Digging in his pocket, he came out with a small packet. 'Look. Let's not fight. I bought you a present.'

Brooke had stared in horror, knowing what it was. 'I don't want it.'

'It's from Tiffany.'

'Give it to Phoebe. My sister. Your wife, remember?'

'Phoebe and I are finished.'

'Not according to her. You ought to be ashamed of yourself.'

'But—'

'Listen to me, Marshall. Your behaviour with me is completely irrational. It's clear you're going through some kind of crisis, and I think you need to seek professional help. Now, I can give you some numbers to call—'

'Yeah, I'm mad,' he'd grunted. 'Mad about you.' And put out his hand to touch her cheek.

She flinched away. 'Don't. I think you should get out now.'

'I can't. I love you.'

'That's ridiculous, Marshall.'

'Oh, right. You love *him*. The soldier.'

'Ben. He's not—' But there was no point in correcting him. 'Yes, I do.'

He flushed. 'How can you be in any kind of proper relationship with someone who lives in another country? Now *that's* ridiculous.'

'That might not be for long, because I'm thinking of moving there to be with him full time. Not that it's any of your bloody business.'

'Has he asked you? Bet he hasn't.'

'Get *out*, Marshall!'

Finally, with threats and as much force as she could use without physically attacking him, she'd managed to get her brother-in-law out of the flat and chained the door in his face. He'd ranted and pleaded a while on the doorstep, then skulked back across the street to his turbocharged Bentley.

In the weeks since, Brooke had been feeling increasingly powerless and confused, angry, even guilty. On the pretext of wanting to spend more time together, she'd arranged to meet Phoebe several times in town for coffee, never at the house or at her own place. It made her feel better to be there for her sister, protecting and supporting her in her time of need; yet at the same time she was more and more miserable for hiding the truth.

Meanwhile, Marshall's barrage went on. She was terrified even to check her emails and texts in case it would be him, and she avoided the phone almost all of the time. Once or twice it had been Ben calling her, wondering how she was and why she hadn't been in touch. Her excuses had been thin, unconvincing at best. She'd kept conversation to a minimum, afraid that she might let something slip. Briefly, during one of her sleepless nights, she'd considered telling him the truth about what was going on with Marshall. But that had been an idea she'd very quickly dismissed.

Ben would be on the first flight to London to beat the crap out of him.

It wasn't that Marshall didn't have it coming – it was the ugly mess that would ensue. She could see it all. Assault charges. Police. Explanations. Ben in trouble. Phoebe devastated.

No chance.

And now, standing here on this beautiful warm sunny day surrounded by the flowers in her garden, Brooke felt completely walled in.

What am I going to do?

Chapter Ten

Once inside the elegant old house, Ben saw he'd entered a private art exhibition. The entrance foyer was filled with stands of posters, pamphlets and guides, and framed prints around the walls gave a taste of what lay inside. He felt very out of place in his jeans and denim shirt. Scanning the crowd he counted roughly thirty-five guests. Apart from one or two elderly couples, most of the people were in their mid-to-late thirties or older, many sporting a carefully-cultivated arty look. With the exception of one or two bohemian scruffs, everyone was very well dressed, and being Italians there was an unspoken war going on as to who could look the most chic. Probably the winner out of the whole bunch was the square-jawed guy in the Valentino blazer who'd clearly been dividing his time between working on his tan and studying old Robert Redford movies. Mr Dashing. Ben smiled to himself and shook his head.

After Gianni, the youngest person in the room was a sullen teenage girl with long curly blond hair, who was doing everything possible to distance herself from her parents and make it clear that she'd rather be anywhere but here.

'Donatella Strada,' the boy's mother said warmly, keeping a tight hold of her son with her left hand while extending her right.

'Ben Hope.' He took her hand. It was slender and felt delicate in his. Donatella was small and petite, almost elfin. He liked the sharp look of intelligence in her eyes. She didn't have that air of pretension that he could sense in many of the others.

'You are English? But your Italian is excellent.'

'Half Irish,' he said. 'I've travelled a bit, that's all.'

'Well, Signor Hope, I must thank you again. Are you living nearby?'

'Just passing through,' he said. 'What is this place?'

'The Academia Giordani,' she said. 'One of the most established and respected schools of fine art in the region. They're celebrating the opening of the brand new exhibition wing, which has just been finished.'

'The modern bit. I saw it from the road.'

She smiled. 'Modern monstrosity, you wanted to say.'

'No, modern is fine. So is old. I like all kinds of architecture.'

'What about art, Signor Hope? Is it something you appreciate?'

'Some. What little I know about it. Not sure I go for sheep in formaldehyde, or unmade beds and dirty underwear – or does that make me a philistine?'

Donatella seemed to approve of his taste. 'Not in my book. You'll be pleased to know there is nothing like that here. No gimmicks, no publicity stunts or con tricks. Just pure art. The owners have put together a wonderful collection of works from across the centuries, on loan from galleries all over the world.'

'Hence the high security,' Ben said. He'd already noticed the glassy eyes of the CCTV system watching from well-concealed vantage points around the room.

'Oh, yes. Smile, you're on camera. A state-of-the-art

system, apparently. Not surprising that the galleries would insist on it, when you have hundreds of millions of euros hanging on your walls.'

'So, do I take it you're part of the art scene around here?' Ben asked as he followed her through the crowd towards where the staff were checking invites and ushering guests through an arch leading to a glass walkway. He guessed it connected the old part of the building to the new wing.

'My husband Fabio is. He's one of the region's top art and antiquities restorers. I just dabble in it, which is nice for me because I get to go to all the exhibitions with him.'

'Is he here today?'

'He's supposed to be,' she said. 'But he phoned earlier to say he might not be able to get here. His company are helping to restore an old church outside Rome, and they ran into some kind of delay. He'll be very disappointed if he can't make it. And he'll be sorry he didn't get to thank you personally for what you did.'

'I didn't do that much,' Ben said.

Donatella showed her ticket, explained to the woman at the desk that Ben was her guest, and they were ushered through the arched entrance to the glass corridor. At the end of it, they stepped into a bright, airy, ultramodern space that was the pristine new exhibition wing of the Academia Giordani. The floor was gleaming white stone, laid out with strips of red carpet that wove around the displays. The paintings were encased behind non-reflective glass, arranged by artist and period. A number of guests had already started doing the rounds of the exhibition, talking in low voices and pointing this way and that. As more people filtered inside behind Ben and Donatella, the murmur of soft conversation gradually filled the sunlit room. Some seemed impressed by the new building, though one or two faces showed disapproval.

'It's hideous,' a stringy, white-haired woman in a blue dress was muttering to her husband. He was about ninety and walked with a stick. 'Maybe not quite as offensive as the Louvre pyramid,' she went on, 'but hideous just the same.'

'I find the concept has a very . . . *organic* quality, don't you?' one of the bohemians commented loudly to the woman he was with. 'I mean, it's so . . . what's the word?' He was padding about the gallery in open sandals, which together with his unkempt hair and beard probably attracted more offended glances from the other Italians than the design of the building. The Redford clone ignored him altogether.

'So what do you think, Signor Hope?' Donatella asked.

'Like I said, I really don't know that much about art,' Ben said. But he knew enough to understand now why galleries across the world had been jittery about lending their pieces for this exhibition. The canvases around the walls bore enough famous signatures to pop any art lover's cork. Picasso, Chagal, Monet. 'And Da Vinci,' he said, raising his eyebrows.

'Oh yes,' Donatella chuckled. 'All the big names are here. They really wanted to put on a show to launch the centre. Fabio told me they wanted to get a Delacroix too, but they didn't have the wall space.' She touched Ben's arm and pointed across the gallery at a man in an immaculate silk suit, forties, carefully groomed. 'That's Aldo Silvestri, one of the owners. And see that man over there, standing beside the Picasso?'

'That little fat guy there?'

'I'm sure he'd love to hear you say that. Luigi Corsini is Silvestri's business partner. But the real money comes from Count Pietro De Crescenzo. Without his influence, the gallery would not have been possible, and certainly not an exhibition of this calibre.'

Donatella pointed out the man to Ben. Late fifties, tall

56

and gaunt with thin oiled hair, he could have passed for an undertaker if it hadn't been for the dapper bow tie. He was standing with a group of people on the far side of the room, sipping a glass of wine. 'The De Crescenzos are one of the oldest aristocratic families of this region, with quite a colourful history,' she filled in.

'You know them?'

She nodded. 'The count has funded several of Fabio's projects in the past.'

De Crescenzo seemed to sense them talking about him. Giving Donatella a smile, he excused himself from the group and approached. Donatella explained to the count that Fabio had been held up, and introduced Ben. 'Please call me Pietro,' De Crescenzo said as he shook Ben's hand. 'I only use the title to open doors and impress stuffy politicians and museum boards. So, Signor Hope, I gather despite your extremely fluent Italian that you are not from these parts.'

'I'm just passing through,' Ben said.

'You are on vacation? Remaining a few days in Italy?'

'Sadly not. I'll be flying to London tomorrow.'

De Crescenzo shuddered. 'Air travel. I cannot bring myself to get on one of those things. Quite irrational, I know.'

'It's a very impressive setup you have here,' Ben said.

De Crescenzo smiled widely, showing uneven, grey teeth. 'Thank you, thank you. We have been extremely fortunate in securing such a fabulous and eclectic range of wonderful pieces.'

'Have your family always been patrons of the arts?' Ben asked, knowing his supply of cultural small talk was going to run out fast.

'Far from it. My grandfather, Count Rodingo De Crescenzo, was a boorish and tyrannical man who despised culture with almost as much passion as he loathed the artistic genius of his first wife, Gabriella. It is to her that we owe the artistic heritage of my family. After doing everything in his power to suppress her talent, my grandfather ironically did the most to nurture it when he expelled her from the family home in 1925, leaving her destitute. Freed from his controlling influence, she eventually went on to find fame and fortune painting under her maiden name, Gabriella Giordani.'

Ben nodded and smiled politely, a little taken aback by De Crescenzo's somewhat dramatic account of his family past. When he suddenly realised that the count was waiting for him to react to the mention of the name Gabriella Giordani, he shrugged apologetically and said, 'As I was telling Donatella, my knowledge of art is pretty limited. I'm afraid I haven't come across your grandmother's work.'

De Crescenzo frowned sadly and shook his head. 'Rodingo and Gabriella had no children. My father was born only after Rodingo had remarried, to a woman of great beauty but little else. Otherwise, I might have had the honour of being related in more than name to the most accomplished and admired Italian female artist of the twentieth century.' He swept an arm enthusiastically behind him at a section of the exhibition.

Ben gazed in the direction he was pointing. 'And that one too?' he said, motioning at an oil portrait of a striking-looking man of about thirty, in a red velvet jacket with a high collar.

'You have a keen eye for style, Signor Hope,' De Crescenzo said. 'Yes, that is also a Giordani.'

Ben took a step closer to the portrait and examined it for a moment. There was something aristocratic about the man in the painting, yet not supercilious or arrogant. The artist seemed to have captured a real sense of humility and gentleness in her subject. The little plaque below the edge of the frame simply said 'Leo', with the date 1925. Ben wondered who Leo had been.

'Just one of her many celebrated works here on display,' De Crescenzo said. 'Including a quite incredible recent discovery.' He said this in a hushed tone of reverence, as though referring to the finger-bone of Christ. Ben waited for more.

'During the recent restoration of my ancestral home, the Palazzo De Crescenzo – it is far too large to live in, of course – workmen came upon a secret room where it seems the young and terribly unhappy countess carried on her art behind her husband's back. He had forbidden her to paint, you see. We found several previously unknown works of hers, which are being exhibited here today for the very first time.' Looking even more excited, De Crescenzo added, 'And sensationally, among the pieces we discovered in her personal collection were several items by other artists – including a most magnificent miniature charcoal sketch by the artist Goya that had long been believed lost.'

Ben turned to look as he pointed out the piece of artwork across the room. It was a small, simple, shaded monochrome image of a solitary man kneeling humbly to pray inside what could have been a monastic cell.

Again Ben could feel De Crescenzo's eyes on him and felt expected to comment knowledgeably, but he just nodded appreciatively and tried not to think about that glass of wine Donatella had promised him. He fought the urge to glance at his watch.

'Naturally it is almost worthless compared to some of the other works here on display,' De Crescenzo went on rather too grandly. 'But I founded this academy in April 1987 to honour Gabriella Giordani's sad passing the previous year, and I cannot tell you how thrilled we are to be able to mark the inauguration of our new centre with a display of her very own collection. For me, it is what makes this exhibition so special.'

'I'm very pleased for you,' Ben said. 'Congratulations.'

'You'll be wanting that wine now,' Donatella whispered as they left the count to carry on the rounds of the guests.

'I don't know what gives you that impression,' Ben said. *What a character*, he was thinking.

Donatella smiled slyly. 'This way.' She led him through the crowd to the far side of the gallery, where two doors led off from the main space. One was shut and marked 'Private'. The other was open, leading into a side room where a long table was covered in expensive finger food and drinks. The glasses were crystal, the white wine was on ice and the red had been opened in advance to breathe at room temperature. Catering done properly. Donatella chose white, while Ben helped himself to a glass of excellent Chianti and suddenly felt much better.

Gianni was allowed to wander about the exhibition on strict orders to behave himself and stay within sight. Away from the chatter of the guests, Ben and Donatella sipped their drinks and talked for a few minutes. She was warm, vivacious and smiled a lot. He found her company relaxing and enjoyable. She told him a little more about her husband's church restoration project, and then asked him about his own business. Ben had long ago learned to answer those kinds of questions without sounding evasive but without getting too specific about the kind of training that went on at Le Val. She'd visited that part of France a few years earlier and was curious to know if his home was anywhere near to Mont Saint Michel, which he told her it was.

As they talked and the minutes went by, neither of them noticed the white Mercedes van that was pulling up outside, or the men who were getting out.

Chapter Eleven

It was exactly 6.45 p.m. when the van appeared on the driveway and drew up in the forecourt outside the entrance of the Academia Giordani. The window rolled down as the two security guys swaggered up to the vehicle, putting on their best officious frowns. Ghini, the one with the moustache, was the first to notice the intimidating bulk of the van driver as he leaned out to talk to them. He could see himself and his colleague, Buratti, reflected like a couple of dorks in the mirror lenses of the guy's wrap-around shades. He folded his arms across his chest to make them look bigger, tried to act tough and let Buratti do the talking.

'Think you're in the wrong place, guys,' Buratti said.

The driver looked puzzled, shook his head. 'This is the Academia Giordani, yeah? Delivery for you.'

'Not that I was told about.'

The big guy produced a yellow printed sheet from his bulging breast pocket. 'See for yourself.'

Buratti studied it carefully. It did indeed look as if the goods had been ordered. 'We have a problem. There's an exhibition on here now.'

'So?'

'So can't you see there are people inside? I can't have a

bunch of workmen spoiling the view from the gallery windows. You're gonna have to come back tomorrow.'

'No way. Not till next month, pal. We're booked solid.'

'We'll see about that when I talk to your boss.'

'I *am* the boss.'

Buratti chewed his lip, his brow twisted in thought. Turning the delivery away was bound to wind up with him getting an earful from someone. 'OK. But make it quick. I want that stuff unloaded and this van out of here in five minutes.'

'Fine.'

Buratti waved the van through and it drove around the side of the building, tyres crunching on gravel, followed the path round the back and pulled up in view of the new modern wing. The diesel died with a shudder.

Rocco Massi swung open his door and jumped down. Bellomo and Garrone did the same, nobody saying a word. Through the tall glass windows Rocco could see the people inside, milling about staring at a bunch of paintings. Chattering, pointing, admiring, one or two standing around sipping wine. Bunch of smug shits. All too preoccupied to notice anything. He grinned. Five minutes from now, things would be a whole lot different for these good folks.

The two security guards were watching impatiently from near the entrance. Rocco jerked his head as if to call them over, and they came stomping across the gravel. Their tough guy act deflated with every step. He was a foot taller than either of them, and the tight black T-shirt showed every muscle. Bellomo and Garrone leaned up against the side of the van, watching in silence.

'What is it?' Buratti said.

'Change of plan, fellas,' Rocco said. 'If you want us out of here fast, you're gonna have to help us unload.'

'What?'

'Won't take long if there's five of us.' Rocco motioned to the rough patch of ground that the builders had left in the wake of the construction project. 'Over there OK?'

'You're shitting us.'

'Nope. There's a lot of stuff here. See for yourself.' Rocco beckoned them round the back of the van, where they were out of sight of the guests inside the gallery.

Buratti was working hard to look fierce and professional, and failing. 'Listen, pal. You do your job and we'll do ours. We're not paid to unload garden equipment. We have a job to do.'

'Yeah,' Ghini said. 'What do we look like to you?'

Rocco gazed at them impassively from behind the curved shades. 'Like a couple of dead assholes,' he said, and opened the back door of the van.

The first thing Ghini saw inside the van was the last thing he'd ever see in this world. Spartak Gourko was crouching just inside the door, watching him impassively. Ghini stared at him, then stared at the strange-looking knife in his hand. The man was pointing it at Ghini's chest, but he didn't move. Then there was a sudden crack and the knife blade was propelled like a missile. Its razor-sharp point drove deep into him, shattering a rib and plunging into his heart. He was dead before he hit the ground.

Buratti backed away in a panic, then let out a wheezing gasp as Bellomo stepped up behind him and buried a combat dagger in his back. He slumped down on top of Ghini.

Spartak Gourko jumped down from the van. In his hand was the hilt of his knife, a long steel spring protruding where the blade should be. A trophy from his Spetsnaz days. He kicked over the bodies and retrieved the detachable blade from Ghini's chest. Slipping it into a metal sheath, he compressed it back inside the hilt with an effort before replacing the weapon in his belt.

Anatoly Shikov jumped out of the van next, followed by the other three Russians, each holding a large black canvas holdall. Strong hands grasped Ghini and Buratti by their collars and belts and bundled them messily into the back of the Mercedes.

The ornamental slabs and edging stones were lying in a ditch miles away.

Anatoly slammed the doors shut, peeled back the sleeve of his jacket, checked the dial of his shiny Tag Heuer. Dead on time, the radio gave a splurt and a fizz. He snatched it up. Petrovich's voice, transmitting from somewhere beyond the woods.

'You're good to go,' Petrovich said in Russian.

'Landline dead?'

'As disco.'

'OK. You and what's-his-name stand by.'

'Caracciolo. Copy. See you when it's done, boss.'

Anatoly shut off the radio. He unzipped a plain black gym bag, took out the cellphone blocker his father had given him, set it down on the van's passenger seat and activated it. Just like that, all communication to and from the Academia Giordani was cut off. Also in the gym bag was the padded case his father had given him, tailored to the dimensions of the Goya sketch. Anatoly put the strap around his shoulder.

The eight men walked fast across the gravel and paused outside the entrance to unzip the holdalls. First, out came the black balaclavas, standard three-hole military issue. Rocco didn't like to remove his shades, but couldn't wear them over the mask. He took them off reluctantly and slipped them into his pocket. Next came the tight-fitting leather gloves; and finally the weapons. Five Steyr TMP ultra-compact 9mm machine pistols with twenty-round magazines; Anatoly grabbed one of those like a kid in a sweet shop, while Rocco Massi helped himself to one of the two AR-15 assault rifles fitted with 40mm underbarrel grenade launchers. Gourko claimed the other. The last firearm to be handed out was the short-barrelled Remington 12-gauge autoloader with folding stock. Good for blowing locks and generally blasting apart anything at close range. That one fell to Garrone.

Between them, it added up to enough firepower to hold off a regiment.

Once everyone was kitted up, all eyes fell on Anatoly. Waiting for his command. He loved this moment.

Chapter Twelve

There was a limit to how much Ben could discuss about fine art, but it turned out that Donatella shared his love of Bartók's music and that was what they were talking about when Gianni came up to complain he was thirsty. While she fussed over the boy and went to the refreshments table to get him a glass of fruit juice, Ben stepped casually across to the window and gazed out at the grounds and the woods that surrounded the property. He noticed the white Mercedes van parked up outside, which hadn't been there before. It looked like a builder's van, well used and streaked with road dirt. Whoever had left it there while he and Donatella had been talking had disappeared out of sight.

Ben didn't give it a second thought as he stood sipping his drink, surrounded by the growing buzz of conversation. The refreshments room was filling with people, wine being poured, the finger food rapidly disappearing from the table. The sullen teenage girl was moping alone in a corner, huffing in exasperation whenever her parents came within a few metres of her. Ben could hear Donatella in the background talking to her boy, and decided that now was the moment for him to make his excuses and get away. She was a charming host, Gianni was a sweet kid and he wasn't sorry to have spent a while with them, but he needed to get back to his own affairs.

Just then, someone bumped into him from behind and a voice said, 'Oh, I'm so sorry.' Ben looked around to see Mr Dashing, the Robert Redford-a-like, standing there with half a canapé in his hand and the other half partially chewed in his open mouth. Ben felt the wetness against his skin. He glanced down at the big dark red patch all down the front of his denim shirt and realised he'd spilled wine over himself. 'Thanks for that,' he said, dripping.

'I'm so sorry,' Mr Dashing repeated.

'Don't worry about it.'

Donatella joined him at the window. She was frowning at the slim phone in her hand. 'I just tried to call Fabio to see what was happening, but I can't get through. My phone's gone dead.'

'Battery?'

'No, it's fine,' she said, puzzled. 'Fully charged, and I'm getting good reception. It just doesn't—' She stopped and looked down at his shirt. 'What happened? You're covered in wine.'

'Just an accident. Not a big deal. It'll dry.'

She shook her head. 'You should go and wash it out before it stains. There are toilets in the foyer but you'll find a bath-room upstairs, on the first floor.' She wrinkled her nose at the stain. 'Really, I think you should. It's a nice shirt.'

Ben was about to explain that a spot on his shirt didn't bother him in the least – but he relented, thinking he didn't want to be soaked in alcohol and smelling like a brewery when he went to find a hotel later. He excused himself and made his way back out through the glass corridor.

Anatoly Shikov was perfectly calm as he led the way into the building. Spartak Gourko followed close behind him, then Rocco Massi, both clutching their bulky AR-15 rifles. Rykov was the last man in, and locked the door behind him.

The entrance foyer was deserted now that all the guests had been shown inside the exhibition, which disappointed Anatoly. He'd been anticipating the squeals of terror from the women at the desk as eight masked and heavily armed men suddenly burst in to blow their cosy little world apart. He'd wanted to see the fear in their eyes, knowing that they were in his power.

It didn't matter. The fun would begin soon enough. Anatoly did a final check of his machine pistol, and then turned to his guys. 'Let's get started,' he said in Russian.

Ben soon found the bathroom near the first floor landing, at the end of a shadowy passage. The door was ajar. He walked in to find an elderly gentleman he recognised as the husband of the woman in the blue dress, stooped over the marble sink. The old fellow's walking stick was propped up against the surface next to him as he washed down a handful of pills with a glass of water. Ben apologised for interrupting him, but the elderly man smiled and replied that he was just leaving. 'Il mio cuore,' he said, showing Ben the tube of heart pills. 'The doctor says I have to take these every couple of hours, or I'll die pretty soon. Then again, what does he know? Maybe I'll outlive the bastard.'

The elderly man introduced himself as Marcello Peruzzi. They exchanged brief small-talk about the exhibition. 'My wife doesn't think much of it,' Marcello said ruefully. 'But then she always hates everything. Married fifty-two years,' he added, and Ben wasn't quite sure whether he meant it with pride or bitterness. With a wave of his hand, Marcello turned towards the door and started making his wobbly way back towards the stairs. Ben asked him if he needed any help, but Marcello assured him he could manage fine, thanks.

The bathroom was large and plush, with French windows

leading out onto its own little balcony with a view of the grounds. Once he was alone, Ben went over to the sink and stripped off his wine-stained shirt. The TYRELL Genetic Replicants T-shirt under it was only slightly wet, and he decided it didn't need washing.

He had the shirt bundled under the hot tap and was rubbing the dark red stain out of the material when he heard the first gunshots blasting out from somewhere down below.

And then came the screams.

Chapter Thirteen

Ben froze. It took him less than a second to process what he was hearing.

The sound was unmistakable, one he'd heard many times in the past. It was the harsh snorting rip of 9mm submachine gun fire, and it was coming from the direction of the gallery wing. Two sustained bursts. Then another. More screams. Pandemonium cutting loose among the exhibition guests.

He wrenched open the bathroom door as he heard more shots reverberate through the building. He glanced left, then right.

Marcello Peruzzi, the elderly man he'd encountered a moment earlier in the bathroom, had made it as far as the top of the stairs when the shooting started. He was standing there paralysed with shock, a frail hand gripping the banister rail.

He wasn't alone. As Ben watched, a pair of men came sprinting up the stairs. From the black ski-masks and the stubby Steyr machine pistols in their fists he guessed they didn't have invites to the exhibition either.

One of them slung his weapon behind his back and grabbed Marcello Peruzzi roughly by the arm while the other jabbed the muzzle of his gun at his head. 'Downstairs with the others, grandpa,' he snarled in Italian.

Marcello struggled weakly, protesting, and tried to lash out with his walking stick. The gunman clubbed him hard across the face with the butt of his weapon, twice, beating him down to his knees. He collapsed onto his belly and the second guy let go of his arm as he began convulsing.

Watching the scene in horror from the shadows of the passage, Ben remembered the heart pills.

The masked men stared down at Marcello as he folded up in agony on the carpet. 'He's having an attack,' one of them said.

'Fuck him, he's dead anyway.' The man pointing the gun casually placed the muzzle against Marcello's neck and touched off the trigger. A deafening triple-shot burst crackled out across the landing and up the passage. The 9mm bullets ripped into Marcello's body and his distressed heart stopped for ever.

Ben recoiled into the bathroom, unseen, and turned the lock.

Down below, Anatoly and the rest of his team had rounded up the crowd of exhibition guests. The gallery was filled with shouts of rage and frightened screams and the blast of fully-automatic fire as the intruders let off bursts into the ceiling. It was a technique intended for one purpose only – to strike terror into their victims and reduce them into a state of complete helplessness – and it was very effective. The thirty-five or so guests gave no resistance, allowing themselves to be herded like sheep across the gallery, their shoes crunching on the broken glass from shattered overhead lighting. It took under half a minute to shove everyone into the corner of the side room and make them huddle on the floor across from the refreshments table. The white-haired woman in the blue dress was looking around desperately for her husband

and wailing loudly in panic. Rocco yelled at her to shut up, and when she kept on wailing Anatoly grabbed a half-finished bottle of Chianti from the refreshments table, took a long swig out of it and then hurled it at her. The base of the bottle caught her across the forehead and she fell back with a gasp. Another woman and the bearded guy in the sandals caught her as she keeled over.

'How dare you!' the bearded guy shouted. 'This is an outrage!'

Gourko delivered a kick to his stomach that folded him double before slamming a knee into his face. He collapsed, wheezing, blood pouring out of his busted nose into his beard.

Gourko laughed.

The Robert Redford type in the Valentino blazer glowered at him, but did nothing. Crouching among the other hostages, Count De Crescenzo exchanged looks of horrified disbelief with his business partners Corsini and Silvestri. The bearded guy huddled into the arms of the woman he was with. The woman in the blue dress was slumped against the wall in shock, blood running from the cut on her forehead.

'Am I going to get any shit from you fuckers?' Anatoly screamed in Russian at the cringing assembly. '*Am I?*' He didn't care that they wouldn't understand him. They'd understand this. He aimed his machine pistol at the table and let off a rattling blast that smashed bottles and plates into flying pieces. '*Am I?*' he screamed again. Wine and food spilled onto the floor. The hostages cowered in terror.

Gianni Strada was pale and shaking as he clung to his mother. The boy was holding her so tightly that it hurt. Donatella struggled to contain her own panic as the armed men strode up and down the room. The one who frightened her the most was this maniac with the blond ponytail sticking out from under his mask. Was that Russian he was talking? Sounded like it to her. What was happening? *How* could this be happening? Was no alarm being raised?

Gianni suddenly let out a strange, high-pitched keening sound that dissolved into racking sobs. He clung to her even tighter, grasping handfuls of her hair. She could feel his tears wet against her neck.

'You. Make that little ratshit quiet or he dies in the next two seconds,' Anatoly raged, jabbing the gun an inch from her face.

Donatella didn't need a translator. She closed her eyes and stroked her son's hair, murmuring words of comfort in his ear. Gianni's sobs quietened to a low whimper.

Anatoly unslung the padded case from his shoulder and laid it down on the table. He beamed at the hostages.

'Good. Now let's get down to business,'

Chapter Fourteen

Ben paced the bathroom, thinking hard. There was no telling how many armed men were down there, and how many other people had been hurt. He dug in his jeans pocket for his phone.

It was a rare thing for Ben to call the cops. In the kinds of situations his work had often involved him in the past, the last thing he needed was the police getting under his feet. But today he was just a tourist. He was unarmed, he had no idea what was happening, and he had no other options.

He punched 112 into the phone keypad, the emergency number for the Carabinieri. Italy's paramilitary gendarmerie were widely disliked but in a situation like this, with their rapid firearms response capability, they were the best people for the job. Fractions of seconds felt like drawn-out minutes as he waited for the dial tone.

And nothing happened. His phone was dead, just like Donatella's. His battery was about three-quarters charged and he was getting a good reception. Yet the phone was utterly useless. There was only one explanation, and that was that the intruders were using a cellphone blocker. The kind of equipment that police and counterterror units used to isolate cells of suspects before moving in. Which meant that what was happening downstairs was no ordinary armed raid – and with no way to call for outside help, Ben was going to have to deal with it on his own.

Another burst of shots from down below made him think of Donatella and Gianni Strada. He imagined the boy's terror. Felt his blood turn from icy cold to burning hot at the thought of anyone harming either of them. He thought of old Marcello Peruzzi lying dead at the top of the stairs. Thought of all those other people down there, helpless, vulnerable, frightened. His teeth clenched so hard that they hurt.

The muffled clump of footsteps running up the passage was audible through the bathroom door. Voices outside.

Ben glanced around him. In a moment like this, just about any household item could be turned into an improvised weapon. His gaze locked on the mirror above the sink. He was just about to smash the glass with the heel of his shoe when he heard the marching footsteps run right up to the bathroom door.

The handle turned. The door rattled furiously. That flimsy lock wasn't going to last long.

As the first heavy kick pounded the door, Ben leaped across the room and out through the French windows onto the balcony. It was too high to jump down to the concrete below without risking injury. He craned his neck upwards and saw that there was another balcony window directly above. The old house was built from solid stone, and the masonry had been expertly pointed, with recesses between the blocks that looked just about deep enough to climb.

As more kicks thudded violently against the bathroom door, he jumped up onto the balcony rail, turned to face the wall and dug his fingers into the cracks in the stonework to the left of the window. He swung his legs off the balcony.

For a few painful seconds, his fingertips took his weight as he brought up his knees and scrabbled against the wall with the toecaps of his shoes until he found a crack. He was clear of the window now, clinging to the sheer wall like a spider. He reached up with his right arm, groped for another handhold and found it. Then the left foot, feeling around for a good purchase, then pulling himself up so he could grab another hold with his left hand. The second floor window was still tantalisingly far above him. He climbed faster.

Down below, the bathroom door burst open with a crash and the two gunmen rushed in, weapons at the hip, knees bent to brace themselves against the recoil. A storm of automatic fire shattered tiles and blasted apart the sink, riddling the walls with holes. Before the men even realised the room was empty, it was destroyed. One of them motioned to the French windows. They ran over to them and burst out onto the balcony.

Ben was clambering over the rail of the balcony above when he looked down and saw the masked gunmen below him, craning their necks down at the ground. They hadn't spotted him. For a moment he was tempted to jump down and try to take them both – but some kinds of heroics could get you killed in a hurry.

By the time they'd looked up from the balcony below, Ben had disappeared out of sight and was going in through the second floor window.

The two men heard the smash of glass above them and knew what it meant. One grabbed a radio handset from his pocket, hit the press and talk button and said in Italian, 'This is Scagnetti. I'm with Bellomo. We have a runner.'

The reply that came over the radio was 'Find him. Kill him.'

Chapter Fifteen

It didn't take Anatoly long to find the piece of artwork his father had sent him all the way to Italy to obtain. The framed Goya sketch looked pretty much the way it had in the photo he'd seen in the old man's study. Just a plain and, to him, frankly pretty fucking boring picture of some scraggy dude crouched down on his knees. The poor bastard was barefoot and had a desperate expression on his thin face. He was wearing a shapeless robe that could have been a bit of old sacking material, and his hands were clasped together in supplication as he prayed fervently to God for something or other. Salvation, Anatoly supposed. Or maybe just a decent suit of clothes.

Anatoly looked at the picture for a long time and the same two questions kept coming back to him. Why would anybody bother drawing such a dull and depressing picture? And why the fuck would anybody want to own it? You'd have thought the old man would have picked something better.

There was a small plaque on the wall next to the display cabinet that housed the picture. It said *Francisco Goya, 1746 – 1824*. Underneath was a blurb about how it had recently been rediscovered after being thought to have been lost for years, blah, blah, blah. Anatoly gave it only a cursory glance. Shaking his head, he moved away and spent a few moments gazing pensively at the other paintings around the walls of the gallery. Big, bold, rich-looking oils and ornate gilt frames.

Now *this* was more like it. He didn't much rate this kind of stuff but he'd heard of fancy names like Da Vinci. Who hadn't? And you didn't have to be an art snob to know there was a bloody fortune hanging on these walls, right here for the taking. Just a single one of these others would surely fetch him the cost of a new Lamborghini, even after deducting the fence's cut. It made him wonder all the more why he'd been sent to steal a poxy colourless drawing of a skinny bloke saying his prayers. It didn't even have a nice frame, just a plain black wood surround.

But what the hell. Anatoly sighed and turned back to the Goya. Raising his Steyr, he was about to whack the protective glass casing when he remembered what that prick Maisky had said about the impregnable security shutters that would come slamming down to seal off the whole place if anyone messed with the artwork. Before it could be taken off the wall they had to enter the three codes to disable the secondary alarm system. Right. *Some* parts of his father's plan did make sense.

Anatoly walked back to the side room, swinging his gun as he went. Passing the food table he scooped a handful of stuffed olives from one of the plates he hadn't blown apart earlier on. He popped it through the mouth hole of his balaclava and chewed noisily as he approached the clustered hostages. Gourko and Rykov were standing over them with their weapons trained menacingly. Turchin was over by the window, refilling a magazine from loose rounds in his pocket. Rocco Massi and one of his guys were slumped in a couple of canvas chairs, holding their guns loosely across their laps. The two Italians Rocco had sent upstairs hadn't returned yet.

Anatoly popped another olive and surveyed the crowd of

frightened faces, feeling supremely in control. His gaze stopped at the young girl who was in the arms of her mother. Her face was hidden by a mass of blond curls, but running his eye down the curve of her body he liked what he saw. The strap of her pretty little dress was just off the shoulder, showing the flimsy bra strap underneath. She couldn't be more than fifteen, he thought, and wondered if she was still a virgin. A budding little flower, just waiting to be plucked by ol' Anatoly. Nice. Very nice.

A couple of the hostages gasped in fear as he stepped forward and reached down abruptly to grab the girl's bare arm. She let out a whimper as she felt his fingers close tightly on her skin. He hauled her away from her mother, yanking her body round so he could see her face. So adorable. He stroked her cheek lightly. It was sticky with half-dried tears, and that really turned him on. He cocked his head a little to the side, looked into those sweet, moist blue eyes and gave her a crooked smile. 'Later, babe, later,' he muttered in Russian.

First, though, he had more pressing matters to take care of. He dumped the girl back down on the floor. Scanning the rest of the hostages he quickly picked out the faces of the three men whose photos his father had shown him. 'You, you and you,' he said, pointing with his Steyr.

Rocco Massi stood and jerked his thumb at the three men. 'Get up,' he barked in Italian. De Crescenzo, Corsini and Silvestri nervously got to their feet, stiff and rumpled from crouching on the floor. The count was deathly pale. Silvestri dusted off his suit and tried to look dignified. Corsini's chubby face flushed with indignation; he opened his mouth to say something, but it never came out, because Gourko slapped him hard across the face and then grabbed a fistful of his collar and shoved him brutally towards the door. Corsini stumbled, and Anatoly aimed the toe of his boot at those fat buttocks, sending him sprawling on his face through the doorway.

'There is no need whatsoever for this violence,' De Crescenzo stammered. 'Whatever it is you want, we're more than happy to comply.'

'Oh, we know that,' Rocco Massi said. De Crescenzo and Silvestri were prodded through the door at gunpoint as Corsini picked himself up with a moan.

Anatoly pointed at the closed door a few metres along the end wall. 'Ask them what's in there,' he said to Rocco. The big Italian translated. De Crescenzo cleared his throat and replied, 'That is the office from which we control the security system.'

'Open it.'

The count fumbled in his pocket, took out a key ring and unlocked the office door. Anatoly shoved it open and led the way inside. The room was small and quite bare, except for a couple of steel filing cabinets, a worktop with a bank of computer equipment and some office chairs.

The three gallery owners were made to sit. Anatoly leaned against a filing cabinet, twirling his weapon. Rocco stepped up to Corsini's chair, bent down so that his nose was just inches from the man's sweaty face, and said, 'Each of you has a separate passcode to disable the secondary alarm system. You have five seconds to enter it.' He grabbed the back of the chair and wheeled the fat man brusquely over to the worktop. The computer was on standby mode and the screen popped up into life as Rocco nudged its wireless mouse. He tapped a few keys and an empty box opened up, a blinking cursor at its far left inviting someone to enter the code.

'I won't do it,' Corsini mumbled.

'What did the fucker say?' Anatoly asked, raising an eyebrow.

'He says he won't do it,' Rocco said.

'Thought so. We'll see about that.' Anatoly walked purposefully past the seated men and out of the office. There was a commotion from next door. Moments later, Anatoly came back into the room, dragging a kicking, screaming woman by the wrist – the girlfriend of the bearded guy whose nose Gourko had broken. Anatoly kicked the office door shut, let the struggling woman slump to the floor and knocked her half senseless with a backhand blow to the jaw. Standing over her, he racked the bolt of his Steyr. Pressed the muzzle to her head.

Corsini had turned from purple to white. Silvestri and De Crescenzo both stared at him.

'Luigi,' De Crescenzo said in a trembling hoarse whisper. 'For the love of God, do as he asks.'

Corsini looked from his colleagues to the woman, from the woman to Anatoly. His face twisted with the agony of responsibility. A nervous tic made his left eye flutter wildly.

'The code,' Rocco Massi said.

Chapter Sixteen

Every second that ticked by was a torment as Ben explored his new surroundings on the second floor. The room he was in might have been a plush bedroom at one time during the building's history, with ornately carved ceiling beams and a magnificent double doorway. In its more recent past, the owners of the art academy had converted it into a classroom. A large oak table at the side of the room bore a slide projector and a portable TV hooked up to a VCR. Bookshelves were stacked high with books and old video cassettes with titles like *Art of the Renaissance* and *Grand Masters of Florence*. Rows of chairs faced the teacher's desk, on which lay assorted pens and writing pads, a heavy paper punch, a roll of tape.

Ben glanced out into the corridor, thinking hard and fast because he knew the gunmen were combing the building every moment he hesitated. He could almost hear their running steps closing in on him. He snatched the paper punch from the desk, weighing it in his hand and imagining its best use as a weapon.

He desperately needed to gain some kind of advantage. Escape was an option – it was only a few minutes' sprint back to the village he'd passed through earlier. If he could get to a phone, he could alert the Carabinieri; but he couldn't stop thinking about what could happen to those people down there during the precious minutes he'd be gone.

A few metres down the corridor, an antiquated fire hose on a big red metal reel the size of a tractor wheel was fixed to the wall. It looked as though it had been sitting there unused since the war. Next to it, held by steel clips behind a panel of dusty glass, was an old fire axe. Ben ran over to it, used the paper punch to break the glass and tore the axe away from the wall. The hickory shaft felt thick and solid in his hands.

Now he really could hear footsteps. They were some way off, resonating through the empty building, but approaching fast.

He propped the axe handle against the wall and tore a strip of cloth from the hem of his T-shirt. *Sorry, Brooke.* Snatching a long, pointed shard of broken glass from the floor, he wrapped the cloth around its base to create an improvised knife. With a hard spin of the reel, metres of pipe spilled like entrails over the floor. He used his makeshift blade to slash four lengths of the thick rubber, then spun the reel back the other way to wind up the trailing hose. Grabbing the axe again, he sprinted back towards the classroom.

'Luigi,' Count Pietro De Crescenzo repeated urgently. 'Do what he says.' Corsini seemed paralysed with indecision. His eyes bulged as he glanced back and forth between his colleagues, the gently stirring woman on the office floor and the submachine gun that Anatoly had pressed hard up against the back of her skull.

'Too slow,' Anatoly said. He touched off the trigger of the Steyr. De Crescenzo's cry of protest was drowned out by the ripping blast of the three-shot burst.

Corsini's jaw gaped. Silvestri rocked back and forth in his

chair, jamming his fist in his mouth to keep from screaming in horror. De Crescenzo stared in numb despair as the last twitches of the woman's central nervous system made her limbs jerk and the smell of death and cordite filled the small room. Vomit erupted in his throat like hot lava and he threw up.

Rocco Massi said calmly to Corsini, 'We can keep doing this all day until you give us the code.'

The fat man had had enough. There were tears in his eyes as he grabbed the remote computer keyboard and tapped in a series of numbers, swallowed hard, and hit the enter key.

Anatoly nodded in satisfaction as the screen flashed up a 'CODE VALID' message. He pointed at Silvestri. 'Now it's your turn.'

Chapter Seventeen

Scagnetti and Bellomo tore through the second floor of the house, kicking open every door as they went. Bellomo was a couple of metres ahead when he held up a clenched fist and jerked his head towards the end of the corridor as if to say, 'Wait. I hear something.'

Up ahead in the shady corridor was a carved double doorway. The doors were open inwards a few inches, sunlight streaming into the room from the window beyond. The men listened. Behind the doors, a man's voice was talking. He spoke in rapid Italian, something about Botticelli. The voice sounded tinny and reedy, and they realised it was coming from a TV speaker.

'That just came on now,' Scagnetti whispered. Bellomo nodded. As they listened, the sound stopped abruptly, as if whoever had turned it on by mistake was turning it off again in a hurry.

The two gunmen kicked open the doors and raced into the room.

Straight into a massive impact that knocked them sprawling backwards and their weapons spinning out of their hands.

Ben rode the heavy oak table as it came swinging violently down from its perch over the double doors. The lengths of

85

rubber hose he'd tied from two of its legs to the classroom's ceiling beams brought it down in a perfect arc so that the thick tabletop rammed into the men's bodies as they entered the room and laid them flat. It was as if they'd been hit by a train. He leaped off, landed nimbly on his feet, and stepped out of the way as the table swung back towards him.

One of the men was out cold; the other was groaning and struggling to raise himself up off the floor. His face was bloodied. Ben remembered him as the one who'd murdered Marcello Peruzzi as calmly as stepping on a beetle. He picked up the fire axe from inside the door and placed its blunt nose against the man's throat, pressing him back down.

'What's your name?' he asked softly.

'Go fuck yourself.'

Ben put some more weight behind the axe blade, and the guy's face turned a mottled purple. Blood dribbled downwards from the corners of his mouth where the table had smashed his lips against his teeth.

'What's your name?' Ben said again.

'Scagnetti.'

'You're in the wrong place, Scagnetti. You have a first name?'

'Antonio.'

'What about him?'

'Bruno Bellomo.' It came out as a groan as Ben leaned a little harder on the axe.

'Who are you working for?'

Scagnetti spat blood at him and snorted. Ben lifted the axe away from his throat. He took a grip on the smooth hickory handle and swung it down with a loud crash of steel on floorboards. Wood splintered. Blood flew, and with it the four severed fingers of Scagnetti's left hand.

'That'll save you money on guitar lessons,' Ben said.

Scagnetti's screams echoed down the corridor as he writhed and rolled in agony, his bleeding hand clamped hard under his right armpit.

'I think you were just telling me who you work for,' Ben said, crouching beside him with the axe handle against his shoulder.

'The Russian,' Scagnetti whimpered. 'I don't know his name. I swear.'

Ben knew the look on the man's face. It was the look of a guy who'd just realised exactly what he was dealing with: an enemy perfectly willing to take him apart, calmly, piece by piece. That was one scary moment, even for a cold killer like Antonio Scagnetti. In Ben's experience, someone in that seriously rattled state of mind was willing to say anything to make the horror go away. The first thing out of their mouths was generally the truth.

Ben stood up. 'OK, Antonio, I believe you. You can save the rest for the cops. Time for a nap now.' He swung the axe at Scagnetti's head, side on so that the flat face of the blade whacked into his skull with a meaty thud. Certainly not hard enough to kill him, unlikely to cause permanent damage, but he'd have something to help take his mind off his sore hand for a while.

Ben stepped over the unconscious body to the other guy, who was beginning to come to. Sweet dreams, Bruno. *Crack*.

Putting aside the axe, Ben frisked the men and found two identical radio handsets. He tossed one aside and examined the other. It was a wide-band VHF Motorola, a complex pro-level device covered with knobs and switches. Ben made a mental note of the channel it was set to, then used its scanning facility to skip through multiple frequencies in search of a police channel. The Carabinieri, officially part of the Italian military, used encrypted frequencies that couldn't be unscrambled on a civilian radio set, but after a minute or so of scanning through white noise and static, he hit on a channel that sounded like a Polizia Municipale control room. The Italian municipal cops were mainly a civilian force, limited to directing traffic, enforcing minor local laws, getting stuck kittens out of trees – but that was good enough right now.

Or so he hoped. He kept his voice low and calm as he explained to the stunned operator on the other end that heavily armed robbers had taken control of the Academia Giordani near Aprilia, had taken hostages and were acting with lethal intent. He repeated that last part again, slowly and carefully.

'This is not a hoax. People are being shot. You must alert the nearest Carabinieri station immediately and have as many rapid response units sent here as poss—'

Ben was able to say no more before the signal dissolved into fuzz and static. He could only pray that the municipal cops would take it seriously and relay the alert to the Carabinieri. This was Italy. No telling how efficient their systems were. Until something happened, if anything did, he was on his own.

Silvestri had been quick to snatch the computer keyboard away from Corsini, who was slumped in his chair weeping openly with shock and guilt. A moment later, the second security code had been entered and accepted by the computer. Then Anatoly thrust the keyboard towards Pietro De Crescenzo with a sneer.

The count took a deep breath, looked at the Russian with bloodshot eyes, poised his long, thin fingers over the keys and typed in the third and last set of numbers to disarm the secondary security system. His hand shook over the enter key. By pressing it he was enabling this gang of ruthless thugs to walk away with every single piece of artwork in the gallery. A massive cross-section of five centuries of the pinnacle of human cultural achievement, delivered at a stroke into the hands of men like these. If he'd been made to launch nuclear missiles, he'd have felt no worse.

He pressed the key. In his mind, its tiny click sounded like the crack of doom. He hung his head and closed his eyes. When he opened them, a new message had appeared on the computer screen: 'SECURITY DEACTIVATED'

'There,' De Crescenzo groaned. 'It's done. Take what you want and go.'

'We're not finished yet,' Anatoly told him.

Chapter Eighteen

Ben dragged Scagnetti's unconscious body through the classroom, leaving a trail of blood from the guy's mangled hand all the way to the balcony. He heaved him upright and slung him half over the parapet, so that just a light shove would send him tumbling over the edge. He did the same with the other man, Bellomo, then ran back to the corridor, unravelled more of the fire hose and slashed off a length. Back out on the balcony, he quickly knotted one end of the thick rubber around their ankles. He estimated the drop to the ground below, subtracted three metres and then secured the other end of the hose to the balcony before shoving both men over the edge. They dropped over the side like the world's calmest bungee jumpers and then were jerked up short by the hose's elasticity before their brains could be dashed all over the ground.

Ben peered down at the two swinging bodies. They weren't going anywhere. He slung one of the Steyrs over his shoulder, stripped the magazine from the other and stuck it in his back pocket. Tossed the empty weapon off the balcony together with one of the radios, and moved quickly on.

Glass flew as the butt of Anatoly's Steyr smashed into the display cabinet that protected the Goya drawing. He used the weapon to knock away the jagged pieces around the edge, then slung it over his shoulder and reached in with both hands to grasp the sides of the plain black wooden frame.

He gave a hard yank and felt something give. The piece of artwork came away easily from the wall, and he lifted it out of the broken cabinet and stepped back.

Nothing happened. No alarms, no slamming down of steel shutters. He grinned to himself. It was his.

And so was the rest of the stuff, as much as he could carry out of here. The old man might be nuts, but he, Anatoly, wasn't.

Anatoly strolled back into the office, holding the Goya against his chest. Rocco Massi was fiddling with his radio, frowning through the mask. 'I can't raise Bellomo and Scagnetti.'

Anatoly ignored him. 'Thank you for your co-operation, gentlemen,' he said in Russian to the three gallery owners. 'That will be all.' He set the frame down on a filing cabinet, then unslung his Steyr and turned to Corsini. The fat man's face was covered with sweat. He began to raise his hands, and his eyes widened in horror as he saw the gun muzzle swing his way. Anatoly made a clucking sound with his tongue, stretched a grin and the gun jolted in his hand. Corsini sprawled heavily backwards, tipping up his chair and crashing to the floor. Anatoly swivelled the Steyr towards Silvestri and pulled the trigger.

'Shit.' He looked at his gun. 'Empty.'

Rocco Massi tossed him a spare mag. Anatoly grunted, dumped the empty one, slotted the new one into the receiver and racked the cocking mechanism.

'You animals,' Silvestri said. His next words were drowned out by the blast of gunfire that spilled him sideways out of his seat and misted blood up the wall behind him.

Pietro De Crescenzo was curled up in a ball like a trapped animal, shaking with terror as Anatoly turned towards him. A thin wisp of smoke curled out of the barrel of the Steyr. Anatoly blew it away and laughed. He took a step closer to De Crescenzo.

'Bellomo, Scagnetti, come in. Where the fuck are you? Over,' Rocco Massi said into his radio.

Ben was walking fast down a corridor when he turned on the radio handset and dialled it back to the frequency the gunmen had been using. He heard the harsh voice crackle out of the speaker. 'Bellomo, Scagnetti, come in. Where the fuck are you? Over.'

The red plastic rocker switch on the side of the radio was the press and talk button. Ben thumbed it and said, 'Uh, I'm afraid Antonio and Bruno won't be joining us. They're kind of tied up at the moment.'

Stunned silence.

'I want to talk to the Russian,' Ben said. 'Now.'

There was another moment's silence, then another voice rasped out of the radio. Speaking Italian, but with a heavy accent. The Russian. 'Who the fuck is this?'

Ben's Russian wasn't as fluent as his Italian, but good enough to get his point over. 'If you're here to steal artwork, it's my guess you're interested in doing business. Correct? Over.'

Pause. 'Go on,' the voice rasped.

'I have a business offer for you,' Ben said. 'Here are the terms. The police are on their way. You and your men put down your weapons and surrender to me immediately, and you have my word that eventually you'll live to be a free man. Not for a couple of decades, maybe, but eventually. And I hear the food's very good in Italian prisons. Over.'

The pause was longer this time. 'Interesting. What if I decide to take my chances?'

'Harm any more of those people down there, and today is the last day of your life.'

'I see. You must be one of those one-man armies, that right? You're gonna kick my ass, and the asses of all my friends down here? All on your own.'

'Scagnetti and Bellomo didn't take much.'

'You don't know who you're dealing with. I think you're the one who should surrender to me. I'd like to meet you.'

'Maybe you will.'

'Maybe I'll just go on shooting hostages until you turn yourself in.'

'Then I'll withdraw my offer. You and all your men die.'

'That's a bold statement.'

'It's a promise,' Ben said. 'The offer is on the table. Think about it.' He turned off the radio.

Chapter Nineteen

Anatoly tossed away the radio with a snort. He'd forgotten all about Pietro De Crescenzo, who was still cringing in his chair, shaking badly and expecting a bullet at any moment.

'Who is this bastard?' Rocco Massi said.

'How the hell should I know who he is?'

Spartak Gourko had walked into the office, cradling his rifle in his arms. He barely glanced down at the bodies of the woman and the two dead men, or the blood that was pooling all over the floor.

'He called the Carabinieri?' Rocco said.

'Fuck the police,' Anatoly said, and Gourko let out a short laugh.

'We should get out of here,' Rocco said.

Anatoly snatched the Goya. 'Come with me,' he muttered, and burst out of the office. The others followed as he strode into the side room where Rykov, Turchin and Garrone were guarding the rest of the hostages. The guests were all much more subdued now, just a quiet sobbing from the young boy as his mother rocked him gently in her arms. A few faces peered up in fear as Anatoly walked in. He stuffed the Goya into its tailor-made case. It fitted perfectly, lying snug against the padding. He zipped it shut, then motioned to Rykov and

Turchin. 'Ilya, Vitaliy, some bastard is loose upstairs and thinks he's John Wayne. Get him for me.'

'He could be anywhere in the building,' Rocco said. 'You've got what you came for. Now let's go.'

Anatoly gave him a long, hard stare. 'You too. Get up there now. And you,' he snapped at Garrone. The four men swapped glances, then headed for the gallery exit.

Now it was just Anatoly and Spartak Gourko left in the room. The fear among the hostages had intensified palpably.

'Spartak, you stay here and make sure these pieces of shit keep still,' Anatoly said. 'Give me your knife.'

Gourko drew the weapon from his belt and tossed it to him. 'Where are you going?'

'I came to Italy to have some fun and that's what I'm going to do.' Anatoly marched over to the hostages. The teenage girl he'd admired earlier was sitting with her parents, watching his every move and not daring to make a sound. He reached out, grabbed her arm. Her face creased in terror and she whimpered.

'Let's find somewhere nice and private we can get better acquainted,' he said, dragging her to her feet. The girl's mother began to howl and tried desperately to hang on to her daughter. Gourko knocked her back with a hard stamping kick to the chest, and aimed his gun at her father with a look that said, 'Go on, make my day.' The other hostages were silent, apart from Donatella who stared at the two Russians and muttered something under her breath.

'Maybe when I'm done with this bitch I'll come back for that one,' Anatoly chuckled. Gourko's lips twitched into a faint smile. Anatoly hauled the girl away from the others and dragged her, screaming and writhing, towards the gallery.

* * *

While Massi and Garrone headed up a backstairs that doubled as a fire escape, Rykov and Turchin stalked the main stairs to the first floor. On the landing was the body of the old guy who'd died there earlier, his blood soaked into a wide area of carpet. They stepped over him as though he were roadkill and made their way through the maze of corridors. Every door they came to, they kicked open, ready to blast anything the other side of it. They found storage spaces, lecture rooms, classrooms. All empty.

Pushing through a set of fire doors, they came to a short flight of steps and then to what looked like a ceramics department with a couple of large workshops flanking the corridor. One of them had display units filled with clay pots and vases, and long benches covered in materials and tools. The other room contained a row of heavy-duty iron kilns, like gigantic ovens with sturdy deadlocks to seal their doors tightly shut and thick layers of insulating material to protect the wall and nearby surfaces. Fat metal flues disappeared into the heat-discoloured wall.

The Russians took a brief glance around the workshop, just long enough to ascertain that the guy they were looking for wasn't hiding under a table or in a cupboard. Satisfied, they were just about to turn to leave when they heard the soft voice behind them.

'Hey.'

The Russians spun around.

Chapter Twenty

Ben had often wondered if you could improvise a silencer out of an empty plastic bottle. He'd never quite got around to experimenting, until now. The litre Pepsi bottle had been left in a waste bin, and he'd used some Sellotape he'd found to fix it to the muzzle of the Steyr. From the doorway of the workshop, he aimed down at the floor and let off a short flurry of muffled shots, sweeping left to right. The two men dropped their weapons and crumpled to the floor, shouting out in agony, clutching their feet.

Ben ripped the burst remains of the Pepsi bottle from his Steyr as he walked over to them. 'That's not bad, is it?' he said, kicking away their fallen guns. The guy on the right let out a stream of obscenities in Russian. Ben silenced him with a kick to the throat and he went straight down on his back. He clubbed the other over the head with the Steyr, and suddenly the room was quiet again.

Crouching beside them, he checked them for hidden weapons and then relieved them of their radios. He stood up and swung open the door of the nearest kiln. It was all blackened inside, with metal grille shelves like those in a domestic oven, only much larger. He pulled out the shelves, tossing them aside with a clatter. There was plenty of space for both men in there, as long as they weren't expecting comfort. He dragged each one inside in turn, kicked their legs out of the way of the door, then clanged it shut and rolled the heavy deadlock into place.

There was a big red power-on knob and a thermostat control on the bottom panel of the kiln. Of course, he was far too nice a guy to turn it up full blast and roast these bastards like turkeys inside.

Their lucky day.

Unless things went badly and they'd harmed more of those people down there. Then, he'd be back and things would be warming up.

Ben stepped over to the doorway, peered left and right and listened hard for a few seconds, then pressed on, running lightly and silently through the corridor. No sign of the cops yet. Of course. But maybe, just maybe, as long as he could maintain the element of surprise and keep taking down the gunmen two at a time, he could stop this thing.

That plan fell apart within twenty seconds when Ben rounded a corner and almost ran into another pair of masked thugs. One was a giant mastiff of a man. He was clutching an AR-15 military rifle at hip level, two thirty-round magazines taped back to back the way it used to look cool in mercenary movies. The other was lean and tough as rawhide, with a short black shotgun in his hands.

For an instant they all stared at one another. The big guy's eyes were locked on Ben's, and in that suspended instant of frozen time Ben noticed that his pupils were different colours, the right one dark brown and the left one hazel. It was a minor anomaly that most people would have missed, but Ben was so practised in taking in the physical details of any situation he found himself in that he spotted it right away.

But he didn't have time to linger over it, because in the next half second the big guy's teeth bared in a snarl and his fists tightened around his AR-15. The rifle muzzle lit up with strobing white flame and the deafening roar of automatic gunfire wiped out all thought. By then, Ben was already in mid-air, diving to avoid the high-velocity blast that ripped a snaking trail of devastation just one inch behind him.

One thing Anatoly Shikov valued was his privacy. He could have just flung the crying girl down on the floor of the art gallery and done her there – but not with Spartak Gourko and the others watching. That would just be barbaric. He dragged his struggling trophy out of the gallery, through the glass walkway and out into the old part of the house, looking for somewhere suitable. Across the hallway, a door lay open and the room beyond looked perfect for what he had in mind. Tightening his grip on the girl's arm, he hauled her inside.

The room was a library or reading room. The walls were lined with high shelves of old books, the furniture was plush and the carpet was soft. There was an elegant marble fireplace, and in the corner was a velvet chaise longue. Anatoly dumped the girl on it. She brushed the tangle of blond curls away from her face and gaped up at him as he stood over her and pulled off his mask. Gourko's knife dangled loosely in his other hand.

'My name's Anatoly,' he said in his best Italian. 'What's yours?'

Chapter Twenty-One

The world erupted in a wall of noise. Ben hit the floor painfully on his shoulder and rolled twice as the hurricane of bullets and debris whipped all around him. There was no time to return fire. He lashed out with his foot, kicking open a fire door. Scrambling through it, he caught a glimpse of gleaming tiled steps spiralling steeply down below him in a tight square pattern. He realised he was on the landing of a fire escape stairwell.

In the next instant, the two gunmen crashed through the swinging fire door after him. Ben threw himself down the steps. The heavy boom of the shotgun resounded in the stairwell. A window shattered, showering Ben with broken glass as he went tumbling down the tiled steps. The next landing was just a few metres down. He hit it on his back and returned fire upwards, one-handed, feeling the snappy recoil from his Steyr twist his hand up and round. The three-shot burst caught the shotgunner across the chest and his knees buckled.

First kill. Ben hadn't wanted it that way, but sometimes you didn't get the choice.

The dead man came tumbling down the fire escape, carried forward by his own momentum, and landed on Ben with an impact that drove the air out of his lungs. The big guy straddled the top of the stairs with his feet apart and aimed the AR-15 down the stairwell. Ben knew all too well that those rifle bullets would punch effortlessly through car doors, toughened glass, even masonry. A human shield wasn't going to slow them down much. He aimed the Steyr over the shoulder of the corpse and squeezed the trigger.

Nothing happened.

The whole problem with small automatic weapons was that they tended to shoot themselves dry in a matter of seconds. A twenty-round mag in a fast-cycling action like the Steyr's didn't last long at all. Worse, the spare he'd tucked in his jeans pocket had fallen out as he'd rolled down the steps. He could see it lying there halfway between him and the landing. No way to get to it in time.

But it wasn't just Ben's gun that had run empty. The big guy swore, released the taped-together mags of his rifle and reinserted them upside down. Before he could release the bolt and hose the stairwell with bullets, Ben had slid out from under the body of his colleague and was leaping down the stairs. He made it to the next bend before the big guy could get him in his sights again. Bullets hammered off the wall where he'd been a second ago. Leaping down the stairs, Ben spotted another landing with two doors leading off it. He made a split-second choice and ripped open one of the doors, praying it wasn't a broom cupboard.

It wasn't. A dark corridor opened up in front of him. Before the big guy could see which way he'd gone, Ben had slammed the door shut behind him and was sprinting hard down the corridor. He tore through another door, hit a fork in the corridor and took a right.

As he ran, he was getting his bearings. He was on the ground floor now, and had probably come down the same way the guys he'd locked in the kiln had come up. The second two must have come round the other way, heading him off in a pincer movement.

Moving more slowly and cautiously now that he'd managed to lose his pursuer, Ben wove his way onwards until he found himself in a familiar-looking hallway. To his left was the foot of the main staircase, ahead of him was the entrance to the glass walkway through to the gallery.

He stopped, listened. He could hear no movement from the gallery. Maybe everybody was dead already and the rest of the gunmen had escaped. Or maybe they were all watching him on CCTV, waiting quietly for him to walk in there so they could riddle him with bullets.

It was as he stood there figuring out his next move that he heard the cry from the half-open door on the far side of the hallway.

A woman's cry. Someone in distress.

A vision of Donatella Strada leaped into Ben's mind. He raced across the hall and slipped into the room.

Sprawled helplessly on her back across a chaise longue was a young girl of about fifteen or sixteen. A man stood over her with his back to Ben. The first thing Ben noticed about him was the long blond ponytail. He'd removed his mask, and thrown it on the floor together with his gun, a Steyr machine pistol identical to the empty weapon in Ben's hand. The man's gun was just a couple of steps out of reach. Careless.

Ben moved a little closer, and recognised the girl as the sullen teenager from the exhibition. Her hair was dishevelled, her face contorted and streaked with tears.

The next thing Ben noticed about the man was the six-inch double-edged combat knife that he was using to cut away the girl's clothes piece by piece. Her dress was slashed up the middle and hung open. He had the blade up inside her bra and was sawing slowly through the middle of it, talking softly to her as he sliced the flimsy material.

The girl's eyes opened just a little wider as she saw Ben. The man seemed to tense, sensing a new presence in the room. He turned.

'Who the fuck are you?' People tended to revert to their native tongue in moments of surprise. The Russian.

Ben raised the empty Steyr. He took a step closer. 'Have you forgotten our conversation? I thought we agreed you weren't going to harm anyone else.'

The Russian blinked. 'It's you,' he said, switching from Russian to English. He spoke it with an American accent. Too many Hollywood movies.

'Get away from her,' Ben said, motioning with the gun.

'I haven't touched her. See for yourself.'

'Get away from her.'

The Russian stepped away from the girl, but he kept hold of the knife. The teenager immediately covered herself with the tatters of her dress and curled up tight on the chaise longue, making small sounds and shuddering as though she'd been thrown in icy water.

'Who are you?' the man asked, with what sounded like genuine curiosity.

'My name's Ben Hope.'

'What are you doing here?'

'I'm just a tourist,' Ben said. 'Came to see some art.'

'Looks like I picked the wrong gallery.'

'Looks that way to me, too,' Ben said, and took another step.

The Russian chuckled. For a man with a machine gun aimed directly at his face, he was a little too composed. 'You are from England.'

'I don't live there any more. And you're Ukrainian,' Ben said.

103

'Excellent guess. My name is Anatoly Shikov.' He said it as though it should mean something to Ben. It didn't, but just the fact that the Russian had told him meant a lot. It meant he was confident Ben wasn't leaving the room alive. The guy had some kind of angle – what it was, Ben didn't know yet.

'I think you should lose the knife, Anatoly,' Ben said. 'Things will go better for you that way. Then you can take me to where you're keeping the hostages. It's time to give this up.'

Anatoly's blue eyes twinkled with a glacier light. 'I disagree. I think you should drop the gun. I think you would have shot me by now. I think I am the only one armed here, yes?' He waggled the knife loosely in his hand, then pointed the tip of the blade at Ben.

Ben shrugged and tossed away the Steyr. 'Someone's going to get hurt, Anatoly, and it's not going to be me.'

'Let us find out.'

In the next split second, Ben's eyes darted to the knife. It was a strange-looking weapon, with a large nub on the top of its hilt that wasn't a bayonet-fixing lug. The Russian was holding it oddly in his hand, and the way he was pointing it . . .

Almost as if it were a gun . . .

There was a sharp crack and something blurred through the air towards Ben. At the same instant he realised what the weapon was, he was ducking out of the way. Fast, but not quite fast enough to avoid the hurtling blade. It ripped through the left shoulder of his T-shirt, slicing the flesh on its way past before embedding itself with a judder in a bookcase behind him.

Ben had heard of the infamous Spetsnaz ballistic knife, but he'd never seen one in action before. That strange nub was a release catch for the blade, which was propelled faster than a crossbow bolt by the powerful spring inside the hilt. Combat dagger meets flick-knife meets harpoon gun. Very KGB. Very effective. He touched his left shoulder and his fingers came away thick with blood. No pain yet, just a burning tightness. The pain would come, though.

'Handy little toy,' Ben said. 'You should practise more with it.'

Anatoly tossed away the empty hilt and backed off several steps, moving round in a curve towards the fireplace. Groping behind him, he grabbed hold of a heavy cast iron poker and swung it wildly as Ben closed in fast. Ben stepped out of the range of the blow, felt the humming *whoosh* of the poker as it passed an inch from his nose. He moved back in, threw a kick at the Russian's knee that didn't connect hard enough to break it. The Russian cried out in pain and rage, bared his teeth in hatred and swung the poker again. Ben ducked. The poker smashed into the mantelpiece, breaking off a big triangular chunk of marble that fell with a crash to the hearth. Ben bent low, scooped it up and hurled it with all his strength at the Russian's head.

Anatoly saw the lump of marble flying towards him and tried to bat it out of the way like a baseball player. The world's thinnest bat against the world's heaviest ball. The poker hummed through the air and connected with nothing. The chunk of marble caught him on the cheekbone with a solid crunch. He dropped the poker and looked dazed for just an instant, then staggered back across the room with blood pouring from the ragged gash below his eye.

'I told you not to harm these people,' Ben said. He picked up the poker. 'You should have listened to me.'

Anatoly staggered across the room to the bookcase in which the Spetsnaz blade had embedded itself. He twisted and ripped it out of the wood. His eyes were filled with maniacal hatred. He screamed and came running at Ben like a wild man, holding the blade high.

He was three metres away when Ben brought the poker down hard and fast and let go. It sailed like an iron spear, and Anatoly ran right into it. Their combined momentum drove it deep into his brain. He went down on his back as if hit by a cannonball and lay still. He was still clutching the blade and his eyes remained fixed on Ben's, but there was no life in them any more.

Ben could feel the warm wetness of the blood running down his shoulder, making his T-shirt stick to him. A trickle went down his arm and dripped from his elbow. He turned to the girl, went over to the chaise longue where she was still curled up tight, shaking, staring at nothing. He felt her brow. Clammy and cold. She was going into shock.

He was about to say something reassuring, when he heard the front door of the Academia Giordani burst in.

Chapter Twenty-Two

The dark blue Land Rovers with the white tops and the red stripes down the side and CARABINIERI in big white letters across the doors had rolled silently up the drive to the Academia Giordani and were clustered outside the front entrance. The assault team, clad in back paramilitary gear, helmets and goggles, took down the front door with a battering ram and stormed inside. In seconds, the entrance foyer and hallway were swarming with armed cops.

Spartak Gourko had burst through the gallery the moment he heard the crash of the front door. At the same instant, Rocco Massi emerged from the passage that led towards the fire escape. Neither of them hesitated. As the police stormed into the hall waving their submachine guns and riot shotguns, Massi and Gourko opened up on them. The crossfire was wild and devastating. Five, eight, ten cops went down before the return fire drove Massi and Gourko together back down the glass walkway. Panes shattered around them as they sprinted back to the gallery. 'Anatoly?' Gourko roared at the Italian. Massi shook his head, as if to say 'I haven't seen him'.

A dozen Carabinieri gave chase. Their commander's eyes opened wide behind his assault goggles when he saw the displays of artwork. His department would have hell to pay if a single canvas was ruined by a stray bullet.

Massi and Gourko didn't share his concern. As the Carabinieri emerged into the open gallery space, they were waiting for them. Gourko levelled his AR-15 and let off a long burst at the invading cops that took down one man and sent the rest scurrying for cover. Three display cabinets exploded into spinning fragments. Tatters of canvas that had once been a Picasso worth eight million euros floated down through the gunsmoke.

In the side room, the hostages were yelling and screaming in panic. Donatella clutched Gianni tightly to her, covering his eyes. Another deafening exchange of shots, and they could see the two masked gunmen retreating towards them just beyond the doorway.

One of the hostages saw his chance. Until now, the Robert Redford lookalike in the Valentino blazer had said and done nothing. Now he crept to his feet, eyes glued to the gunmen's backs.

'No,' Donatella said. 'Don't do it.'

Pietro De Crescenzo tugged at the man's sleeve. 'Get down,' he implored. 'You'll get us all killed, you fool.'

The guy wasn't listening. He snatched his arm away from De Crescenzo's grip and before they could stop him he was across the room and had attacked Gourko from behind, grasping for his gun and trying to wrest it from his hands.

Gourko was twice as strong and twice as fast. He'd once held off an entire squad of Chechen guerrillas, armed with nothing more than a sharpened entrenching tool, for five hours until reinforcements arrived. This guy wasn't going to cause him much trouble. He tore the man's hands from his weapon and sent him flying with a head-butt that drove his teeth into his throat. The guy screamed and started crawling back towards the other hostages, as if he thought he could hide among them. Crazy with rage, Gourko rushed after him into the side room with his AR-15 down at the hip, pulled the trigger and held it back. More than twenty rounds of high-velocity rifle bullets ripped the room apart, drowning out the screams of the hostages. He didn't stop firing until the magazine was empty.

By then, the screams of the hostages had been silenced.

Spartak Gourko gazed dispassionately at the carnage inside the room, then turned away. Spotting the padded case containing the Goya picture, he snatched it up and slung it over his shoulder. When he ran back out into the gallery he saw the place was being overrun with cops. Massi was pinned down by gunfire. Gourko spat. Raised his AR-15 and let rip with the underbarrel 40mm grenade.

The explosion shook the room and blew out most of the windows. Glass rained down like an ice storm from the ceiling. Where the Carabinieri had been gaining ground a moment earlier, a lake of fire washed over scattered bodies. Burning cops staggered and fell. A shattered Rembrandt turned a blazing cartwheel across the floor.

Gourko and Massi dashed through the smoke and leaped out of the smashed windows and into the grounds, running like crazy. They vaulted over a low wall, and then were rapidly disappearing across the lawns towards the woodland in the distance.

Chapter Twenty-Three

Ben had raced out of the library just in time to see the heavily armed Carabinieri come swarming into the hallway. He waved his arms and yelled 'No! There are hostages!' at the top of his voice – but his shout was lost in the noise as the two gunmen opened fire and drove the assault team back towards the entrance foyer. Ben had just enough time to recognise one of the shooters as the hulk he'd encountered earlier; then he had to duck back inside the library, shielding his face from flying splinters as the two thugs shot everything to pieces with their automatic rifles. He ran back to the girl, trying to shield her as best he could from stray bullets, his mind racing to think what he could do to protect her if the gunmen came in here.

But moments later he realised that the gunfight had moved to the gallery room. He ran back out into the hall and was met by the gun muzzles of the Carabinieri. He raised his arms and laced his fingers over his head. As they closed in on him, he explained that he was one of the exhibition visitors. Rough hands started hauling him away towards the entrance foyer.

That was when the grenade went off inside the gallery. The whole building seemed to rock.

'Jesus Christ!' yelled the Carabinieri sergeant who'd been clutching Ben's arm. He let go of Ben and ran with the rest of his men towards the shattered glass walkway as thick black smoke billowed out into the hall.

Nobody was stopping him in the chaos, so Ben followed them through the acrid smoke. For the first time since the robbery had started, he found himself back inside the exhibition room.

However many more gunmen there'd been, they were all gone now. In their wake they'd left a battlefield. Burning bodies of fallen cops, some dead, some maimed and trying to roll out the flames and crawl to safety. Broken glass covered everything. Many of the precious exhibits were destroyed.

Ben didn't care about those. His heart was in his mouth as he looked around him, peering through the smoke. No sign of the hostages anywhere – then he looked through the open door to the side room and saw something.

A foot. Someone lying motionless. Ben ran. He burst into the room.

He stared.

He'd found the hostages.

Or what was left of them. Thirty or more bodies lay strewn and piled across the floor. Some lying flat. Some propped against the wall. Blood everywhere, and plaster and dust and debris and scattered bottleneck shell cases from an automatic rifle.

Ben heard a groan. A survivor. He rushed over and saw a dusty hand groping out from the piles of bodies, and a pale face staring at him streaked with dust and blood. It was Pietro De Crescenzo, the count. As Ben looked around him, he realised one or two others were stirring.

And then he saw Donatella and Gianni.

Ben staggered back and slumped against the opposite wall and closed his eyes and felt sick and then the room was filling with shouting Carabinieri.

He scarcely even noticed them haul him to his feet and half-carry him away. Barely registered the chatter of radios and the screech of the sirens, the chaos around him as he was led outside, or the paramedics who sat him down and covered him with a blanket.

The ambulance ride was just a faraway dream.

Chapter Twenty-Four

Dark was falling by the time the fleet of ambulances wailed into the ER bays at San Filippo Neri hospital in Rome and the injured were urgently whisked away by medical staff. Ben refused the wheelchair that the paramedics tried to shove under him. After a few minutes he was taken into a brightly-lit treatment room where he was given a form to fill in and left alone for a while. He sat on a bed with his head in his hands. Didn't look up when he heard the nurse come to attend to his shoulder. Didn't speak to her as she gently cut away his bloodied T-shirt and began cleaning his wound. He hardly noticed the sting of the surgical spirit or the prick of the anaesthetic needle as she prepared to stitch him up. He was far away, caught up in a dark storm of rage and guilt and despair.

For the first time in his life he'd voluntarily allowed the police cowboys to compromise a delicate, volatile hostage situation. It went against all his training, all his experience. And look what had happened as a result.

What were you thinking?

I had no choice.

Yes, you did. You could have saved those people.

It didn't matter how tightly he closed his eyes or ground his fists against them. He couldn't shut out the image of

Donatella and Gianni lying dead. Their staring eyes. Their clothing ripped up by bullets, the pool of their merged blood glazing on the floor. He saw the boy's face looking up at him as they'd walked down the road together earlier that day. Saw the young mother's expression of relief and joy as he'd brought her son back to her. She'd been so warm, so vivacious. The kid so inquisitive and smart, his whole life ahead of him.

Now the two of them were lying on slabs somewhere in this very hospital. And that could have been prevented.

It was insupportable.

Ben didn't notice the nurse leave the room. Time passed – it could have been minutes or days, he had no sense of it. Then a voice broke into his thoughts, speaking his name. He looked up to see two men standing there, both wearing dark suits.

He instantly figured them for police. One of them stood back near the doorway as the other stepped towards him. 'Signor Hope?' he repeated. 'I am Capitano Roberto Lario of the Arma dei Carabinieri here in Rome.' His English was accented but fluent.

For a long moment, Ben stared at him and said nothing. A hundred emotions welled up inside him, and a thousand things to say. But he wasn't the only one who was hurting. The sense of shock and grief hanging over these men was palpable, and he could see the tight grimness in their faces and the dark circles around their eyes that signified more than just fatigue from working late shifts. There was little to gain from unleashing his anger at these guys.

'I'm Ben Hope,' he said.

Lario held something out to him. A white shirt, neatly pressed and folded. 'I hope it is the right size.'

Ben took it and put it on. It was tight around the chest

114

and uncomfortable against the thick dressing the nurse had wrapped around his shoulder. 'Thanks,' he muttered.

'I must ask you some questions,' Lario said. 'A car is waiting downstairs.'

Ben sat quietly and closed his eyes as the unmarked police Alfa Romeo 159 sped through the streets of Rome. Nobody spoke. Fifteen minutes later, the car was ushered inside a secure compound by armed guards. Lario and his silent companion escorted Ben into a building with heavily barred windows. Inside, Italian flags and the heraldic symbol of the Carabinieri adorned a broad foyer. The same grim atmosphere hung over the whole place as Lario led the way up an echoing flight of steps and along a corridor to an office. His quiet companion disappeared as Ben was shown inside. Lario offered coffee. Ben politely refused.

The police captain's desk was littered with a ton of paperwork. He cleared a pile to one side, laid a notepad and a file in front of him and launched into what sounded to Ben like the beginning of a long spiel about the terrible events of that day.

Ben cut in. 'How many survived?'

Lario puffed out his cheeks. 'Eleven.'

'Out of thirty.'

'Thirty-one visitors to the exhibition, the gallery's three owners and two receptionists. Plus the boy. Thirty-seven in all.' Lario paused, watching the expression on Ben's face. 'I have also lost many men. Seventeen dead, three who may not survive, a further eight severely injured.'

'Not what I would call a highly successful operation,' Ben said.

Lario spread his hands, seemed about to say more, then held it back. 'No.'

'What happened to the girl?' Ben asked. 'About fifteen, blonde. She was in the library.'

'Claudia Argento. She is being treated for shock. Her parents also survived.'

'I'm glad,' Ben muttered, and he meant it.

'Now, Signor Hope. I know it has been a long and difficult day. But I need you to tell me everything you know.'

Ben explained how he'd become separated from the rest of the guests as the attack started. 'So I didn't see all the intruders. But we're obviously dealing with a professional outfit. Some of them were Italian, some Russian. How many have you arrested?'

'Two,' Lario said. 'And this is something I have been anxious to understand, Signor Hope. We found the two men hanging from a window, their feet bound by a length of fire hose.'

'I was able to overpower them,' Ben said. 'I got lucky, that's all.'

Lario nodded. He tapped the file on his desk with his fingertips, then flipped it open. Ben recognised the faxed sheet inside. 'I have read your military record,' Lario said. 'That is to say, as much of it as the British Home Office has allowed me to see. I understand you are a man – how shall I put it – of very specific skills.'

'Used to be,' Ben said. 'I'm retired now.'

'Of course. Tell me, Signor Hope. One of the arrested men has several fingers missing from his left hand. My officers found the fingers in the building. I would be interested in hearing your thoughts as to how this injury could have occurred.'

Ben shrugged. 'I really couldn't say. Maybe the guy caught his fingers in a door, or something.'

Lario's mouth twitched into what could have been a tiny smile. He made another note on his pad.

'Did you find the two inside the kiln?' Ben said.

Lario looked blank.

Didn't think so, Ben thought. 'There's a ceramics classroom on the second floor. Inside one of the kilns you'll find two of the Russians. Alive, of course, if they haven't suffocated by now.'

Lario looked at him for a second, then snatched up his phone and fired a stream of commands in rapid Italian.

'Make a note of this too,' Ben said when he'd finished. 'Out of the robbers your men allowed to escape, one has a particular distinguishing feature. An ocular heterochromia.' When Lario looked blank again he explained, 'Different colour eyes. One brown, the other hazel. It's not that obvious, but you'd see it if you looked closely. What's even more distinctive about him is his physique. Not hugely tall, probably no more than six-three. But built like a tank. A bodybuilder, possibly a steroid user.'

Lario was making notes as Ben talked. 'And this man was Russian or Italian?'

'I didn't hear him speak.'

'This is useful information nonetheless,' Lario said. 'Thank you.' He paused, and pursed his lips thoughtfully. 'I am wondering whether you can also enlighten me regarding the two dead criminals we have found. One was in the fire escape, and had been shot with a 9mm automatic weapon. The other was in the library where we found Claudia Argento.'

'Anatoly Shikov,' Ben said.

Lario wrote it down. 'You seem well acquainted with his name.'

'I overheard their conversation.'

'I see. That was careless of them. Now, this Shikov. The nature of his death was unusual, to say the least. I suppose you would have no idea as to how he came to have an axe buried in his skull?'

An axe. Ben suppressed a grim smile and kept his face expressionless. As if he'd fall for that old trick. 'I'm afraid I really have no idea.'

'I see.'

'Except that there seemed to be some kind of quarrel going on between the thugs,' Ben said. 'Don't ask me why, but it seemed to me that they were fighting among themselves. That's how I was able to overpower the two I locked up. They'd shot each other in the foot. So perhaps that also accounts for the axe. Maybe the severed fingers, too. Who knows?'

Lario looked at him. 'Excuse me. Did you just say "in the foot"?'

'That's right. Your officers will confirm it when they find them.'

Lario stared at Ben for a long time, as if searching behind his eyes for any sign of a lie. His lip curled up into another faint, wry smile. 'I suppose we shall never know what really happened.'

'It was a very confusing time,' Ben said. 'It all happened so fast.'

'I imagine you are no longer used to being, how do you say, in the thick of the action?'

'As you've seen from my record, it's been a few years since I left the army. These days, the scariest thing I have to face is completing my tax returns.'

'Then I do not wish to tire you. I think our business is concluded for now, Signor Hope.' Lario got to his feet. He jutted out his chin. 'On behalf of the government and people of Italy,' he said grandly. 'I thank you for what you have done.'

Ben stood, and they shook hands. 'I really did very little.'

'As you say. Nonetheless, we are grateful to you.' Lario

pointed out of the office window at the gated forecourt down below. 'You will find your car outside. My men found your passport and personal belongings inside and I took the liberty of having it brought here. Ask the duty sergeant for the keys.'

'So I'm free to go?'

Lario nodded. 'Though I regret you may be requested to return to testify at some stage during the investigation. Should that need arise, I presume you can be reached at your business address in France?'

'That's right,' Ben said, and headed for the door.

'Signor Hope?'

Ben turned. Lario was leaning against his desk, watching him with a curious expression. 'I would not of course allow you to leave so freely if I thought for one moment there were any . . . *irregularities* in your account of the events. You follow my meaning?'

'Irregularities such as . . . ?'

Lario waved his hand. 'No matter. I am sure it is quite plausible these men shot one another in the foot. Just as I am sure there must also be an explanation for this poker incident, as well as the severed fingers.'

'So it was a poker,' Ben said.

'My mistake.'

'When thieves fall out . . .' Ben said. 'You know better than me how these things go.'

'Quite,' Lario replied graciously. 'It is of little consequence. And I am sure I need not worry about any . . . *irregularities* taking place during the rest of your stay in Italy?'

'Not in the least.' Ben smiled. 'Why would you?'

'You are right. Why would I?'

'In any case, I'm leaving for London tomorrow.' Ben glanced at his watch. It was after one. 'Or should I say, later today. My flight's at four in the afternoon.'

Lario was about to reply when the phone rang on his desk. 'Excuse me.' He picked up. 'Lario.'

There was silence for a few seconds as he listened, a deep frown spreading across his face. He sank down against the desk, sighed and ruffled his hair.

Whatever it was, even on a night like this, it was bad news.

'Is Strada going to be OK?' Lario said in Italian.

Ben's heart went cold at the mention of the name.

Lario's brow creased into an even deeper frown. 'Poor guy. To lose his family like that and then . . . OK. Yeah. Thanks for letting me know.' He hung up the phone, sighed loudly and rubbed his face with his hands.

'Strada,' Ben said. 'As in Fabio Strada?'

Lario looked surprised. 'You know him?'

'I met his wife Donatella and son Gianni at the gallery.' It was hard to say their names. 'What's happened?'

'Fabio Strada has been involved in a serious car accident. He was apparently driving home late from work when his sister called him with the news of the deaths of his wife and son.' Lario made a face. '*Una isterica.* Silly woman. It should not have happened this way. Strada was so stricken with shock that he lost control of the car.' Lario shook his head sadly. 'Thank God he was not too badly injured. He was taken to the same hospital you have just come from.'

Chapter Twenty-Five

The moment he climbed into the Shogun, Ben could tell that the cops had been through every inch of the vehicle. Just the subtle telltale signs that only a professional could discern, like the grubby prints all over the dashboard, the sweet wrapper in the rear footwell and the undone straps on his old green army bag. His leather jacket was still on the passenger seat where he'd left it, but with consummate skill, whoever had checked out the contents of his wallet had replaced it in the wrong pocket. At least they hadn't managed to lose his air tickets, or dipped their fingers into the thick wad of banknotes he preferred to carry rather than use cards. The driver's seat had been adjusted for someone with legs about the length of a mandrill's. Ben made himself comfortable, then fired up the engine and drove out of the forecourt of the Carabinieri headquarters. The armed guards waved him laconically out of the gate.

The night was warm, and Ben rolled down his windows as he drove out into the street. He felt tired. It was late, but in Rome it was never too late to find a hotel. All he wanted right now was to get to bed and close his eyes and wipe the last few hours from his memory forever.

In the glow of a streetlight a few metres away, three people were hanging about a parked silver Renault Espace. Two guys, one unshaven with spiky hair and a loud shirt, the other chubby in a denim jacket, talking to a tall, attractive brunette. The men were both smoking and the three were sharing a joke about something. The woman's laughter carried across the street.

As Ben drove out of the police HQ and the gates closed behind him, he noticed the chubby guy glance his way through the Shogun's open window, narrow his eyes in recognition and then tap the woman on the arm and mutter something in Italian that might have been 'here he comes'. The woman and the spiky-haired guy turned to stare at him; then the spiky-haired guy quickly threw down his cigarette and crushed the butt with his shoe, ducked into the back of the Espace and came out with a lightweight TV camera that he slung over his shoulder like a surface-to-air missile launcher, while the chubby one produced a set of earphones and a boom mike. They all came striding across the street towards the approaching Shogun, and Ben had to brake to avoid running them down.

The woman held up her hand. 'Excuse me?' she called out in English. 'Signor Hope? Silvana Lucenzi, TeleGiornale 1 News.'

Ben swore under his breath. Lario's grip on secrecy was about as refined as his men's hostage rescue skills. He waved the crew out of the way, but they circled the car and wouldn't let him pass. The spiky-haired guy aimed his camera through the Shogun's open passenger window at Ben while the woman came up to the driver's side, smiling in that rapacious way ambitious reporters had when they were hot on the trail of an exclusive.

'Signor Ben Hope? You are the hero of the gallery robbery. Can I have an interview?' She put her hand, with long pink nails, on the door sill and trotted along beside the Mitsubishi as he nosed between them, trying to get past without running over their feet. That was all he needed. *Art gallery hero cripples TV reporter.*

'You have the wrong person,' he said in an American accent. 'Hugo Braunschweiger, US Embassy attaché.'

'How did it feel to be facing death, Signor Hope?' she asked, evidently not fooled. Ben could see the camera's autofocus lens zeroing in on him for a response. He stabbed the window control and the woman jerked her hand away as the glass wound up. He put his foot on the gas, forced the three of them aside and roared off down the street. In his mirror, Silvana Lucenzi pulled a face and waved her arms in frustration at her colleagues.

The streets of Rome were never asleep. Ben was immune to the spectacular sights as he drove by the illuminated Colosseum and up Via Fori Imperiali. A few cafés were still open, people sitting drinking in the beautiful evening. Lovers walking arm in arm, sports cars zapping through the streets and impetuous young guys on noisy little motorcycles popping wheelies to impress girls. After a couple of misses, Ben found a hotel with vacancies near the Piazza Venezia and wearily carried his bag over to the reception desk and booked a single room. The woman behind the desk seemed uninterested in him at first; then she suddenly looked at him more closely, frowned and cocked her head.

Uh-oh, he thought, seeing the look of recognition dawn on her face. *Don't tell me.*

But she did, wide-eyed with animation and waving her incredulous colleagues over. Within seconds a whole group of women had gathered to stare at him as though he'd landed from Jupiter. Was he really the same man they'd just seen on the TV news? The one who'd helped the police to rescue the hostages from the masked gunmen? He was a real live hero. What was happening to the world? What could ordinary, innocent people do, without such heroes to step in and save them from evil men?

An angel, the eldest of the women said, gazing at him adoringly. '*Siete un angelo.*'

Ben escaped as politely and as quickly as he could before anybody proposed marriage, and rode the lift to the third floor. The room was small and neat. He dumped his things on an armchair, peeled off the ill-fitting shirt Lario had given him and put on a fresh light blue cotton one from his bag. He turned the lights down low and lay back on the bed, closing his eyes, and rolling over on his side. A lump in his pocket pressed into his leg. It was his phone. He sat up and dug it out. When he tried to switch it on, there was no response. The badly cracked screen and dented keypad offered some clue as to why. Ben guessed his tumble down the fire escape hadn't done it any favours.

Another reminder he didn't need of that day's events. It was impossible to shut out the constant replays that kept running round and round inside his brain. He tossed away the broken phone. His head was spinning with fatigue, but he knew he couldn't sleep.

The mini-bar had two miniatures of blended whisky. Infinitely better than nothing. He poured both into a tumbler, grabbed his cigarettes and Zippo from his jacket pocket and leaned out of the window, watching the lights of the night traffic and the architecture lit up gold across the city. He finished the rough-tasting liquor too fast and wished for more, then thought it was probably just as well the room didn't come with a litre of the stuff. He kept smoking and staring out of the window. By the time he was properly wound down and ready for sleep, it was nearly four in the morning and the first glimmers of dawn were rising over the seven hills of Rome.

Chapter Twenty-Six

Georgia

The airstrip was a long straight tongue of concrete running through the middle of the shallow valley on the edge of the isolated Shikov estate. It was deserted except for a black Humvee with tinted windows, and two men. One of the men sat at the wheel of the hulking vehicle, gazing idly into space. It wasn't his job to be concerned with who they might be waiting for out here, or why.

The other man had a great deal to be concerned about. Yuri Maisky stood a few metres away from the Humvee with the warm morning sun on his back, and gazed west. The snow-capped mountains were crisp and clear against the blue sky, but he hadn't come out here to take in the beauty of the landscape.

Maisky had been working for his uncle for nearly twenty-five years, and in all that time he'd had no illusions about the nature of the business. They were all soaked in blood. If he'd been a religious man, he'd have felt damned to hell.

But fourteen months ago, things had changed. One of those unexpected events that could turn a man's life around.

It had been during a business trip to Moscow that he'd met Leyla in the empty bar of his hotel one night. She was a sales rep from Kiev, there for a conference. One drink together had turned into three. One night together became a week. Two months later, they were married and Leyla had quit her job and moved to Georgia to live with him on the estate. He'd told her that his uncle was involved in government work.

Within a year, Leyla had given birth to little Anja. The day he'd held his newborn baby daughter in his arms had been the happiest of Maisky's life.

But with the responsibility of fatherhood had come the beginning of Maisky's problems. For the first time in his life, he'd become afraid. Afraid of his uncle's increasing unpredictability. Afraid of what would become of his wife and baby daughter if anything happened to him. He was a new man, and suddenly he was terrified.

He was even more terrified at this moment.

His watch read 7.06 as he heard the incoming light aircraft. Just a low buzz in the distance growing steadily louder, before his eyes picked out the white dot in the sky a hundred metres above the forest. He kept his eyes on it all the way as it approached and the pilot banked steeply in to line it up with the airstrip. The landing was perfect. A yelp of rubber as its fixed undercarriage touched down, then the pilot taxied the craft to within a short walking distance of the Humvee. The side hatch opened, and Maisky walked over to meet the man who was getting out.

Just one man.

Spartak Gourko's face was expressionless as he stepped down from the plane. His only luggage was the black rectangular padded case hanging from a strap over his shoulder.

They didn't shake hands. No greetings. No explanations. No 'glad you made it'. No 'sorry about what happened'.

'Where is he?' Gourko said.

'In his study. He hasn't come out since we heard. Hasn't moved. Hasn't spoken.'

Gourko said nothing. They got into the Humvee. As they drove away, the pilot was taxiing the plane around 180 degrees for take-off. Twenty minutes later, the Humvee passed through the gates of Shikov's complex and pulled up in the concrete yard. The two men got out and walked towards the boathouse. The sun was getting warmer. Clouds of midges floated over the shimmering lake behind the house.

'You're very quiet, Yuri,' Gourko said.

Maisky glanced into the man's inscrutable eyes. He found it hard to look at Gourko without staring in disgust at the scar on his face. 'It's been a difficult time,' he said.

Gourko didn't reply.

They reached the boathouse. Two guards armed with AKS assault rifles opened the wrought-iron gate for them, and they stepped through into the ante-hall and down a broad, marble-floored passage filled with the scent of tropical plants and flowers. Another armed guard stood at the heavy oak door. Maisky waved him aside and showed Gourko into the study.

Shikov still had not moved from behind his desk. His face was as ashen grey as the rumpled suit he'd been wearing all night. White stubble coated his jaw and his hair was in disarray. An empty container of his pills lay in front of him, and next to it a whirring notebook computer showing the large, full-colour photograph of the man being hailed as a hero on the website of the Italian paper *La Repubblica*. On the small TV screen on the sideboard to his left was a muted DVD playback of yesterday's RaiUno news, playing on a loop. It had been playing all night. Over and over.

Maisky motioned to Gourko to stay back. He cleared his throat nervously as he approached the desk. Shikov seemed not to register their presence at first; then his gaze came into focus. His breathing sounded laboured.

'Are you all right, uncle?' Maisky asked hesitantly, glancing at the empty pill bottle. He knew the answer to that. The old man's illness was growing worse all the time.

'You have it?' Shikov asked Gourko. His voice was a hoarse whisper.

Gourko said nothing, just nodded.

'Bring it to me,' Shikov said softly.

Gourko stepped over to the desk. He unslung the pouch from his shoulder, laid it down carefully and unzipped it all the way around before stepping away. Shikov shoved the laptop to one side and peeled back the lid of the pouch to reveal the framed picture. He ran his fingers over the glass, and for a few moments he seemed lost in thought. Then his eyes snapped upwards and fixed intensely on Gourko.

'I want to know,' he said. 'Tell me everything.'

And Gourko did, in a flat tone that conveyed no emotion. He described Anatoly's idea to change the original plan. Said how he'd wanted to honour his father by bringing home the trophy more efficiently. How he'd proved his strength of leadership and his tactical skills. And how the man called Hope had somehow managed to trick him and then murder him.

As Gourko spoke, Maisky was watching his uncle with growing horror. Shikov's face seemed to collapse into itself, as if a silent, slow-motion nuclear mushroom cloud was unfolding inside him. The light in his eyes dulled. He faltered, then gradually crumpled lower and lower, inch by inch, until his forehead was resting on the desk.

Maisky had never seen him this bad. He raised his hand, and Gourko stopped talking.

'Uncle? Are you OK?'

No reply. For a few seconds, Maisky was convinced that the old man had suffered another heart attack. The big one they'd all been grimly waiting for. Visions of him lying dead in his casket, of the long winding funeral procession, unfolded in his mind's eye. A hundred black limousines crawling in single file towards the cemetery.

On the sideboard was a carafe of water and some crystal tumblers. Maisky hurried over to it, poured a glass of water and was about to start opening desk drawers to look for another bottle of pills when he saw the old man raise his head and open his eyes. No tears. No red. Just a depth of silent rage that sent a chill down Maisky's backbone.

Shikov drew in a long breath. He held it for what seemed like forever, then let it out, slowly. His lips rolled back from his teeth. He reached down and tore open the middle drawer of his desk, thrust his hand inside.

And came out with a gun.

His old Mauser automatic pistol. An ancient nineteenth-century collector's piece, but still in perfect condition. The weapon gleamed dully with oil. Its barrel was long and tapered. Maisky stared at it, and for one terrible moment he believed the Tsar was going to shoot them both. Gourko, for having failed to save Anatoly's life. Him, Maisky, for having failed to warn him against sending his son to Italy.

Unfair. Brutal, even. But then, unfairness and brutality were traits Grigori Shikov was well known for. Maisky waited for the muzzle of the gun to swing his way. Waited for the explosion of the shot, the punch of the high-velocity 7.63mm bullet ripping into his body.

It didn't happen. Instead, Shikov flipped the pistol over in his right hand, gripping it like a hammer by its long barrel. He reached out with his left, grabbed the edge of the framed sketch and smashed the rounded wooden butt of the gun into the glass. Kept hitting it over and over again, until the frame was hanging in pieces, the card mount was battered and buckled and the picture itself was a crumpled mess.

Then Shikov dropped the ruined artwork down on his desk among the broken glass and splinters and dust, breathing hard. The sketch tore in two as he ripped it from the wrecked frame. He shoved his fingers between where the sketch had been and the twisted backing board, and with a deep grunt of satisfaction he drew his hand out clutching a yellowed old piece of folded paper. His hands trembled with excitement as he unfolded it. He hunched over it, studying it intently.

Maisky had never seen Gourko look baffled before. Only Shikov and his nephew had known what had lain hidden inside the sketch's frame for more than eighty years.

Shikov finally tore his gaze from the paper and looked up at Maisky.

'Get the Gulfstream ready,' he rumbled.

'Where are we going?'

'To a ruined church near St Petersburg, in Russia,' Shikov said. 'To bring back the Dark Medusa.'

Chapter Twenty-Seven

Rome

Ben was up before eight, took a long shower, dressed and sneaked out of the hotel before anyone could collar him. For all he knew, his face was plastered on every news channel and paper in Italy by now. It wasn't a comfortable feeling. He'd always been able to move around unseen, and anonymity had become second nature to him. All at once, it felt as if a giant spotlight were following him everywhere he went, and planes flying overhead trailing banners saying 'Ben Hope this way'.

The sun was already hot, and the traffic was insane as he ploughed the big Shogun across Rome to San Filippo Neri hospital. The hospital reception desk was as chaotic as the rest of the city. Ben beat a path through the bustle and managed to find out that Fabio Strada was in Room 9 in a private ward on the fifth floor. He avoided the overcrowded lifts and used the stairs.

It was only as he was approaching Room 9 and reaching out to knock softly on the door that he stopped. Until that moment, he'd been driven by pure impulse to see the man. But now that he was here, he didn't have any idea what to say to Strada face to face.

131

Hi, I'm the guy who wasn't able to save your family. How are you feeling today?

At the end of the corridor, sunlight was streaming through tall windows into a little sitting area with armchairs and racks of magazines and a dispensing machine. The place was empty. It would give him a few minutes to get his thoughts in order. He slotted coins into the machine and carried a plastic cup of scalding espresso over to a corner. In Italy, even dispensing machine coffee was good.

He took a seat in the far corner of the room, and sat for a moment thoughtfully sipping his coffee. Someone had left a newspaper on a table nearby, with its front page facing down. He flipped it over.

The first thing he saw was the paper's title. It was that day's edition of *La Repubblica*. The second thing he saw was his own face looking up at him from behind the wheel of the Shogun, and beside that two more full-colour photos showing scenes of the devastation at the Academia Giordani. He swore, then scanned quickly through the article below.

It didn't get any better. His name was printed maybe six times in two inches of text. The media loved a sensational slogan, and the one they'd picked for him was *'L'eroe della galleria'*. The art gallery hero. The article lingered gushily over the unconfirmed reports that the saviour of the hostages was a former British Special Forces operative, before moving on to quote from Capitano Roberto Lario of the Rome police and the Carabinieri officer who had led the storming of the building. Below was a further quote from Count Pietro De Crescenzo, the gallery's only surviving owner, lamenting the shocking destruction of several irreplaceable pieces of priceless artwork in the robbery.

Ben wasn't too interested in the count's impassioned, outraged attack on the animals who had done this. It was the generic 'something must be done to bring these monsters to justice' type of rant he'd heard before, a thousand times. He skipped down a few lines.

Then his eye landed on something that caught his attention. The investigation team had immediately turned up one interesting, and mystifying, detail. At least two robbers had managed to get away clean – whereabouts currently unknown. Which meant, barring some of the larger canvases that would have been impractical for a running man to carry, they could have helped themselves to pretty much any painting they wanted. And yet, the only item that appeared to have been stolen – and the only one, as far as the investigators could make out, the gang had even *attempted* to steal, as opposed to merely destroying – was a relatively valueless sketch by Goya.

Ben raised an eyebrow at that one. He raised it higher as he read on: while some of the works that had been irreparably damaged or left untouched were worth tens, even hundreds, of millions of euros, the valuers' estimate of the worth of the Goya was around the half million mark, maybe less.

Now that *was* strange. Ben guessed he couldn't be the only *Repubblica* reader that morning to be wondering what the robbers had been thinking. Had they simply panicked and grabbed whatever they could as their plans fell apart and all hell was breaking loose around them? They might have had no idea of the relative values of the pieces of art in the exhibition.

On the other hand, just grabbing the nearest thing to hand and legging it seemed like the work of opportunists – and these guys hadn't seemed like mere opportunists. The way they'd managed to get past the security showed a high degree of preparation, of professionalism. They'd done their homework. Then again, Ben thought, professional art thieves didn't compromise themselves by hanging around the scene of the crime to murder and rape hostages at their leisure. They just took what they wanted in the minimum possible time, then got the hell out of there.

The crime seemed schizophrenic in nature, a contradiction in terms. It was as though the planning phase had been carried out by exactly the kind of person best suited to the job: someone extremely careful, meticulous and thorough; and then been passed down the line to be executed by someone temperamentally altogether different. Someone psychopathically insane.

Ben put the paper down, sipped some more of his cooling coffee and thought about the glaring inconsistencies of the case. His photo stared up at him from the newspaper front page. He shoved it away, feeling even more self-conscious and uncomfortable about being here. It struck him that maybe he should just leave a card for Strada expressing his condolences. There had to be somewhere in the hospital he could buy one. Even just a sheet of paper would do. He could slip it under Strada's door, or simply hand it in at reception. Then he could get out of here.

Art gallery hero sighted skulking away from hospital.

Just as he was about to get up to go, Ben heard low voices and looked up to see a group of two men and three women shuffle into the sitting area, trailing a couple of sobbing children behind them. All had red eyes. The eldest of the women was sniffing into a handkerchief as they sat down in a circle of armchairs on the far side of the room. One of the men put his arm around her shoulders. Ben watched them from the corner, and saw that one of the women looked like a slightly older, plumper version of Donatella Strada.

The men were looking over at him. One of them nudged the old lady, and she turned her teary gaze on him as well.

They all stood, hesitated, and then the old lady stepped over to him. He got to his feet as she approached.

'We saw you on the news,' the old lady said in Italian. 'We know who you are, Signore.' She put out her hand. 'Donatella was my daughter.'

'My deepest sympathies,' Ben said.

'You have come to see Fabio?' she asked.

Ben nodded. 'But I don't know if he'd like to see me. I was just about to leave.'

'Fabio would want to meet the man who tried to save his wife and child,' the old lady said firmly, and Ben found it impossible to refuse her as she took his arm and led him back out of the sitting area. She knocked on the door of Room 9. 'Fabio? It's Antonella.' Ben heard a weak voice from inside, little more than a whisper. They went in.

Fabio Strada lay on the bed with his right arm and leg in traction. His head was wrapped in bandages, his neck in a brace. His face was a mass of livid bruises.

The rest of the family followed them inside the room. Little was said. The old lady grasped her son-in-law's hand and held it tight. She pointed at Ben, and the injured man slowly rolled his eyes across to look at him. The old lady whispered in his ear. Fabio Strada gave an almost imperceptible nod. The grief in his eyes was so deep that Ben had to force himself to return his gaze. For a moment they seemed to exchange a silent conversation that went way beyond anything words could say.

I'm sorry I couldn't do more.

You tried. What more can anyone do? I'm grateful.

Then Strada closed his eyes, as if the effort had exhausted him. The old lady smiled at Ben and squeezed Fabio's hand. Fabio squeezed hers in return. Donatella's sister was crying softly, one of the children clinging to her leg.

There was a knock at the door, and a tall man of about fifty-five, with chiselled good looks and a trim waistline, thick silver hair and a finely-tailored cream suit, stepped confidently into the room. The heels of his expensive-looking shoes clicked on the floor.

Through the half-open doorway, Ben could make out a group of other men out in the corridor. He couldn't see their faces, but the way they held themselves looked stiff and official.

'Excuse me,' the silver-haired man said in Italian. 'I came to pay my respects to Signor Strada.' He glanced around the room, and Ben thought he noticed a momentary frown of recognition as the man's gaze landed fleetingly on him. Then the man turned round and muttered a command to the people out in the corridor. 'Wait for me downstairs. Not you. You come on in.' A photographer with a long-lens Nikon SLR came into the room before the silver-haired man shut the door behind them.

Ben couldn't place the silver-haired man, though his face looked strangely familiar. Fabio Strada's family clearly had no doubt about who he was, and they seemed to act deferentially towards him as he stepped over to the bedside and bent low over the injured man. The photographer snapped away as he spoke.

'Signor Strada, I am Urbano Tassoni.'

The name was one Ben couldn't help recognising, even though he made no effort to keep up with current affairs. Tassoni was a top Italian politician, a prime contender in the upcoming Presidential elections. And you didn't have to follow the news closely to have heard the stories about the guy's glamorous playboy lifestyle, the dalliances with actresses and supermodels. The media worshipped him almost as much as he exploited them.

136

Nice PR opportunity, Ben thought. Making sure you got your picture taken paying your respects to the injured widower. Strada's family seemed to accept the intrusion; in their position Ben would have thrown him out of the window, and the photographer's Nikon with him.

'Words cannot express my sorrow at your loss, Signor Strada,' Tassoni went on gravely. 'I myself am divorced and have never known the joy of parenthood. It makes it all the more heartbreaking for me to hear of this terrible tragedy that has befallen your family. May there be some comfort in knowing that Donatella and Gianni will never be forgotten. And I give you my personal guarantee that I will not rest until every last perpetrator of this terrible crime has been brought to justice.'

As Tassoni spoke, Ben noticed the one flaw in his immaculately-groomed appearance – a red weal on his cheekbone, as though he'd recently been punched. The photographer had clearly been ordered to shoot his good side only. Tassoni finished expressing his condolences, nodded solemnly to all, and then graciously exited the room with the photographer in his wake. Ben saw his chance to slip away at the same time. He said his last respects to the injured man and his family, then left them to their private grieving.

He'd done what he'd come here to do. It wasn't enough. Nothing would ever be.

Tassoni was talking to the photographer in the corridor. Seeing Ben coming, he turned and gave a well-practised smile. 'Signor Hope,' he said, and Ben groaned inwardly.

'I wish to thank you for your heroic efforts,' Tassoni said in English. 'All Italy is in your debt.' He shook Ben's hand with such vigour that it tugged painfully on the stitches in his shoulder. Ben winced a little.

'I'm sorry. You were injured.'

'Don't worry about it. You've been in the wars yourself, it seems,' Ben said.

Tassoni touched his fingers to the weal on his face. 'This is nothing. A minor fracas.'

Ben looked at his watch. 'Now if you'll excuse me, I should get going. I have a flight to catch later on.'

'You are leaving Italy?'

'Is that a good thing or a bad thing?'

'I regret very much that you could not stay longer,' Tassoni said. 'As it happens, I am free for the rest of the day. A rare luxury, I can assure you. I have some paperwork to go through at home this afternoon, but you would be a most welcome guest for dinner there this evening. I am a simple bachelor, but I do appreciate the finer things in life.'

'So I've heard,' Ben said.

'You are a connoisseur of wine?'

'I've been known to pull a cork or two.'

'Then it would be my pleasure to introduce you to some of the treasures from my little cellar, over a dish of home-made *pollo ripieni.* My mother's recipe. I once had the honour of cooking it for your prime minister.'

'He isn't my prime minister,' Ben said.

'You are not a political animal, as they say?'

'Just not a hopelessly gullible one.'

Tassoni smiled. 'But a man of strong opinions. I respect that. What do you say, Signor Hope? Just you and me, man to man, setting the world to rights?'

'You, me, and half of Italy's press. How cosy,' Ben wanted to say, but he kept it to himself. 'That's a generous offer. Thank you, but I'm afraid I'll be in London by this evening.'

'Then perhaps you are free for lunch? I know an excellent restaurant not far from here.'

'Another time, perhaps,' Ben said.

'As you say, another time.' Tassoni slipped a business card from his jacket. 'Should you ever find yourself in Rome again.'

'You never know,' Ben said, taking the card. He stuffed it in his jeans pocket without looking at it. They parted with a nod, and Tassoni headed for the lifts while Ben made his way back to the stairs.

Chapter Twenty-Eight

There was a somewhat cryptic message from Roberto Lario waiting for Ben at the hotel reception desk. Ben hesitated, reached for his phone and then remembered it was broken. When he asked if he could use the hotel phone, his new fan club were only too happy to fuss him into their cluttered little office behind the reception area and pester him with offers of coffee and cake. It took several minutes to beat them politely away.

'I have received an unusual call this morning,' Lario said. 'You might wish to know about it. It was from a woman desiring most eagerly to speak with *L'eroe della galleria* after seeing you on the television news.'

Ben groaned inwardly. 'I'm not feeling like much of a hero, Roberto. What did she want?'

'She would not say. But it sounded very urgent. An Italian woman, living in Monaco. Her name is Mimi Renzi.'

'What did you tell her? You didn't tell her where I was staying, did you?'

'Just that I would try to pass the message on. Nothing more.'

'Good. It's obviously just another bloody reporter.'

'She sounded old,' Lario said. 'Very old. I do not think she is a reporter.'

'I don't really care, Roberto. I'm leaving soon, and I'm not interested in old women in Monaco, whoever they might be.'

Back upstairs, Ben took his time packing his few things together. He was still aching from the tumble down the fire escape, and his cut shoulder hurt. He dozed a while, catching up on lost sleep and happy to give his mind a rest.

It didn't quite work out for him that way. Fitful dreams full of noise and pain woke him sometime before two. The room was stifling. He took another shower, then dressed stiffly and grabbed his bag and went down to the desk to settle his bill. The owners wouldn't take any money, and he had to fight to persuade them. Eventually managing to tear himself away, he hacked across Rome and made the 30-kilometre drive southwest to Fiumicino airport. He handed over the Shogun at the car rental office, and checked in only to find that some technical problem had delayed the flight by an hour. Take-off wouldn't be until almost five o'clock.

He found a payphone and used it to call Jeff Dekker at Le Val. When he got no answer, he left a message to say he was at the airport waiting for a delayed flight and would be back home from London in a couple of days or so. The truth was, he had no idea what awaited him in London and he didn't really want to think about it until he got there.

After leaving the message, he chose a quiet spot at the edge of the departure lounge and watched the people go by. Time passed. He watched parents with their kids. The tender and romantic couple in one corner who couldn't get enough of each other, the sour-looking couple in the other corner who'd had way too much of each other. The businessman going through his papers with worry written all over his face. The captive audience of bored shoppers lured into the departure lounge's various boutiques and stores by duty-free goods made to look glitzy and tempting under the lights. An electronics boutique window display was filled with an array of screens of different sizes, some of them showing an explosive movie while others displayed a news programme. Ben kept expecting to see himself appear, splashed across the window for all to see. The next thing, people would be recognising him, pointing at him, and there'd be nowhere to hide.

To his relief, that didn't happen. Instead, the news focused on the arrest of one Tito Palazzo, an environmental protester charged with throwing a lump of coal at Presidential candidate Urbano Tassoni a few days earlier, as a protest against the politician's election promise to build more coal-fired power stations in Italy.

That accounted for the damage to Tassoni's face, Ben thought with a smile.

Footage showed police officers dragging Palazzo out of an apartment building and stuffing him into the back of a car. The environmentalist was yelling, 'Yes, I threw it at the *stronzo*; and I'd do it again!'

Some people were watching the TV screens. 'Good for him,' a man laughed. 'I wish he'd shot the bastard.'

Onscreen, the stony-faced talking head paused for effect, then said that police were investigating Palazzo's possible connections to the radical environmentalist terror organisation known as the Earth Liberation Front, or ELF, who had claimed responsibility for acts ranging from spiking trees marked for deforestation to blowing up mobile phone masts. Then the screens cut to footage of the assault itself: Tassoni looking unflappably self-possessed as he strode towards a waiting limo, flanked by his bodyguards in dark suits and sunglasses. They were all large, heavyset men; one in particular looked as if he must have his suits specially tailored to contain

142

his muscular bulk. The press were all over Tassoni, cameras flashing and the air full of questions and jeering while the police struggled to hold back the crowd. As Tassoni was about to climb into his limo, the environmentalist Tito Palazzo was clearly to be seen forcing his way through the police line and hurling a black fist-sized object at Tassoni's face from just three metres away.

Tassoni staggered from the blow. The crowd went wild, the police barely able to contain them. The video cameraman shooting the film zoomed in close to catch the shot of the bleeding politician being helped into the limo. The big bodyguard rushed over to shove the camera away. A protester pushed him, knocking off his sunglasses. A scuffle ensued, and the picture froze with an extreme close-up of the bodyguard's angry face looming into the lens.

It was only onscreen for a second, but Ben could see the image clearly in his mind's eye even after the newsreader had moved on to the next item.

He was so stunned that he didn't even realise he'd spilt his coffee.

He didn't give a damn about Urbano Tassoni's election manifesto, or how popular or otherwise it was with Italian voters. It wasn't that.

It was what he'd just seen.

A big, muscular man. With one dark brown eye.

And one hazel eye.

Ben was still staring at the television screens when he dimly heard his flight being called. He looked at his watch. 4.51 p.m. Moving as if dazed, he picked up his bag and followed the line of people filtering out of the departure lounge.

As he walked, the sounds and sights around him seemed to blur out and become an indistinct jumble. He slowed his pace, staring down at the floor. Someone lugging a heavy suitcase bumped into him from behind and tutted irritably, but he was only vaguely aware that he was in everyone's way.

The men outside Fabio Strada's door at the hospital. The way Tassoni had ordered them away after seeing Ben inside the room. It made sense now – and there was only one possible reason why the politician would have sent his bodyguards away like that. It was because there was a witness present who might have recognised the big guy from the robbery.

And that meant Tassoni was in on it.

Ben was still a hundred metres from the plane when he stopped dead in his tracks. Passengers streamed past either side of him like a fast-flowing river current divided by a rock.

No, he thought. And said it out loud. 'No.'

And turned round and started walking back the other way. His step became a purposeful stride as he headed back towards the arrivals lounge. Stopping at a row of lockers, he removed enough cash from his wallet to be getting on with, put the wallet in his bag and stuffed the bag into locker 187. Better to travel light, for what he had in mind. Then he went outside into the sunshine and looked for the taxi rank.

Chapter Twenty-Nine

Richmond, London

Brooke Marcel's current contract as a hostage psychology consultant with the specialist risk assessment firm of Sturmer-Wainwright Associates Ltd allowed her to manage her time quite freely and spend a lot of hours working from home on her latest research paper. One of the benefits of managing her own schedule was that she could train in her local gym in the middle of the afternoon, like today, when the place was all but empty. After the running and rowing machines, the ab exercises and the free weights it was nearly four o'clock and she was finishing her workout with a last two-minute full-on sprint on the stationary cycle. Breathing through her nose, staring straight ahead as her body arched over the handlebar and her legs pumped hard and fast, she could feel the muscles in her thighs flooding with blood and oxygen, her calves burning, her heart stepping up to meet the challenge.

Ten seconds to the two-minute target, her phone buzzed inside the pocket of her shorts, and she eased off the pressure and stopped pedalling. The call was from her sister.

'You sound a lot more cheerful today,' Brooke said, noting the upbeat tone of Phoebe's voice.

'I think I've made a big mistake,' Phoebe said, sheepish and relieved at the same time.

'Marshall?'

'Yes. I think I got him all wrong. I completely overreacted and I'm so sorry about it.'

Brooke listened and said nothing.

'Remember that receipt I found?'

'Tiffany's.' *How could I forget*, Brooke thought.

'You were right. He got it for me. Gave it to me last night over dinner. A beautiful gold necklace.'

'That's wonderful, sis,' Brooke said. She didn't quite know how to react.

'I feel terrible. How could I have been so suspicious? You were right. He told me he was sorry he'd been a bit out of sorts lately. This really big deal at work looked about to fall through, something they'd been working on for months, and it's been driving him up the wall, apparently.' Phoebe sighed. 'I only wish he could have told me.'

Brooke said nothing.

'But everything's fine now,' Phoebe went on brightly. 'Anyway, that's one reason I'm calling, just to let you know and to thank you for having been there for me. I really appreciate it, and when I get back from Devon I'm going to take you out for a fancy lunch.'

'Devon?'

'That's the other reason I'm calling, Brooke. You know we arranged to meet on Thursday for coffee? I'd totally forgotten I have this continuing professional development Pilates course that I enrolled on ages ago, and I just looked at the calendar and realised the bloody thing starts tomorrow. So I'm rushing off to Exeter tonight, for five days. Really sorry.'

'Don't be silly. Have a great time. Call me when you get back.'

'I will. Bye.'

Brooke slipped the phone back in her pocket and let out a long sigh of relief. So it was over. No more worrying about how she was going to deal with the situation. Marshall must have finally got the hint that she wasn't interested in him. Maybe it *was* true that he'd been going through some crisis. But whatever the cause of it, his infatuation with her had obviously burnt itself out and things were going back to normal. Thank God.

Brooke showered, changed and left the gym. Dusk was falling, and the car park was quiet as she walked to her Suzuki Grand Vitara.

She heard footsteps coming up behind her, and turned abruptly.

'Marshall!'

'Brooke—'

'What are you doing here?'

He shrugged. 'I followed you.' As if it were the most obvious, natural thing.

'So you're stalking me now, is that it?'

'I had to see you.'

She stared at him. 'Why?'

'You know why.'

'I don't understand. Phoebe's just been on the phone, all happy because you gave her that necklace.'

'I gave Phoebe the necklace because I love her,' Marshall protested. 'But I'm *in love* with you. I know I shouldn't say it—'

'Then why do you keep saying it?'

'I just can't help myself. I don't have any control over my feelings. You think I *enjoy* deceiving Phoebe like this?'

'You're seriously confused, Marshall. Go away and leave me alone.' She reached her car, unlocked the back and threw her gym bag inside. When she turned to walk around to the driver's door, Marshall grabbed her by the shoulders and tried to kiss her on the mouth. She pushed him away. 'You do that again and I'll punch you. I swear it.'

'Brooke—'

'Piss off, Marshall. Keep away from me.' Brooke clambered into the Suzuki, slammed the door and roared away, leaving him standing at the side of the road, red-faced and wild-eyed. A hundred metres down the street, she slammed her palms on the steering wheel. 'Jesus *Christ!*' she burst out in frustration.

By the time she'd reached her place in Richmond, the realisation had dawned on her that Phoebe's five days in Devon were only going to make things worse. Marshall wasn't going to leave her alone, the whole time. Five whole days free to pursue and harass her to his heart's content. The situation was bound to escalate, and then she'd have little choice but to tell her sister what was happening. *Shit.* God only knew how things would go from there. Unthinkable.

As she parked the Suzuki and walked to the entrance of her ground-floor apartment, Brooke was thinking that maybe she *should* call Ben and get him to have a word with Marshall after all. Maybe the threat of a black eye was the only language Marshall would understand.

But then a better idea came to her. It wasn't going to cure the problem, but it would put some distance between her and Marshall and buy her some time to figure out what to do.

She dumped her gym stuff in her apartment and then trotted up to the first floor and knocked on her upstairs neighbour's door. His name was Amal, and he was a twenty-something 'aspiring playwright' who kept himself to himself and tended to be around during the day. In fact, she doubted he ever went anywhere. How he paid the dizzying rent was one of life's great mysteries, but she didn't ask. She was content to have a nice, dependable guy living upstairs on whom she could call from time to time and get him to water her plants while she was away.

The door opened. 'Brooke. Hi!' Amal grinned at her like a long-lost friend.

'Need to ask you another favour, Amal,' she said apologetically.

He clicked his fingers and pointed at her. 'The plants, right?'

'You don't mind?'

'My pleasure. Off to Bob's place in France again? How is he?'

'It's Ben.' She'd been deliberately vague about him with Amal, and had never revealed too much about the nature of her work trips to Normandy. 'Not this time. I'm nipping over to Portugal for a few days.'

'Right. Holiday?'

'More like a retreat. I have a place there, out in the countryside.'

'Very fancy.'

'You wouldn't say that if you saw it. Believe me, it's tiny – you'd hardly even call it a cottage. And very, very basic.' In fact it had been a rustic hovel when Brooke had bought it, five years earlier. On her salary, it was the best she could afford. The plan had been to visit at least twice a year, doing the place up, renovating and decorating one bit at a time. That had been before Ben Hope had come into her life and she'd started spending more and more time in France. The tranquil, isolated little *finca* in the hills near Vila Flor was something she'd been neglecting lately, to the point where she'd been thinking of selling up.

Right now, though, she couldn't think of a place she'd rather be.

'You're a star, Amal. I worry about that amaranthus.'

'Leave it with me. It'll be ten feet high when you get back.'

'One thing, though. If anyone comes looking for me, don't tell them where I've gone, OK? And I do mean *anyone*.'

'No problem. I won't breathe a word.' Amal frowned in concern. 'Everything all right, Brooke?'

'Everything's fine. I just badly need to get away from it all. And thanks. I owe you one.'

A quick phone call to Sturmer-Wainwright Associates was all she needed to square the time off work with her bosses. Five minutes later, she'd booked a flight online for seven-thirty the next morning. With a little luck she'd be at her place in Portugal for lunch.

As she started packing her things for the morning trip, she felt a pang of guilt at the thought of Ben. She desperately wanted to see him – and she would, the moment this stupid situation with Marshall was resolved. That couldn't happen soon enough. She called his mobile number. No reply. After the tone she left her message:

'Hey, babe, it's me. You've probably been wondering why I haven't been in touch. I promise I'll explain everything as soon as I can, OK? Anyway, I'm going to my place in Portugal for a few days. Maybe a week or so. I need a break. Remember there's no mobile signal there, so you won't be able to call me – but don't worry about me and I'll see you soon. Miss you. Love you.'

Chapter Thirty

172 kilometres southwest of St Petersburg, Russia

The gleaming black Mercedes S-Class limo pulled up on the lonely, empty stretch of country road. When its engine cut out, the only sound was the murmur of the wind and the cawing of a faraway crow. It was the kind of place few people ever passed through, and even fewer people stopped. The road was reduced almost to rubble by the ravages of too many hard winters. The few trees around looked starved and oppressed under the grey sky. The only feature in the bleak landscape was the ruined church steeple a few hundred metres away, its spire just visible from the road over the top of a grassy mound.

Grigori Shikov hauled his bulky frame from the rear of the limo and stretched away the stiffness that had crept through his limbs on the long drive. Spartak Gourko climbed out of the other rear door, while Yuri Maisky stepped down from the driver's seat.

Barely a word had passed between them since St Petersburg. Gourko hadn't spoken once. Maisky watched him walk around to the back of the car, pop the boot and take out a green military duffel bag and a large black combat shotgun. It was loaded with solid rifled slugs the size of wine corks, capable of blowing a man in half at thirty metres. Not that anyone was likely to disturb them out here in the middle of nowhere; though Maisky knew that Gourko would have relished the opportunity.

Shikov reached across his chest to his inside jacket pocket, took out a single sheet of paper and unfolded it. For the hundredth time since leaving Georgia, he studied the copy of the document he'd retrieved from inside the broken Goya frame. He glanced up from the paper to look at the distant church ruin. He licked his lips and nodded. 'This is the place.'

They left the road, and Shikov led the way through the long grass. He was soon breathing hard with the exertion of crossing uneven terrain, but pressed on eagerly.

He'd waited a long time for this moment. Paid a heavy price for what he knew was waiting for him here.

He imagined turning it over in his hands. Caressing it with a lover's touch. To be able to hold it, own it at last. The excitement was almost more than he could bear. Part of him couldn't help but question whether acquiring the priceless lost relic – so long dreamed of, so far beyond his reach all these years – had been worth the death of Anatoly. Another part of him hated himself for thinking it.

And yet another part told him he'd thought, and done, things in his time that were far, far worse. He had little time to waste on idle sentiment, especially when something like this was about to become his.

Maisky followed. Gourko brought up the rear, the duffel bag slung over one shoulder and the shotgun dangling lazily at his side. At the top of the grassy rise, the old ruined church came into view. Crows had nested in its steeple, and all but one of the walls had long since crumbled to the ground, their fallen grey stones covered with moss and half obscured by wild flowers. A tree had grown up where the nave used to be.

The paper trembled in Shikov's hand. The lie of the land was exactly as Borowsky had described. 'This way.' He led them over a low broken-down wall to the neglected graveyard beyond. Some of the graves had been grand once, but now the imposing monuments and statues were weathered and streaked with green lichen. Other gravestones were broken or misaligned, like bad teeth. Across the far side of the cemetery was the crumbling outer wall, and next to it an old oak tree.

The tree was the marker. Near to its foot, three simple graves were arranged in a row, the stones lying flat on the ground and half grown over. The resting places of three poor folks, three undistinguished lives that had met unremarkable ends and melted away into history. Shikov lowered his heavy bulk into a crouch and studied the weathered inscription on the first of the three gravestones. He shook his head and stepped over to the next one.

Not this one either. His face darkened. Just one left. He dropped down awkwardly on his haunches and tore away the clump of weeds obscuring the markings on the third gravestone.

'Andrei Bezukhov,' he muttered. 'Born 1794, died 1853.' He took a deep breath and looked up at Maisky, standing nearby. 'This is it.'

'I wonder who he was,' Maisky said.

Shikov raised himself upright with a grunt of effort and gave his nephew an empty stare. 'Who gives a damn who he was? It's here.' He nodded at Gourko.

Gourko propped the gun against the tree, unslung the duffel bag, reached inside and came out with a heavy iron wrecking bar. He rolled up his sleeves and then stabbed the chisel end of the bar deep into the grass at the edge of the gravestone. The muscles in his forearms bulged and veins stood out from his skin as he heaved it upwards, levering the heavy slab off the ground with a ripping of dead grass. Beetles and woodlice scuttled away from the rectangular patch of bare, damp earth it left behind.

Gourko tossed the wrecking bar down on the grass. He shoved his hand back into the duffel bag and took out a folding military entrenching shovel. As he began to dig, Maisky glanced around him nervously and Shikov looked increasingly restless.

Within less than a minute of fast digging, Gourko's shovel blade struck something that sounded metallic.

'Quickly,' Shikov said. 'Get it out.'

Gourko stabbed and chopped at the earth and uncovered the top of a metal box, like a small casket. It would have been too small for even a baby's coffin, and was buried far too close to the surface. Gourko dropped the shovel and got down on his knees to dig around the casket with his hands. He prised the object from the ground and placed it on the grass at the graveside.

Maisky hadn't seen the Tsar look this excited since the execution of Vladimir Drago and the heads of the four ruling families in '94. He seemed to savour the moment like a gourmet dish being placed in front of him. He was almost rubbing his hands with glee.

'So this is where Borowsky hid it.' His voice was strangled and croaky with emotion. He cleared his throat and ordered Gourko to open the casket.

Gourko grappled with the domed lid of the metal box, but it was rusted shut. He reached down his leg, slipped a small double-edged commando dagger out of the hidden sheath he wore in his boot, and used its sharp tip to force the box open. The lid gave with a crack. Gourko wiped his blade carefully on his trouser leg and slipped the knife back into the boot sheath. He opened the casket and looked inside. His expression didn't change. He glanced at Shikov. Stared back at the box.

'Show me,' Shikov said, panting with anticipation.

Gourko slowly turned the casket round so they could see inside.

Empty.

Shikov left the cemetery looking as though he'd just attended the funeral of a dear friend. His shoulders were slumped in grim defeat as they walked back to the limo.

Inside the car, Maisky let out a long sigh. 'Well, that's that.' He thought the old man was as grey as a corpse. 'I'm so sorry, uncle. Maybe Borowsky went back for it,' he added after a pause.

Shikov shook his head. 'No.'

'Maybe he lied about the whole thing.'

Shikov shook his head again. 'Impossible.'

'Then someone else must have taken it,' Maisky said.

Shikov was silent for a long time. 'And my boy died for nothing,' he said quietly, and closed his eyes.

In the driver's seat, Gourko said nothing.

Shikov was taken by a racking fit of coughing. He grabbed a pill from the tube in his pocket and gulped it down. When he'd finished coughing he said, 'Spartak.'

Gourko slowly turned to look at him. His eyes stayed blank.

'One item of business remains unfinished,' Shikov said. 'Until it's done, you work only for me. Is that understood?'

'Yes,' Gourko said. It was the first word he'd uttered since they'd left Georgia.

'You'll return to Italy, or wherever necessary, and for as long as required. You'll have unlimited resources. Men, money, transportation, weapons, no object. Eliminate anyone who gets in your way.'

Gourko nodded. A thin smile tugged at the scar.

'Find this man who killed my boy. However long it takes. Whatever it takes. You find me this . . . this *Ben Hope*.' Shikov's eyes brimmed with sudden tears, and he wiped them with the back of his hand and sniffed, then collected himself. 'You may hurt him if you wish. Hurt eliminate very badly. But keep him alive, and bring him to me. I want to be there at the end. I want to be the one who finishes him. As he deserves to be finished. Is that clear, Spartak?'

Gourko nodded again, smiling more widely.

Shikov snapped his fingers. The tears were gone. 'Start the car.'

Chapter Thirty-One

Rome

The taxicab Ben took from the airport was a faded yellow Merc that had seen a lot of hard service and looked like it was a second home for the driver, a cheerful, chubby guy with curly hair. Ben read out the address on Tassoni's business card, and the guy seemed pleased. It was right across the other side of Rome.

Almost 5.20 and the traffic was intense. As they hustled across town the driver played Iron Maiden loudly from rattling speakers, drummed on the wheel and sang along. His English was even less comprehensible than the lyrics the lead singer was belting out.

'OK if I smoke?' Ben said over the noise.

The guy made a casual gesture that said sure, do what you like. Not the fussy type. Ben leaned back in the worn seat and took out his Gauloises and Zippo. He offered one to the driver. The guy was happy to accept. Ben smoked and watched the city go by, and thought about Urbano Tassoni.

When the politician had invited him to dinner earlier that day, Ben had made the assumption that he simply wanted to curry public favour by being seen to hobnob with *l'eroe della galleria*'. Visions of himself walking into a storm of camera flashes, platoons of paparazzi stampeding over one another to get a shot. Having to pose shaking hands with the politician, the whole tedious grip 'n' grin media ritual that he'd have done anything to avoid.

But Ben realised now that his assumption had been false. Dinner probably would most likely have been a very private affair after all. Just the two of them, over good food and good wine, exactly as Tassoni had promised. A pleasant, quiet couple of hours during which the politician would have used all his well-practised smooth-talking guile to pump Ben for just how much he knew, or might have figured out, about the gallery robbery. Whoever had set up the operation, they hadn't figured on their plan being interrupted by someone like him; and whatever Tassoni's involvement, it made sense that he would want to assess the level of threat Ben represented now, in the aftermath.

This surprise visit was going to be interesting. Even a politician could be made to tell the truth. All it took was a little pressure of the right kind. By the time their discussion was over, Tassoni was going to feel all squeezed out.

It was after quarter past six by the time the taxi pulled up in the quiet street where the politician lived. Judging by the average value of the cars parked along the kerb, Tassoni had picked himself one of the most prestigious neighbourhoods in the Roman suburbs. The houses were widely spaced apart, and stood well back from the road at the end of long paved or gravelled driveways. The late afternoon air smelled of flowers and freshly-mown lawns. Tassoni's place was bounded by a high wall. The house was a graceful white villa, its facade elegantly half-hidden behind drooping willows. Outside the front entrance, a sparkling white Porsche Cayman was parked up next to a burgundy Cadillac SUV. If Tassoni was a patriot, it didn't show in his automotive tastes.

Cameras peered down from the tall gateposts. Ben wasn't going in there to kill anyone. Not yet. So it wasn't nervousness about being caught on a security recording that made him stop and peer back up at the little black lenses that were watching him from above. He was thinking again about inconsistencies. An untrained eye would have missed them, but Ben was already picking out details that seemed to jar.

The politician clearly valued his security; yet the tall wrought-iron gates were wide open. Not just open, but wedged with wooden chocks so that their automatic closing mechanism was blocked. Not the most secure perimeter Ben had ever had to cross.

He walked through the open gates and up the driveway. The lawns were prim, the flower beds neat. Fancy gravel, not just rough quarry chippings but the expensive ornamental stuff. Ben only noticed it because of the tyre grooves cut so deep into the surface that in places it was down to the black synthetic membrane underneath. As though someone had driven away from the place in a real hurry. More inconsistency. Tassoni's place looked well-tended enough to be pretty well staffed. The kind of place you'd expect two little guys to come out from behind the bushes to rake the gravel up after you. The urgent skidmarks struck the wrong note. A subtle sense of emptiness, a certain desolation that Ben couldn't put his finger on.

He walked on towards the house. At its end the driveway forked into two and swept across the front of the villa in a U-shape. He climbed the steps to the entrance and his eyes searched for a bell push. Before he found one, he saw the inch-wide gap between door and frame. He nudged with his foot, and the door swung open silently.

159

The hallway was large and elegantly furnished, with huge polished stone floor tiles that probably each cost the price of a small car. It made Ben think of the old part of the Academia Giordani building, on a showier scale. The broad double staircase was carpeted in red and the banisters gleamed with fresh wax. A perfect backdrop for a photo session for *Grazia* or *Paris Match*.

Not today, though. Not without some major cleaning up first.

Ten metres away from the entrance, two men in dark suits were lying sprawled on their backs on the gleaming floor. Tassoni's bodyguards. They hadn't been there very long, because the blood pools around them hadn't fully glazed yet. Ben put it at about twenty minutes. Both men had been shot.

Ben walked up to them. He wasn't interested in the smaller, blonder of the two guys. It was the big one who caught his attention, and held it. Standing up, he would have towered over Ben by maybe four inches. The cut of his suit couldn't hide the weight-room bulk of his chest, shoulders and arms. But no amount of muscle could stop a bullet. One had punched through his left pec, straight through to the heart. That one probably hadn't killed him outright, though. The fatal shot had split his dark glasses in half before blowing out the back of his head. Everything above the eyebrows was pretty much mulch. Below the eyebrows, the face was mostly intact. The dark glasses had fallen away to reveal the guy's eyes, which were open and staring.

One brown. One hazel.

The big man had been going for his weapon when he'd died. The chunky .45 Ruger automatic was cupped loosely in his outflung hand. Ben scooped it up. It was loaded. Better to have it and not need it than need it and not have it. First lesson Boonzie McCulloch had ever taught him, a long time back, and it had stuck.

He glanced around him, and that was when he noticed the foot poking through the banister rails. The shoe was shiny. Expensive Italian leather. He trod up the stairs to see more, but he already knew whose foot he was seeing.

Which was just as well, because Tassoni's whole face was missing. The generous blood spatter and the bullet hole in the staircase wall told Ben that the politician had taken one shot to the head while still on his feet, then a second after he'd gone down.

Not the messiest headshot Ben had ever seen, but not too far from it.

It ain't a lump of coal, he thought.

That first shot had gone right through Tassoni's head and into the wall. Ben stepped carefully over the body and examined the hole in the plaster. It was neat and clean, about the right size to have been drilled by a .38 or .357 handgun bullet. He could see through it into the next room. There were no shell casings lying about, which meant either the shooter had picked them up, or he'd used a revolver. Three targets, two shots each, added up to six. A revolver made sense. It also tallied ballistic-wise. The most penetrative handgun calibre Ben had used in an automatic pistol had been the .357 SIG cartridge, back in his army days. It had been conceived by a military mind with the purpose of providing a little more power than the standard 9mm auto rounds. But not even the .357 SIG could punch through a man's skull and out the other side, removing most of his head before going straight through the wall behind him.

Whereas a revolver round like the .357 Magnum was a whole different concept. That hadn't been developed by a soldier, but by a big-game hunter called Elmer Keith, back in 1934. Keith had been more concerned with taking down elk at three hundred metres than a man at room distance. Forty-four thousand pounds per square inch of pressure, enough to drive the bullet through an engine block. Which was precisely why no soldier would use one for close-quarter work. Too penetrative. Not even the SAS could see through walls and tell who might be standing in the next room, waiting to catch a stray round. A comrade. An innocent civilian. A hostage. A kid. And the calibre's sheer power was also the reason why no professional assassin would choose it, especially not for close-up indoor kills in a residential area. A .357 Magnum revolver was impossible to silence. Not just difficult. Impossible. And ear-splittingly loud, a brutal high-pitched bark combined with a supersonic crack, that added up to just a few decibels short of standing next to a jumbo jet on take-off. A sound that could carry for miles.

So in the three seconds Ben spent assessing the situation, he knew he was seeing more inconsistencies. A professional kill, executed in a decidedly unprofessional manner. More odd notes struck in his mind.

But now wasn't the time to try to figure it out. He trotted back down the stairs to the hallway and began checking rooms. The first was a dining room with a long table and a grand piano. The next was some kind of scullery. The third door he tried led to a small room with a row of security monitors on the wall and a table covered in electronic equipment. The stack of four DVD recorders on a professional rack-mounting system looked state of the art. The spaghetti of wires running from the backs of the machines trailed across to a splitter box that it wasn't hard to guess was wired up to the CCTV system. All four disc ports on the machines were open. The discs had been removed, and with them the cameras' testimony to the events of the day. The security system was a blind witness to everything that had happened since.

Ben would have liked more time to spend going through Tassoni's home. He was short on clues as to what the hell this was all about. But the sound of police sirens outside, still some way off and getting steadily closer, told him that his time was running short. He ran back out into the hall and through a door to the right of the stairs that led into a plush living room. Beyond that was a sprawling conservatory and sliding glass doors that led out to back garden. Skirting the L-shaped pool, he made his way across the patio to the long stretch of lawn that led all the way to the far garden wall. Quickly climbing over it, he dropped down into the neighbouring garden. Kiddies' swings, a tennis court, a patch of woods. He slipped into the trees and was gone before the first in the wailing convoy of police cars made it to Tassoni's front gates.

Chapter Thirty-Two

London

Inside a sealed operations room, on the top floor of a tall, modern, closely guarded building whose real identity and purpose was kept strictly secret from the public, nine people were gathered around a table. If the room had had any windows, the view would have been a spectacular panorama that took in the Thames, Westminster Bridge, Big Ben and the Houses of Parliament. The things that were seen and discussed inside were kept carefully away from prying eyes and ears, but through the giant LCD screen that dominated the far end of the room, those granted access had a window on the world whose reach was virtually limitless. From the comfort of their chairs they could monitor events in any location of the world as they unfolded. Zoom in on individual players close enough to count the hairs on their heads and track them anywhere they wished. All beamed to them from space in crisp hi-definition colour, controlled by the small team of technicians in uniforms and headsets who were seated on the other side of a wall of soundproof plate glass.

The most senior member of the group, presiding from the head of the table, was a slender, grey-haired man called

Mason Ferris. Even to his closest aides, seasoned veterans like Brewster Blackmore seated to his right and the steely-eyed Patricia Yemm on his left, Ferris was a legend. His present occupation was even less a matter of public record than the details of his past military career. His mere presence in the room commanded absolute deference.

Of all the people around the table, nobody was more in awe of Ferris than Jamie Lister, at twenty-nine by far the youngest and rawest recruit to the team, freshly promoted from the GCHQ spy centre at Cheltenham. He just hoped that he wouldn't look like these guys when he got to their age. Ferris was a gnarled skeleton of man. By contrast, Blackmore looked like he lived on an exclusive lard diet, with skin that hadn't seen sunlight for decades. None of the rest looked much better. Lister tried not to stare too much.

This was Lister's first time in the operations room, and he felt as rigid and awkward as the stiff, prickly new suit he was wearing. From the moment he'd been admitted through security and taken his place in the room, he'd been aware of Brewster Blackmore's watchful eyes darting his way every so often. From the little office gossip Lister had managed to pick up during his short time with the department, he'd learned that Blackmore lived to serve his lord and master Ferris. The man missed nothing, and reported everything.

The giant screen showed a crisp aerial view of a large villa set in well-manicured gardens in a quiet suburb of Rome. The image was crisscrossed with gridlines, technical readouts and co-ordinates that constantly changed as the satellite panned slowly to follow the lone figure emerging from the rear of the house. They watched as he moved stealthily across the grounds, vaulted the wall at the bottom of the garden and slipped into the trees in the neighbouring property. The satellite's gaze followed him as he made his way through the quiet streets. The watchers had no interest in the fleet of police cars swarming at the entrance of the villa he'd just left.

All nine at the table had an identical copy of the same classified file open in front of them. Everyone was by now thoroughly familiar with the details of the man whose movements they'd been following for the past twenty-four hours. They'd observed him being taken from the scene of the gallery robbery to hospital. Tracked his route to and from the Carabinieri HQ in Rome, and had been watching him via the CCTV airport security system when he'd strangely missed his flight and apparently decided to remain in Italy.

'What are you up to, Mr Hope?' Patricia Yemm said with a half-smile, watching intently as the figure onscreen walked the quiet suburban streets. The satellite image was magnified large. They could see the thoughtful bow of his head as he walked, the glow of his cigarette.

'You mean, apart from destroying this entire operation?' Blackmore said.

Ferris made an impatient gesture. 'The question is, what do we do with him?'

Across the table from Jamie Lister, a large, square-shouldered man called Mack spoke for the first time. 'I think we'd all agree that Hope's involvement in this delicate situation represents a potentially disastrous liability for us. I mean, it's sheer luck that he got out of there before the bloody police arrived. This was a carefully laid plan and he's blundered into the middle of it – not just once, but twice now. He's a loose cannon. I can see only one solution.'

'I concur with that,' said a woman to Lister's left. She had dark brown hair cut short like a man's, and bright red lipstick that glistened under the lights. The name tag on her jacket read Lesley Pollock.

There were nods and murmurs of assent from around the table. Lister looked down at the file in front of him and said nothing. His mouth was dry. There was a carafe of mineral water and nine glasses in the middle of the table, but he was aware of the unwritten rule that nobody would drink until Ferris did, out of deference.

'Therefore I propose that we act to take him out of the picture,' Mack said, looking solemnly up and down the table at his colleagues. 'And try to see a clear way out of this God-awful mess we're in.'

Patricia Yemm turned away from the screen and swivelled her chair close into the table. She tapped long red fingernails against the open file in front of her. 'Are we sure we want to initiate terminal action against this man? He's not the easiest of targets. It could get very ugly.'

'Naturally, it needs to be quick and quiet,' Mack said. 'Difficult, not impossible. Nothing is impossible. That's been proven time and again, by this department and others.'

Lesley Pollock pursed her lips and nodded. 'It's simply a question of selecting the most appropriate asset to allocate the task to. We have people on standby. Just takes a text message. Problem deleted.'

Lister's mouth felt more parched with every passing minute. He'd known what to expect when he applied to join the department. Even so, the conversation seemed quite surreal to him. *Problem deleted.* They were discussing a man's life here.

He thought about his father. He swallowed.

'Have you read Hope's file?' Yemm said doubtfully, turning to look down the table at Mack and Pollock.

Mack flushed with irritation. 'I'm perfectly aware of his capabilities. But he's not the only one we've trained to that level. He can be taken out. And that's the course of action

I would advocate at this point. I frankly don't think we're left with a choice in the matter.'

Ferris had been listening carefully with his chin lowered to his chest. He clicked his tongue, and all eight heads turned, instantly attentive. 'It's my feeling,' Ferris began, then interrupted himself to reach a long, bony hand across the table and pick up the carafe of water. He took his time pouring himself a glass, and sipped slowly. Lister seized the opportunity to fill a glass for himself, too. He drained it in a gulp. Blackmore watched him.

Ferris resumed, measuring his words carefully. 'It's my feeling that, while our friend here has most certainly been a liability for us up until now – and in principle I might agree with my esteemed colleague's assessment – there's an alternative course of action none of you appears to have considered.'

All eyes were fixed on Ferris, except for Mack, who seemed to have taken a sudden profound interest in the strap of his watch.

'As I see it, Major Hope's sudden and unexpected intrusion into the Urbano Tassoni situation works rather neatly in our favour,' Ferris continued. 'Under the circumstances, deletion is not the appropriate course of action. And I don't want this dealt with privately. I want this man brought in alive, as noisily and publicly as possible.'

'Sir, I'm not sure I follow,' Lesley Pollock said, frowning.

Ferris smiled a dry smile. He leaned back in his chair and clasped his hands together. 'Let me tell you about my grandfather,' he said. 'He was a colonel in the British army. During the twenties he spent some time in India, where, as a professional tracker and rifleman, he was commissioned by the rulers of several provinces to hunt down and destroy rogue tigers that were attacking and eating rural workers. Which he did, very successfully, thanks to certain methods.'

'Sir?'

'It's really quite simple,' Ferris said. 'Bear with me. If I explain a little about how my grandfather worked, you'll understand my thinking on this.'

Ferris went on, and his line of reasoning soon became clear.

Jamie Lister's mouth went dry again as he listened. It was warm in the operations room, but fingers of ice seemed to be working their way around him. He stared at the table, knowing Blackmore was watching every twitch of his face for a response, and stayed resolutely blank.

'And that's how you catch a tiger,' Ferris finished. He scanned the faces of his team. 'Now do you understand? It's a logical conclusion.'

Nobody argued.

'So it's agreed,' Ferris said. 'I want Hope in custody within the next twelve hours. Alert the Italian police.'

'You expect them to bring him in, just like that?' Mack said.

'I do not. That's why I want to send in one of our own to head up the task force.'

'Department?'

Ferris shook his head. 'Let's keep back from this.'

'We're going to need someone very good,' Yemm said, 'if we're to have a chance of catching him. Someone every bit as capable and smart as he is.'

Blackmore looked at her. 'Did you have anyone in mind?'

Chapter Thirty-Three

Manchester

Visibility was minimal as the black unmarked Vauxhall V6 Vectra tore northwards through pouring rain along the M60 Manchester ring road at a shade under a hundred miles an hour. Each of the three occupants of the speeding car was occupied with their own thoughts, and nobody spoke. They were in that quiet space where tension and alertness combine with disciplined training to create a sense of purposeful calm.

They'd been waiting months for this moment. Now, at 11.26 p.m. on this dismal night, it looked like they were finally about to score.

Vince McLaughlin was sitting in the back, wearing the same faded jeans and field jacket he always wore. Across his knee was the police-issue Heckler & Koch MP-5K that he'd just finished checking for the fifth time. In the front passenger seat, Mick Walker was nursing the secure frequency radio they were using to communicate with station HQ and the pilot of the unmarked SOCA helicopter whose blinking lights could be seen high above them through the drifting rain.

The third occupant of the Vectra was a woman named Darcey Kane. Her slim, strong hands were relaxed on the wheel as she skilfully wove the car through the light traffic.

Her black hair was tied back under a black baseball cap. Walker and McLaughlin were both very well acquainted with the fierce glint in their team commander's slate-grey eyes and that set to her jaw she always had when going into action. She was as focused as a hawk on its quarry. She pressed her foot down a little harder and the speedometer crept up past the hundred and ten mark. The roar of the engine filled the car.

The target Darcey was bearing down was two hundred metres ahead, and closing. The occupants of the TDV8 Range Rover had spotted them five miles back, and its driver was steaming ahead at full throttle to get away. As it came speeding up behind a cluster of slower-moving cars it blasted its horn and sent them swerving aside. Darcey could tell from the Range Rover's erratic course that its driver was within a fraction of losing his nerve. That was fine. She had plenty.

She wondered which of the drug gang was at the wheel: Wolonski? McNiff? Or could it be Gremaj himself? Whichever of them it was, his foot hard on the gas, glancing nervously in his mirror at the car behind and the chopper overhead, he had every reason to be scared shitless. He had the Serious Organised Crime Agency, British law enforcement's best-kept secret weapon against his kind, right up his arse and he wasn't getting out of this one.

After three months of working her team round the clock and to the verge of madness and collapse, Darcey knew beyond a shadow of a doubt that stashed under the false back seat of the Range Rover were over two hundred kilos of pure uncut heroin. She knew where it had come from, where it was headed, how much the gang had paid for it, how much each man stood to receive as his cut of tonight's deal. She even knew what they'd been planning to spend it on – except they wouldn't be spending a penny of it. Their number was up. Right here, right now.

Darcey knew she was taking a gamble. If she was wrong and the drugs weren't on board, she wasn't going to come out of this well. But it was a risk she was willing to take, and she was committed now.

'Let's cut the foreplay, shall we?' she said, letting rip with the blues and twos. The siren wailed through the rasp of the souped-up V6. Any remnant of doubt the guys in the Range Rover might have had about the identity of their pursuers had just been blown away.

The SUV accelerated to over a hundred and twenty miles an hour, but there was trouble ahead as it caught up with a pack of traffic moving at the speed limit and taking up all three lanes. The driver's fist was on the horn as he bullied several cars out of his way before ramming the back of a Ford Focus that didn't move aside fast enough to let him pass. The Focus gyrated out of control across three lanes, sending other cars skidding out of its path.

There was a flurry of collisions. A spinning people carrier hit the crash barrier at over fifty miles an hour, bounced back into the path of a Nissan Micra that smashed into it side on and went into a tumbling flip-roll. Suddenly the road flashing towards Darcey was a minefield of bouncing wreckage. Her face didn't show a flicker of emotion as she took evasive action, weaving the Vectra nimbly through the carnage. The chopper was closer now, and she could hear the thud of its rotors over the noise of the car engine. Walker was talking fast on the radio, issuing commands, calling in the rest of the troops.

Up ahead, the Range Rover kept battering onwards, its taillights burning through the rainy haze. Darcey was keeping pace at a hundred and twenty-five miles an hour as they flashed under the looming arches of the Stockport viaduct. Moments later, the signs came up for the A560 Stockport turnoff. The driver of the Range Rover held back until the last moment, then veered wildly across the glistening lanes and went skidding off down the sliproad, only barely in control of the vehicle.

Darcey gave chase. They weren't going to shake her off that easily. And the target had just made a big mistake.

'This guy is fucking insane,' McLaughlin muttered from the back seat. Walker yelled fresh co-ordinates into the radio. More signs darted by: REDUCE SPEED NOW. The Range Rover was still doing over a hundred as it bore down on a light-controlled intersection across a large grassy round-about. A dozen or more cars were waiting for the red lights to change. The last car in the queue was a blue BMW road-ster. The Range Rover wobbled violently as its driver stood on the brake, and then it went slamming into the back of the BMW with a crunch of metal that Darcey heard even over the growing roar of the helicopter. Glass exploded across the road. The Range Rover was badly damaged but it kept going, hammering a destructive path through the chaos and storming through the red lights and across the intersection, right into the path of oncoming traffic. There was a chorus of horns and screeching tyres.

'They're gonna get wiped out,' McLaughlin said.

Somehow, the Range Rover made it across the intersection.

Almost. Its driver was too panicked or too bold to get out of the way of an articulated Tesco lorry that sideswiped it at over forty and sent it flying like a tin can. The Range Rover flipped end over end, crushed a barrier and ploughed a massive furrow in a grass verge before coming to rest upside down in the dirt.

The chopper was hovering right overhead, roadside shrubbery pressed flat under the wind of its blades. Voices yelled urgently on Walker's radio. There was a screech of sirens in the distance.

Darcey rolled in over the sea of smashed glass and wreckage. The road looked like a bomb site, vehicles and glass and pieces of twisted bodywork strewn everywhere. The driver of the Tesco lorry had climbed down from his cab. There was blood on his face from a gash above the eye. He gaped at the Range Rover, then up at the descending helicopter, shielding his eyes from the white glare of its spotlamp. A car horn was stuck on, wailing loudly. Other passengers were venturing out from their cars, looking dazed and frightened.

No sign of movement inside the Range Rover.

Darcey unclipped her seatbelt and took out her pistol. She instinctively checked the breech. A glint of shiny brass against matt black steel.

'Here we go,' McLaughlin said, taking up the MP-5K.

'Watch yourselves out there,' Darcey said, not taking her eyes off the Range Rover.

The three SOCA agents climbed out of the car. Swirling blue lights appeared through the drizzle as a fleet of police cars came swarming in from all directions.

The driver's door of the upside-down Range Rover opened a crack, and then swung out wide. A hand appeared, groping about, then a balding head that Darcey instantly recognised.

Gremaj. She'd been staring at the same grainy black-and-white image of the elusive drug baron for three months. Now he was hers, helpless and vulnerable as he tumbled free of his tangled seatbelt and sprawled out onto the muddied grass. Darcey felt flushed with victory as she walked towards him, clutching her Glock tightly in a double-handed grip. It

174

was an end to the cruel suffering he and his minions had been bringing onto the streets of Britain for the last seven years. A bullet in the brain of his nefarious career – and a defining moment in hers. God knew she'd grafted for it.

Gremaj had blood trickling from the corner of his mouth as he crawled away from the overturned Range Rover. He spat red. His jacket fluttered in the blast of the landing helicopter, and the flashing blue lights were reflected in his glasses. One lens was cracked. The butt of a nickel-plated custom .45 auto stuck out of his waistband; it was a typical showoff gangsta weapon, the kind of impractical piece of tinsel a pimp would like to flourish about. It had probably never been fired. Gremaj got other people to do that kind of thing for him.

He glanced up at Darcey as she approached, and the look in his eyes made it clear that he understood she had every intention of shooting him dead if he didn't play this right. He gingerly slipped the pistol out between index finger and thumb and tossed it away. He raised his face to the sky, held up his arms.

Darcey opened her mouth to say the words she'd been dreaming of saying for far too long: 'Thomas Gremaj, you are under arrest.' But before she could speak, she heard Walker's radio fizz, and a new voice issuing a clipped command that she could only barely make out over the chaos of noise all around her.

She froze. Turned. Had she heard right?

Walker was striding towards her, holding out the radio. 'You need to hear this, guv.' She took it from him, and this time she heard the order loud and clear.

'*Base to Alpha One – you are to stand down, repeat stand down immediately. Your presence urgently required at head-quarters. Do you copy? Over.*'

McLaughlin and Walker looked aghast.

'Fuck them,' Darcey said under her breath. And for one heady moment, it felt good to defy the faceless superiors who were trying to snatch away her moment of glory. This was *her* case. *Her* arrest. Nobody was going to deprive her of it.

But then she thought better of it. She swallowed hard. Her heart felt like a lead brick behind her ribs.

How could this be happening to her?

She watched in a daze as tactical firearms officers came pouring out of their rapid response vehicles and circled the Range Rover, clutching MP-5s and taser guns, bulky in their bulletproof vests. They knew their job. Darcey had been one of them once, not so very long ago, and she couldn't deny that Gremaj was in capable hands. In seconds, he and three more injured occupants of the vehicle had been laid out face down on the wet grass with their wrists trussed behind their backs. Weapons were seized and bagged. One of the officers emerged from the wreckage of the Range Rover holding a white object: shrink-wrapped, the size of a house brick. He jabbed a gloved finger towards the back seat as if to say 'come take a look at this'.

So her gamble had paid off. Darcey smiled, but it was a bitter smile as she watched the situation slipping away from her. More officers were spilling out of the vans that came screeching up in the background, taking control of the crowd that was rapidly forming around the demolition derby of strewn vehicles. Three ambulances were already on the scene, and paramedics were attending to the injured.

The chopper had touched down, rotors slapping air at idle speed, side hatch open. Its co-pilot was a SOCA agent Darcey and her team knew well. He was waving his arms for her to get into the aircraft.

The voice on the radio was demanding acknowledgement.

Darcey hesitated. Her mind was reeling at the enormity of what was being done to her. From the looks on their faces, Walker and McLaughlin couldn't believe it either. It was a body-blow for all of them. Nobody spoke for a few seconds until McLaughlin said, 'You'd better respond, guv.'

'Bastards,' she muttered, then pressed the talk button. 'This is Alpha One. Copy instruction, returning to base. Out.' She tossed the radio back to Walker in disgust.

'Shitty call,' Walker said.

'Yup,' was all she replied. Then she made her weapon safe, clipped it back in its holster and started walking towards the helicopter.

Chapter Thirty-Four

Rome

A person who'd just stumbled over the scene of a murder could do one of two things. The first option was to do what most normal people would do: call the cops. In Ben's case, it was too late for that. And he wasn't inclined to stick around to find out what Capitano Roberto Lario would make of this further 'irregularity'. The questioning wouldn't be so laid back this time, and he was in no mood to spend the rest of the night back in Carabinieri HQ trying to convince a bunch of very angry police that he hadn't shot Tassoni and his guys, hadn't dumped his .357 Magnum in some clever hiding place nearby. It was all just a bit too complicated. Ben didn't need those kinds of complications until he'd figured out the answers for himself.

So option one was out. The second option, if you couldn't behave like a law-abiding citizen, was to act the way the killer would act and put as much distance between yourself and the scene of the crime as possible, as quickly as possible. Ben had walked fast for a long time through the suburbs, keeping his mind blank, not letting his spinning thoughts slow him down. Night had fallen as he kept moving. Eventually, as he left the suburban sprawl behind him and the streets got busier, he'd flagged down a second cab. Another taxi, another hotel.

By ten, he'd been sitting downstairs in the empty bar and flouting the no-smoking regulations over a triple whisky on the rocks as he tried to understand what had just happened.

He laid out what he knew. Fact: Tassoni's big ape of a bodyguard was one of the gallery robbers. Fact: Tassoni knew something about it too. Now Tassoni was dead, along with his man and a second heavy who might or might not have been involved as well. All of which meant that someone was cutting their ties. Which in turn meant that the politician hadn't been top of the food chain. He'd been in league with someone else, someone higher and more dangerous.

And that offered the solution to a question that had been burning a hole in Ben's mind for the last twenty-five or so hours. The robbery had clearly been some kind of co-ordinated joint operation. Italians and Russians. The two nationalities seemed to have been keeping themselves to themselves. Maybe partly for reasons of communication, but maybe also because each side knew each other and had worked together before. A bringing together of two gangs, one Italian, one Russian, required someone in each country to organise their side of things: recruitment, transportation, logistics.

Maybe Tassoni had been the guy behind the scenes on the Italian side. Whoever had killed Tassoni might then have been his Russian counterpart. Why would they do that? Fighting over the spoils, maybe, such as they were. Or perhaps Tassoni was being punished as a result of the plan going sour. The reasons why didn't matter so much. What mattered was who was top of the food chain.

Ben lit another cigarette and thought about the man he'd killed. Anatoly Shikov. Clearly someone used to violence. Clearly someone used to getting his own way. A dangerous guy to have around. Unruly, undisciplined. Possible psychotic tendencies. Not an effective leader, not someone who could remain in command of an organised criminal gang. Yet he'd been put in charge.

By whom? An influential contact? Had Anatoly had a friend in a high place? A relative? Was he someone's brother?

Someone's son?

By the time he'd finished his second triple shot of whisky, Ben's instincts were telling him that the top man, beyond any doubt, was a Russian. And no mere art robber, not sending their boys in that heavy.

Russian mafia. That went a long way towards explaining these men's ruthlessness, the violence, the lack of hesitation when it came to pulling the trigger.

And Ben had a name to go on. Shikov.

He thought again about Donatella, and Gianni. Remembered the ghastly, haunted look on Fabio Strada's face in the hospital.

Then he thought about justice. Who was going to deliver it to the Stradas, and to the rest of the victims, the survivors, their families? Roberto Lario? Ben didn't think so.

It was pushing midnight by the time the hotel bar closed and he headed back up to his small room on the first floor. The door clicked shut behind him. He left the light off. By the intermittent dull glow of the blinking neon hotel sign on the wall outside, he walked over to the armchair where he'd dumped his leather jacket and picked it up. It was heavy from the weight of the .45 Ruger he'd taken from Tassoni's place. He slipped the hotel room card key into the other pocket, then slouched back on the bed, closed his mind to the night traffic rumble wafting up through the open window, and shut his eyes.

Chapter Thirty-Five

Georgia

Far away over the hills, a wolf's howl pierced the deepness of the night: a plaintive, mournful sound, like a lament for lost souls. Grigori Shikov turned away from the railing of his balcony and walked slowly back into the shadows and silence of the house to refill his glass with chilled vodka.

He had spoken to nobody since hearing of the murder of his old friend.

First Sonja. Then Anatoly. Now Urbano. So much death. Death all around him.

And there would be more. Always more.

In his study, Shikov opened one of the display cabinets. He laid his hands on the smooth, cool veneer of the old cherry-wood box inside, carefully lifted it out and laid it on his desk. He opened the lid and gazed for a few moments at the pair of antique percussion duelling pistols nestling inside the red velvet lining. The finest Italian craftsmanship, from a more civilised era when gentlemen could settle their disputes honourably, in blood. He ran his fingers lovingly down the guns' slender barrels. His mind drifted back twenty-six years.

It had been 1985, around the time he'd first seriously

contemplated a career in politics, that the then twenty-nine-year-old Urbano Tassoni had presented his friend with the magnificent gift. For a serious amateur historian like Shikov, the cased pair of duelling pistols would have made a fine addition to his collection whatever their background, but Tassoni had had particular reason for picking those specific guns. Aware of his friend's passion for all things even indirectly connected with the bygone epoch of Imperial Russia, he'd known that the weapons' unique history would hold a special appeal.

The pistols had once belonged to an Italian aristocrat by the name of Count Rodingo De Crescenzo, a man of small historic consequence save for the little-known fact that, exactly sixty years earlier, he was rumoured to have used these very same weapons to fight one of the last illegal duels in European history. What made the duel especially interesting for Shikov was that the count's rival had been an exiled Russian prince, who had subsequently died from his wound. By its very nature, the duel had been something the count's agents had been keen to cover up. No formal charges had ever been brought, nothing had ever been proved. Only a handful of historians, including the antiquarian who had sold Tassoni the pistols, had ever known of the scandalous episode.

On receiving the gift, Shikov had been mightily touched by his friend's gesture. But when Tassoni had told him the name of the Russian prince who'd been involved in the duel, he'd been completely staggered, blown away to the point of stupefaction. It was too incredible to be a coincidence. For the first and only time in his life, Shikov had been convinced that the hand of Fate was at work.

Prince Leonid Alexandrovich Borowsky. Born into one of the richest and most powerful noble families in Imperial

Russia, second only to the ruling Romanov dynasty and Tsar Nicholas II himself. Exiled to Europe after the 1917 revolution and the fall of the Romanov empire and – according to the whispered legend that decades of short-sighted dismissal by egghead historians could not snuff out – the owner of a priceless relic, a unique and exquisite treasure worth killing, even dying for.

In the exclusive circles of wealthy, dedicated, hardcore antiquities collectors to which Shikov belonged, the relic was known as the Dark Medusa. All his adult life, ever since he'd made his first real money and taken his first tentative steps into amassing artefacts of historic value, Grigori Shikov had lusted after it, imagining himself owning it, willing to offer any price to acquire it.

And trying to picture what it looked like. In all the long years since the disappearance of the magnificent relic, nobody had come forward claiming to have actually seen the Dark Medusa. No photographs or drawings of it were known to have survived, and only the sketchiest of descriptions existed in the historic archives. From his arrival in Europe after the Russian revolution to his death in 1925, there were no recorded witness accounts of Prince Leo showing his treasure to anyone; and after his untimely demise at the hands of the Italian count, the Dark Medusa had never again resurfaced.

None of which had been able, now that fortune had gifted him with this incredible discovery, to deter Grigori Shikov from his renewed quest to find it. He'd been forty-eight years old then, at the height of his power and ready and willing to use every bit of it to cut as wide and bloody a swathe as necessary to get what he wanted.

His experience had taught him that men would do anything to protect a secret of this value. That was why, when he'd traced the antiquarian who'd sold the pistols to

Tassoni, intending to press any information out of him that might shed light on what had happened to Leo Borowsky's priceless possession, the brutality of the interrogation had made even some of his hardest thugs blanch. By the time Shikov had been persuaded that the antiquarian really didn't know anything useful, the man was too badly damaged ever to walk or talk or eat again. Shikov had personally ended his suffering by cutting his throat with a razor.

The search had continued fruitlessly. It had often occurred to Shikov, back in those days, that Rodingo De Crescenzo might have known where the relic was – might even have taken it for himself after killing its owner. If so, where had it gone? The leads were few and far between. Investigations revealed that the count had succumbed to tuberculosis in 1934. His son Federico had been killed in Sudan during World War II. The only surviving descendant was Rodingo's grandson, Pietro De Crescenzo, not yet thirty but already a leading patron of the arts and very much in the public eye.

The young count's celebrity wouldn't have deterred Shikov in the slightest from using brute force to gain information from him. But in October 1986, just when he'd been about to issue the order that would have seen Pietro De Crescenzo strapped to a chair with a gun to his head, Shikov's search had suddenly veered in a whole new direction. De Crescenzo would never know how lucky he'd been.

It had been while tearing through an obscure, out-of-print book on the European aristocracy of the twentieth century that Shikov had found out about Rodingo De Crescenzo's short-lived first marriage to the woman who had later gone on to become one of Italy's most celebrated female artists, Gabriella Giordani. From what he could glean from the brief text, the relationship had ended abruptly in 1925. The same year as the duel.

The discovery had sent Shikov's imagination into overdrive. The possible motives for two men fighting a duel to the death over a woman were easy enough to speculate about. The question was, what secrets might the former countess have learned from Leo Borowsky before her husband had ended his life?

Shikov had delved deeper. None of the biographies of the artist made any reference to that part of her past. The fact that Gabriella had kept so silent for so many years intrigued him all the more.

His investigators had had little trouble tracking her down. She'd been pushing eighty by then, leading a solitary and reclusive existence in a rambling old country villa outside Cesena in the north of Italy. So alone. So vulnerable. So easy.

Shikov could still remember that starlit night when he and his men had paid their visit to her. He recalled the delirious sense of elation he'd felt as they'd smashed their way into the isolated villa, convinced that he'd found his prize at last. He hadn't.

What he'd found instead was the cracked, worn old diary, its writing faded with age. For the next twenty-five years, not a week had passed without his returning to re-read it obsessively, like a devout believer drawn to his bible, certain that it contained the key. And he'd been right, in the end. Yet now, just when once again he'd thought he was about to lay his hands on the lost relic of his dreams, his hopes had been dashed a second time in a forgotten Russian cemetery. The map inside the picture frame had been accurate enough – but someone had got there before him.

Could the search for the Dark Medusa finally be over?

Maybe it was, Shikov thought. Maybe he'd be in his own grave before it was done.

At least he could console himself that he wouldn't be the only one.

He picked up one of the duelling pistols. The antique lockwork gave a delicate *click-clunk* as he cocked the hammer. He held the gun at arm's length, sighted down its barrel. Pulled the trigger. The hammer fell with a dry snap.

'Ben Hope, you are dead,' he said. And that thought, at this moment, was the only thing in the world that gave him any joy.

Chapter Thirty-Six

Manchester

Just after midnight, Darcey Kane was escorted from the helipad on the roof of the SOCA regional HQ by plain-clothes agents who checked her name, rank and number into a register and took away her weapon to be logged into secure storage. Less than three minutes later she was whisked into a large, plush office on the top floor, and found herself alone with a man she'd only ever heard of before but never met.

Sir William Applewood, SOCA's Senior Director of Intelligence, personally appointed by the Home Secretary, was a heavyset man of sixty-two with skin turned the colour of chalk by the strain of his job. Behind his half-moon spectacles, there were dark rings around his eyes. Maybe the whispered legend that he needed only three hours of sleep a night wasn't true after all. He glanced up as she was shown into the room, and expressionlessly waved her to a chair across the broad, polished desk from him.

Darcey stayed on her feet. 'Sir, I would appreciate an explanation as to why I was snatched away from an oper-ation I've been working day and night on for three months, just at the point when—'

Applewood flashed a steely look at her. 'Take a *seat*, Commander,' he said firmly.

Darcey shut her mouth and did as she was told. Applewood said nothing more for a few moments while he sifted papers on his desk. She could see the open file in front of him was hers. He scanned the text, his eye lingering on a section here and there with a slight flicker of an eyebrow. It was probably as impressed as he could look. Finally he shut the file, leaned back in his reclining swivel chair and gazed at her over the desk.

'Darcey Kane. Age thirty-five. Joined the force as a constable in April 2000. Rapid promotion, then three years with Merseyside police Matrix rapid response team. From there, graduated to CO19 Specialist Firearms Command. Top of your division for speed and accuracy both on the range and the field. Showed exceptional leadership and decision-making qualities. Fluent in five languages. Proficient in all forms of combat. Extensive experience of hostage and raid situations, eighteen major arrests to your credit. Left the police service at thirty-four to take up present duties at SOCA. How's your first year with us been?'

'Excellent, sir.' She felt like adding, 'Until some arsehole decided to compromise my operation.'

Applewood's stare was cold and penetrating, as if he could read her thoughts. 'You've come a long way, Darcey. As you know, we monitor the performance of our agents very closely. Certain people believe you're capable of a great deal more than your current position allows. They feel we might be wasting your talents.'

So now she had an inkling of what this was about. She fought back a smile. 'Certain people, sir?'

Applewood raised his index finger at the ceiling, as though pointing to some imaginary floor above. 'Let's just say, the *gods.*' He allowed himself a brief chuckle, then became serious again. 'An assignment has landed on my desk tonight that requires an exceptionally gifted agent. I'm in agreement with the suggestion that it might be time to let you spread your wings.' The cold stare bored into her. 'What do you think?'

Darcey's mind was racing and she could barely sit still. In her mind she was turning cartwheels across the desk. But she controlled herself and remained completely impassive, with her hands folded neatly in her lap. 'I think I'd like that very much, sir.'

'Thought you would.' Applewood kicked his chair back from the desk, pulled out a drawer and reached for another file, which he skimmed across the polished surface at her.

The front of the file was printed with the usual eyes-only heading in bold red capitals that went with a high-level clearance document.

'Operation Jericho?' she said.

'Read it,' Applewood replied.

Darcey flipped the file open. The first thing she saw was the face of the man whose photo was clipped to the top page. Good-looking guy, she thought as she instinctively memorised his likeness. Blond hair, not too short. Strong features. The blue eyes showed a depth of intelligence. And pain, too, somewhere in there. She scanned quickly down the accompanying text, soaking up information. In police evaluation tests she'd shown she could read a complex eighty-page document in under three minutes and retain every single detail. The police psychologists had called it eidetic memory. They'd also done their best to prove she was cheating, until she proved them otherwise.

She'd got faster since then.

It took her just a second or two to see that this guy was more than just a pretty face. The military resumé that filled the page was enough to make her purse her lips. She read down the list, flipped the page, read more. Everything was heavily stamped with dire Ministry of Defence confidentiality warnings. There was enough detail of unofficial black ops missions to war zones the British army weren't even supposed to have been involved in to cause some serious embarrassment within the highest echelons of government. It wasn't the kind of information that a few decades of Official Secrets Act suppression could dilute enough to be allowed into the public domain. The data in this file would never be seen by anyone outside the corridors of power while anyone remotely connected to it was still living.

Darcey was extremely aware that in the last few short moments she'd taken a bigger leap up the security clearance ladder than in eleven long years of her career to date.

The gods, indeed. She'd been chosen. All her hard work had finally paid off and now the doors were opening for her. The feeling was giddying, and her heart began to thump.

'Ben Hope,' she muttered to herself. 'Full name Benedict. Age thirty-nine, retired from 22 SAS, rank of major, now resident in France, occupation specialised security consultant.'

'Specialised security consultant,' Applewood said. 'Covers a lot of ground, doesn't it?' When he grinned he looked like an alligator. 'I want you to familiarise yourself with this man. He's your next target. I *expect* results, Commander.'

Darcey narrowed her eyes. There was just one small piece of information missing. 'Why do we want him?'

'You'll be fully briefed in the air.'

What might Hope have done to attract this kind of attention, Darcey thought. Her mind sprinted through the possibilities. Terrorism, arms dealing, drugs. Another ex-hero gone rotten. It didn't really matter how, or why. She was locked on her target. From this moment until the moment he was hers, he was all she'd care about.

'Where am I going?' she asked.

'Rome. Naturally you'll have full command of the operation, answerable only to me. How fast can you be ready?'

'I'm ready now,' Darcey said.

'Tired?'

'Not on your life, sir.'

'Then go and get your man, Commander,' Applewood said. 'There's a car waiting for you downstairs. Your plane leaves in exactly twenty-four minutes.'

Chapter Thirty-Seven

Rome

Ben was wandering slowly, alone, down a tunnel that went on forever, listening to the faraway echo of his own footsteps. The walls, floor and ceiling of the tunnel were white and bathed in a bright glow that came from everywhere and nowhere. As he walked on and on, he became aware of the strange works of art suspended either side of him. Their colours seemed to jump out at him, swirling, moving, though he couldn't make out the images or what they signified.

He hit against something he couldn't see. Reached his hands out and sideways and groped around until he realised there was a glass wall blocking his path. He could go no further. Narrowing his eyes, he peered through to the other side – and saw the figure standing there. A man in a mask. They gazed at one another, and then the man seemed to smile. He had a gun in his hand. In front of him were two kneeling, huddled shapes – or it could have been a hundred. Ben knew that the man intended to harm them. He thumped against the glass and yelled as the man raised the gun, taking aim at the kneeling figures; but no sound came out, and he was suddenly powerless and trapped as more glass walls seemed to press in from all sides. The man in the mask laughed as he pulled the trigger. His victims were screaming now.

The gun boomed. And again. A deep thud that reverberated through the walls. The victims went on screaming and screaming.

Ben woke suddenly and jerked upright in the darkness, blinking away the fog of sleep. For a few instants part of his mind seemed unwilling to detach itself from his nightmare – and then he realised he really could hear voices shouting, and the heavy thumping that was coming from beyond the rectangular strip of white light that outlined the door.

Reality was suddenly sharp and clear. He glanced at his watch and saw that it was 1.14 a.m. He was still fully dressed, wearing his shoes. He must have fallen asleep on the bed.

'*Polizia!*' yelled a voice from outside. The next thump on the door was a shattering crash that splintered the frame. The lock was still holding, but another impact like that and they'd be in.

Three options. One, stick around and find out what they wanted. Two, grab the .45 Ruger and start blasting holes in the door. Ben glanced back at the open window as another massive thud filled the room. He decided he preferred the third option. He snatched up his jacket and slipped it on.

The door crashed open in a shower of splinters. Armed police burst in, yelling and waving their pistols.

Before they'd even stepped over the threshold, Ben was already out of the open window, dropping down out of sight below the ledge and shooting out his right hand to grab hold of the bracket of the neon sign fixed to the wall a metre away. It held his weight. As he hung from it, his legs kicking in space, he could hear the cops crashing about in the hotel room. More yells. Another loud thud as they burst into the bathroom. Probably expecting to find him in the shower.

He glanced down. It was a pretty long drop to the street below, about seven or eight metres. The pavement seemed about an inch wide. Traffic rolled by, skirting around the two police Alfa Romeos that were pulled up outside the hotel entrance.

All he had to do was get down to the street before someone spotted him. He guessed that would happen within about the next fifteen seconds. He scrabbled the toecaps of his shoes against the wall, trying to get a purchase on it, but the stonework was covered in a smooth render that offered no footholds. Two metres to his right, an iron drainpipe was solidly attached to the wall. If he could get to it . . .

But it was too far to reach. He dangled helplessly. Any second now, the cops would be at the window.

Two more police-marked Alfas came screeching around the street corner and skidded to a halt outside the hotel. The doors flew open and four more Carabinieri scrambled out clutching pistols. They made straight for the hotel entrance.

All they had to do was look up.

'I *told* you we should have taken a right back there!' Gary Parsons seethed at his wife from behind the wheel of the six-berth motorhome as it lumbered through the night traffic. 'Christ, you're the one with the map!'

'This thing's all wrong,' his wife Annabel complained, flapping the unfolded map across the dashboard. 'I'm telling you I followed it perfectly—'

'How can it be *wrong*? It's a fucking *map*, for God's sake. You read it, it tells you where to go. How hard can it be?'

'Don't yell like that. You'll wake the kids.'

'We should have been at the campsite hours ago,' he grumbled bitterly. 'Now we're lost in the middle of Rome, thanks to you. I think I'm perfectly justified in yelling.'

'What's going on here?' his wife said, pointing, as they passed a lit-up hotel entrance that was swarming with police.

'How the hell should I know?'

They both shut up as they heard a soft *thump* from somewhere above them.

'What was that?' she said.

'Dunno. Sounded like something landed on the roof.'

'Or you've gone and hit something, more like,' she said archly.

Gary looked in the mirrors, then craned his neck out of the window, thinking the high top of the vehicle must have snagged a streetlight or a road sign that he'd failed to notice while they'd been arguing. But he could see nothing. He damn well hoped he hadn't damaged the new satellite dish.

His wife said, 'Better stop and see what you've done.'

'I've got nowhere to pull over,' he replied through gritted teeth. 'Can't you see I'm in the middle of traffic? Look at all these police cars. You want me to get bloody arrested?'

'Stop yelling!'

'This is all *your* fault!'

The couple went on arguing as the motorhome lumbered on by the hotel and continued up the street.

Chapter Thirty-Eight

Ben lay pressed flat against the broad white expanse of the motorhome roof, feeling the vibrating thrum of the diesel engine through his body as they rolled away from the hotel.

Not exactly the ideal getaway vehicle. The thing couldn't be doing more than thirty kilometres an hour, and he was plastered across the top of it for all to see. He craned his head to look behind him. Over the top of a large cargo storage box and two kids' bicycles lashed to a luggage rack he could see the window of what had been his hotel room until just a moment ago. Dark silhouettes of the cops were milling around in the lit-up windows. Nobody was pointing after him, shouting 'There he goes!'. As long as they all stayed focused on the inside of the room for another few seconds, he was clean away.

The motorhome kept moving, and Ben kept his gaze fixed on the receding hotel window. Nothing happened. Then, as the vehicle reached the corner of the street, it turned sharply to the left and he held on tight to the luggage rack to stop himself sliding sideways. These things hadn't been designed with roof passengers in mind. He looked back once more as the side of a tall building blocked the hotel and the parked police cars from view.

Nobody came round the corner in pursuit. It wasn't the

most elegant escape ever made, but it was the end result that mattered. Ben imagined the police storming about the place, wondering where the hell he'd disappeared to, kicking in doors all through the hotel and arguing with the receptionist who'd be insisting that the guest hadn't left the building. In different circumstances it might have made him smile. Maybe he could smile about it later, once he knew what all this was about. Maybe Roberto Lario had decided to have another polite chat about the gallery robbery. More likely, it had something to do with the late Urbano Tassoni.

The joys of celebrity, Ben thought. Someone must have spotted him going into the politician's place and recognised him from the newspapers or TV. Just great.

Two hundred metres further up the street, he felt himself sliding towards the bulky overcab section of the roof as the motorhome braked for a red light. 'This is my stop,' he muttered as he scrambled back towards the rear of the vehicle, looking for a way down. An aluminium access ladder ran down from the roof. He swung nimbly over the edge, climbed down the narrow rungs and dropped to the road as two young guys in a little Fiat pulled up behind. The lights turned green and the huge white boxy motorhome rumbled off, a giant fridge on wheels with British plates and a big GB sticker on the back.

Ben stepped aside to let the Fiat pass. The two young guys inside were staring at him, and one of them tapped a finger to his temple and said something to his friend that was probably 'These Brits are crazy'.

Ben didn't hang around waiting for them to recognise him, too. He ran across the road and began walking fast up the pavement, past closed shop doorways and windows. The streets were mostly empty, which made him feel conspicuous and vulnerable. Another police Alfa sped by, lights flashing.

He paused and turned away from the street to gaze at a bright boutique display. Just a casual window shopper out for a night stroll. Then he realised the window was full of half-naked female mannequins modelling lacy underwear, and moved on quickly. The pervert thing wasn't an ideal way to avoid police attention.

The Alfa passed on by. Ben kept walking. But then, fifty metres down the road, it suddenly pulled a screeching U-turn and came back after him. He broke into a run, the clapping echo of his footsteps loud in the empty street. The car chased him. A squeal of brakes; he heard its doors open. A voice yelling *'Alt! Polizia!'*

Ben ran faster. Music was thumping from an alleyway up ahead. He darted into it, and the music got louder.

The alley terminated in a cobbled yard at the entrance to what must once have been some kind of warehouse or factory, but was now a late-night dance club. Its doorway was a pair of steel shutters, and the red light strobing from inside made it look like the gates of Hell. A mob of rowdy guys in their twenties were clustered around the cobbled yard, clutching beer bottles and yelling drunkenly in Dutch at some skimpily-clad Italian girls teetering inside the club in high heels. From the way the Dutch boys were taunting the bouncers, Ben guessed they'd been refused entry to the place. The bouncers were both heavy guys, bowling-pin forearms folded across bench-press chests. One wore a goatee and the other had a shaven head with tattoos over his ears. Their body language screamed *do not fuck with us*, but the Dutch guys were either too drunk or too cocky to heed it. It looked like a situation about to kick off. Sure enough, when Ben was still a few metres from the door, one of the Dutch crew lobbed a bottle. It narrowly missed the shaven-headed bouncer and shattered against the brick wall behind him.

The bouncers moved surprisingly fast for such big men. They waded in, and in two seconds three of the Dutch guys were on their backs. Ben slipped into the unguarded entrance before the scuffle turned into a full-on war. In his wake he could hear the yelling as the cops came racing down the alley and found their path blocked by a fistfight in progress. There was a screech of sirens and brakes at the top of the alley as at least two or three more police cars arrived on the scene.

Ben walked quickly through a bare brick corridor, the thump of the music building up to a head-filling roar. The corridor turned a corner and then opened up into a large, murky space that was heaving with bodies and smelled of beer and spirits and hot skin and the mixed perfume of the girls. The lights stuttered red, green, white over the sprawling mêlée of people dancing, making everything look like slow motion.

Beyond the crowded bar, Ben saw what he was looking for – the dim neon exit sign over the back door. He pressed on through the throng. Hearing an angry clamour behind him he glanced back over his shoulder and saw maybe eight, maybe ten Carabinieri swarming into the club, provoking jeers and catcalls from the dancers. They shoved people out of the way as they pressed aggressively through the crowd, scanning left and right. Their hands were on the butts of their holstered pistols and they looked serious.

Ben pushed on towards the exit. A hand on his arm made him turn abruptly, and he saw it was a girl. She was about twenty, skinny with dark hair and heavy eyeshadow. Her face and neck and the bare shoulder where her loose-fitting top had slipped down were shiny with sweat; her eyes were bright as she smiled at him and mouthed inaudible words that he guessed were an invitation to dance. She looked a little high, a little unsteady on her feet.

He hesitated a moment. Two of the cops were drawing close through the crowd. They'd be searching for a guy on his own. Someone nervous and furtive and aiming to put as much distance between himself and them as possible. Someone who'd stand out a mile in here. Ben smiled at the girl and nodded, mouthed 'Yeah, sure'. She pressed up close to him and began to sway her hips. He danced with her, matching her movements. She closed her eyes and threw back her head and raised her arms high in the air.

The cops came brushing by. Ben took the girl's arm, whirling her round so his back was to them, and she laughed, and so did he. He grabbed an empty beer bottle from a nearby table and pretended to swig out of it, acting drunk. She laughed louder, her teeth flashing red in the lights.

A few metres away, a tallish guy with fair hair and a slim build was making his way over to the bar. The two cops grabbed his arm and whisked him round. They shone a torch in his face, glanced at one another, then shook their heads and shoved him away.

Time to go, Ben was thinking. He'd picked up the dance moves pretty well by now. Basically you thrashed around, looked completely out of control and grinned like an idiot: that way you blended perfectly into the crowd. Still gyrating his hips and waving the beer bottle about, he guided the girl away from the dance floor and through the exit.

It didn't lead outside, but through to a lounge where the mood was a lot more sombre and the emphasis seemed to be squarely on getting quietly slaughtered. Some guys were playing pool in one corner, and a few couples and assorted drinkers were clustered round the bar. A little grey guy in a rumpled suit was drowning his sorrows, an attaché case resting against the legs of his stool. Bad day at the office, maybe. A little way from him sat a tired-looking blonde in a low-cut outfit, knocking back what definitely wasn't her first gin and tonic that night. Nobody was doing much talking. A few faces were turned towards the small TV over the bar, gazing uninterestedly at the passing images even though the sound was muted. From the opposite corner came a draught of cooler air, and Ben noticed another doorway marked TOILETS leading out to a narrow passage littered with beer crates.

The girl he'd been dancing with was watching him expect-antly, either because she thought he was going to buy her a drink, or else take her somewhere more private. She stag-gered a little as she clutched his arm. He asked her name, and in a slurry giggle she told him it was Luisa. He took her wrist and pushed her gently back. 'Thanks for the dance, Luisa,' he said. 'Make sure you get home safe tonight, OK?'

She frowned at him.

'Hey,' someone said, nodding at the TV. A few people glanced over.

The smiling face of Urbano Tassoni was plastered all over the screen. Then the picture cut to a dark street, swirling lights of emergency vehicles and a lot of official milling around as a good-looking brunette Ben recognised as the reporter Silvana Lucenzi talked soundlessly into a mike. The heading 'BREAKING NEWS: URBANO TASSONI MURDERED' scrolled in bold white letters across the bottom edge of the screen. The barman idly reached for a remote and turned up the volume. The next image to flash up on the screen was Ben's face, the photo he used for his business website.

'. . . suspect is believed to be armed and extremely dangerous,' Silvana Lucenzi was saying. 'The public are being warned not to approach him under any circumstances . . .'

Faces at the bar turned slowly to stare at Ben. The guys

playing pool had laid down their cues and were standing there, frozen. Luisa frowned more deeply, the confusion in her eyes turning quickly to a shade of fear.

Ben shrugged. 'Don't believe everything you see on television,' he said, and then moved for the exit.

Just a little too late. As he made it to the doorway, there was a shout and he turned and saw five cops push through into the lounge bar. The barman pointed but they'd already spotted him. Their pistols were drawn. One was clutching a taser gun.

Ben didn't much feel like having sharp wire darts embedded in his flesh, connected to an incapacitating electric current that would have even the biggest, most violent guy down on the floor in seconds, struggling as helplessly as a landed fish while cops surrounded him and trussed him up in handcuffs. He ducked away out of the exit, kicking over a stack of crates that blocked his path. Cool night air washed over him and made his clothes feel clammy as he ran down the narrow passage, slammed through the ramshackle door at the end and out into a deserted backstreet.

Racing footsteps and yelling voices came right after him. He ran harder, didn't look back. After a hundred metre sprint, the backstreet spat him out on the main road. His pursuers weren't far behind him. He could hear them radioing for support.

He bolted across the street, narrowly avoiding being hit by a passing car. On the other side of the road was an iron railing and a sign for a subway station. He vaulted the railing, went thundering down the concrete steps, shouldered hard through the swing doors. He passed the ticket office without slowing down, and an unshaven guy in a uniform yelled as he hurdled the turnstile. Signs pointed this way and that as gleaming white-tiled tunnels branched off in different directions. Ben sprinted down the nearest one, then hammered down a slow-moving elevator. Another junction, another split-second decision, another snaking tunnel.

Deep under Rome, the atmosphere was thick and stifling. As Ben approached the station platform, a breathy, whistling slap of warm air woofing up the tunnel and a crescendo of wheels on tracks told him that a train was coming.

Chapter Thirty-Nine

Fiumicino airport, Rome

After the dank Manchester weather and then the air-conditioned Cessna Citation jet, the sultry Rome night felt like a sauna to Darcey as she stepped down to the tarmac of the private runway. She knew right away that the thin black cotton polo-neck sweater she'd changed into on board was going to be way too heavy. First time in Italy, and she was caught out like a damn fool tourist.

Three vehicles were waiting nearby, two unmarked Interpol BMWs and a police Alfa Romeo. Next to them were clustered a group of four plainclothes agents, watching her expectantly as she walked up to them. A quick round of businesslike handshakes, and one of the agents did the introductions. He was tall, bald and rail-thin in a tailored jacket and open-necked shirt. His English was excellent. 'And my name is Paolo Buitoni,' he finished. 'I'm your liaison officer in Rome. Anything you need.' He stole a puff of his cigarette and exhaled through his nose.

'Buitoni?'

'Like the pasta. No spaghetti jokes, please.' Buitoni smiled, wrinkles creasing at the corners of his eyes.

'I don't like spaghetti,' Darcey told him.

'That's a pity.'

'And I'm not here to appreciate humour,' Darcey said.

'So I see.'

'And lose the cigarette, Paolo.'

Buitoni shot her a look, then flicked the cigarette away and orange sparks tumbled across the tarmac. He motioned towards one of the BMWs. 'There has been a development within the last few minutes,' he told her as they walked over to it. 'The suspect Ben Hope evaded arrest earlier tonight and is on the run in the city as we speak.'

She narrowed her eyes at him. 'Uh-huh. The first I hear of this is now?'

Buitoni shrugged. 'We only just heard ourselves.'

'Nobody was to make a move until I got here.'

'You'll find things tend to work that way in Italy.'

'Not any more. What's the target's location?'

'Our officers chased him into the subway system just seven minutes ago.'

'Wonderful,' Darcey said as he showed her to the rear of the BMW. The driver had the engine running. 'A city subway system is an easy place to lose a fugitive. And this one's already shown once tonight that he's smarter than your police.' She yanked open the door.

'Not as easy as you might think,' Buitoni said. 'The Rome underground is still under construction. It has just two lines and only thirty-eight kilometres of track, compared with over four hundred kilometres in London. Believe me, there are few places for him to hide.'

'Then I want the whole system sealed before he finds a way out of there. Set me up a cordon. Nothing goes in or out without my say-so.'

'Being done. We'll catch him. No problem.'

Darcey climbed into the back of the BMW with one of

the other agents and slammed her door. 'Let's get moving, people.'

Buitoni got in the front passenger seat, and the car took off with a squeal of tyres. The second unmarked BMW followed, with the police Alfa bringing up the rear. As they left the airport the Alfa started up its flashing lights and siren. The night traffic parted for them as they hit the road for the city.

Buitoni turned round in his seat to pass Darcey an ID card and badge, and a handgun in a black fabric holster. She unclipped it. A Beretta 92FS, standard Italian police issue. It was heavier than the Glock she was used to, just under a kilo of chunky steel. The fat grip contained seventeen rounds of 9mm Parabellum.

'How far to the scene?' she asked, nodding at the speeding road ahead.

'We'll be there in fifteen minutes,' Buitoni said.

'Anything I need?'

'You're the boss, Commander Kane.'

'Then get me there in ten.'

The driver put his foot down and the little procession of cars tooled into Rome in just a shade over eleven minutes. They screeched up outside a metro station that was teeming with police cars, vans and motorcycles and a milling crowd of uniformed cops. It was Darcey's first glimpse of Italian Carabinieri with their red-striped trousers and Beretta machine pistols slapping their sides as they strode. She wondered how cocky they'd be if she told them how camp they looked in their knee-high leather boots. Buitoni must have seen her looking at them because he leaned close to her and said, 'Your first time in Rome?'

'And let's get it over with,' she said.

They were getting of the car when Buitoni received a radio call that left him frowning. 'Hurry,' he said, taking Darcey's elbow to lead her towards the subway station entrance. She jerked the elbow away. 'Talk to me, Paolo.'

As they ran down down the steps he explained: 'We have CCTV footage of Hope boarding a train three stops down the line from here, just minutes ago.'

Darcey batted through the swing doors. 'Is every station sealed?'

'We're working on it. But he hasn't got off. Which means he's still on board. The train is due to stop here any second now.' They strode fast through the tunnels, surrounded by cops bristling with weaponry. Darcey scraped back her hair as they walked, fastening it with an elastic tie. She took the folded baseball cap from her back pocket, shook out the crumples and pulled it down tight over her head.

A moment later they emerged onto the platform where about a thousand guns were trained on the black mouth of the tunnel. Darcey did a check of her Beretta. Outwardly, she was calm, relaxed and totally in charge. She didn't want Buitoni or anyone else to see that her heart was racing and her knees like jelly with the nervous excitement of waiting for the train to roll into the station. She almost let out an involuntary cry when she saw the lights in the dark tunnel. With a rumbling whine and hissing of brakes, the train emerged into the light and pulled up.

Darcey was so tense she thought her neck was going to snap. There was a wheeze of hydraulics and the train doors slid open. This time of night, there were just one or two passengers on board, and they stared in horror at the arsenal of weapons suddenly trained on them. Cops poured into every carriage. Up and down the length of the train, radios fizzed and chirped and officers milled around checking every inch inside and out.

It didn't take long for the signal to reach back to Darcey.

'He's not here.' Buitoni looked suddenly drained.

Darcey said nothing.

'Don't be angry,' he said, watching her eyes.

'You'll know when I am.'

'I don't understand how this could have happened.' Buitoni jabbed a finger back at the empty train. 'He was *on* it.'

'Then he's obviously got off it, no? He just didn't use a station.'

Buitoni looked blank.

'You don't understand what you're up against here, do you?' Darcey snapped at him. 'Ben Hope isn't your typical criminal, some little mafioso you're going to scoop up off the street or nab asleep in the whorehouse with his nose full of coke. He's SAS. You have no idea of the training these people have.'

'How come you know so much about it?'

'Because I've had more than a taste of it myself,' she said. 'My old unit, CO19, sends its personnel to train with SAS instructors. Physical fitness. Armed and unarmed close-quarter battle. Defensive driving. Hostage rescue. Escape and evasion. That's just for breakfast.'

Buitoni raised an eyebrow. 'Tough.'

'Believe me, there isn't a word for how tough it is. Just like there isn't a word in English or Italian to describe just how royally you people have fucked up here.' Darcey went on talking over the top of him as he started to protest. 'Get it through your head. This man is ready for anything. He can disappear, resist capture for weeks on end, slip through the net of even the most dedicated manhunt. The hardest target you've ever gone after, and what do you guys do? You make it easy for him. You let him make fools of you. Not that it was so hard. Don't argue with me, Paolo. You know I'm right.' She glanced up the empty tunnel, past the immobile train and the hordes of cops now leading the dazed passengers away. 'I guess that even in Italy they must occasionally service and maintain the underground system?'

'Though we could surely never live up to your superior example.'

She ignored his sarcasm. 'Then it must be possible to shut down a section of electrified rail but keep some lighting going in there.'

'I think we can manage that.'

'Do it.'

Buitoni talked in his radio. A moment later he got a call back and told her it was done.

'Good. We're going in.'

Buitoni stared at her. 'Who's going in?'

Darcey pointed at him, herself and the crowd of cops on the platform. 'All of us. And I want another fifty searching from the other end, where Hope boarded. Somewhere along the line he's got to be there.'

Within three minutes Darcey and Buitoni were at the head of the party flushing out the underground tunnel. Away from the station, the atmosphere was stifling and oppressive. She wasn't used to this heat. The cotton polo-neck was sticking to her back. Every so often a dim lantern glowed against the sooty walls, but the lighting was poor and for most of the time the tunnel was in darkness except for the bobbing beams of their Maglites. There was nothing moving ahead of them, only the occasional black scuttling shape of a rat disturbed by their approach.

'This is fun,' Buitoni said as they trudged on, a few metres ahead of the rest of the troops.

'How come your English is so good?' she asked him.

'My mother was from Gloucester. We lived in Britain until I was nine, then we moved to Rome. I've lived here ever since.'

'You know this city pretty well, then.'

'Better than most,' he said. 'What about your Italian? Not bad either.'

'Night school,' she replied.

They walked on in silence. Buitoni seemed deep in thought. 'I just don't get it,' he said after a while. 'I mean, a lot of people had their suspicions about Tassoni. There have been allegations about him for years, never proven. But to gun the man down in his home . . . And why? How is this Hope even involved?'

'I don't care if Tassoni was shaping up to be the next Mussolini,' Darcey said. 'I don't care if Hope was doing the world a favour taking the guy out. And I don't care why he did it. He's mine, and he's going down.'

Buitoni turned to look at her as a flash of torchlight passed across her face. He noticed the expression in her eyes and was going to say, 'I can see why they sent you,' then thought better of it and kept his mouth shut.

Another twenty minutes passed. 'This is no use,' Buitoni said as they trudged on in the dark. 'I'm sure Hope was never here.'

'He was here. Can't you smell it?'

'Don't tell me. The SAS instructors also taught you to detect the scent of your prey, like a hunting predator.' That wouldn't have surprised him. He was beginning to get a pretty sharp idea of what kind of person his new commander was.

She didn't reply. Buitoni sniffed at the stale, humid air. 'All I can smell in this hellhole is rats and filth and damp and the sweat of fifty Carabinieri.'

'I can smell something else as well,' she said. 'Burnt lighter fluid.'

Chapter Forty

The flickering yellow flame of a Zippo wasn't quite as useful as a torch for finding your way up a black tunnel. Better than groping about blindly, though it had other disadvantages. The lighter's brushed steel body was getting uncomfortably hot in Ben's fingers, and he was beginning to worry about the fuel-soaked cotton inside reaching flashpoint. But singed fingers were some way preferable to zapping yourself into a piece of crispy bacon in about a millisecond when you happened to step on the electrified rail in the dark.

He reckoned enough time had passed by now for the police to seal off the whole underground network. Call it instinct, call it experience, but his sense of growing unease as he'd ridden the near-empty tube train through two stations had made him want to bail out before reaching the third. Three was pushing his luck. And he was fairly sure that, before too long, they'd be swarming through these tunnels like ferrets down a rabbit hole.

As he walked down the dirty gravel path between the rails, his shoe scraped against something solid and heavy. In the dim flame he saw that it was an old wrench. It was rusted and pitted and had probably been dropped by a workman decades earlier. A thought came to him, and he picked the wrench up and lobbed it gently against the electrified rail.

No flash, no bang. The wrench lay against the dead steel. He had suspected that would happen, and it could only mean one thing – that he'd been right, and that the cops had shut down a section of the line and were already coming after him on foot. The next station back down the track was probably swarming with them by now, and they'd be working their way back to trap him in the middle. 'At least, that's what I'd do,' he muttered to himself.

And he couldn't afford to be spotted. He snuffed out the lighter, dropped it in his pocket next to the Ruger, and pressed on in darkness. At least he didn't have to be concerned about where he stepped. He passed the dim light of a service lantern, then moved on blindly. Every few metres he reached out his left arm to touch the tunnel wall to orientate himself. The stonework felt gritty and loose against his fingers. A few hundred metres further, his hand brushed something smooth and soft, that gave way with a rustling crackle when he pressed it. It was a thick plastic sheet, and it was covering a hole in the wall that seemed to go on for quite a few metres, nearly as wide as the tunnel itself. He found the edge of the plastic and pulled it away from the stonework. A breath of cooler air chilled the sweat on his face.

Wherever this was leading him, it was taking him away from where he didn't want to be. He stepped through the hole into even blacker darkness. Taking small, careful steps, he found his way to the nearest wall. After a few minutes' groping around he came across what he quickly realised was a plastic switchbox attached to the wall. He threw the lever, and blinked as a dozen powerful floodlights came on. He looked around him, shielding his eyes from the blinding glare. He saw towering lattices of scaffolding. Heavy earth shifting equipment. Electrical cables as thick as anacondas snaking across the floor, hooked up to humming transformers the size of small cars. Keep-out and hard-hat-zone warning signs everywhere. It was a construction site for a new tunnel, branching off perpendicular to the one he'd just walked up. The heavy plastic sheeting had to be there to screen off the site so that work could carry on while the trains were in service.

Except that it looked as if no work had gone on here for a while. A fine layer of black soot had found its way in around the edges of the plastic sheeting and settled over everything. No prints or marks on any of the machinery to suggest they'd been used lately. There was mould growing inside an abandoned Thermos flask of coffee.

The new tunnel curved away to the left. Ben was about to check it out when he heard a sound from beyond the plastic curtain. He stiffened, listening. Voices. An echo of footsteps. Maybe ten people, maybe twenty, maybe more. A walkie-talkie fizzed. The sounds were still a long way down the main tunnel, but closing steadily.

He ran back to the electrical switch and threw it. The hum of the transformers died and he was plunged back into total darkness. Glancing again from behind the sheeting, he saw the first trembling pool of torchlight sweep the curved tunnel wall in the distance.

They'd be here in minutes.

Tracing a path from memory in the dark, Ben made his way across the construction site and followed the line of the new tunnel – and his heart sank when, just forty or fifty metres down the line, he bumped into another wall of plastic sheeting. Dead end.

Only, it wasn't quite. He pushed against the plastic and could feel another opening in the solid wall. He reached for his Zippo, risking a little light. Punched a hole in the plastic and tore his way through.

What he found there was something that definitely hadn't been part of the subway network plans. His flame shone off massive stone blocks that were craggy and pitted with age and looked as if they'd been here since biblical times. It was some kind of chamber, and from the jagged hole he'd just climbed through and the fresh scrape marks on the stone, he guessed that one of the excavation machines had made an unexpected discovery down here.

The chamber was long and narrow, just a metre and a half wide, disappearing into darkness. Its ceiling was a high arch, the floor compacted earth thick with the dust of centuries. Long, deep recesses were set into the walls at intervals, stretching all the way up to the ceiling. The recesses housed towering, crumbling wooden structures with stacked platforms like shelving.

The place smelled dank and ancient. Like a grave.

And when Ben walked on a few metres down the passage, he realised that was exactly what it was. By the amber glow of his lighter flame, thousands of sightless eyes stared at him from the darkness. He was looking at human remains. Mountains of them, heaped high on the wooden towers either side of him; fibias and tibias and femurs and others he couldn't identify, stacked carefully like firewood kindling. Many of the skulls were intact, grinning at him, while others were missing jawbones or bore the marks of the injuries that had killed them.

How long had they been here? Two thousand years? Three?

Ben kept moving along the passage as it opened up in front of him. He came to a fork, then another. A whole labyrinth of corridors. He couldn't begin to estimate how many dead had been stored down here. Fifty thousand, a hundred thousand, a million.

He pressed on. There had to be a way out of here.

The Zippo gave a sputter, then seconds later the flame choked and died. He stopped, his heart beginning to beat hard. He shook the lighter, flipped the hot striker wheel a couple of times. Nothing except a strong smell of evaporating fluid. He swore, and his voice sounded dead and flat in the cramped underground space.

He fumbled and groped his way forward. His fingers caressed something brittle and jagged. Teeth raking his skin. He jerked his hand sharply away from the skull's mouth and stumbled on. He was fighting hard to deny it, but the realisation was growing on him.

That he was lost and buried in a forgotten mass grave beneath the city.

The lingering petrol scent of her prey had been subtle at best, and now Darcey couldn't smell it at all any more. She'd lost the trail, and that perplexed her.

Where have you gone, Hope?

She didn't want to say it out loud, didn't want Buitoni or the others to know what she was thinking. She kept walking, feeling the tension in her neck spreading to her shoulders. The tramping footsteps of the Carabinieri echoed around her. Her heart jumped and her fist tightened on the Beretta when she saw the glimmer of light ahead in the tunnel – but the flush of excitement quickly died to disappointment when she realised it was the torches of the police team coming the other way down the tunnel. At least forty of them, to add to the fifty with her and Buitoni. The place had never been so crowded.

'Shit,' Buitoni said. As they all met, he began talking in rapid Italian to the officer in charge. There was a lot of arm-waving, and pretty soon a general argument had broken out and shouts were echoing through the tunnel.

Darcey left them to it. This couldn't be right. She doubled back on herself. A hundred metres back down the tunnel, her torchlight flashed against shiny plastic. She cursed herself. How could they have missed it? She poked the torch through the hole, then called Buitoni over. He came running.

She showed him. 'This is where he went.'

'How can you be sure?'

'It's where I would have gone.'

Buitoni shouted for the rest of the team. In moments he and Darcey were running across the construction site with ninety uniformed officers in their wake. Darcey flashed her light from side to side, following the path of the beam with the muzzle of the Beretta. They followed the bend in the tunnel and came to the second plastic curtain. 'Gotcha,' she muttered, seeing the ripped hole in it. 'Come on.'

There was no Ben Hope on the other side, but her light flashed on the passage's other, more permanent, occupants and she let out a breath. 'Jesus. What the hell is this place?'

'Some kind of crypt or catacomb,' Buitoni said, looking around him in fascination. 'Why do you think the Rome metro is still so underdeveloped after all these years? They're forever having to suspend digging because of some unexpected archaeological find. There may still be thousands of archaeological sites under the city, just waiting to be discovered, and armies of conservationists and historians lobbying for the protection of our ancient heritage. A treasure trove for them, but a nightmare for the city planners.'

But Darcey wasn't listening to him. 'It's hot down here.' She quickly peeled off the polo-neck and tossed it away. She was wearing a tight black sleeveless vest underneath. 'Let's go.' She took off at a run down the passage with her pistol out in front of her.

Buitoni sighed, then followed.

Chapter Forty-One

Ben was making slow progress, and he wasn't happy about it. His muscles were quivering with pent-up adrenalin as he inched his way up the dark passage.

His heartbeat jumped up a notch as he heard the sound behind him and whirled round. Torchlight flashing from around a bend, just fifty metres back. He moved faster, but he was running blind and his pursuers weren't. Seconds later, the torchlight filled the tunnel behind him.

The sound of a woman's voice cut sharply though the dead atmosphere. Hard, calm, controlled. 'Armed police. Stop right there. Get your hands where I can see them.'

Ben stopped, turned, strained his eyes against the searing white light. The woman wasn't alone. He could make out her silhouette in the torch beam of the man trotting to catch up with her. Her arms were bare, the muscles toned and tight, and the gleaming steel in her fist was as rock steady as her voice. She was breathing hard and looked like a panther ready to spring at him. Even without seeing her face, he could tell this was no lightweight they'd sent after him.

'I'm Commander Darcey Kane of SOCA,' she said. 'Ben Hope, you're under arrest.'

Two heartbeats went by and nobody moved. Then Ben raised his hands to chest level.

'Lose the weapon,' she said.

As Ben slowly hooked out the Ruger from his jacket pocket and let it dangle from a finger through the trigger guard, he was wondering what a SOCA agent was doing on a case that should have been a matter for Italian police. He tossed the pistol down in the dirt near his right foot.

'Kick it away. Hands high.'

Ben nudged it a few inches with his toe. 'I didn't kill Tassoni. He was dead when I got there.'

'Innocent men don't run.' Her tone was matter-of-fact. Someone just doing their job.

'You have the wrong person, Darcey.'

'Then you have nothing to fear.'

'There's more to it.'

'I don't want to know. Tell it to the judge.'

As she spoke, she stepped closer to him. Now just a few metres away, he could see her more clearly by the torchlight bouncing off the stone walls in the narrow space. Her jaw was set tight and there was a glint of quiet ferocity in her eyes. A stray wisp of black hair had broken out from under her cap. Without letting the gun waver a millimetre, she tucked her torch under her right arm. Reached into her back pocket with her left hand and fished out a pair of cuffs. Her partner was just one step behind. Ben didn't think he looked as confident as she did. Then there was more clamour behind them, and torchlight flooded the passage as a whole pack of uniformed Carabinieri appeared around the corner guns drawn. Seeing the situation ahead, they crouched and took aim as more came up from behind. It looked like a whole army of them.

The odds were definitely getting interesting, but Ben guessed he had more to worry about from Darcey Kane than from the rest put together. He moved forward a step. To his left, the hundreds of piled skulls watched like silent witnesses from an alcove as he held out his wrists to be cuffed.

'Looks like you got me.'

She smiled. 'Wasn't hard, either.'

'No bones about it,' he said.

And lashed out with his left foot. His shoe connected with one of the supporting struts holding up the tall wooden framework on which the human remains were heaped. A few centuries ago, the wood might have been solid. Not any more. Ben's kick cracked it in two with an explosion of dust and the whole towering edifice gave a lurch and came crashing down in a splintering bony avalanche that filled the passage. Ben threw himself back out of the way as a hundred bouncing skulls rained down where he'd stood a second before.

Darcey barely had time to react before she was swiped off her feet and half buried in the slide. Her torch fell and rolled away from her, cutting a milky swathe in the billowing dust. Her face and hair were white with it. Coughing and spluttering, she tried to struggle to her feet. Her partner was down on his knees and elbows, a streak of blood above his eye where a section of the falling wooden framework had caught him a glancing blow. The passage behind them was almost completely blocked with debris and swirling dust.

Ben snatched up Darcey's Maglite and swung it like a club, knocking the Beretta out of her hand. She cried out in pain as the weapon clattered away from her.

'Sorry, Darcey,' Ben said. 'Maybe another time.' His Ruger was buried. He grabbed her Beretta instead and bolted away up the passage, leaving the agents floundering among the wreckage.

Chapter Forty-Two

Ben ran hard through the passages, shining the Maglite this way and that, searching for a way out. Gleaming metal flashed in his beam, and he spotted a ladder running up through an open shaft in the ceiling. A winch cable dangled down from above, holding up a platform with a safety rail around its edge. At the foot of the ladder was scattered an assortment of cases and boxes. He guessed they contained whatever kind of archaeology equipment was needed for the excavation of the discovered catacomb. He stuck the torch in his belt and climbed the ladder.

The next level up was still underground, some kind of gloomy circular tunnel that was just about high enough to stand up in. It looked like a disused sewer. It was getting hard to believe there was any solid ground at all under Rome. Maybe one day the city would just cave in and disappear.

Ben shone his torch around him. There was more equipment lying about near the shaft, and across on the other side of the tunnel. Next to it was another ladder, climbing up to a freshly-cut trapdoor that he was certain led to street level.

He was halfway to the ladder when the tunnel filled with the stunning noise of a gunshot and a bullet wailed off the stonework near his head. He whipped round to see Darcey

Kane clambering out of the shaft behind him, clutching a Beretta identical to the one he'd taken from her.

There wasn't time to stick around to say, 'You just don't give up, do you?' There wasn't even time to draw the gun from his belt and return fire. He'd have been dead before he could release the safety lever. He took off at a zigzagging run, keeping low.

She fired again. The ricochet howled off the wall and rattled around the tunnel like a pinball. She was shooting at the light. He ditched the torch. Heard the clatter behind him as she did the same. Not stupid, that Darcey Kane.

Rats slithered out of Ben's path as he sprinted through the gloom. He was a fast runner, but it was clear that his pursuer had been putting in some serious track practice. Her pounding footsteps weren't far behind him as he went flying around a corner, nearly losing his footing on the slippery stone. His shoulder connected painfully with the tunnel wall, and he felt the hard edge of an iron rung embedded in the brickwork. He hauled himself up, found another, then another. There was a cast iron manhole cover above him. He punched out hard with the heel of his hand, praying the lid wasn't rusted in place or bolted down. It gave way with a grinding clang. He shoved it aside, and fresh air flooded down the round hole. He clambered up to the top rung, thrusting his head and shoulders out into the night air.

A screech of air horns almost blew out his eardrums. He twisted his head around to see the blinding headlights and massive front grille of a truck bearing down on him like some kind of monster. The truck's tyres screamed, smoke pouring from its wheel arches. Ben ducked his head down in a hurry. A fraction of a second later, and it would have been torn off. The manhole was filled with roaring noise and grit and diesel stink as the truck passed overhead.

By the time it had come to a shuddering halt fifteen metres further down the road, Ben was clambering out of the hole and kicking the cast iron lid back into place. He was in a broad, straight street with old buildings and shops and parked cars and scooters gleaming under the street lights. He glanced around him for something to lay across the manhole cover to delay the SOCA agent – but large, heavy objects weren't readily to hand in the middle of the road. All he had was himself. He stood on the plate, feeling just a little self-conscious and all too aware this didn't present a lasting solution to his predicament. A car sped down the street and swerved to avoid him. Ben ignored the stream of abuse that came at him from its open window. The truck driver had pulled into the side of the road and had jumped down from his cab, storming over with clenched fists to yell obscenities at him. Ben ignored him, too. He had other things to worry about.

Under his feet, the plate gave a lurch as something hit it hard from below. *Here she comes*, he thought. A second's pause, then there was a muffled explosion and something struck the underside of the cast iron plate with a loud clang and an impact that rattled him all the way up to his knees. She was trying to shoot her way out. She must have been deafened down there.

Ben looked up as he heard the buzz of a motorcycle approaching. A tall, skinny trail bike was coming down the road towards him. Its helmetless rider was a young guy of about twenty. He slowed the bike uncertainly as he got closer, probably thinking Ben was a drunk who was about to stagger into his path and bring the bike down.

Ben slipped the Beretta out of his belt and yelled *'Alt! Polizia!'* at the top of his voice.

Seeing the pistol, the truck driver instantly stopped

screaming abuse and beat a hasty retreat back to his vehicle. The motorcyclist's eyes opened wide as he brought the bike to a sliding halt. Up close, Ben could see the Honda legend on the shiny blue tank and the letters '250cc' on the side panel beneath the seat.

'Sorry about this,' he said. Still pinning the manhole cover with his weight, he grabbed the young guy's arm and hauled him roughly out of the saddle. He caught the bike as it began to topple, swung his right leg over it and gunned the throttle.

The instant Ben took his weight off the manhole cover, the iron lid flipped up with a clang. Darcey Kane came bursting out of the hole, pistol first. Her eyes were wild, her face streaked with sweat and dirt.

Ben flashed her a grin, stamped the gear lever into first, opened the throttle wide and dumped the clutch. Before she could make a move, the Honda's front wheel lifted a foot in the air and the machine took off like a startled horse.

As he raced down the street with the warm wind whistling in his ears and fluttering his jacket, Ben glanced in the handlebar mirror. Darcey was already waving down an approaching car with her drawn pistol. Not just any kind of car, but a low-slung gleaming red sports convertible that looked worryingly like a Ferrari under the street lights. She bundled the protesting driver out, leaped in behind the wheel. Over the tinny howl of the Honda's engine, Ben heard the roar and screech of spinning wheels as she accelerated after him.

'This damn woman's unstoppable,' he muttered. He ground the throttle against its stop and the little 250cc engine screamed in protest. Parked vehicles and buildings flashed by in a blur. He snatched another glance in the mirror. The sports car was already gaining on him fast.

It *was* a Ferrari. Not good. No way he could outrun her on this sewing machine on wheels.

Do what you can with what you've got. Boonzie had taught him that one.

Ben kept his eyes on the mirror just an instant too long. When he looked back at the road ahead, there was a fat man crossing the street dragging a chihuahua on a lead. He swerved violently to avoid them, narrowly missing crunching into the side of a parked Fiat Cinquecento. He hammered up onto the kerb and rode down the pavement. A corner café was closing for the night, with plastic chairs and tables strewn outside and a waiter gathering up glasses. Ben ducked down behind the bars, gritted his teeth and went ploughing through the tables, sending the waiter diving for cover. The little Honda wobbled furiously but he somehow managed to keep it upright. He jumped the bike back down off the kerb between two parked cars, hit the road with a screech and accelerated away.

It was only as he sped off down the street that he realised the bumpy ride had jolted the Beretta out of his waistband. Any thoughts he had of going back for it were quickly scotched as the Ferrari came hurtling round the bend just a few metres behind him, glued tight to the road, bearing relentlessly down on his tail.

A street sign flashed by: Via dei Coronari. Buildings parted, and Ben could suddenly see the city lights glinting off the smooth waters of the Tiber to his left. A line of lanterns traced the shape of a bridge spanning the river and illuminated the facing rows of angelic white statues along its sides. But it wasn't the graceful beauty of the architecture that made Ben swerve the Honda hard left and take a closer look at the bridge – it was the fat concrete bollards set across its entrance, blocking the way to anything wider than a skinny little trail bike. He passed between them and sped out across the smooth paving stones of the bridge. Heard the scream of tyres behind him as the Ferrari skidded to a halt at an angle in the road.

Halfway over the bridge, Ben stopped the bike and looked back. Darcey Kane was out of the car, standing under the glow of a street light, gun in hand. Even at this distance he could see she was virtually dancing with frustration. Her shout of rage echoed across the river.

Ben had to smile to himself as he rode away into the night.

Though somehow, he had the feeling he hadn't seen the last of this Darcey Kane.

Chapter Forty-Three

The De Crescenzo residence, Rome

Ten to two in the morning and Count Pietro De Crescenzo was too tired to pace up and down any more, too tired to think, too tired to do anything except sit slumped in his armchair and stare dully across the large living room at his wife Ornella. She was lying with her back to him, her glossy blond curls fanned out over the arm of the sofa. The flimsy material of her dress had ridden up to mid-thigh and her legs were kicked out carelessly over the cushions. One white high-heeled shoe had fallen to the rug; the other was dangling from her toe, ready to drop at any moment like the last autumn leaf from a twig.

Once upon a time, Pietro De Crescenzo would have got up and gone over to her, brushed the hair from her face and straightened her dress for modesty's sake, maybe covered her with a blanket, or else carried her tenderly to bed. But he didn't move. Just sat there and listened to her soft snoring, watching the curve of her hip rise and fall as she slept.

Though, he reflected bitterly, 'asleep' wasn't quite the right word for someone who'd spent the last almost three hours passed out in a comatose stupor. She'd hit the vodka particularly hard that night, and he had no sympathy for the selfish bitch. *He* was the one who should be drinking himself stupid all day, after what he'd been through. The tremors in his hands and knees were slowly fading, though there were moments when the horrors came flooding back and he was rendered virtually prostrate with nerves. The trauma was going to stay with him for the rest of his life – he was sure of it.

He looked at his watch and sighed. He dreaded going to bed. Night was the worst time. Night was when the ghosts came out to revisit him. Aldo Silvestri and Luigi Corsini, and the woman who had died in front of them all on the office floor, and all the other poor souls who had lost their lives. Their sightless eyes staring at him in the dark, their bloody fingers groping out to claw at him until he woke gasping and covered in sweat. Then he'd be awake till dawn, with only more horrors to look forward to – more agonised phone calls with Aldo's and Luigi's relatives, more terrible funerals to attend, more wrangling with obtuse insurance company directors and more hysterical gallery owners threatening dire litigation. It was a mess on a cataclysmic scale.

And meanwhile, the police investigation was drawing blanks every way it turned. Pietro had no faith in any of the detectives who'd been assigned to the case. Lario was a fool, and when he failed he'd simply be replaced with another fool. Though Pietro had to admit that he was having just as little success in solving the enigma that haunted him feverishly day and night.

Why the Goya? Why? *Why?* Its personal value to him, as a tangible connection to the woman he'd always wished could have been his own grandmother, was inestimable – but its monetary value was minimal compared to so many works that the robbers had just seemingly ignored. To walk past prizes that could have enriched them for the rest of their lives, for whose recovery the art world would have paid whatever gigantic ransom they demanded, in favour of a simple sketch that had spent most of the last century hidden away among the forgotten personal effects of a dead artist: no amount of obsessive brain-racking could help Pietro to see any sense in it.

Something else perplexed him even more deeply. This wasn't the first time that Gabriella Giordani's personal possessions had attracted the attentions of dangerous men.

He was worn out from trying to figure out the connection. His eyes were burning from fatigue and his neck and shoulders ached. He rose stiffly from his armchair, turned off the living room light and shut the door behind him.

Pietro's office was across the other side of the large villa. When things weren't going well between him and Ornella he often took refuge to sleep on the couch in there. They hadn't argued, but he felt that way tonight.

As he walked into the office, he noticed the flashing light on his answer machine telling him there was a new message. It had been left after midnight.

Pietro let it play on speaker. The caller spoke Italian with a Spanish accent. His voice was deep and rich, like old wine.

'Signor De Crescenzo, my name is Juan Calixto Segura. It is extremely important that I speak with you. Please call me immediately, night or day.' A pause, then: 'It concerns your stolen Goya.'

Pietro replayed the message with a trembling finger.

He hadn't dreamed it.

Segura. The name was vaguely familiar. A wealthy art collector and dealer in Salamanca, De Crescenzo remembered – though they'd never met.

Frantic with anticipation, Pietro snatched up the phone handset and returned the Spaniard's call. Segura picked up on the third ring. He didn't sound as if he'd been asleep.

'This is De Crescenzo.'

'I thought you would call.'

'My Goya,' Pietro said breathlessly.

'Charcoal on laid paper. "The Penitent Sinner".'

'That's it. What have you to tell me?'

'I think it better that we meet,' Segura said. 'I have something to show you.'

'If you know something, I beg you . . .' Pietro's voice quavered; he was near to a sob as he spoke.

Segura was silent for a moment, as though unwilling to disclose too much on the phone. 'I will tell you this much,' he said. 'How can it be that "The Penitent Sinner" was stolen from your gallery in Italy?'

Pietro was stunned. 'What do you mean? It *was* stolen.'

'Then you may care to explain to me,' Segura said, 'why it is sitting here safely in my private collection, where it has been for many years.'

Chapter Forty-Four

It was after two in the morning when Ben rode the little Honda along the cobbled streets and through the Porta Settimiana, a Renaissance-period stone gateway that led into the Trastavere quarter on the west bank of the Tiber. Before ditching the motorcycle in a narrow, winding lane, he searched through its side panniers and found a pair of sunglasses and a floppy hat. He slipped the shades in his pocket. From there it was a short walk to Rome's botanical gardens. He scaled a locked gate, and minutes later was walking free among moonlit parkland. The night air was sweet with the scent of flowers. He stuck to the shadows, silent and invisible.

Always seek out the high ground. A long hill led him to a wooded ridge overlooking the city, where a hollow among some shrubs offered a vantage point to rest up for a few hours. He sat immobile among the leaves and let nature absorb him until he was scarcely even there any more. He watched the stars and the city lights and wondered how Fabio Strada was doing. Thought about Darcey Kane and the things that were happening to him. Thought about Jeff Dekker and the rest of his team back home in France. They must surely have seen the news by now. Jeff would be worried, but he'd know better than to expect a call from Ben. First, the phones would be tapped. Second, it wasn't Ben's way to involve his friends in his own troubles. Jeff was ex-SBS. He'd have done the same. Sometimes, a guy just had to work things out on his own.

And then Ben's thoughts turned to Brooke, and dwelled on her for a long time. He'd never missed her this much. She'd never seemed so far away from him.

By sun-up, he was on the move again.

The obvious place to find an Italian count would have been in his ancestral palazzo – except that Pietro De Crescenzo had said he didn't live there. Resorting to the Rome phone directory, Ben found four possibles and figured out a route that would take him roughly west, then north, then northeast across Rome. He wore the sunglasses as he made his way across the city. Wear them in Britain, and you drew instant suspicion, as though their only purpose was as a disguise for crooks and terrorists and murderers on the lam. But in Rome, everyone wore shades and he was just another face on board the crowded buses and trams that he used to criss-cross the city.

Someone had left a morning paper on a bus seat, and Ben picked it up. The screaming headline article covered most of the front page. As more details of the Tassoni murder began to emerge, British government officials were remaining tight-lipped over speculation that the killer on the loose was a former soldier of 22 Special Air Service.

On the next page, Ben read an interesting article about himself, written by a leading criminal psychologist called Alessandro Ragonesi. According to Ragonesi, the ruthless training undergone by Special Forces soldiers, notably the British SAS, was designed to strip away any modicum of humanity, programming once-decent men into robotic killing machines capable of committing the worst atrocities without question, pity or remorse. Even years later, the slightest psychological trauma or other stressor could potentially reawaken that programming and trigger random acts of psychopathic behaviour. Amid a welter of scientific jargon, Ragonesi explained how the experience of the gallery robbery might have sent this former black-ops soldier into a state of mental confusion that had resulted in the tragic killing spree at the home of Urbano Tassoni. Who knew where the deranged assassin would strike next?

The wonders of modern neuroscience, Ben thought. Give that man a cigar.

The first De Crescenzo residence he visited, just before 8 a.m., was a tiny terraced house with an ancient Volkswagen Beetle outside and two scraggy german shepherd dogs snarling at him from behind a mesh fence. He couldn't imagine the dapper count living here. At the second place, he was told the old man called Pietro De Crescenzo had died a year ago. Two down, two to go.

It was after nine by the time Ben found the third place on his list, a crumbling eighteenth-century apartment building that retained a certain elegance and could potentially have been the home of the Pietro De Crescenzo he was looking for. But when he knocked on the door, a stunningly pretty, dark-haired girl of about twenty-two answered and told him her boyfriend was at the office. She could have been a model.

De Crescenzo didn't seem the type.

Three down. One left.

It was pushing on for ten in the morning and the sun was warming up fast when he stepped off the bus and made his way on foot through what looked like an even wealthier suburb than Tassoni's. Tall cypress trees screened the houses from the road. As he approached the tall wooden gates, two things told him he was in the right place. The first was the enormous, sprawling white house he could see through the greenery. It was impeccably tasteful and refined: all the things he'd expect from a man of De Crescenzo's artistic sensibilities.

The second was the metallic silver Volvo saloon that came speeding out of the gate, scattering gravel over the road in its wake. Ben instantly recognised the hunched, gaunt figure clutching the wheel. The count was going somewhere in a hurry – too much of a hurry to notice Ben standing there on the pavement watching as he sped off into the rising heat haze.

Ben walked in through the open gates before they whirred shut automatically, and made his way up to the house. The front door wasn't locked. The entrance hall was cool and white, with frescoes on the walls and a tasteful arrangement of gleaming white nude statues. Wandering into a large white living room, he saw a blonde in a flimsy dress sitting on a sofa with her head in her hands. On the coffee table nearby was a fancy lighter set into a block of onyx, and next to it a bottle of vodka and an empty cut crystal tumbler. Both the level in the bottle and the woman looked as though they'd taken a fairly serious hammering the night before.

Ben was standing just a couple of metres from the woman by the time she registered his presence and squinted up at him through a morning-after haze. She looked about forty-five, but if the vodka was a regular thing she might have been eight years younger. Her hair was flattened on the right side where she'd been sleeping on it, and her mascara was smudged. She didn't seem to care that the strap of her dress had slipped down her arm.

Ben took off his shades.

'Do I know you?' she slurred in Italian. Obviously too busy to keep up with the TV news, Ben thought.

'I'm a friend of your husband's.'

'He's not here.'

'I know. I just saw him driving off. What's got him leaving in such a hurry?'

She made a contemptuous gesture, and the dress strap slipped a little further. 'What do you think?' she muttered. 'Numbnuts is only interested in one thing. Art. Always art.'

Ben sat down next to her. She smelled of Chanel No.7 and stale booze. She gazed at him unsteadily for a second, her eyes still bright from the vodka. 'Who did you say you were again? This isn't about that thing that happened, is it?'

'Just a friend,' Ben said. 'The name's Shannon. Rupert Shannon.' He took out his pack of Gauloises. 'Smoke?' She nodded and plucked one out between long red nails. He lit it with the onyx lighter, and then one for himself.

'Ornella De Crescenzo,' she said through a cloud of smoke, and held out her hand for him to shake. She clasped his fingers for a few seconds too long, but that might have been the hangover fuzzing her senses.

'Pietro's told me so much about you,' Ben said. 'I feel as though I know you.'

She nearly choked. 'You're kidding, right?'

'Did he say where he was going?' Ben asked her. 'It's important that I speak to him.'

Ornella made a vague gesture. 'Some guy called him late last night. Art dealer or something. I forget the name. It's all the same to me. And this morning, he's all in a rush packing up his shit, tells me he has to drop everything and go to Spain, some place near Madrid. Of course he won't fly, wants to take my car, it's faster than his. I said, touch that car and it's divorce.' She laughed giddily.

'Madrid is long way away.'

'So I won't have to see the *stronzo* for a day or two. Leave me in peace to do my own thing.'

'Like drink yourself to death?'

She snorted, took another long drag on the cigarette. 'Sounds good to me.'

'It can get expensive trying,' he said. 'I know.'

Ornella sidled up to him, and he caught a whiff of her vodka breath. 'Rupert Shannon. That's a beautiful name.'

Ben had borrowed it from the biggest, dumbest swinging dick of an ex-soldier he'd ever known, a brigadier's nephew who'd miraculously held it together for three years in the Paras – and later, for a brief time, had somehow worked his way into Brooke's affections. 'Kind of you to say so, Ornella.'

She arched an eyebrow and moved closer. 'Have you come to stay with me a while, Rupert?' she said in a low purr.

Ben smiled. 'I think maybe you could do with a coffee.'

The kitchen was a cavernous affair off the entrance hall, with a state-of-the-art cappuccino machine that looked as though it had never been used. Ben fired it up and made two strong black coffees, put the cups on a tray and carried them through to where Contessa Ornella De Crescenzo was lounging back on the sofa, still nursing her hangover. He made an excuse about needing to use the bathroom, and left her alone to sip the coffee as he trotted upstairs.

It was a big place, and it took a few wrong turns and a lot of doors to check before Ben found what looked like Pietro De Crescenzo's home office. There was a good deal of art on the walls. The antique desk bore a framed snap of the count and countess in their younger days, somewhere alpine – Switzerland, maybe. He had more hair and looked less cadaverous; she obviously hadn't discovered vodka back then. Happier times.

Next to the picture was all the usual desk stuff – a phone, a jar full of pens and pencils, a lined writing pad, an exhibition brochure and a pile of opened mail, bills and letters. Ben glanced at the one on top long enough to see it was from the director of a gallery in Amsterdam that had loaned De Crescenzo one of the grand masters for his exhibition. The words 'destruction' and 'tragic' and 'severe consequences' featured heavily in the text.

Ben picked up the writing pad. Its topmost sheet had been torn away in a rush, leaving a serrated ribbon of paper trapped in the wire binding rings. He angled the pad towards the light. Whatever had been hastily scribbled in biro on the missing page, the pressure of the pen had left faint marks on the paper under it.

Ben grabbed a pencil from the jar. Using the side of the tip, he carefully shaded over the pressure marks. The hand-writing that appeared in white was the jagged scrawl of someone scribbling in a hurry while talking on the phone It took him a few moments to make out the name Juan Calixto Segura. Under it was an address in Salamanca, Spain.

Ben turned on De Crescenzo's laptop and did a Google search on the name. Segura had no website of his own, but he came up in listings of European fine art dealers. It seemed he specialised in Spanish painting from various periods: El Greco, Velázquez, Zurbarán, Picasso. Ben's eye skipped down the list, then stopped at a certain eighteenth-to-nineteenth-century Romantic painter and print artist called Francisco José de Goya y Lucientes.

'Now we're getting somewhere,' Ben murmured. He remembered what De Crescenzo had said about not liking to fly. It was a long drive across three countries to Salamanca, which made it all the more interesting that the count would feel the need to rush off to see this Segura so suddenly.

Whatever the guy had told him on the phone, it had to be worth hearing. Ben copied the address more clearly on another sheet of the writing pad, tore it off and folded it into his pocket, then burned the original in De Crescenzo's fireplace. He erased the computer's memory of the Internet search, then headed back downstairs.

Ornella had finished her coffee and half of his and was up on her feet, only a little wobbly on her high heels. She'd cleaned up the smudged makeup. As Ben came into the room she teetered over to him with a big smile and ran her hand down his arm.

'Will you stay for lunch, Rupert? I'm so lonely here, all by myself in this great big house.'

'Lunch isn't for two hours.'

Ornella De Crescenzo pouted innocently. 'You're right. However shall we pass the time?'

When the count's away, Ben thought. 'It was truly a pleasure to meet you, Contessa. I'd love to stay longer, but sadly I have a prior engagement.'

Her face fell. 'Shame. You've been so sweet to me. There must be something I can do for you in return?'

'Maybe another time,' Ben said with a smile, and Ornella's eyes sparkled like champagne. She thumped him playfully on the chest.

'You're a *bad* boy.'

'You have no idea.'

On his way out the front door, Ben spotted a set of car keys in an ornate silver dish on a stand in the hall, and the shiny leather fob embossed with a distinctive trident emblem. Interesting.

Touch that car and it's divorce.

Maybe there was something Ornella could do for him, after all. She wasn't in a fit state to drive it, anyway. Ben snatched the keys and went out into the hot sun to look for where she kept it.

The ivy-clad three-door garage was around the back of the house. He used the remote bleeper attached to the key fob to open the middle door, and when it whirred up he let out a low whistle at what was inside.

Psychopathic SAS fugitive makes off in countess's Maserati. Silvana Lucenzi would lap it up.

As he jumped in behind the wheel of the sleek bronze GranTurismo, he was already planning his route. From Rome towards Genova, then passing by Nice and Marseille, through Andorra, then westwards through Spain to Salamanca. A twelve-hour drive, maybe thirteen. But when he twisted the ignition and the throaty roar of the 4.7-litre V8 filled the garage, he reckoned he could do it in less.

It was 10.34 a.m.

Ben slipped the shades back on, and hit the gas.

Chapter Forty-Five

Vila Flor
Portugal

Brooke's flight had been dead on time, and it was only 11.45 a.m. when her taxi rolled up to the end of the country lane that was as close as it was possible to get to her cottage by car. She got her luggage out of the back, paid the driver and watched the car turn round and disappear in a cloud of dust.

It felt immensely liberating to be here again. The heat was intense and dry, and the air was filled with the chirping of cicadas. She set off down the rambling, rocky path that wound through the trees, across a small valley where butterflies flitted in vast numbers, and up a gentle slope to the grassy mound where her little cottage glinted white in the sunshine. As she walked, she heard the puttering motor of a quad bike in the golden fields and saw the small, wiry figure of Fatima Azevedo riding along with her dog in pursuit. Brooke waved. Fatima and Luis were her nearest neighbours. Their little organic farm a quarter of a mile up the road produced fruit, herbs and a tiny yield of wine that they kept mainly for themselves and their friends. When Brooke was around, the warm-hearted couple would sometimes pop over to visit her with a bottle and a box of fresh eggs.

The rocky path turned to fine gravel on the approach to the cottage. The old stone *finca* nestled comfortably among sprawling wildflowers and shrubs. After Ben's place in France, it was Brooke's favourite place to be. So peaceful here. No noise, no aeroplanes roaring overhead every ninety seconds the way they did in Richmond. Nothing could disturb it. Apart from the growth of the shrubbery, it looked exactly as it had last time she'd been here.

With Ben, she remembered with a smile. It had been the end of June, just a couple of weeks after their long-standing close friendship had developed into the full-blown relationship she'd secretly dreamed of for longer than she liked to admit. It had been a wonderful few days here together. They'd eaten out on the little terrace every day, and gone for long walks together through the surrounding woodland. No worries, no distractions, just their love and laughter. Ben had seemed so happy, happier than she'd ever known him.

She wished he were here with her now. Wondered what he was doing at that moment, and whether he'd got her message. She couldn't wait to see him again. It was all the more infuriating that Marshall's behaviour was forcing her to run and hide like this. She could only hope that a few days' absence would help to cool him down and make the man come to his senses.

Fat chance.

No way was she going to let her troubles spoil the moment, though. An ancient dry-stone wall ran up the side of the path leading up towards the front door. Brooke paused to reach her fingers into the gap between two of the warm stones, where she kept the front door key. She unlocked the door and felt a surge of relief as she stepped inside the cool, fragrant hallway.

Chapter Forty-Six

Rome

Urbano Tassoni and his two bodyguards had long since taken up residence in the morgue downtown, but the villa was still swarming with police and forensics. Darcey and Buitoni left their car in the street and threaded through the cluster of vehicles parked up in front of the house.

Darcey was feeling tired, hot and ratty as they walked in through the entrance hall. A few snatched hours' sleep, a cool shower and a change of clothes hadn't done much to alleviate the smarting frustration of letting her target slip through her fingers the night before, and she'd just spent the whole morning in a fruitless attempt to get hold of the surveillance tapes that the Italian police had, according to some vague information from on high, taken from Tassoni's place shortly after the killing. But now, after she'd bludgeoned Buitoni into chasing up a hundred people who either didn't answer their phone or simply passed callers from this desk to that department to some other idiot who didn't seem to know what day it was, it seemed that the whereabouts of the key evidence showing the assassin Ben Hope escaping from the scene of the murders were a complete mystery. It riled Darcey Kane to boiling point when things stood in her way like this.

'I don't know why you wanted to come here,' Buitoni said at her shoulder. 'They've already gone through the place.' A large plaster covered the cut over his left eye where the falling timber had gashed him.

'Same reason I wanted to see those bloody tapes,' she told him without looking at him. 'To pick up the details that other people usually miss.'

'How lucky we are to have you,' Buitoni muttered. He'd been testy all morning. She fired him a glance, but let it go and scanned the crime scene in front of her.

Three sprawled outlines on the floor and the stairs showed where the dead men had lain. Judging their angle and position, Darcey walked over to where the shooter would have been standing when the shots were fired. A mirror on the far wall had been shattered by a bullet that had passed through one of the bodyguards. Behind the smashed glass, the round had chewed a hunk of masonry the size of a pineapple out of the wall. The same had happened with one of the shots fired at Tassoni himself. The bullet had travelled at an upwards angle over the stairs, done its work on the man and gone on to penetrate the plasterwork a metre or so behind where his head had been.

Darcey stepped over the police tape and climbed the stairs. Peering into the bullet hole in the wall, she could see daylight shining through from the other side. She walked across the landing to a door, nudged it open with her toe and found herself inside a brightly lit room that was all glossy wood panels and expensive repro antiques. After expending maybe two-thirds of its muzzle energy blowing out Tassoni's brains, the bullet had punched through in here and finally come to a stop in the heart of an ornate grandfather clock that stood against the far wall. It looked like the forensics people had already been here to retrieve the bullet for testing and matching. There wouldn't be much left of it, just a flattened, distorted mushroom of lead alloy bearing only faint traces of the rifling marks from the gun barrel.

Darcey crossed the thick cream carpet and examined the dead clock. Its gold-tipped hands were frozen at precisely three minutes to six. The piece was dressed up to look like something from an eighteenth-century chateau, but through the splintered mahogany case she could see where the bullet had taken out a thoroughly modern radio-controlled quartz movement. The kind of clock that would lose maybe a second every couple of million years or so. Which meant its testimony could be pretty well trusted. Tassoni had met his maker at exactly three minutes to six.

But Darcey was less concerned with that than the fact that the bullet had made it as far as here in the first place. It didn't fit Ben Hope's profile to use such a weapon for this kind of job. It clashed with her instinctive understanding of the guy. A big, noisy, over-penetrative .357 Magnum hand cannon was more the kind of gun you'd expect to find stuck in the belt of a crass thug like Thomas Gremaj. A bad boy piece, for cocky little dickheads who modelled themselves on what they saw in bad action movies, holding the thing sideways and screaming 'Fuck you, asshole!' at their victims before spraying bullets all over the place with reckless abandon. That wouldn't be the style of a man who had been through the SAS training mill. From the killing house at Hereford to the jungles of Borneo and the battlefields of Iraq and Afghanistan, the lessons were ground so deeply into these guys that they never forgot. Darcey would have bet her left thumb that Ben Hope's instinctive choice for a killing like this, as second nature to him as brushing his teeth or tying his shoelaces, would have been a suppressed 9mm automatic using subsonic ammunition. Neat and discreet, clinical and professional. No excess noise, no hideous mess, no going up against three opponents with only six rounds in the cylinder.

Still, she thought, even the best of them can lose their edge.

Then again, had the man who'd escaped her last night seemed like someone who'd lost their edge?

Her phone buzzed in her pocket. She carried two, one SOCA-issue and the other her personal phone, which she seldom used. It was her own phone that was ringing. She wondered who could be calling her.

'Darcey Kane.'

No reply.

'Who is this?'

Still nobody spoke. Just the sound of heavy breathing on the other end.

'Fuck off, then,' she said, and ended the call. She checked the incoming call records. The number had been withheld.

She was still frowning about it when Buitoni turned up. 'I've seen enough,' she told him. 'Take me back to the office.'

An hour later she was in Roberto Lario's empty office in the Carabinieri headquarters. She'd had no stomach for lunch. The police cafeteria coffee was strong enough to stand a spoon up in, and was keeping her going just fine.

As she'd pretty much expected, the Tassoni surveillance tapes still hadn't materialised. Nor had a single trace of Ben Hope. The streets of Rome seemed to have just swallowed him up.

She was thinking seriously about lobbing her coffee cup at the wall when Lario walked into the office looking rumpled and harassed. He tossed a file on the desk in front of her.

'Interpol agents visited Hope's business premises in

Normandy early this morning,' he said. 'That is the statement they took from his colleague, Jeff Dekker.'

By the time Lario had slumped in a chair, rubbed his eyes and straightened his tie, Darcey had scanned to the end of the statement. Loud protestations of Hope's innocence, naturally. She swivelled her chair round, grabbed a laptop with a wireless Internet connection and tapped in Ben Hope's business web address. She scrolled through the site until she came to Jeff Dekker's name, clicked on it and studied the image of the dark-haired man that came up onscreen. Dekker's military record was clipped to the statement Lario had given her. He was a couple of years younger than Hope. Royal Marines, followed by five years in the Special Boat Service. Then a spell doing private contract work, before he'd left to join Hope's operation in France.

Darcey kicked the swivel chair away from the desk and faced Lario. 'You talked to Ben Hope, before the Tassoni killing.'

Lario nodded. 'Right here in this very office.'

'What kind of man did he seem to you?'

Lario shrugged. 'Articulate. Calm. Intelligent. Capable.'

'You were sitting here face to face with him, and you didn't see anything out of the ordinary?'

Lario spread his hands. 'What can I say? The man sat there. He was rational. He was perfectly normal, considering what he had just been through. He told me he was here on business—'

'Did you ask him what kind of business?' she cut in.

'It did not strike me as being important. In any case he was due to fly back to England the next afternoon.'

'And you believed that?'

'Why would I not?'

'Did you check it out?'

'There was no reason to. He was not under suspicion at the time. He was *l'eroe della galleria.* I had no cause to suspect this man presented any threat to Tassoni or anyone else—'

She raised a hand to interrupt him. 'So you just let him walk out of here, and the rest is history. More than a little slack, don't you think?'

Lario's face reddened and his eyes bulged. 'How old are you?' His tone was hard and challenging.

'If it's any of your business, I'm thirty-five.'

'I have been a police officer since you were just a small girl. I'm not going to be treated like a fool by some *raggazina.*'

Darcey let him have a cool smile. 'Let's say I have every respect for your vastly superior experience and intuition. So educate me, Roberto. Why did Ben Hope kill Tassoni?'

Lario said nothing.

'Maybe you think he didn't do it?'

Lario was silent for a moment longer, then got up and headed for the door. 'I have nothing more to add at this time, Signorina,' he said brusquely.

'That's *Commander,*' she fired at his back as he strode out of the room. But he was already out of the door and slamming it behind him. 'Prick,' she muttered under her breath and went back to the website to get the number for Le Val. She snatched up the phone and dialled. 'Jeff Dekker, please.'

'Speaking,' said the voice on the other end. He sounded pleasant, but tense with worry. When she introduced herself, the pleasantness vanished and the worried tone turned to hostility.

'Get lost. Drop dead.'

Darcey took a breath. She kept her voice soft and steady. 'Don't hang up, Mr Dekker. Please.'

'I haven't anything more to say than what I told the other arseholes who turned up here early this morning,' Dekker said angrily. 'You want to know what I told them, read my statement.'

'I'm looking at it,' she said.

'Then you know exactly what I think. You're hunting the wrong man.'

'If he's innocent, he has nothing to fear from us. He needs to come in. He needs to talk to me.'

Dekker chuckled grimly. 'You're wasting your time, you know. All of you. You haven't a clue what you're dealing with.'

'I have a pretty fair idea,' Darcey said.

'And meanwhile, whoever did this is laughing their pants off.'

'Have you heard anything from Ben?'

'What makes you think I'd tell you if I had?'

'Because you want to help your friend,' Darcey said calmly. 'He can't run forever. I know how clever he is, but he's not Superman. He'll surface. They always do, and when that happens some trigger-happy cop fresh out of the academy is liable to put one in his back. So I suggest that the best thing you can do for Ben is to help me do my job and resolve this situation.'

Jeff Dekker paused, and when he spoke again, the defensive tone in his voice seemed to have slackened a little. 'Ben called here.'

Darcey stiffened. That information wasn't in Dekker's police statement. 'When?'

'Yesterday afternoon. He left a message on the office phone, but I didn't pick it up until just a couple of hours ago, after the Interpol people had left. We've been getting storms here. The phone lines go down sometimes.'

Darcey snatched up a pen and a notepad. 'What did the message say?'

'Don't get too excited,' Dekker said. 'He was just checking

in. He was calling from Rome airport. Said he was just about to leave for London, and that he'd be back home again in a couple of days or so.'

'What time was this?'

'Around four.'

'And he didn't say anything else?'

'Only that his flight was delayed. I told you not to get too excited.'

Darcey's heart had sunk again. 'And you have no idea where he is now?'

'No, I don't. As though I'd tell you if I did.'

'Why was he travelling to London?'

'That's personal.'

'Nothing is personal in a murder investigation, Mr Dekker.'

'Because it's where his girlfriend lives,' he said after a beat.

'Name and address?'

Dekker sighed irritably, and then told her. Darcey wrote it down. 'Brooke Marcel. Is she French?'

'Half French, on her father's side. Don't think she'll tell you anything different from what I've said.'

'What was the purpose of Ben's trip to Italy?'

'I think he mentioned something about wanting to kill this guy called Tass-something.'

'Please, Mr Dekker.'

'He was there to offer a job to someone.'

'A job?'

'Here at Le Val. I imagine you've seen the kind of work we do.'

'And I imagine you can tell me the name of this person he was looking to employ?'

'Yes, I can,' Dekker said. 'Though it won't do you any good whatsoever. And if you're thinking of calling him, let me tell you he's not as warm and fuzzy as me.'

'Thank you for the warning. I'd appreciate that name,' Darcey said patiently.

Jeff Dekker told her.

She made him repeat it, then wrote it down on her pad underneath the details for Brooke Marcel.

She thanked Dekker, put the phone down and sat for a long time staring at the name of the man he'd just given her.

Chapter Forty-Seven

Richmond, London

Marshall killed the purring engine of his Bentley, took a deep breath and then got out and started walking towards the familiar red-brick Victorian house that featured in his nightly dreams. He could think of nothing but Brooke. Couldn't sit still, couldn't watch TV or read the paper. Britain could be at war, the prime minister could have been caught with a rent boy, and he wouldn't have known or cared.

Marshall paused at Brooke's door, cleared his throat and knocked loudly, twice, heart thumping under his Versace suit. He blinked in surprise when the door opened and there was a young Asian guy standing there holding a small watering can.

'H-hello,' Marshall stammered.

'Hi. You're Marshall, right?'

'What?'

'We met. Brooke's party, a few months ago? You're Phoebe's husband.'

'And you're Amal. I remember now.'

Amal smiled, but he seemed a little edgy. 'Listen, if you're looking for Brooke, I'm afraid she's not around.'

'Oh,' Marshall said, scrutinising him closely.

'She's gone away for a few days. I'm looking after her plants.' He raised the watering can, as if to make his point.

Yup, Marshall thought. This young guy was definitely acting guarded. He wondered why that might be. 'Off to France again?' he said breezily.

'No,' Amal said. 'I mean yes. Yeah, that's it. Right.'

Marshall dealt with much better liars than Amal every day at the office, and years of practice had taught him he could get around anyone. He was known, and widely feared, for having a mind that stored information like a bank vault and the ability to retrieve instantly any shred of detail that could serve him, even years later.

He smiled warmly. 'That's a real shame about Brooke. Never mind. Hey, how's the writing going? I remember you said you were working on a play.'

Amal looked surprised for a moment, then smiled back, the ice melting suddenly. 'That's right.'

Vanity. The most exploitable vice under the sun. 'Actually, I was thinking about you just the other day,' Marshall went on.

'You were?'

'Absolutely. One of my clients is just about to take over this big, big theatre. Guy's worth a trillion quid. I can't say too much about it now, not until the deal's finalised. But I think he's going to be on the lookout for talented playwrights. Top notch productions, big budget. I think your stuff could be right up his street. If you wanted, I could put in a mention. Could be a good opportunity for you.'

'Wow. That'd be great. Thanks, Marshall.'

Marshall grinned his most generous grin. Once you softened them up, it was time to press your advantage. 'Listen, the reason I'm here is that Brooke had this novel she wanted to lend me. I was in the area and thought I'd come by to

251

pick it up. I know where it is, on the bookcase near her desk. Mind if I pop inside and get it?'

Amal was all smiles now, his guard completely dropped. 'Sure, no problem. Be my guest.'

Seconds later, Marshall was making a bee-line for the door of Brooke's study while Amal was safely out of the way watering the flower beds outside. Marshall was an expert snoop, and he knew exactly where to look for what he wanted. A quick scan of Brooke's desk yielded no clues as to where she might have gone, so he fired up her Mac and went into her emails.

'France my arse,' he muttered as he found the ticket booking confirmation. She'd gone to Portugal.

And Marshall knew precisely where in Portugal. He thought back to the terrible week last May he and Phoebe had spent at Brooke's rundown rustic getaway. The worst holiday of his life. No pool, no nothing, not even a mobile signal that he could use to keep in touch with the office. Phoebe had loved it, but he couldn't leave the place fast enough. For some reason Brooke thought it was just heaven. That was where he'd find her, for sure.

Marshall quickly powered down the computer, snatched a book at random from her shelf to back up his cover story with Amal, and left the apartment.

Chapter Forty-Eight

Rome

'Where are we going?' Buitoni asked as Darcey led him down to the police car pool. She was clutching the keys to one of the unmarked Carabinieri pursuit Alfa Romeo GTs.

'To the airport,' she said, glancing at her watch. It was 2.47 p.m.

He gave her a blank look.

'Because Ben Hope called his business partner from there just over an hour before the Tassoni shooting,' she explained. 'The question is, what was he doing there?'

Buitoni thought about it as they approached the car. 'He could have been going there to meet someone. The weapon might have been in a luggage locker there.'

'Hope called from the departure lounge. He was waiting for a flight.'

'Are you sure?'

'I checked it out. The 16:03 to Heathrow. Take-off was delayed for nearly an hour. Hope was on the passenger list. Business class. You want to know the seat number?'

Buitoni looked baffled. 'He was heading for London?'

'Certainly looks that way.'

'But he didn't get on the plane.'

'Apparently not.'

'Why would he do that?' Buitoni said. 'Was he just going through the motions to throw us off?'

'You think he'd be that stupid? Nobody walks in and out of an airport without being filmed on a million cameras. That's why I want to go there. The security footage might tell us something.' Darcey tossed the Alfa keys in the air, and Buitoni caught them. 'You drive,' she said.

After a stuttering journey through the snarled Rome traffic, they blasted the 30 kilometres of open road to Fiumicino. At the airport security section, a couple of surly guys in uniform led them into a control room where banks of screens fed back constant live footage from the hundreds of cameras throughout the complex. Everything was backed up on a massive hard drive that was hooked up to yet more screens, so that live and recorded footage could be viewed simultaneously. Darcey had Buitoni request to view playback from the previous afternoon, from around the time Ben Hope might have turned up in the departure lounge.

Things did not move fast. By the time the technicians had eventually dug out the right section of recordings, Darcey had paced miles up and down the corridor outside the control room. She and Buitoni sat on plastic chairs to view the screens while a technician worked the computer.

Actually spotting Hope among the thousands of tiny figures that came and went, moving comically in speeded-up motion, was a painfully slow task. After an eternity of staring hard at the screens and sipping a Coke, Darcey's eyes felt as raw as steaks. But then, finally, her searching gaze found its mark. The blond hair, the leather jacket, the easy way he moved. He was carrying a green canvas bag with a lot of miles on it.

'Got you,' she said with a smile.

'You see him?'

Darcey pointed. 'There.'

She and Buitoni watched as Hope walked calmly over to a seat on the far side of the lounge and sat quietly. He had that capacity she'd only ever seen in Special Forces soldiers, to sit completely immobile for long periods. In a sea of fast-moving bodies he was the only one frozen still. Unnoticed by the crowds that came and went – but watching everything around him.

Then, at a certain point, something seemed to catch his eye and his position shifted.

'What's he looking at?' Buitoni said.

'Those.' She pointed at another screen, which showed a different angle on the departure lounge and a boutique window filled with televisions. 'Can we get a close up?' she asked, and Buitoni relayed the request to the technician. The image swelled on the screen, pixellated momentarily and then sharpened.

'I know what that is,' Buitoni said. 'It's the report on the arrest of Tito Palazzo, the guy who assaulted Tassoni.'

'Keep watching.'

The screens displayed the time 16:51 as Hope suddenly rose from his seat and headed out of the lounge with a crowd of other passengers.

'Nine minutes to five, his flight was called,' Darcey said.

'He really looks like he means to get on that plane,' Buitoni mumbled, looking more baffled than ever.

They followed his progress on another screen. But something was wrong. As their man approached the walkway to the plane, he began to slow down. His body language was strange, his head carriage low. People jostled him from behind as he finally ground to a halt and just stood there.

'What the hell is he thinking?' Darcey said.

Buitoni shook his head, staring in fascination as the figure on the screen turned around and started heading back in the opposite direction. 'I think this is it. The moment where something snaps in his mind. A switch was triggered.'

Darcey glanced at him. 'Maybe.'

'For sure. He'd just been watching Tassoni on TV. He decides not to take the flight. He turns around and heads for the villa. It all makes sense again.'

'He's just gone through airport security. Where's the .357?'

'Stashed somewhere else. To pick up en route, maybe.'

'Hold on. He's already stashed a weapon *before* "something snaps"?'

'Does it really matter? We know he did it.'

Darcey bit her lip and went on watching as the cameras followed the fugitive through the airport. Now the uncertainty in his body language had evaporated and there was purpose in his stride.

'There,' Buitoni said as they watched Hope going to the lockers and opening one up. 'Just like I said. The whole thing was a feint. He's only come here to pick up the gun. It's in the locker.'

Darcey stared closely. 'You're wrong, Paolo. He's not picking up anything. He's leaving his bag there.'

The time readout was just seconds after 17:17 as Ben climbed into the taxi and it pulled away.

'There he goes,' Buitoni said with conviction. 'Straight to Tassoni's and bang, bang, bang.'

Darcey didn't answer. She stood up. 'Let's go for a drive.'

Back in the airport parking lot, Buitoni was walking around to the driver's side when she plucked the key from his fingers and jumped in behind the wheel. The inside of the Alfa felt like a pizza oven after a couple of hours standing in the sun. Darcey checked her watch again. It was 4.42 p.m. She fired up the engine and wound down the windows. 'You navigate.'

'Where to?'

'Casa Tassoni,' she replied.

Buitoni was thrown back in his seat as she took off and went skidding out of the car park. She used the siren to carve a path through the traffic as she headed back towards the city with the speedometer nudging the hundred and seventy kilometres an hour mark.

'Mind telling me what this is about?' Buitoni asked her.

'Call it an experiment,' she said as she zipped past a speeding BMW so fast it looked like it was standing still.

She barely slowed for the city. By then, Buitoni was rigid and pale, holding his door handle in a death grip. 'Three guys are sitting in a bar,' he said in a strained voice. 'One of them is telling a Carabinieri joke. The second guy thinks it's the funniest thing he's ever heard, but the third one's all serious. First guy asks him, "What's wrong?" He replies, "I'm a Carabinieri." First guy says, "Don't worry, I'll explain it to you later."'

Darcey laughed as she took the racing line through a busy junction at over ninety, ignoring the chorus of horns from swerving drivers. She dived through a gap that was maybe an inch wider than the Alfa, changed down and put her foot to the floor.

'See, you do appreciate humour,' Buitoni said.

'I'm laughing at *you*, Paolo. Look at you. White as a sheet. Practically chattering your teeth. I thought Italian drivers liked to go fast.'

'We also like to reach our destination in one piece. Are you sure you wouldn't prefer that I drove?'

'And you call yourself a red-blooded male.'

He muttered something in Italian, and she grinned. 'Just navigate, all right?'

'You're enjoying this too much.'

Buitoni was soaked in sweat by the time Darcey screeched the Alfa to a halt outside Tassoni's villa. She killed the engine, did another time check. 5.36 p.m. She sighed loudly.

'What?'

'Do you think I could have gone any faster?'

He stared at her. 'Are you the one making jokes now?'

'Maybe I was wasting my time on all those high-speed pursuit driving courses I took. Maybe the taxi driver that brought Ben Hope here from the airport was just completely, insanely, reckless. Or maybe Hope's discovered the secret of teleportation. I don't know. All I know is that he only had between 5.18 and 5.57 to get here in time to shoot Tassoni and it's just taken me fifty-four minutes and twenty-two seconds to cover the same distance.'

'Perhaps the taxi driver knew a short cut.'

'You told me you knew this city.'

'I do,' Buitoni said. 'Then it's possible we have the wrong time of death. Tassoni's clock could have been inaccurate.'

'Those kinds of clock mechanisms don't go wrong, Paolo. NASA wouldn't use them otherwise.'

'Then Hope must have been working with someone else.'

'Not if we apparently have video of him walking out of here with the smoking gun.'

'Which we haven't seen,' Buitoni admitted.

'Which we haven't seen,' she repeated.

Buitoni was about to reply, then gave up and flopped in his seat. 'I don't understand.'

'Neither do I. But don't tell anyone about this, Paolo. That's an order.'

At that moment, Darcey's mobile went off in her pocket. It was her personal phone again.

'I need a cigarette,' Buitoni said, and stepped out of the car as she answered the call.

The heavy breather had called back.

'How did you get this number?' she said angrily.

Silence on the line. Just the quick, agitated rasp of his breathing.

'Fine. Play your little games. But hear this. You ever call me again, I'll find out who you are and come and kick you so hard your balls'll pop out through your nose. That's a promise. Get it?'

She was about to flip the phone shut when the man spoke.

'Don't . . . don't hang up. Please. Listen to me.'

A young-sounding voice. Maybe late twenties at the oldest. Educated accent, maybe Cambridge. This was no habituated phone pervert. The slur in his speech told her he'd needed a couple of drinks too many to pluck up the courage to make the call, but it nonetheless couldn't hide the nervousness. He was almost breathless with it.

'There are things you need to know,' he said. He paused. 'Are you still there?'

Darcey could see Buitoni pacing the pavement a few metres from Tassoni's gates, anxiously puffing on his cigarette. There were still a few police vehicles parked up in the background, outside the house.

'I'm still here,' she said to her mystery caller. 'But I won't be for long.'

'My name's Borg.'

'Borg,' she repeated dubiously.

She heard him swallow hard on the other end. 'Look. Christ. I don't know where to begin . . . Operation Jericho isn't what you think it is.'

She frowned. Operation Jericho. If he knew about that, he definitely was not a prank caller.

Alarms were whooping and red warning lights popping like flashguns in her mind. She needed to back off. Right now. Report this to Applewood. Do the right thing, before she opened up a hornet's nest and got herself stung to pieces for it.

But it was stronger than her. She wanted to know more.

'I don't like this anonymous bullshit. You need to tell me who you really are or I'm hanging up.'

A long, nervous pause. She could sense he was thinking about it. Weighing up the pros and cons. He knew he needed to gain her trust. But his hesitation smelled of fear. This was a lot more dangerous for him than it was for her.

Or maybe it wasn't. But she still had to know.

'All right. Let's stay with Borg for now,' she said, talking in a low, soft, reassuring voice. Her negotiator's voice. 'Tell me what you know.'

He took a long, quavering breath. 'It's best we meet.'

'That would be fine,' she said. 'Where?'

'You need to come alone.'

'I'll do that, Borg. Tell me the place and the time. I'll be there. Just me. That's a promise.'

Another hesitant silence. Buitoni was still pacing up and down near the car, drawing on his cigarette like a dying man sucking oxygen.

'OK, listen,' Borg said. His voice lowered to a whisper, sounding muffled as if he was cupping his hand over his mouth. 'I – oh, fuck. Someone's co—'

There was a scuffling sound, and then the call cut off. Darcey was left staring at a dead phone.

Outside in the street, Buitoni flicked away his cigarette as his radio came to life. Darcey saw his eyes open wide at what he heard. He came running over to the car and she whirred down her window.

'What's happening, Paolo?'

'Remember De Crescenzo, the gallery owner? His wife

just phoned the police to say she had a gentleman caller this morning.'

'Don't tell me. Hope?'

Buitoni nodded. 'Made her coffee, apparently.'

Darcey couldn't believe the audacity of the man. 'We need to go and talk to her right away. You drive.' She shifted across to the passenger seat as Buitoni got in gratefully behind the wheel.

'Who was that on the phone?' he asked as he started the car.

'Wrong number,' Darcey told him.

It took another forty-five minutes to butcher their way back across the city to the De Crescenzo place. The contessa took her time answering the door, and when she did, Darcey could smell the booze on her breath. She rolled her eyes at Buitoni. He shrugged and gave a look that said 'let me do the talking.'

Ornella De Crescenzo wobbled her way to an airy sitting room, where they all sat on soft armchairs and Buitoni had her run through the events of that morning.

'He told me his name was Rupert,' she said. 'It wasn't until later, when I saw the TV . . . ' She bit her lip. 'I was so shocked. To think I was alone here with a brutal killer. Here, in my own home. What if he had murdered me, too?'

'You say he left here around ten, ten-thirty? Yet you didn't call us until late afternoon.'

'I was resting,' she said defensively.

Darcey glanced at the half-empty bottle and single glass on the sideboard across the room. Resting.

'What did he want?' Buitoni asked Ornella.

'To see my husband. But Pietro went off to Spain early this morning.'

'Spain?'

261

'Near Madrid. Visiting some art person.'

Buitoni and Darcey exchanged looks. 'Do you think Hope might have gone there after him?' Buitoni asked Ornella.

Darcey took out her phone and quickly dialled up an online distance calculator. Rome to Madrid was eight hundred and fifty-five miles. On maximum thrust, the Cessna could get there in under ninety minutes.

'He certainly seemed terribly keen to talk to him,' Ornella said, and her face crumpled into a look of terrified realisation as connections came together in her mind. '*Mio dio*, you don't think he means to—'

'It's very important that we know exactly where your husband went,' Buitoni told her seriously. 'We are dealing with a highly dangerous criminal here.'

Ornella touched her fingertips to her mouth, working hard to recall. 'He did tell me the man's name. It starts with . . . it starts with S.' Her eyes lit up momentarily. 'Sangio— no, that's not right. Seg— Seg something. Segovia.'

'Segovia?'

'Yes, I'm quite sure it was Segovia.'

'The famous Spanish guitarist,' Darcey said. 'Where was your husband planning on meeting him? The dead people's concert hall?'

'I'm trying,' Ornella said irritably. 'I don't remember. Hell, I need a drink.' She got up and stumbled over towards the bottle on the sideboard. Darcey was on her feet and snatched the bottle away before Ornella could get to it.

The countess snarled at her. 'Who do you think you are? You can't—'

Darcey ignored her and coolly turned to Buitoni. 'Tell her that if she doesn't remember, it's withholding evidence and she could go to jail,' she said in English.

'*I* can't tell her *that*,' he protested.

'Then I'm going to take her into custody and have her pumped full of coffee until she gives us that name. See if we can get hold of her husband. In the meantime, you and I are going to Madrid. Get on the radio and have them prepare the jet for take-off.'

Chapter Forty-Nine

Salamanca, western Spain

After the long journey west under the hot sun, the Maserati's dashboard clock was reading 10.31 and dusk was turning to darkness as Ben finally closed in on his destination.

Salamanca, northwest of Madrid, not far from the Portuguese border on Spain's northern plateau. Ben felt just a little wistful about being here. He hadn't set foot in the historic city before, but it was somewhere he and Brooke had once talked about coming to visit. Take some time exploring, see the sights, wander around its churches and museums, check out the little backstreet Castilian restaurants where the tourists didn't venture. Ben remembered reading that Salamanca had been dubbed 'Ciudad Dorada', the Golden City, for its magnificent old sandstone buildings. Once besieged by the Carthaginian army under Hannibal, in later centuries it had gone on to become a major battlefield between the Moors and the forces of Christendom.

But Salamanca's long, colourful history and cultural heritage were the last things on Ben's mind right now, and he staunchly refused to let himself get all melancholy dwelling on thoughts of Brooke as he followed the Maserati's onboard sat-nav into the old city towards the home of the fine art collector Juan Calixto Segura. The sun was setting in a blaze of reds and purples that shimmered gently on the waters of the Tormes River and glittered off the dome of the distant cathedral. Spires and minarets reached for the darkening sky, casting long shadows across the rooftops.

Ben left the Maserati in a deserted side-street a kilometre or so from Segura's place. It had done its job in getting him here quickly, but to hang on too long to such a distinctive car in his position was just begging for trouble. Double-checking the address he'd copied down back in Rome, he stretched his legs after the long drive and set off towards Segura's home on foot. Night was falling fast. It was hot and close. Rain was coming.

The art collector lived in a four-storey townhouse, a noble and imposing sandstone building with balconies, shutters and a red-tiled roof, high on a hill overlooking the city and surrounded by neatly-tended flower gardens. The street was quiet, the only people in sight a young couple out walking who smiled pleasantly and wished Ben good evening as they strolled by.

Ben glanced up and down the line of cars parked on the kerbside. Pietro De Crescenzo's silver Volvo wasn't one of them. He kept his eyes open for it appearing round the corner as he walked up to the house. It didn't show. It didn't surprise him too much that he'd managed to beat the count here by some margin.

As Ben had expected from a guy who kept a lot of expensive art in his home, Segura's security was pretty good. It took Ben four whole minutes to get inside. He moved from room to room unseen and as silent as shadow.

The scent of aromatic pipe smoke lingered throughout the house. Nude art adorned much of the wall space, some of it risqué enough to make Ben think that either Signora

265

Segura was an extremely permissive wife or else Juan Calixto was a single guy. A woman's touch on a home left an unmistakable trace; the more Ben saw of the house, the more convinced he was that there was no Mrs Segura. That was fine by him. Fewer occupants to become alerted to his presence.

From somewhere above, he could hear the strains of a violin. He followed the music up the stairs, treading on the edge of each step to avoid creaks. At the top of the staircase was a dark landing. The music was clearer now – maybe Bach, or Haydn – and the smell of smoke stronger. Three doors led off the landing, one in the centre, one left and one right. The door on the right was ajar a couple of inches. The music was coming from the room beyond, as well as a shaft of light. Ben stepped softly over to it and peered through the crack.

The room was a study. Sitting on a deep green leather chair at an antique desk was a large, solidly-built man in his fifties with a mane of grey hair swept back from a high forehead. He was wearing an open-necked shirt with a silk necktie, and toying with the stem of a half-filled glass of red wine as he pored through what looked like a fine art auction catalogue. A curved pipe hung lazily from the corner of his mouth, its smoke drifting in the light of his desk lamp. Segura seemed preoccupied, glancing frequently at his chunky silver watch as if waiting for someone.

Ben very quietly turned the handle of the landing's middle door and opened it a crack to reveal a bedroom. Unless Segura was the world's tidiest bachelor, it had to be a guest room. Ben gently closed the door and returned to watching Segura in his study, hanging well back in the shadows.

The art collector's desk clock was reading almost 11.15 when the door chimes sounded suddenly from below. Segura

266

laid down his pipe, got up and bustled towards the study door. Ben slipped quickly into the guest bedroom as the Spaniard trotted heavily out onto the landing and hurried down the stairs.

A moment later, Ben heard voices, indistinct at first and then growing louder as Segura led his visitor back up to the study. Ben bent down to peer through the keyhole and saw De Crescenzo climbing the stairs behind his host. The count's suit was rumpled from the long drive. He looked pale and nervy, wringing his hands and showing his grey teeth. They were speaking English; Ben guessed that was the only language they had in common. Segura led the Italian into the study and pulled the door to behind him.

As Ben emerged cautiously from the guest bedroom he was relieved to see that the Spaniard had left the door open a few inches. The two men were visible through the gap. Ben moved closer, and listened.

'To business,' Segura was saying in his rich accent.

De Crescenzo looked so nervous he could hardly breathe. 'The Goya,' he whispered. 'Show me.'

Segura nodded. He slid open a desk drawer, took out a remote control and pointed it at a large oil painting mounted on the study wall. The painting slid aside with a whirr of an electric motor, revealing a hidden safe door with a wall-mounted keypad to one side. Shielding the keypad with his left hand, Segura punched in a number with his right index finger. Twelve digits, twelve little beeps. The door swung open.

'Naturally,' he said, turning to De Crescenzo, 'the vast majority of my collection is stored in my basement vault. I brought this up here earlier, knowing you would wish to see it.'

He reached into the safe with both hands, and came out

holding a rectangular object wrapped in white cloth. Ben watched as Segura carried it over to the desk and laid it down as though it could crumble into powder at any moment. As the Spaniard drew the cloth away, De Crescenzo let out a gasp and whispered, 'May I hold it?'

'Carefully, please,' Segura said with a smile. The count picked it up. He was standing with his back to the door, so Ben had a clear view of the picture in his hands. It looked identical to the charcoal sketch at the exhibition, a drawing of a man on his knees praying to God with a look of devout passion, as though his life depended on it.

The same picture that had been stolen.

Ben stared at it. What was going on here?

De Crescenzo was swaying on his feet with amazement as he stood gaping at the sketch in his hands.

'Now you understand why I asked you to be here in person,' Segura said, reaching for his pipe. 'This is not something I could merely describe by telephone. This, my friend, is the real "Penitent Sinner". As certifiably authentic as it could possibly be.' He relit the pipe with a lighter from his pocket and puffed clouds of smoke.

Ben was so stunned he had to bite back a choking cough. *The stolen piece had been a forgery?*

'How – how do I know—' De Crescenzo stammered.

'That this is the genuine article?' Segura smiled. 'I have been cautious. More cautious than you, my friend.' As Ben listened, the Spaniard launched into a whole technical spiel about white lead dating, X-ray diffraction, infrared analysis, dendrochronology and stable isotope testing and a whole lot of other things Ben didn't understand a word of but which seemed pretty convincing to Pietro De Crescenzo.

'You have had this for—'

'Seventeen years,' Segura finished for him, nodding. 'Like

the private collector from whom I bought it, I prefer to avoid publicity. For the same reason, I generally refuse to loan out items from my collection.' He gave a dark smile. 'As I think you know, it can be a risky business.'

The count laid the Goya down gingerly on the desk and slumped into a nearby chair. Segura was watching him closely, and Ben could read the look on the Spaniard's face. Segura was no idiot. He was looking at all the angles. Studying De Crescenzo for any sign of play-acting that might have indicated he'd been up to some kind of scam here. Have a fake painting knocked up by a discreet forger, arrange for it to be stolen in such a way that you could never be suspected, claim on the insurance, then feign total innocence when someone comes up with the original.

But whatever suspicions Segura might have had were clearly dissipated by the Italian's reaction. Nobody could have acted so well. De Crescenzo suddenly looked about two hundred years old. For a few moments Ben was as concerned as Segura obviously was that the Italian might be about to keel over.

'Would you care for a drink?' Segura asked, motioning towards a decanter on a sideboard.

De Crescenzo dabbed at his brow with a handkerchief, tried to smile and shook his head. 'Thank you, no. I'll be all right.'

'This must come as something of a shock, I know,' Segura said with a note of sympathy. 'Though I must say I am somewhat surprised you did not conduct similar testing to verify the authenticity of the piece yourself.'

De Crescenzo sank his head in his hands. 'I assumed—' he said weakly. His voice trailed off.

Segura laughed. 'I have made similar assumptions in the past, and paid the price for them. It happens to us all.'

But De Crescenzo wasn't listening. He sat there quaking, as if the full force of realisation was suddenly hitting him. 'If I had known – if I had taken the trouble to check, instead of being blinded by sentiment, none of this tragedy might have occurred. This whole thing has been my fault.'

Segura stared at him. 'How can you have been responsible for what those animals did?'

De Crescenzo shook his head furiously. 'No, no. You don't understand. The thieves were targeting the Goya specifically.'

'But why would they have done that? They must have known how little it was worth, compared to—'

'I don't know why,' De Crescenzo cut in. 'All I know is that, had I not chosen to include it in the exhibition, innocent lives would have been spared.' He fell into thought for a moment, then his face crinkled into a grimace and he gave a sour laugh. 'And so history repeats itself. The first time, the crooks left with nothing. The second time, they left with a fake.'

Listening in the shadows, Ben wondered what he meant by that.

Segura shrugged, not seeming to understand. 'You do look as though you need a drink, Pietro. I cannot begin to imagine what you have been through.' Chewing on the stem of his pipe, he stepped over to the sideboard and picked up the decanter and a glass. 'Here. Some cognac will settle your nerves.'

De Crescenzo shook his head again. 'I think I will leave you now, and find a hotel.' He rose unsteadily to his feet, held out his hand. 'Thank you. Tomorrow I will return to Rome and inform the authorities.'

'I would have preferred that my ownership of the Goya remain a secret,' Segura said. 'But I appreciate I no longer have that luxury.'

'I'm grateful for your understanding,' De Crescenzo said in a hoarse croak.

It was two minutes after midnight when Segura showed De Crescenzo back downstairs. The Italian took his Burberry raincoat from the ornate antique coat stand in the hallway where he'd hung it, then the two art scholars shook hands and exchanged goodbyes.

De Crescenzo left the house and walked out into the sultry night. His mind was awhirl as he headed across the road to where he'd parked the Volvo. He patted his coat pocket for the ignition key. Not there. He was so distracted that he couldn't remember if he'd locked the car or not – maybe he'd even left the key in it. In a daze, he reached for the door handle. It opened and he got in.

The key wasn't in the ignition. He cursed softly and felt in his other pocket.

'Good evening, Count De Crescenzo,' said a voice behind him.

Chapter Fifty

Torréjon military base
24 kilometres northeast of Madrid

The airfield's floodlights gleamed off the sleek fuselage of the SOCA Cessna Citation jet as it waited on standby a hundred metres from the giant hangar where Darcey had set up her temporary command centre. The huge space was alive with heavily-armed police and soldiers, technical personnel and government agents, and filled with vehicles and military trestle tables and flight-cased racks of radio and computer equipment. At the rear of the hangar, silhouetted in shadow, stood the official planes of the King of Spain and the country's President.

Darcey was deep in a meeting with Comisario Miguel Garrido, one of Madrid's most senior-ranking police chiefs, when, just after midnight, Paolo Buitoni came sprinting across the hangar and broke in on their conversation. He was out of breath and clutching a card file, full of apologies for the interruption but bursting with news.

'I just had a call from Rome,' he said excitedly. 'Your idea to bring Ornella De Crescenzo into custody and put some pressure on her? We'll probably get our balls – that is to say, we'll probably get disciplined, but it worked. She remembered. She got it.'

'Don't beat about the bush, Paolo,' Darcey said. 'Tell me.'

'The name of the man her husband rushed off to meet is Segura. That was all she could remember, but I ran a search using "Segura Spain fine art". I came up with this guy.' He plucked a glossy printout from the file. Darcey took it. It showed a serious-looking man in his fifties, with swept-back silver hair and broad shoulders, pictured at some kind of arts event, shaking hands with another man in front of a huge canvas.

'Juan Calixto Segura,' Buitoni said. 'A well-respected art collector based in Salamanca.' He snatched a sheet from his file. 'I have the address right here. Million to one, Ben Hope followed Pietro De Crescenzo there tonight. And there's more. Our men just discovered that Ornella's car is missing. She says her husband left for Spain in his own Volvo.'

'Ben Hope took it,' Darcey said.

'We're looking for a bronze Maserati GranTurismo. Not too many of those around.'

Darcey turned to Garrido. 'Comisario, we need your tactical teams and every available patrol officer in there, hard and fast.'

Garrido was already summoning his aides and issuing commands.

'Darcey, Salamanca is just a hundred and fifty kilometres from here,' Buitoni said. 'The jet can get us there in less than fifteen minutes and I'll have a police chopper waiting for us at the military base outside the city.'

'Nice work, Paolo.' Darcey flashed a brief smile at him, and then her jaw tightened and the fierce glint came into her eye. She grabbed her Beretta from a nearby steel table.

As she strode towards the mouth of the hangar she jacked a round into the breech, flipped on the safety and shoved the weapon into her hip holster. 'Ben Hope isn't getting away this time.'

'She has that look again,' Buitoni muttered under his breath as he ran after her. 'God, I love that look.'

Chapter Fifty-One

Salamanca

Pietro De Crescenzo's eyes became huge and round in the rear-view mirror. He twisted round in horror to stare at the man who'd suddenly appeared in the back of the Volvo.

'Good to see you again,' Ben said. 'Remember me?'

'*Mio dio*. The murderer.'

'That's right,' Ben said. 'I'm a sick, sick man. A raving psychotic, just like the papers say. I killed Urbano Tassoni and I enjoyed doing it, just like I enjoyed killing a hundred other men, women and children before him. And I'll kill you, too, Pietro, unless you do exactly what I say.'

De Crescenzo cowered behind the steering wheel. Ben dangled the Volvo keys from his fingers. 'This town's pretty by night. Why don't we take a scenic tour while we talk?'

De Crescenzo took the key from him with a trembling hand. He was shaking so badly it took him three attempts to fit it into the ignition.

'Don't drive too fast,' Ben said. 'Don't drive too slowly. Don't do anything that might attract attention to us.'

De Crescenzo nodded frantically, took a deep breath and pulled away. The Volvo glided through the night streets. Traffic was thin. As they skirted the old city, the ancient sandstone buildings and domes and steeples were lit gold under the moonlight.

'How did you know where to find me?' De Crescenzo quavered.

'The contessa was a great help,' Ben said. 'She even lent me her car.'

'Ornella! You did not—'

'You can relax, Pietro. She's fine, apart from a hangover. Needs to ease up on the Smirnoff a little. As soon as I'm finished with you, you should think about getting home to her before she overdoes it. You're not giving her the attention she deserves.' Ben Hope, marriage counsellor.

De Crescenzo's shoulders slumped at the wheel. 'What is it you want from me?'

'I came to ask you what the hell's going on,' Ben said. 'But now I can see you don't know any more than I do.'

De Crescenzo glanced back at him in the mirror. 'You were there? In Segura's home?'

'I heard every word you said, Pietro.'

'Then I can tell you no more. Please. Let me go. I promise – I *swear* – I will tell nobody that I saw you here tonight.'

'Tell me one thing, and you won't see me ever again,' Ben said. 'Tell me about the first time.'

'The first time?'

'Something you said to Segura. "The first time, the crooks left with nothing." You weren't talking about the gallery heist, were you?'

De Crescenzo was silent for a few moments, then let out a long, sad sigh. 'When Gabriella Giordani passed away in October 1986 from a heart attack, it was as the direct result of a violent intrusion at her secluded home outside Cesena. She was all alone when it happened. Her former maid and longtime companion and confidante was no longer living with her. When Gabriella was later found dead at the scene, the coroner's conclusion was that the heart attack had been induced by acute terror.'

'What were they looking for? Cash? Valuables?'

De Crescenzo grunted bitterly. 'That is the strange thing. Gabriella Giordani had been an established artist for quite a few years and her work was worth a fortune. She was *extremely* wealthy, her home filled with beautiful things. Antiques, jewellery, artwork, every piece itemised for insurance purposes. The burglars could have helped themselves to everything. And yet, they touched not a single item of her possessions, though they searched the house violently from top to bottom. What they were looking for remains a mystery.'

Ben could see a pattern forming here. Criminals broke into a house full of valuables, were willing to cause death in order to obtain what they wanted, yet left the place apparently empty-handed. Twenty-five years later, an armed gang committed multiple murder, just to obtain a relatively valueless drawing once owned by the same person, which now moreover turned out to have been a fake. When history repeated itself like that, there had to be a reason.

'You think they were looking for "The Penitent Sinner" the first time round?' he asked.

De Crescenzo shrugged helplessly. 'I have asked myself this many times. There is no way to know the answer.'

'I can think of one way. Talk to the people who did it.'

De Crescenzo said nothing.

'Tell me again about this drawing,' Ben said. 'What was it, a pencil sketch?'

'Charcoal, drawn on laid paper.'

'Laid paper?'

'A special kind of art paper, thick, textured rather like a fabric print. But essentially just a piece of paper, nothing more. The sketch itself is interesting and masterfully executed but, as you have seen yourself, it is by no means a spectacular piece of art. Its only possible value was the signature at the bottom. If it had only been genuine,' De Crescenzo added sourly.

'The sketch couldn't have been superimposed on some other piece of artwork?' Ben asked. 'The original painted out, then redone over the top?' He was thinking that maybe whatever the thieves had been after was hidden underneath – but he was clutching at straws and he knew it.

'Impossible,' De Crescenzo said. 'On canvas, this could be feasible. On paper, however, such an overpaint would be immediately apparent, as well as highly impractical. No artist would do such a thing. The mystery is simply unsolvable.'

Ben leaned back against the seat as De Crescenzo drove on, and thought for a while in silence. Then an idea hit him. 'You mentioned Gabriella had a longtime companion. Someone she might have confided in. Maybe that person would know something.'

'I do not know what happened to her after she left Gabriella,' De Crescenzo said. 'If Mimi is even still living, she would be impossible to trace.'

'Did you say Mimi?'

De Crescenzo looked blank. 'Yes.'

'That wouldn't be Mimi Renzi, would it?'

'Her surname was unknown. In all the biographical accounts of Gabriella's life, she was referred to only as Mimi.' De Crescenzo's bemused look turned to one of desperation. 'Now you know everything I know. That's it. There is nothing more I can add. Will you please let me go?'

'I'm true to my word,' Ben said. 'I'm not who you think I am.'

'Why did you kill Tassoni?' The question burst out of De

Crescenzo's mouth as though it had been burning on his tongue all day.

'You really think I did?'

'It was on television.'

'I thought you were smarter than that, Pietro.'

At that moment, something caught Ben's eye out of the car window. He turned and saw it again – a blinking light suspended high in the air over the rooftops. He whirred the glass down a few inches, felt the hot sticky night air on his face.

And heard the thump of helicopter blades over Salamanca – as well as the high-pitched chorus of police sirens.

Ben reached into his pocket for the Maserati keys. It was time to be out of here.

Chapter Fifty-Two

Within minutes, the dark, quiet street outside Juan Calixto Segura's home was filled with noise and activity as a whole fleet of police vehicles pulled up outside and armed officers spilled out. Segura was standing at his front door wearing a silk dressing gown and a bewildered expression as eight cops came storming up the steps, bundled him aside and poured into the house with their weapons drawn. Within moments, the radio signal came back that the place was clear.

Two kilometres across Salamanca, a black Eurocopter deployed by the Grupo Especial de Operaciones, Spain's specialist tactical firearms police unit, was hovering low scanning the streets with its powerful spotlamp when the co-pilot spotted the bronze Maserati GranTurismo making its way out of the city. In a flurry of radio calls the chopper overtook the car, banked round one hundred and eighty degrees and came down to block the Maserati's path. Ropes tumbled down from the aircraft's open sides and six heavily-armed cops in black fatigues, helmets and goggles came abseiling down and hit the road running.

The Maserati halted in the middle of the road as they circled it, six bullpup FN submachine gun muzzles trained steadily on the dark figure behind the windscreen. The men had all been briefed on the nature of their target. They were taking no chances. Over the roar of the chopper the team leader yelled into his throat mike, 'Fugitive apprehended!' The others were shouting at the car: 'Get out of the vehicle NOW! Hands on your head! Move SLOW or we WILL shoot!'

The Maserati's door swung open. In the blazing spotlight from the chopper the driver got out very nervously and dropped to his knees on the road with his fingers laced over his head. Laser sight dots danced around his head and chest like a swarm of red insects as the cops advanced warily. But the man didn't seem like the fearsome adversary they'd been briefed to expect – in fact he didn't match the description of the fugitive at all. This guy was much older, skinny and gaunt. The team leader signalled to his men to bring him in anyway.

'I didn't do anything!' Pietro De Crescenzo screeched in Italian as they put him face down on the road and fastened his wrists behind his back. 'He told me to take my wife's car home—' His protests were lost in the noise as an armoured police van skidded up to the scene and he was dragged into the back.

Three minutes' fast sprint away in a quiet backstreet overshadowed by tall houses, Ben was working his way up a line of parked vehicles looking for a ride out of Salamanca. Stealing cars wasn't something he liked doing, but when he saw the rusted-out Renault 5 at the kerb he had a feeling the owner would probably thank him for taking it. No alarm, no immobiliser. Auto theft, the old fashioned way. The passenger side window gave after just a couple of hits. Ben popped the locks, and then he was in and working on the wires behind the steering column. The engine fired with a rattle.

He pulled away and drove calmly through the empty night

streets. Not fast, not slow, attracting no attention, observing the rules of the road. Over the wheeze of the Renault's engine he could hear the rhythmic thud of the police helicopter and a chorus of sirens that sounded as if every police vehicle in the region was heading for the vicinity of Segura's house.

Ben stopped for a red light at the mouth of a wide T-junction, indicating right to follow the signs out of town and toeing the gas to help the Renault maintain its idle speed. The junction ahead was deserted. After a few seconds, the lights changed and he pulled out.

A massive impact tore the steering wheel from his grip and threw him sideways as the Renault was sent spinning sideways, mounted the kerb and hit a wall.

For a few moments, Ben was stunned. His vision floated unsteadily, his hearing muffled. Seconds passed before he understood that the dazzling light shining through the cracked windscreen was the remaining headlight of the car that had been speeding across the junction and hit him. It was stationary at an angle a few metres away in the road, its nearside wing badly crumpled and a smashed mirror dangling like a half-severed ear.

Two figures got out of the car, moving towards Ben's Renault. As his senses cleared, he realised they were wearing uniforms – and that their car was a dark blue Citroën C4 with a light bar on the roof and POLICIA written across its side.

One of the cops was an older man, mid-fifties. There was a smear of blood on his mouth where the airbag had punched his lip into a tooth. The other was maybe late twenties, already on his radio reporting the accident. Ben tried to open his car door, but it was jammed. He turned sideways in the driver's seat and kicked out with both feet together. The door burst open with a grinding of buckled metal. As he clambered out, the two cops met him with humble and apologetic looks, and the older one launched into an explanation in rapid Spanish.

Then stopped. He frowned at Ben, peering at him closely under the streetlights. He turned to his colleague, who was staring too. A rapid nod, a heartbeat's silence, and both cops went for their pistols.

The younger cop's SIG was the first to clear its holster, but it never made it to aiming position. Ben was on him in one step and about half a second. He slapped the pistol downwards and twisted it out of the guy's hand, throwing a solid elbow in his face. At the same time his left foot lashed out in a straight low kick that connected with the older cop's knee and sent him tumbling on his back. Before the younger cop had hit the ground, Ben had stepped over to his colleague and knocked him out with a kick to the head.

Neither of them would have any permanent damage. Ben shoved the younger cop's SIG in his waistband, scooped up his partner's weapon and ejected the mag and pocketed it. The pistol was quick and easy to dismantle. With the slide off the frame rails, the barrel fell out and Ben dropped it through the slots of a nearby iron drain cover. He tossed the other useless pieces into the shadows, then picked up the cops' radios and smashed them on the road.

The Renault was undriveable, but the police Citroën still had the keys in it. As he took off, Ben knew that it was tactically a bad move and that he'd have to ditch the car within the short time it would take for the alarm to be raised.

Only a few seconds passed before he knew it was already too late. As he rounded a bend, there were suddenly two more police C4s right behind him. They weren't after him – not yet. He could either stay with them and gamble on their not spotting him behind the wheel, or he could take evasive action before fifty more of them joined the party, together with air support and the whole of Spain's rapid response firearms units combined. That was a little more trouble than he needed right now.

It wasn't a difficult decision to make. He floored the gas and threw the Citroën into a screeching hard left turn. The two following cars seemed to hesitate, then turned in after him. His in-car radio began to shout at him. He ignored it. No point pretending any more. He hammered the car up onto the kerb and the revs soared as he sent it over the top of a flight of concrete steps that descended steeply down to a pedestrianised street below. The Citroën bucked and juddered down the steps. There was a loud *whang* and a shower of sparks as he hit the bottom. As Ben took off again he glanced in the mirror and saw that his pursuers hadn't dared risk the steps. Four cops were out of their vehicles. He heard a ragged series of popping pistol shots. His rear window shattered. There was a junction twenty metres ahead. Ben threw the Citroën into a skidding right-hander out of pistol range and then redlined it. He was heading away from the old city, into the modern urban sprawl that had grown up around its edges.

He was scanning left and right for a good spot to pull over and ditch the police car when he heard the thud of the chopper overhead. An instant later, he was caught in the strong circle of white light it was throwing down over the street. He pressed harder on the gas, leaving the chopper behind momentarily as the speedometer climbed past a hundred and twenty and buildings and parked vehicles zipped past on both sides in a blur. Pedal to the floor, his stomach rose into his ribcage as the road dropped down through a flyover tunnel. The chopper banked steeply to clear the bridge, then it was on him again as he zipped by signs for an industrial estate. Tall warehouse buildings loomed against the night sky. The chopper dropped down low, keeping pace just thirty metres to his left. Its side hatch slid open and a police shooter in a black tactical vest hung out with one foot on the skid and a large shotgun in his gloved hands. He was aiming for the front of the car.

BOOM. Ben felt the heavy buckshot load punch into the front wing, sending the car skittering to one side. The shooter was going for the tyres. At this speed, a blowout could send him into a spin, flip and roll that would turn him into corned beef. He hit the brakes and skidded around another bend. He was heading deeper into the industrial estate.

A scream of sirens tore his eyes from the road to the mirror. Police cars were joining the chase from all directions, converging into a fleet that filled the road in an ocean of swirling blue lights.

Not good. But the chopper worried him more. It was swinging back parallel to him, closer now, and the shooter was lining up for another shot. Ben could see the guy's black-gloved hand tighten on the weapon's pistol grip. Quarter of a second before he heard the shot, he stabbed the brakes and the blast of pellets passed in front of the Citroën's nose.

But braking meant he'd lost precious speed, and now the pursuing cars were coming up fast behind him. More shots rang out. Ben felt the impact as bullets punched into the bodywork of the car.

The shotgunner fired again from the chopper. This time he scored. The front corner of the C4 dipped hard as the tyre exploded into flying ribbons of rubber. Ben sawed at the wheel and just about managed to control the skid that sent him screaming into a narrow alley between warehouse buildings. The helicopter pilot pulled up into a violent climb.

Ben's car was lurching and bumping wildly as he gunned it down the alley as fast as it could go. There were extensive building works going on up ahead – a yellow JCB, a concrete mixer and a giant dumper truck with its flatbed elevated to tip a load of gravel by the roadside. The chopper's lights were reflected in the windows of another tall warehouse directly opposite the exit of the alley.

Another police C4 was right on Ben's tail. As he wrestled with the erratic steering, it nipped past his right flank and overtook him, trying to block his path. The alley was narrowing for the building works. As the car in front braked heavily, Ben realised with a shock that he was running out of road.

With half the Spanish police behind him, there was no way he was about to slow down. He flattened the pedal to the floor and aimed the speeding car at the heap of gravel behind the dumper truck.

If this didn't kill him, it might even work.

Fuck it. Ben braced himself for the impact.

As the car raced towards the gravel pile at almost a hundred and sixty kilometres an hour, more shots rang out over the scream of the engine and his windscreen suddenly turned into an opaque web of cracks. Something thumped his upper left arm hard, but his senses barely had time to register it before the car crashed into the gravel pile with massive force and the airbag exploded in his face. He felt the crunching shock through the steering wheel as most of the front suspension and the underside of the Citroën's chassis were sheared away. The car's nose jerked brutally skywards as it hit the uptilted flatbed of the dumper truck and sailed up it, tearing through the wire mesh barrier at its end and flying upwards through the air like an F-16 fighter launched from the deck of an aircraft carrier.

For a snatched moment in time that seemed to linger for an eternity, everything was almost peaceful. Ben thought of summer breezes and wildflower meadows. He thought about Brooke. Heard her laughter echo in his mind.

Then he was engulfed in a maelstrom of deafening noise and pain and chaos and bone-crunching destructive forces as the airborne car hit the building opposite. A dozen metres above the street, the Citroën went smashing through the plate-glass warehouse windows. It careened into the building in a storm of flying glass and spinning masonry and timber. There was a massive shower of sparks as it ploughed across the concrete floor. Stacks of wooden pallets and crates cannoned off the shattered windscreen. The car spun across the warehouse and buried itself in one of the brick pillars holding up the roof.

Suddenly, all was still and quiet again, just the ticking of hot metal from the wrecked car. The police sirens sounded muffled and a long way away.

Ben groaned, stirred and painfully released his seatbelt. There was no need to open the driver's door, because it wasn't there any more. He stumbled out of the Citroën and stared at the devastation around him illuminated by the flashing blue lights from down below. A moment earlier, the place had obviously been some kind of furniture warehouse. Now it looked like the ruins of Dresden, February 1945.

It was only then that Ben felt the burning agony in his upper left arm and remembered the impact he'd felt. He couldn't move it properly. Touching it, his fingertips came away dripping red. He could feel blood trickling down inside his sleeve. A cold wave of nausea gushed through his body and his heart began to hammer at the base of his throat. He blinked sweat out of his eyes, willed himself to keep moving.

Stepping over the wreckage to the shattered warehouse

window, he could see the police piling out of their vehicles down below, pulling guns and scattering into teams searching for an entrance to the warehouse. The police helicopter that had chased him was still hovering over the industrial estate.

Then, as Ben watched, a second chopper came thudding in out of the night sky and settled beyond the cluster of police vehicles. Before it had fully touched down, its hatch flew open and a figure in black jumped out.

Her black hair flew loose in the wind from the rotor blades. Even at this distance, Ben could see the look of ferocious determination on her face.

Darcey Kane.

Ben almost smiled. He'd known he'd see her again. What was it with this woman?

Behind her came a tall, bald man whom Ben instantly recognised as the man who'd been with her in the catacomb in Rome. The two of them were quickly briefed by uniformed officers and some of the paramilitary tactical firearms team who had rolled up in an unmarked black van. Darcey Kane looked up at the warehouse, then drew her weapon and started striding fast towards the wrecked building.

Ben moved away from the window and looked around him for a way out.

Darcey led the tactical firearms squad into the warehouse. Weapons cocked and ready and darting torch beams left and right, they covered each other as they climbed from level to level up clattering iron stairs.

Emerging onto the third floor, the sharp odour of spilled motor fluids and hot metal reached their nostrils, and they shone their torches on the car wreck.

'Jesus Christ,' Buitoni murmured. 'He can't have walked away from this.'

Darcey was already approaching the vehicle, her weapon out in front of her.

The car was empty. There was no sign of Hope anywhere.

Then she saw the trail of blood spots that led away from the car and followed it with her Maglite across the concrete floor to the window, where it pooled in a gleaming puddle.

'He's hurt,' Buitoni said.

'Not that badly,' she said. 'He was watching us from here.'

A further blood trail led back in the opposite direction. 'This way,' she called, and Buitoni and the team followed.

The blood spots ended below a round ceiling hatch that was accessed by a metal ladder. Some of the rungs were smeared red and there was a red handprint on the trapdoor overhead. Darcey hauled herself up the ladder, pushed through the trapdoor and stepped out onto the flat roof. She cast her torchbeam through the darkness, and saw the row of warehouses whose rooftops stood close enough together for Hope to have made his escape that way.

Darcey felt the first heavy patter of rain on her cheek. Then a second. She looked up at the sky.

'Fuck,' she said.

And the gathering rain clouds opened up. In seconds, everyone except Darcey was taking cover from the deluge and the warehouse roof was running slick with water.

She could only stare as the blood trail washed away, and with it her chances of catching Ben Hope that night.

'*Fuck*,' she said again.

Chapter Fifty-Three

The rain was pounding down like warm hail as Ben staggered away from the industrial area. The pain in his arm was intensifying, and he tucked his wrist through his belt to keep the limb supported as he ran. He made for the side of a tin building where old pallets were stacked in five-metre-high piles. Ducking in among them, he stripped off his shirt and examined his wound. The blood was oozing out as fast as the rain could wash it away. The bullet was still in there, lodged somewhere up against the triceps muscle. He didn't think it had struck bone. He tore the right sleeve off the shirt and tied it as tightly as he could around his arm to stem the bleeding. Not much of a field dressing, but it would have to do for now.

He bundled the rest of the shirt out of sight into a gap between the pallets, then peered through the hammering rain to get his bearings. The other side of a wire fence, two hundred metres across a piece of wasteground, was a road. He ran to the fence and scaled it using just his good hand. Dropping down the other side, he crossed the wasteground and walked along the road for a couple of hundred metres, glancing back frequently for the police cars he kept expecting to see bearing down on him at any moment.

None had appeared by the time Ben heard the diesel

rumble of a big articulated truck coming his way. He cleared the rain out of his eyes, stuck out his thumb.

The truck slowed and pulled up at the side of the road with a hiss of airbrakes. Ben clambered up into the cab, thanking the driver for stopping and doing his best to hide the bloody bandage with the sleeve of his T-shirt.

'Travellin' light, mate,' the driver said in English with a grin and a strange look as he pulled away and the truck picked up speed. His accent was strongly South African.

Ben looked at the guy in the dim cab lights. Early-to-mid-forties, scraggy, hollow-cheeked and unshaven, with greasy sandy hair tied back under a flat cap.

'Name's Jan,' the driver said, putting out his hand. 'Jan the man.'

'*No comprendo Inglese,*' Ben said. He didn't take the hand.

Jan shrugged and withdrew his hand, then gave another knowing grin and winked exaggeratedly. 'That's all right, mate. No hard feelings. You don't have to pretend with me, know what I mean?' He laughed, flicked the windscreen wiper lever and the wipers stepped up a notch, batting away the pouring rain.

Ben said nothing.

'I recognised you right away,' Jan said. 'Never forget a face, that's me.' He tapped a finger against his temple. The grin was etched on his lips as if someone had carved it with a blade. Maybe somebody had, Ben thought. He wondered whether he could break the guy's neck and take over at the wheel without needing to stop the truck to do it.

'Hey, I'm not gonna *report* you, man,' Jan said, wrinkling his nose as if this was the most distasteful idea imaginable.

'No?'

'Ha! You do speak English. Gave yourself away there, mate.

291

Nah, I'd never shop you to the fuckin' pigs.' Jan spat somewhere onto the cab floor. 'We're cool, you know? Not enough of us around. See?' He jerked up the sleeve of his grimy T-shirt and Ben saw the faded, crudely tattooed compass rose insignia on his withered arm. It was the emblem of the South African Special Forces Brigade. It looked fake to Ben. In his experience, the guys who really had been in Special Forces were those who didn't talk about it.

'We fear naught but God,' Jan said, quoting the SASFB official motto. 'Angola, '82. I was there, man. We kicked some kaffir arse, let me tell you.' The laugh again. 'Those were the days, man. I left South Africa after the fuckin' kaffirs took over in '94. Now I have to drive these fuckin' tractors for a living.' He gave a loud snort. 'But hey, man. Imagine *you* gettin' in my truck.' He thumped his fist on the horn, twice. 'Unbe-*fuckin*-lievable, eh? Must be fate, or what? You know, what you did back there in Rome was sweet. You ask me, we ought to be droppin' the hammer on a lot more of these politician bastards. If we'd had more guys like you, guys with bollocks, we'd still have a country back home instead of a fuckin' zoo, know what I mean? Jesus fuckin' H Christ.'

Ben sank back in his seat. Maybe tearing Jan's windpipe out through his mouth would have to wait until he felt a little stronger. 'You have a first aid kit on board this thing?'

'I can abso-fuckin-lutely do better than that,' Jan said, reaching down between his knees for a green moulded plastic case. 'You catch one back there, yeah? I saw the fuckin' lights, man. What the fuck?'

Ben took the case and opened it.

'Jan the man's personal survival kit,' Jan said proudly. 'Just like the fuckin' old days, eh? Eh?'

There was a tube of codeine pills, a syringe with sterile needles and a vial of broad-spectrum antibiotic, a good supply of bandages, a surgical suture kit and a scalpel. In a separate compartment was a tiny folding stove complete with a cube of solid petroleum fuel and matches, some water-purifying tablets and a packet of dehydrated army rations. Jan must have been reading his issues of *Combat and Survival* pretty faithfully. Everything a wannabe warrior might need for the day he got to live his fantasy. Ben opened the codeine tube and popped a couple of pills.

'So where you headed, bro?' Jan asked.

Ben hesitated before replying. He wasn't wild about divulging his plans to this guy – but under the circumstances he didn't have an awful lot of choice. 'Portugal,' he said.

He'd been thinking about it ever since he'd escaped the warehouse. Salamanca was just fifty kilometres from the border, and Brooke's little rural Portuguese hideyhole wasn't too far on the other side. He badly needed somewhere quiet to lie low, get this injury seen to and figure out what the hell his next move would be.

'I'm takin' this load of shit from La Coruña to Seville,' Jan said. 'I can drop you right on the fuckin' border. Be an honour, man.'

Ben's head was spinning. He popped two of the codeine pills, closed his eyes and felt himself drifting through the void. Jan was still talking on in the background, but he was too tired and weak to care. Once the effects of the codeine kicked in he dozed fitfully, waking every so often to the monotonous rumble of the truck and Jan grinning wolfishly at him. Ben didn't speak to him. Eventually, he fell into a deep, dreamless and dark sleep.

When he awoke again, the truck was pulled up at the side of a winding road in open countryside. The driver's seat was empty. Ben checked his watch. It was after three in the morning. He slipped painfully down from the cab and walked around the side of the truck. The rain had stopped, and the stars were bright.

Jan was squatting in the bushes a few metres away, making no attempt to hide what he was doing.

'Just takin' a shit, man,' he called over, grinning broadly.

'You carry on,' Ben said, and walked back towards the cab.

'I was thinkin', bro,' Jan called after him. 'When I'm done here, you let me take a look at that arm. Get that pill out for you. Maybe you'd let me keep it, eh? Little fuckin' souvenir – what d'you say?'

While Jan was still occupied, Ben took the green plastic case from the truck cab and slipped away over the hill fifty metres beyond the other side of the road. He crouched down in a stand of trees and watched as the South African searched for him, then stamped his foot in anger a couple of times before getting back into his truck and driving away.

Using the stars to set his course westwards and light his way, Ben set off cross-country. After a while, he was pretty sure he'd passed into Portugal. He walked onwards through the night, feeling his strength draining like fuel from a tank, falling back on the old habits he'd learned all those years ago on SAS training marches in the Brecon Beacons. You didn't think about your destination. You emptied your mind of all thought of the distance still to be covered, and focused instead on an object closer by, like a tree or a hill. Once you reached it, you set yourself a new marker, plodding doggedly from one to the next.

The pain from his bullet wound gradually worsened. He was going to have to attend to himself soon, or he'd end up in an unconscious heap in a ditch for someone to find him and report it to the cops. He used that thought to force himself to keep going.

By the time Ben's energy was fading to a critical point,

the first rays of dawn were cracking the rim of the dark horizon and he could see some farm outhouses in the distance. It was in a broken-down barn that he found the dusty hulk of the old Daihatsu four-wheel drive and climbed in. He dosed himself with more painkillers, lit the little stove on the passenger seat and used it to sterilise the scalpel blade. He then removed his improvised dressing, took a deep breath and set about performing surgery on himself.

A bad hour later, the copper-nosed 9mm bullet was lying wrapped up in a bloody wad of gauze on the passenger seat, and Ben had finished cleaning out the hole and stitching himself up. He injected a dose of antibiotics into a vein, then leaned back in the Daihatsu's seat and passed out for a while.

Chapter Fifty-Four

London

Mason Ferris had got to the office before seven that morning and been at the desk in his private office for nearly an hour when his secure line rang. The caller ID said Brewster Blackmore.

Ferris picked up. 'I see we're having little success apprehending Major Hope,' he said coldly, without waiting for Blackmore to speak.

'I'm not calling about that,' Blackmore said. 'I think we may have a problem with our man Lister.'

Ferris breathed out through his nose. 'The park. You know where. Give me thirty minutes.'

Twenty-two minutes later, Mason Ferris had his driver drop him at Canada Gate, the south-side entrance to Green Park, just a stone's throw from Buckingham Palace. He told the driver to circle for a few minutes, then straightened his tie and walked under the gilded gates, making his way through the wooded meadows to the prearranged location. They never met at the same place twice.

Blackmore was sitting on the end of a park bench reading the morning's *Times* as Ferris approached him. There was no greeting. Ferris casually perched himself on the other end of the bench and took out his own paper. He waited for Blackmore to speak.

'It seems that our boy is getting himself into trouble,' Blackmore said quietly, without looking up from the page. 'He was in his office yesterday afternoon when Lesley Pollock walked in on him making a call to someone he shouldn't have. He hung up fast, acted extremely nervous with her, made his excuses and left in a hurry. Hasn't been seen since.'

Ferris remained expressionless as he listened.

'The problem is this,' Blackmore went on. 'As you know, we monitor Lister's phone, as we do everyone's in the department. And we now know with whom he's been in contact.'

Ferris slowly turned and looked at him coldly.

'The SOCA woman. Kane.' Blackmore paused. 'There's something else. Something worse, I'm afraid. Lister's copy of the operation file is missing. We think he's taken it.'

Mason Ferris was silent for a long minute. 'Do we have his location?'

Blackmore nodded. 'Silly sod apparently didn't learn a lot at GCHQ. Seems to think he can give us the slip by going to stay in some backwater hotel in Surrey. Should I issue the order?'

Ferris thought a little longer, then shook his head. 'Not just yet. Let the boy run. See where he leads us. If this goes where I think it will . . .' He pursed his lips. 'Then you know what to do. And do it quickly.'

Salamanca
8.19 a.m.

After a fruitless night searching the city for a fugitive who seemed determined to evade and humiliate her at every turn, Darcey had finally returned in defeat to the police HQ in central Salamanca's Ronda de Sancti Spíritus, where she'd knocked back four coffees and two aspirin before curling up exhausted on a couch in the top-floor office they'd given her.

In her dreams she was chasing Ben Hope. Just as she was about to catch him, her phone rang and woke her up.

'Who is it?' she asked sleepily, straightening up on the couch and brushing a strand of hair away from her eyes.

'It's Borg,' came the whispered reply.

Darcey swallowed, waking up fast. 'You again.'

'Where are you?'

Darcey paused a beat. Maybe she ought to hang up right now, but what the hell. 'Spain,' she said.

'I'm leaving for Paris in an hour,' he said. 'Can you make it there this afternoon?'

'All right.'

'Café de la Paix, three o'clock. Come alone.'

Chapter Fifty-Five

Café de la Paix
Central Paris

Darcey sat alone at a table on the terrace of the famous café, watching the traffic shoot by on the Boulevard des Capucines and the people around her eating brioche and drinking coffee and *bière blonde*. She wondered if this Borg was even going to show up. He was now four minutes late.

Until he did, there was nothing much for her to do except sip on her Orangina and enjoy the Paris atmosphere. There had been just enough time to book into a hotel, take a shower and change into a white blouse, crisp blue jeans and a denim jacket, and she now felt refreshed and alert.

At exactly five minutes past three, a grey Renault Laguna pulled up abruptly at the kerbside a few metres from her table, and a young guy with soft brown eyes and dark hair leaned nervously out of the driver's window. He glanced up and down the café terrace, then his gaze landed on her.

'Get in,' he said in a jittery voice.

Darcey got up and climbed into the front passenger seat next to him. 'So you're Borg,' she said. 'What happened to the headband?'

'Very funny,' he said, waiting for a gap in the traffic. He was just about to pull out when Paolo Buitoni appeared as if out of nowhere, wrenched open the back door and got in.

'My associate, Mr McEnroe,' Darcey said.

'Jesus Christ, I said come alone.'

'My mother taught me not to get in cars with strange men,' Darcey said. 'Especially ones who won't tell me who the fuck they really are.' She slipped out her Beretta from under her denim jacket and shoved it in his side. 'Now drive, and start talking.'

They pulled into the traffic and headed up Boulevard des Capucines.

'I'm listening,' Darcey said.

'OK, first things first. My name's Jamie. Jamie Lister.' Lister glanced down at the gun. 'Listen, would you mind not pointing that thing at me? It makes me feel very uncomfortable.'

Darcey put the Beretta away. 'Just remember it's there. So who exactly are you, Jamie Lister?'

'I'm with MI6. Or was, until yesterday. This isn't exactly the greatest career move for me.'

She raised her eyebrows at him.

'You don't believe me?' As he drove, Lister reached into his jacket pocket, took out a laminated ID card and tossed it to her.

She inspected it, held it up for Buitoni to see, then skimmed it onto the dashboard. 'Where did that come from, inside of a Christmas cracker?'

Lister looked pained. 'It's vital that you believe me. I'm MI6, all right? How else would I have known about Operation Jericho?'

'I don't like all this furtive crap,' she said. 'There are channels.'

'It's necessary. If they knew I was talking to you, they'd kill us all.'

'Forget the them-and-us stuff. Who d'you think it is you're talking to here?'

'Don't kid yourself, Agent Kane. You're not one of them, because if you were, they wouldn't have you raking through a load of falsified evidence. You're just a pawn in a game you don't even know exists. This whole thing with Tassoni is fucked up. They've sent you after an innocent man.'

Darcey exchanged glances with Buitoni. 'Why would they do that?' she asked Lister.

'To get to Shikov,' Lister replied, steering past the Madeleine church and heading southwest towards Place de la Concorde.

'Who's Shikov?' Buitoni asked from the back seat.

'Grigori Shikov,' Lister said. 'He's a Russian mafia boss. High up. They call him "the Tsar".'

Darcey shook her head. 'Never heard of him.'

'You wouldn't have,' Lister told her. 'He's well connected. And very careful. Even his fronts have fronts. For decades, agents have been prying around the edges of his business empire looking for the smallest chink in his armour. Nothing. They can't even get him on tax evasion. He's smarter than Al Capone.'

'Why are MI6 going after Russian mafia? That's SOCA's territory.'

'Not since Shikov branched out into a new line of business. Drugs and prostitution and people trafficking aren't enough for him any more. He's dealing in arms. A very specific class of weaponry, destined for a very specific client.' Lister gave her a sideways look. 'The Taliban.'

Darcey shook her head. 'Unlikely. The Taliban already have more weapons than the entire Russian mafia put together.'

'Not like these, they don't,' Lister said. 'What do you know about the Ka-50?'

'Russian military attack helicopter. Their answer to our Apache Mk1, maybe even more advanced in some ways. Known as the Black Shark.'

Lister nodded. 'Seven weeks ago, a pair of Russian air force Black Shark helicopters went missing from a base in the Ukraine. Inside job. Major bribery and corruption. When Russian military intelligence tracked down the personnel involved, all they found were dead bodies. At this moment, nobody knows where the helicopters went. According to our own sources, we have reason to believe that Shikov has them hidden somewhere. But Russia's a pretty big place. Nobody knows where.'

'And he's planning to sell them to terrorists?'

'That's what the intelligence sources suggest. If it's true, it could turn the tide of the war in Afghanistan against us. Forget hit-and-run RPG attacks, forget suicide bombers. We're talking about a rise of the terrorist threat to a whole new unprecedented level.'

'Hold on,' Darcey said, raising her hands. 'I'm lost here. What does all this have to do with Ben Hope murdering Urbano Tassoni?'

'Ben Hope no more killed Tassoni than you did.'

'So who did kill him?' Darcey said, stunned.

Lister looked at her. 'We did.'

Chapter Fifty-Six

Lister let out a humourless laugh at her expression. 'That's right. Us. The good guys.'

'I don't believe it,' Buitoni said.

Lister glanced back at him in the mirror. 'No? That's just for openers.'

A million frantic questions crowded into Darcey's mind at once. Lister had just shared a piece of information which, if it were even half true, could get them all killed. Part of her wished she'd never heard it; the other part wanted to hear more.

'Keep talking,' she said.

Lister talked fast as he drove. The Laguna was in thick traffic circling the Place de la Concorde, with the Champs Élysées to their right. 'OK. Tassoni's public face is pretty well documented. Born into a wealthy, influential family in 1956. Successful, handsome, charismatic, destined from the start to be a major player, one way or another. What the public don't know is that Tassoni was connected to organised crime, going back years. Italian mafia, Russian mob, you name it, but none of it ever proved. As far as we can tell, he first ran into Grigori Shikov in Moscow back in the late seventies, as a young guy heavily involved in the Italian Marxist movement. Those ideologies didn't last long. He and Shikov have

303

been photographed together on numerous occasions since then and are reckoned to be doing a lot of business together. Intelligence services have had surveillance on him for as long as anyone can remember, but he's never put a foot wrong. Not until earlier this year, when he made one mistake that gave our people the opening we wanted.' Lister glanced sideways at Darcey. 'Tassoni liked them young, seemingly.'

Buitoni swore from the back seat. Darcey said nothing.

Lister continued. 'So they didn't waste any time approaching him and offering him the deal. The terms were pretty simple. Sell out Shikov to us and walk free, or else be buried forever by an underage sex scandal. Tassoni was quick to agree. The problem was, not even he could offer anything to nail Shikov down solid. Then, just a few days ago, Tassoni contacted our agents. It looked like the perfect opportunity had finally come up. He said Shikov was planning a heist on an Italian art gallery, and he was giving the job to his son, Anatoly. Real piece of work, that one. He and his gang were going to kidnap the three gallery owners from their homes in the night and force them to give up the security codes. In the end, it didn't happen that way.'

Darcey frowned, working hard to keep up with the welter of details. 'Hold on. You're saying British Intelligence had advance knowledge of the robbery?'

Lister swallowed and nodded. 'It's all there in the Operation Jericho file. The proper file, that is, not the censored version you've seen. My department heads decided to let it play out. The Italian police were never told.'

'This is really fucked up.'

'Keep listening. I don't have a lot of time. It was Tassoni who recruited the Italian team for the job, including his own bodyguard, Rocco Massi. What Rocco didn't know was that he was a stooge. If he'd been arrested and tried to plea-bargain his way out by giving them his boss's name, it would've been buried. As it happened, he got away clean. But what *Tassoni* didn't know was that one of the guys he brought in, Bruno Bellomo, was a deep-cover intelligence agent whose real name is Mario Belli. Are you following this?'

'Go on.'

'If things had worked out, either of two things could have happened. One, Anatoly could have led us straight back to his father, in which case Junior and Senior could be arrested together. Jackpot. Alternatively, if the Shikovs were more careful and there was no direct contact, with Belli's help we were going to pick up Anatoly on his own and lean hard on him. He was a sadistic little bastard, but deep down he was a spoilt weakling who'd have quickly broken down and agreed to give up his father rather than spend the rest of his life in prison.'

Darcey gave a bitter chuckle. 'I just love the way you people operate.'

'Let me continue. That's how it was *meant* to go down. Everything changed when Anatoly Shikov altered the robbery plan at the last minute. Belli could still have led us to him, no problem. But by turning the robbery from a low-key night raid into the full-on daytime heist it became, it allowed a new and completely unforeseen factor to enter the equation.'

'And that factor's name was Ben Hope,' Darcey said.

'Neither side could have predicted a guy like that would become involved. A normal person would have been taken hostage with the rest, or killed.'

'Which was an acceptable risk, as far as your guys were concerned. Collateral damage.'

Lister shot her another sideways glance as he drove. 'Don't look at me like that, OK? I'm just a junior. I don't make these fucking plans.'

'So Ben Hope helped to save as many hostages as he could. I know the story. Or he just made it look that way.'

Lister shook his head vigorously. 'You only know what they want you to know, the stuff that's been allowed into the police report. You don't know that Hope killed Anatoly Shikov with a poker to save one of the female hostages from being raped. And killed, most probably.'

Darcey didn't reply. That definitely hadn't been divulged to her.

'As if that didn't screw up the Shikov operation badly enough,' Lister went on, 'he also apprehended our guy Belli and hung him out of a window. Which completely put paid to the whole plan.'

'So now it's all about containment.'

Lister nodded. 'Simple as that. Tassoni knew too much. Rocco Massi too. They took them both out together, and covered their tracks by making it look sloppy. The initial idea was to blame it on a tin-pot radical environmentalist outfit, ELF.'

'But meanwhile, Ben Hope was figuring out the Tassoni connection, and decided to go and pay him a visit.'

'Which again was completely unforeseen,' Lister said. 'I don't even know how he worked it out.'

'I'll be sure to ask him when I catch up with him,' Darcey said.

'Only this time, instead of messing up the plans, when he turned up out of the blue it offered a way forward.'

'How's that?' Buitoni asked, frowning.

'By framing him for the killing and sending someone like you after him, they regain control. Hope turns from being a liability into a valuable asset.' Lister pointed at Darcey. 'And once you deliver him to them, they're going to use him.'

Darcey blinked. 'Use him?'

'Tigers and lambs,' Lister said.

'I'm sorry?'

'Something my boss said. When you want to catch the tiger, you whack a stake in the middle of a jungle clearing. Tether a lamb to the stake. Then all you have to do is wait up a tree with your rifle. Sooner or later, the tiger will come.'

'I don't think Ben Hope's going to be that easy to catch.'

'You're missing the point. Ben Hope isn't the tiger. He's the lamb.'

Darcey understood. 'They want to use him as bait.'

Lister nodded. 'Shikov is the tiger. They know he'll stop at nothing to avenge his son. They want him to kill Hope, and they want to catch him doing it.'

'Jesus Christ,' Buitoni groaned from the back seat.

Lister whacked his palm against the steering wheel. 'The whole thing is full of shit. It's not what I joined the service for. I can't stand being part of a manhunt against an innocent man. Not just innocent – Hope risked his *life* to save those people. Just like he risked his life for his country, and now the bastards are happy to screw him for it.'

'But you're part of it, Lister.'

'Not any more. Not after this. I quit. Well, not exactly.'

'You just went AWOL?'

'I can't let this happen. Someone's got to stop them.'

'Aren't you taking a risk, talking to me?'

'Bigger than you can even imagine. But I don't know who else to turn to.'

'And you're forgetting one thing. Shikov's deal with the terrorists. If the sources are right—'

'Then the Taliban will be in possession of two Black Shark attack helicopters. I know.'

'Our Apache crews won't know what hit them. Hundreds

of British soldiers will be at risk. All to save one innocent man?'

Lister turned to glower at her. 'My father was a Royal Marines captain. He died in Iraq for his country. You think I want to endanger our troops out there? Shikov's deal can't be allowed to go through. I'm just saying I can't stand by and let things happen this way. I won't.'

'You can't possibly prove any of this.'

'Yes, I can.'

'How?'

'I won't say another word until you agree to help me.'

'Help you do what?'

'We've got to end this.'

'*We?*'

'Please. Like I said, I didn't know who else to turn to.'

Darcey was about to reply, but the words died on her lips as a movement in the rear-view mirror caught her eye. She twisted round in her seat, and Buitoni did the same.

The Laguna had turned away from Place de la Concorde and was heading parallel with the River Seine down the Voie Georges Pompidou. The Louvre was passing by to their left, but Darcey was more interested in the two high-performance sports motorcycles that were weaving through the traffic after them. Their riders were hunkered down low over the bars, passengers perched behind and above them. All four were wearing black leathers, their faces hidden behind opaque visors.

In seconds, the bikes had caught up with the Laguna, peeling apart and drawing up level on either side of the car. The growl of their pipes was throaty and loud. The machine on Darcey's side was so close that she could clearly make out the Kawasaki logo on its tank.

'It's them!' Lister cried out.

As if in slow motion, Darcey saw the Kawasaki's pillion

passenger reach a gloved hand up to his chest. He tugged at the zipper on his leather jacket. His hand disappeared inside and came out holding a tiny black micro-Uzi submachine pistol on a sling.

Buitoni saw it too and was reaching for his pistol. But Darcey acted faster. Knocking Lister's hands out of the way, she grabbed the steering wheel and yanked it a hard quarter-turn clockwise. With a screech of tyres, the Laguna swerved to the right and slammed into the bike. The impact sent the car gyrating wildly all over the road. The Kawasaki went down and hit the tarmac with a shower of sparks, then flipped and slammed down on top of the tumbling rider. The pillion passenger somersaulted into a parked Volkswagen with a bone-shattering crunch that Darcey heard even over the roar of the car's engine.

'Please,' Lister moaned. 'Don't let them kill me.'

'Shut up and drive.' Darcey aimed her Beretta at the weaving second bike. Before she could get off a shot, the machine's passenger aimed an identical micro-Uzi over the rider's shoulder and opened fire. Bullets thunked through the body-work, shattering the windows on Lister's side. The dashboard and inside of the windscreen misted red.

Lister let out a high-pitched cry. He fell forward against the steering wheel. His foot pressed down on the gas.

They were right down by the river now, just metres from the water's edge. The car began to veer towards it. Buitoni yelled something in Italian that Darcey didn't try to catch as she tossed down her pistol and wrestled with the steering wheel, fighting the weight of Lister's body to keep the car on the road and trying desperately to kick his foot away from the accelerator.

They flashed under a bridge, almost colliding with a slow-moving three-wheel delivery vehicle. The motorcycle came at them again, its pillion passenger letting off another stream of bullets from his Uzi. Buitoni cracked off three shots, but they all went wide as the Laguna veered wildly from side to side.

The road curved away to the left, and suddenly there were trees flashing by between them and the river's edge. Lister's body slumped hard to the right as Darcey took the corner, pushing her back and tearing the wheel out of her hand. The Laguna was doing a hundred kilometres an hour as it hit a grassy verge, went into a violent skid, crashed into the trees, flipped and rolled. It came to a rest on its caved-in roof and lay still by the water's edge.

Darcey opened her eyes. She was suspended by her seatbelt in the upside-down car and covered in blood. The shock of it numbed her for an instant, until she realised the blood was all Lister's. He was dangling from the driver's seat, blood bubbling from his lips as he gasped and tried to speak. The inside of the car was littered with spilled debris. Fragments of glass lay everywhere. Lister's phone charger dangled from its wire, and loose change had showered from his pocket.

'Paolo,' Darcey coughed, trying to twist round towards the back seat to face Buitoni. 'You OK?' She released the clasp of her seatbelt, fell onto the padding of the car's ceiling, and crawled across to him. 'Paolo!'

Buitoni didn't reply.

He couldn't. His neck had been broken in the crash.

Through the shattered car window, Darcey saw the motorcycle pull over at the side of the road just thirty metres away. The pillion stepped off first, still holding the Uzi. Then the rider dismounted, let the bike down onto its side-stand and they both calmly started walking across the road towards the river's edge.

Darcey remembered her Beretta. After a few frantic

seconds of searching, she realised with an icy jolt that it must have fallen out of the smashed window as the car rolled. She tried to get to get to Buitoni's, but it was trapped under the weight of his body and she couldn't budge him.

'We need to get out of here,' she said to Lister. '*Now.*'

Lister tumbled from the tangle of his seatbelt and sprawled beside her on the upturned ceiling of the car. He tried to speak, but all that came out of his mouth was a gout of blood. She could see it was too late for him. He'd be dead in minutes, and that knowledge was in his eyes. He reached out with a trembling hand. Extended his bloody index finger.

Darcey realised he was pointing at one of the spilled coins, a mixture of UK currency and euros, that littered the upside-down ceiling of the car. His fingertip prodded weakly at a pound coin. He was fading fast. As his hand fell away, she stared at the bloody fingerprint he'd left on the Queen's head on the back of the coin. Lister raised his hand again, holding up his index finger. His eyes implored her. *Understand. Please understand what I'm trying to tell you.*

Lister splayed out his hand, thumb and fingers together. Then folded the little finger and ring finger in.

He was making a number.

One. Five. Three.

'What's one-five-three?' she asked him urgently. She glanced back at the bloodied pound coin. Did he mean money? A hundred and fifty-three what? Million? 'I don't understand!'

The motorcyclists were now just twenty metres away. The rider had opened his jacket to reveal a shoulder holster. As he walked, he nonchalantly drew a pistol. The pillion passenger held his Uzi at the hip and let off a rasping blast of gunfire. Darcey ducked as bullets punched through the bodywork and ricocheted around the inside of the car.

When she looked up again, Lister was dead. A round had blown out his temple.

She scrambled out of the car. Gunfire ripped up the ground around her as she sprinted away through the trees at the river's edge.

There was only one place to go.

She ran straight for the concrete bank and dived into the waters of the Seine. In mid-air, she filled her lungs and prepared herself for the imminent shock of the cold water. She gasped as her body knifed into the surface, then began swimming ferociously, driving deep underwater with strong strokes. The water roared in her ears. Bullets stabbed past her, leaving little spiralling trails. She swam harder, thrashing through the water until her heart was pounding and her lungs felt ready to burst.

When Darcey surfaced with a gasp, she was a hundred metres downriver, hidden by the arched support of a bridge. She huddled against the side and watched as the two motor-cyclists returned to the crashed Laguna. One of them tossed a small black object in through its broken window.

Almost instantly, flames engulfed the car. The motor-cyclists turned and started running back towards the bike. A police siren began to wail in the distance. Then a second.

As the motorcycle roared off, the burning Laguna blew apart.

Chapter Fifty-Seven

Northeastern Portugal
A few kilometres from the Spanish border

A couple of hours' rest around dawn had done little to make Ben feel refreshed or any stronger, but the fear of being discovered curled up asleep in the old Daihatsu by a farmer or one of the hands had been all the incentive he'd needed to move on early.

Some horses in a nearby paddock had stopped munching and stared at him warily as he took a drink from a rainwater barrel that was fed from their stable-roof guttering. Then the strange, furtive creature seemed to vanish as suddenly as it had appeared, and the horses relaxed and went back to their grazing.

Through the morning and the early afternoon, Ben had kept moving on foot. Public transport was less risky in the city, where people tended to ignore each other and individuals could lose themselves in the crowd. In country areas folks took much more interest, especially in strangers, and a sleepy railway station or half-deserted bus stop could spell disaster out here. All it took was one curious local to recognise his face from the TV news, and he'd have Darcey Kane and her troops back after him like greyhounds running down a hare. Hitching a lift was too risky for the same reason, and trying to steal a vehicle from one of the villages or farms he passed by was just asking for trouble – and maybe a couple of barrels of bird-shot from someone's twelve-gauge into the bargain.

He kept shy of main roads, keeping to the rural lanes as much as he could and avoiding built-up areas. The effort of the long walk quickly tired him again. His arm was burning in agony under the clean dressing he'd wrapped over the stitches. There were still some codeine tablets left, but the narcotic drug could affect judgement and reaction time; he needed to keep his wits about him as best he could.

Just after four in the afternoon, near the town of Castelo Branco, he heard the chug of an old diesel coming up the road and ducked into the trees as it came by. The pickup truck had seen better days. Its motor sounded like a bag of nails and a hazy blue mist of burnt oil smoke hung in its wake. Behind the pickup was a large trailer heaped with loose straw. Ben saw his chance to gain some ground. It was better than hitch-hiking. The driver, an old man with a face like leather and one deeply tanned arm dangling out of his window, looked too half-asleep to notice an uninvited passenger joining him en route. Ben waited until the pickup had lumbered past, then ran after it, grabbed hold of the tailgate of the trailer and jumped aboard. The straw was prickly as he dug in, concealing himself from any vehicles that might come up behind.

After a bumpy, rattling, twenty-five or so kilometres westwards, the pickup lurched off the road and headed up a sun-cracked earth track towards a farm in the distance. Ben parted ways with it, picking bits of straw out of his hair as he carried on walking. By his reckoning, Brooke's place wasn't more than about another nine or ten kilometres away.

The closer he got, the more he kept thinking about her. The thoughts helped him to forget the pain that lanced through him with every step – but brought a different, deeper kind of pain, a sense of desolation and terrible loneliness. He wished he could call her, just to hear the sound of her voice. He wondered where she was, what she was doing. He trudged on.

Another hour passed. His step was getting heavy, as if he were wading through desert sand, and having to skirt around the edge of a village slowed his progress even more. The heat was stifling and oppressive. Ben wiped sweat from his face and looked up at the dark clouds that were rolling in from the distant hills, gradually amassing to blot out the clear blue sky. His lips were dry and his throat was parched, but he had a feeling that before too long he'd have all the water he needed, and more. A storm was brewing.

Chapter Fifty-Eight

Vila Flor, Portugal

After spending most of the day curled up on the sofa with her laptop and a pile of notes to work on her research paper, Brooke had changed into shorts and training shoes and gone for an early evening run through the forested countryside that surrounded her cottage for miles around. She was on her way back, still a couple of kilometres from home, when the sky turned ominously dark and she smelled the electric burning smell of an imminent storm. As the first rumble of thunder rolled across the hills, she felt the first heavy raindrop spatter on her arm. Moments later, the heavens opened. By the time she came running back to the shelter of the cottage, she was soaked to the skin and shivering.

Feeling invigorated after a long, hot shower, she lightly towelled her hair and pulled on a sleeveless T-shirt, a pair of loose jogging pants she used as pyjama bottoms and for general lounging-around duties, and her cosy old dressing gown. She trotted downstairs, put on some Django Reinhardt and idled away some time with a magazine while her hair dried before going into the little kitchen to start putting together a simple evening meal.

As she padded around the kitchen in her bare feet, the

rain was lashing the windows and the darkening sky was lit up every few seconds by the lightning flashes. These late summer storms could go on for hours. After dinner, she planned to read a hundred pages of the paperback she was deep into, before getting an early night and listening to the wind howling and the rain on the roof. She loved storms. They comforted her, somehow.

Dinner was going to be a rice salad with mixed beans and some freshly sliced tomatoes from the garden. Brooke made a dressing with olive oil, garlic and just a little wine vinegar. She was grinding a sprinkle of black pepper onto it when the music paused momentarily between tracks.

That was when she heard the sound from outside. Brooke looked up from her pepper grinder. *What was that?*

It had sounded like footsteps outside, on the gravel path next to the house. She strained to listen, but then the thunder growled loudly again across the hills.

Maybe it was Fatima, she thought. The farmer's wife could be coming by with some eggs or wine, the way she often did.

During a storm?

Brooke went to the front door, opened it and peered outside into the sheeting rain. 'Fatima?'

No reply. There seemed to be nobody there. Brooke shut the door, then bolted it as an afterthought. She was just about to head into the kitchen when she heard it again – the same sound of shoes crunching on wet gravel, footsteps moving quickly round the side of the house.

A fleeting movement past the kitchen window caught her eye. It could have been anything in the falling darkness – leaves blowing from a tree, or a bird wrestling against the wind. But she could have sworn she'd seen the figure of a man hurrying past.

She caught her breath, stepped quickly across the kitchen and drew the largest of the carving knives out of the block on the worktop. She walked back to the front door. Her heart beat fast and her hand was trembling a little as she slid back the bolt and turned the handle.

'Luis? Is that you?'

Still nothing.

Had she imagined it? It wasn't like her to get jumpy in a storm.

Brooke strode back to the kitchen and replaced the knife in the block.

And looked up to see the face squashed up against the window pane.

She let out a gasp.

The man outside was staring at her. His hair and clothes running with rainwater. His face was wild, plastered with mud down one side.

It was Marshall.

'Brooke – let me in,' he implored. The aggression that had burned in his eyes last time she'd seen him in London had fizzled out. He looked utterly forlorn.

Brooke stared at him through the window for a second, then marched to the door and tore it open.

'What the hell are *you* doing here?' she managed to say through her shock.

'I came to see you,' he replied lamely. The rain was still pelting down around him, bouncing off the ground. The small case at his feet looked soaked through.

'You scared the life out of me, Marshall,' she said angrily. 'Sneaking around like a bloody rapist or something.'

'I'm sorry. I thought you wouldn't want to see me.'

'Damn right I didn't want to see you. How did you know I was here, anyway?'

'Your neighbour told me where you'd gone to.'

'You're lying, Marshall. Amal is someone I can trust, unlike you.'

Marshall hung his head. 'OK, OK, I tricked him into letting me inside your flat, and I went into your computer.'

'You really are a piece of shit, aren't you?'

'Yes. I know. I am. You're right. But I had to see you.'

'I don't want you here,' she yelled. 'I came here to get *away* from you!' She was about to slam the door in his face, then something made her hesitate. The wetness on his face was more than rainwater. He was weeping openly. She'd never seen a man so empty, so defeated.

'All right, Marshall,' she sighed. 'You can come in. Have a shower and dry your clothes, and we'll talk. But you can't stay here. Do you understand what I'm saying?'

He nodded. Brooke stepped back from the entrance steps to let him through. He left a trail of muddy steps on the hallway flagstones.

'What happened to you?' she said, looking at the mud caked down his side.

'Bloody cab driver dropped me miles away,' he mumbled. 'I had to walk. Slipped and fell in this stinking bog.'

'You know there's no access for a car here, you silly sod. That's what the path is for. You should have stuck to it.' She pointed up the stairs. 'You do remember where the bathroom is, don't you? There's a clean towel and a bathrobe on the rail. Go.'

While he was cleaning himself up, Brooke paced in the kitchen, cursing loudly. 'What do I do now?' she asked herself over and over. A shutter banged in the wind, and she went round the downstairs rooms closing them. As she bolted the last one, the lights went out and the house went dark.

'Shit. There goes the power.' She'd been half-expecting it.

It didn't take much of a storm to cut her off out here. She lit candles and placed them around the kitchen and living room. A few minutes later, Marshall came downstairs, feeling his way in the dim light. He was wearing the bathrobe. His hair was still wet. He came shuffling into the living room and slumped on the sofa.

Brooke stood over him with her arms folded and glared at him. 'You know your being here is totally out of order, don't you? You're lucky I didn't leave you out there to drown like a rat.'

'I *am* a rat,' he mumbled miserably.

'You came all the way to Portugal to state the obvious?'

'Don't hurt me. You have no idea how I'm feeling right now.'

'Things cannot go on like this, Marshall. You've got to snap out of this fixation, or whatever it is. You may have convinced yourself that you're madly in love with me, but you aren't.'

His face twisted. 'Speaks the great psychologist. Is that a clinical diagnosis? I'm delusional, is that what you're saying?'

Brooke breathed deeply and tried to sound calm. 'I think you're confused, Marshall. Maybe you work too hard and you're going through a crisis, and now you're at risk of losing everything. Phoebe loves you, you know. You'll break her heart if you carry on like this. And you'll end up with nobody, because the simple fact is that I don't love you. I like you, you're a great guy – or at least, you could be if you started acting more normally – and you're family to me. But I could never feel anything beyond that for you and it's important that you get that through your head. I'm with Ben. And even if I weren't with Ben, even if I did have those kinds of feelings for you, do you think for a moment I could ever betray my sister?'

320

There was a long silence. Marshall sank his head into his hands and his shoulders began to quake. When he looked up at her, his eyes were red and his face streaked with emotion in the candlelight. 'I don't know what's wrong with me,' he sobbed. 'I just can't control my feelings.'

Brooke sighed. He was a pathetic sight. 'I think we could both use a drink,' she said, going over to a little cabinet where she kept some red wine, some glasses and a corkscrew. She quickly opened a bottle, poured out two glasses and carried them over to the sofa. Keeping well away from him, she perched herself on its arm and laid the glasses down on the low table in front of them.

Marshall snatched his up and drained half of it down in one gulp. 'Oh, Jesus, I'm such a wreck,' he muttered. 'I've been a real prick, haven't I? You must hate me. I wouldn't blame you if you did.'

'I don't hate you,' she said softly. 'I think you must be in a lot of pain and I wish there was more I could do to help you.'

'What am I going to do?'

'You're going to go back to Britain. You're going to drive straight to Exeter and find Phoebe and take her away from that course she's on. Surprise her. Take her on a cruise. Jet out to the Bahamas. Look after your wife.'

He nodded slowly, sniffed, smeared tears down his cheeks with the back of his hand and slurped more wine. 'Maybe you're right,' he murmured weakly.

'There's no maybe. As for me, I might be moving to France soon – could be when my contract is over, in six weeks' time. That means you and Phoebe won't be seeing so much of me, and you can seek some professional help to forget these irrational feelings you've been having. Get on with your life.'

'Ben is a lucky guy.'

'So are you. You have Phoebe.'

He started to cry again. 'This is so hard.'

Brooke felt a surge of pity for him. She moved from the arm of the sofa to sit closer to him, set down her glass and laid her hand gently on his arm. He sank towards her, pressing his face into her shoulder, and she held him for a few moments.

'It's all going to work out fine,' she said. 'Trust me.'

Chapter Fifty-Nine

All his life, even before army training had sharpened his skills past imagining, Ben had possessed a strong sense of direction. As a child he'd been able to wander for hours in the woods and fields without ever once losing his way. Years later in SAS operations – jungle or desert or mountain wilderness – his inborn talent for navigation had more than a few times saved his life and those of his troopers. If he'd been to a place once, he could always rely on finding his way back there again without map or compass.

And it was the same unerring homing ability that led him right to Brooke's little hideaway tonight. Even in the dark, sagging with fatigue, his morale all but washed away by the relentless rain and bombs of agony bursting in his whole side with every movement, he remembered every tree like a marker, every rock as if it had been put there to guide him. There was the stone wall bordering her property – and there was the grassy mound leading up to the house. He could see the terrace where they'd spent so many happy hours eating, drinking, laughing; and above it the ivy-framed window of the bedroom where they'd lain together watching the stars.

The shutters were closed upstairs and down, as he'd expected Brooke to have left them when the place wasn't in use. It meant nobody was around. Ben couldn't wait to get inside. A safe, secret shelter where he could dry his clothes by the log fire, shower and re-dress his wound, fill his empty stomach with some of the tinned provisions Brooke kept in her larder, then take some badly-needed rest and regain his strength.

The rain was slackening as Ben walked the last fifty metres up the gentle slope towards the house. Running his fingers along the rough stone wall that bordered the path, he felt for the gap where she kept the front door key.

It wasn't there. He paused, wondering where else she might have left it. He didn't want to have to break his way in.

It was then that Ben noticed the faint light through a gap in the downstairs window shutters, and froze.

Someone *was* here.

Had Brooke started letting the place out when she wasn't using it? She hadn't mentioned anything. Maybe she was letting a friend stay there. Ben felt his plan crumbling into pieces. He gritted his teeth and moved closer to the shutter, taking care not to make a noise on the gravel path. He pressed his hand to the cool stone wall, bent down and peered through the gap.

And recoiled as if someone had stabbed a hot needle into his eyeball from the other side of the shutter.

There were two people inside the room. One of them was Brooke. The other was a man Ben had never seen before.

They were sitting close together on the couch. Brooke was barefoot, wearing her pyjama bottoms and her dressing gown. Her hair was frizzed from the shower. The man's hair was damp, too, and he was in a bathrobe. On the low table in front of them sat a pair of half-empty wine glasses. The room was bathed in soft candlelight.

Brooke and the man were embracing. Not kissing, not

passionate. Just the intimate closeness of two people who obviously had a lot to talk about and were very open with one another. As Ben watched in horror, they broke the embrace and Brooke said something to the man. Ben didn't catch the words, but her expression was soft, her eyes full of warmth. The man looked emotional. He smiled and squeezed Brooke's hand, murmured something to her. She nodded, smiled back and her lips mouthed the words 'I know'.

Ben had seen enough. He reeled back from the shuttered window. He felt as winded as if he'd been punched hard in the solar plexus. He fought for air, bent double.

This was it. This explained it all. The lack of communication between them. Brooke's strangely elusive behaviour of the last few weeks.

She was seeing someone else.

Ben wanted to scream. He wanted to charge inside the house and confront them. He wanted to ask her – why? *Why?*

Wanted to tell her how much he loved her.

But in that moment, he knew he couldn't. He turned and stumbled away. When he reached the path that wound back down the slope, he broke into a staggering run, and ran and ran back through the night, until his heart was ready to burst and he fell to his knees in the sodden dirt, gasping in pain. He reached in his pocket for the remnants of his codeine supply, popped the last three pills and swallowed them dry.

All he could see in front of him were Brooke and her lover sitting there inside the house. The voices screamed inside his head until he couldn't bear them any more.

She's happy with this man. If she doesn't love you any more, that's your fault, not hers.

You chased her away. You screwed it all up.

Ben staggered back up to his feet and kept on running

through the darkness. Branches whipped his face. He stumbled over rocks and through mud, losing all sense of time as he kept ploughing on. By the time he saw the village lights through the trees, he might have been running for twenty minutes, or he might have been running for a month – he didn't know.

Half-blind with confusion, he made his way up the village's main street. He heard the muffled thump of music coming from somewhere and turned to see a squat, stretched-out building with a neon sign and a scattering of cars and trucks and a couple of motorcycles parked outside.

Ben headed that way, and walked into the packed bar. After the stillness of the night, the clamour of a hundred raised voices and the heavy rock blast from the jukebox momentarily overwhelmed his senses. Glancing around him, he ambled up to the bar and perched on a wooden stool. The barman was a grizzled guy with long hair and a Harley Davidson belt buckle digging into his overhanging belly. Ben looked past the guy, saw the whisky bottle on the shelf behind him and pointed.

'*Duplo,*' he said.

The barman hesitated, running an eye over Ben's wet, muddy clothes, then shrugged as if to say 'what the hell'. He grabbed the bottle, set a glass down in front of Ben on the bar and poured out the double measure he'd asked for.

Ben knocked it back without tasting it. He slammed the glass back on the bar and pointed at it. '*Outro.*'

The barman poured another. Ben sank it. '*Outro,*' he said again.

By the fifth refill, the barman was frowning at him. Ben ignored him. He didn't care about anything. Didn't care about the people around him, didn't care about the bullet hole in his arm, didn't care that a high dose of codeine mixed with alcohol could cause him to black out – or maybe just drop dead on the spot. None of it mattered.

His glass was empty again. '*Outro*,' he said to the barman. The guy shook his head. Ben reached across the bar and grabbed the bottle. The barman tried to wrestle it out of his grip. Ben hung on to it, dug a damp, crumpled banknote out of his pocket and flicked it over towards the guy without checking whether it was twenty euros or five hundred. Whatever it was, the barman must have thought it was a decent price for a bottle of cheap whisky, because he let go and snatched up the money before the crazy foreigner could come to his senses.

Ben couldn't feel his legs move as he carried the whisky bottle back through the noisy crowd to the far side of the room. He slumped heavily on a padded window seat, clasped the bottle between his knees and sank his head into his hands. When he closed his eyes, he felt himself swirling backwards through a spinning tunnel of nausea. The thud of the music was like one continual roar in his ears. However hard he clamped his eyes shut, he couldn't close the image of Brooke and the other man out of his mind. He opened them again and took another swig of the whisky.

Some guys at a nearby table covered in bottles and glasses were grinning at him and waving drunkenly at him to come over. Ben shrugged, and swayed up to his feet to join them. He didn't understand all of the conversation that followed, but vaguely gathered that they were local guys out celebrating someone's birthday – Ben had no idea whose. In a swirl of blurred impressions, more drinks came, glasses were clinked and in the midst of a lot of shouting and joking, he found himself switching from whisky to beer. He was pretty sure a full glass got shoved in front of him every once in a while, and he just kept numbly drinking the stuff down. The pain in his arm was completely gone now, but there were other kinds of hurt that no amount of alcohol could suppress.

He felt himself muttering her name. Shaking his head, as if he could make it go away just by refusing to accept it.

'*Quem são vocês falam?*' one of his new friends asked, clapping him on the shoulder. Who are you talking about?

Ben muttered a reply. He said more than he meant to. Once he started, it all came pouring out, until he stemmed the flow of words with another long pull of beer.

'*Ela é uma puta cadela,*' a voice from across the table said.

Ben nodded. Then frowned and looked up as the meaning of the words sank slowly in.

'Bitch whore,' the guy repeated in English. 'Like all the rest. You fuck them and then you leave them. Before they can do the same to you. I am right about this, no?'

A couple of the others were nodding and grinning and raising their glasses.

The grins dropped away radically when the guy who'd said it suddenly dived forward in his seat and cracked the table in half with his head. Drink flew. Glasses smashed on the floor.

Ben had hardly felt himself move. He realised he was up on his feet. Tangled in the fingers of his right hand was the big hank of dark hair that had come away from the back of the guy's head. The guy was face down on the floor, groaning and clutching his bloody face.

There was an instant's stunned silence; then the whole group were leaping up from their seats and the place erupted in fury. Ben saw a punch coming his way and blocked it instinctively. He moved his arm and saw another guy go flying backwards into the wall. Someone else grabbed a cue from the nearby pool table and came at him swinging it like a bat. Ben ducked backwards and felt the wind of it whoosh a couple of inches past his face. Moving around the side of the pool table he scooped up a ball and as the guy came in for a second swing he dashed it in his face at close range. There was a short scream. The cue clattered to the floor, together with some small white-red objects that Ben realised were teeth.

Nobody else tried to attack him after that. The crowd parted as Ben staggered away and tried to make it as far as the door. Then the bar-room floor came rushing up to meet him, and someone turned out the lights.

When Ben woke up, his first thought was that somebody had decided to pull his brain out through his temple with a blunt corkscrew – until he realised it was just the cruellest, most punishing headache he'd ever known. He groaned, and blinked his eyes to clear away the blurriness in his vision.

He was sitting on some kind of hard bench. He could feel vibrations coming up through his feet and against his spine, where his back was pressed to a hard wall. When he tried to move, he found that his ankles and wrists were secured tight.

That realisation cleared his senses and he opened his eyes. The first thing he saw was the unsmiling face of the Portuguese cop sitting opposite him in the back of the police van. The second thing he saw was the short-barrelled shotgun cradled over the cop's chubby thigh, its muzzle pointed accurately enough at him to blow him in two if he tried anything. Not that he could – he could see now that his wrists and ankles were chained tight to the tubular frame of his bench.

'Fine,' he mumbled. 'Be like that.' And passed out again.

Chapter Sixty

The Ferris residence
Kensington, London

It was Brewster Blackmore's voice on the line again, and from his tone it sounded as if he hadn't called in the middle of the night for nothing.

'Wait,' Mason Ferris said. He swung his long, thin legs out of bed, stepped into his slippers and carried the phone out of the master bedroom, out of earshot of Mrs Ferris.

'Who is it, Mason?' she murmured sleepily as he left the room. He ignored her, stepped out into the long, broad landing and snicked the bedroom door quietly shut behind him. Moonlight shone in through the house's high windows. He stood and looked out at the view across London, without really seeing it.

'It's after two, Blackmore,' he said into the phone. 'Tell me something I want to hear.'

'Ben Hope's just been arrested in a village in northeastern Portugal,' Blackmore said, and Ferris was suddenly much more alert. 'Local police recognised him after being called out to a bar brawl. He's being flown back to Rome as we speak, to be treated at Sandro Pertini Hospital before being transferred to Regina Coeli prison.'

'Hospital?'

'Gunshot wound to the arm. He managed to get the bullet out and clean himself up. No secondary infections, but he'd lost a lot of blood and there was enough alcohol and codeine in him to kill a horse. We're lucky we still have him. They want to keep him in for observation for a day or two. That should give us enough time.'

Ferris pondered this latest development for a moment. His plan was back on track. A thin smile traced itself across his lips, then disappeared as his pleasure gave way to darker thoughts.

'Kane?' he said.

'Negative so far,' Blackmore said. 'We've lost track of her.'

'Not good enough,' Ferris said softly.

'You told me to deal with the Lister situation,' Blackmore protested. 'I dealt with it, and I'll deal with this. I'm doing all I can. For all we know, she's dead and her body will wash up somewhere down the Seine.'

'Get it done,' Ferris told him. He shut off the phone and turned back towards the bedroom.

Chapter Sixty-One

Sandro Pertini Hospital, Rome
Two days later

It was almost a relief for Ben when the doctors came into his tiny private room early that morning and told him he was going to be moved to the prison pending his first hearing. Two days spent lying in a narrow steel-framed bed hooked up to a drip, with nothing to count the hours go by except for the changing of the guard outside his door, had felt like twenty. Other than the grim-faced police officials who'd come to formally arrest him and read him a long list of charges and rights, two doctors and four different nurses had been his only visitors. The youngest of the nurses, a waiflike thing from the deep south of Italy, seemed mortally terrified of him; while one of the older ones, a steel-haired matron with the heft of a Cape buffalo, gave him looks of such intense hatred that he was worried about being left alone with her in case she tried to inject him with some lethal drug.

So far, he'd managed to stay alive, despite the tasteless boiled vegetables they were feeding him, and some kind of pulpy grey matter that passed for meat. It was like being in the army again.

The whole time, they'd kept him strictly as far away from newspapers and TV as a person could be. He could only imagine the fun the media were having with the arrest of Urbano Tassoni's murderer. His favourite Italian reporter, Silvana Lucenzi, would be right in the thick of it, playing to the gallery and watching her ratings climb.

'How are you feeling?' the doctor asked.

'Like an innocent man about to go to jail,' Ben said. 'How are you?'

The murderous-looking nurse came into the room carrying a bulky paper bag, which she laid on a chair before stomping over to Ben's bedside and unhooking him from his drip with all the delicacy of a person ripping tail feathers out of a dead turkey. Ben gave her his sweetest smile as she left, then climbed out of bed and picked up the paper bag. Inside were his clothes, cleaned and pressed, and his shoes with the laces removed.

'Damn,' he said. 'Foiled again. I was planning to use those laces to throttle everyone on the ward and then escape out of the window.'

The doctor just stared blankly. Ben walked through to his little bathroom, changed out of the hospital gown and dressed. His arm was still a little stiff, but healing up fine now. When he came out again, four armed Carabinieri guards were waiting for him with handcuffs. Ben put out his wrists for the bracelets, and was escorted from the room. More police were outside in the corridor with shotguns. Among their faces was one Ben recognised. Roberto Lario avoided his eye, looked pensive and said nothing.

The guards ushered Ben out of the ward and down a short corridor to a lift. The door whooshed open, and they all piled inside. Ben faced the door, conscious of the loaded and cocked weapons just inches away. His knees were trembling with the thought of what was happening to him, but he was damned if he'd let them see him nervous. As the lift descended towards the ground floor, he turned to the silent Lario.

'I have to say, I'm disappointed,' he said. 'I'd expected Darcey Kane to make an appearance. To thank me in person for letting myself get caught. That's gratitude.'

Lario looked uncomfortable. 'I don't know where she is,' he replied softly, as if even that was saying too much. Ben wanted to ask him what he meant; but then the lift bell pinged and the doors slid open. The guards shoved him forwards, and moments later he was being walked out into the pale morning sunlight.

A group of plainclothes police agents and armed Carabinieri were waiting by a pair of police Alfa Romeos and a bulky white prison van staffed by uniformed security staff. The van's rear doors were open, revealing a stark interior that consisted of two facing steel benches, sheet metal walls and ceiling. No seatbelts. Ben guessed the Italian prison service were concerned about inmates strangling themselves, or each other, in transit. Or maybe they just didn't care about them getting pulped in an accident. The windows were barred with high-tensile mesh on the inside, black-smoked glass on the outside.

As Ben was marched towards the back of the van he saw there was another cuffed prisoner waiting to be loaded on board with him. It seemed he wasn't the only bad boy being transported from the hospital. The second prisoner was a stocky, dark-haired guy of about thirty. He didn't have the look of a hard-boiled criminal. Ben wondered what the guy must have done to deserve being locked up in the back of a mobile cell with a notorious psychopathic killer.

Ben's travel companion remained sullen and silent as the

two prisoners were steered into the back of the van and the doors slammed behind them. It was dark in the back. The steel shell resonated with the growl of the diesel starting up, and then the van pulled away with a lurch. After a moment's pause at the gates, they drove out into the streets of Rome.

Chapter Sixty-Two

With the doors shut, the inside of the prison van quickly turned into an airless sweatbox under the Rome sun. It was a jarring, jolting ride, and Ben steadied himself as best he could against the bare metal wall, trying to keep his mind blank of thoughts of where they were taking him and the fate that awaited him.

Nobody had even mentioned a lawyer yet. No phone calls, no contact with the outside world. Jeff Dekker at Le Val must be tearing the world apart trying to find out what was going on.

And Brooke . . . she'd know, too. She'd know that Ben had been caught just a few kilometres from her place in Portugal. Would she guess that he knew her secret? That he'd seen her there with . . . with whoever this guy was?

What am I going to do, Ben asked himself. If he ever got out of this mess, could he even bear to see her again? Did he want to hear what she had to tell him? Should he just try to forget that the last few months had ever happened? He had no answers. He felt lost, and so very alone.

The prison van must have been on the road for some twenty minutes when a sudden violent swerve sent Ben and his travelling companion sprawling across the bare metal seats. Ben was about to say something when he heard the sound of gunfire outside – a ragged string of single shots cracking off somewhere behind the van, followed by a long sustained burst. The two of them dived for the floor as a flurry of percussive impacts clanged against the flank of the vehicle. But Ben quickly sensed that the prison van wasn't the principal target of whoever was doing the shooting.

The van was suddenly rocked in the shockwave of a huge explosion that was deafening even from inside. Something other than bullets cannoned off its side: flying pieces of whatever it was that had just been blown apart nearby. The van went into a skid, its tyres shrieking as the wheels locked, then hit something solid. With nothing to hold on to, Ben and his companion were hurled forwards, hit the sheet metal partition separating them from the cab, and sprawled to the floor.

A second explosion boomed out. Ben smelled the acrid stink of burning fuel and plastic. They heard the front doors of the van opening, the sounds of men yelling. Then more shots, and yells turned into screams.

Then, as suddenly as it had started, the shooting stopped. Ben turned towards the van's rear doors as he heard running footsteps and more voices. They weren't Italian.

He hadn't heard the sound of the Russian language since that day in the art gallery.

The voices were drowned out by a final blast of gunfire from right behind the van, a ripping flurry of bullets chewing through the locks. The doors flew open. Sunlight flooded into the back of the van.

Two men stood framed in the open door, holding stubby black submachine guns. From the cold efficiency in the guy's eyes, Ben could tell that the one on the left had done this kind of thing before. Ex-military, a gun for hire.

The one on the right, with the buzz-cut hair, who looked

as if he'd had his face torn off and stitched back together with a nail and string – he was different. This wasn't just a job for him. If a shark could smile, it would have contemplated its next meal the way the guy was looking at Ben right now. He jerked the barrel of his SMG. 'Get out,' he said in guttural English.

Ben guessed it was meant for him. Big surprise. He stood up, keeping his head ducked low, stepped towards the back door and jumped out.

The guy with the scar shouldered his weapon, and before Ben could react, he fired a single shot into the back of the van. The second prisoner's head exploded in a red mist and he slumped to the metal floor. The scarred guy's companion unholstered a pistol and aimed it at Ben's heart. There wasn't much Ben could do but stare at the scene around him.

What must have been a normal street on the edge of Rome just moments earlier now resembled a scene from Kosovo at the height of the Bosnian war. The two police Alfas that had been escorting the prison van were burning wrecks. One car was lying roofless and twisted on its side, flames pouring out. A charred arm sticking out of the driver's window was all that remained of the cops inside. The other car was buried under the front of the van, crumpled and blackened like a Coke can tossed in a fire. The bodies of the van driver and prison guards were littered bloodily across the road.

They weren't alone. Through the smoke, Ben could see at least half a dozen dead passers-by strewn about the pavements, cut down as they went about their business. A taxi was stopped in the road, its horn stuck and blaring. The inside of its shattered windscreen was smeared with blood.

One of the Carabinieri had obviously managed to leap clear of his car before it exploded. Not clear enough. He was crawling pitifully away from the burning wreckage, dragging himself with bloody fingers. His legs were ablaze.

Six men had done all this in under a minute. Four of them were heading back in a group towards a big black Mitsubishi SUV nearby, carrying automatic weapons and a couple of ex-Soviet rocket-propelled grenade launchers. As they passed the burning cop, the tallest of the men casually shot him in the back of the head. It wasn't meant as an act of kindness. One of the others let out a laugh.

The badly-scarred Russian shoved Ben roughly towards the Mitsubishi. 'Walk,' he said.

Ben walked. The hijackers didn't even seem to be in a hurry as they climbed aboard the seven-seater SUV. Ben was bundled in the middle of the centre row with the pistol still aimed at his heart. The man with the scar sat beside him. He gave a command to the driver in Russian, and the Mitsubishi took off.

Chapter Sixty-Three

The Mitsubishi's driver was fast and skilful. Ben sat quietly among his captors with his cuffed hands in his lap as the car sped away from the scene of the hijack and headed for the city's outskirts. A couple of Carabinieri vehicles flashed by in the opposite direction, but nobody came after them.

Beyond Rome's outer fringe of suburbs and used car lots, furniture superstores and discount warehouses, the Mitsubishi passed through a dilapidated iron gateway, crossed the weed-strewn concrete forecourt of a dingy industrial building that looked like a disused factory or packing plant, and drove inside. The SUV's engine boomed in the empty building, then died. The six men climbed down from the vehicle and hauled Ben out at gunpoint.

The abandoned building smelled of urine and decay. The place was scattered with empty bottles and other debris left behind by itinerant homeless people. Rays of sunlight shone in through tall, grimed windows. A pair of pigeons flapped about among the rusty iron roof girders, their wing-beats echoing in the huge, empty space. The only furniture in the building was a cracked plastic office chair that sat alone in the middle of the concrete floor. The scarred man shoved Ben over to it. 'Sit.'

Ben figured that unless he was going to try and take down

six heavily-armed men with his wrists cuffed together, he might as well sit down.

The scarred man motioned to one of his crew, the tall one who'd executed the burning cop earlier. The tall guy approached Ben with a grin and crouched down. He grabbed one of Ben's feet and yanked off one of his laceless shoes, then the other, and tossed them over to his boss.

'First place we look,' the scarred man said in his guttural English. 'Then we look other places.' He propped his weapon against a concrete pillar. Holding Ben's left shoe by its toecap, he smashed the heel hard against the pillar's edge, two, three, four times, until the shoe's heel broke apart. He inspected it, then did the same with the other. Ben watched, confused, as the right heel fell off to reveal a hollow compartment inside. The man dug his fingers inside, pulled out a small black device, and the mass of scar tissue crinkled into a mirthless smile.

Ben stared at the thing that had been in his shoe. How long had he been walking around with a GPS tracker attached to him?

'They are not so smart,' the scarred man said, tossing it away. 'We have jammer.'

They, Ben thought. Whoever *they* were.

The man walked up to him. 'Nobody can find you here, Mister Ben Hope. Now we have business.'

Ben knew there wasn't much point in playing the 'you've got the wrong man' card. Not when he was Italy's most overexposed celebrity of the moment.

'Let me guess,' he said. 'You've just found out the Goya you and your boys stole is a fake, and you want to know where the real one is.'

The man snorted. 'We do not care about the Goya. The Goya is shit.'

'But you still thought it was worth killing for.'

341

'You know nothing. You are ignorant man. You know who I am?'

'Someone who stuck his face in a combine harvester.'

The scarred man slapped Ben hard across the face. 'My name is Spartak Gourko. Spetsnaz, Russian Special Forces. Now private contractor.'

Ben had a feeling he knew what was coming next. Anatoly Shikov hadn't bought that Spetsnaz ballistic knife from a mail-order catalogue.

'And I was friend of someone you kill,' Gourko said. 'I know Anatoly for many years. Now he is gone. This makes me very sad.'

Ben's cheek was burning fiercely from the slap. 'I'm glad I killed him. He was a piece of shit and he had it coming.'

Gourko's face hardened, the patchwork of gristle across his jaw pulling tight. 'For this you must die. You die slow and in lot of pain. I wanted you to know this. But you will not die now. I must let you live.'

'That's considerate of you,' Ben said.

'You think you are tough guy?'

'I've known tougher.'

'You will not be so tough when my boss is going to work on you. Grigori Shikov is not gentle man like me.'

'I take it we're going on a trip, then,' Ben said. 'I'm guessing east.'

Gourko nodded. 'First there is matter to take care of. You have taken away the son of Grigori Shikov, and for this he will take away your life. But you have also hurt me. You have taken away my friend. And so now I will hurt you.' He shrugged, as though this were the most straightforward and reasonable thing in the world.

The men were grinning. Ben ran his eye along the row of gun muzzles, wondering if there was some way to disarm

342

five men and shoot them all without getting pumped full of bullets himself. Nothing leaped immediately to mind.

Gourko went on. 'You will be . . .' He paused, searching for the right term. 'Mutilated.' He seemed to enjoy the sound of it. 'You understand this word, "mutilated"?'

'I only have to look at you,' Ben said.

Gourko pointed at the tall guy who had removed Ben's shoes. 'But Maxim will keep you alive for Grigori. Maxim is expert medic. He put my face back together after grenade. Make me pretty again.' He laughed, then signalled to another of the men. The guy lowered his weapon and walked over to the SUV. Opened the rear hatch, reached inside and came out with a pickaxe.

Ben stared at the axe. It looked like it had just been bought from the local hardware store. The shaft was orange fibreglass. The blade was painted blue steel. A long, slightly curved spike on one side. A chopping edge on the other. The guy hefted the heavy tool in both fists, slung it across his shoulder, then reached back inside the Mitsubishi. This time he came out with a blowtorch. It was a heavy-duty industrial model, with a long butane canister hooked up to its pistol grip and a blackened heat shield around its flame nozzle.

'I am not animal,' Gourko said to Ben. 'I let you choose.' He spread his hands. 'Which you choose?'

Ben said nothing.

'I put spike through your body,' Gourko said. 'I pin you to floor like insect and make you wish for death. Or maybe we do some cooking together. You like make barbecue? I roast your balls, your toes, your hands, your face. I only leave enough so that Grigori recognises man he is killing. Maybe you prefer. What you choose, Mister Ben Hope?'

Ben wasn't going to give this man the satisfaction of a reply.

'You cannot choose? Then I choose.' Gourko grabbed the pickaxe from his colleague. 'I choose this.'

It took five of the men to pull Ben out of the chair and get him down on the concrete. His cuffed hands were yanked up over his head. His legs were held out apart.

Gourko walked up to him, taking his time, flipping the axe shaft round in his hands. He paused to set the pickaxe down for a moment to take off his jacket, hung it neatly on the back of the plastic chair. Then his eyes glinted, and he raised the tool above his head. The sharp point of the hardened steel spike paused high in the air for a moment, and then Gourko gave a grunt and brought it down with all his strength. Ben saw it descending towards his body. He struggled desperately to twist out of the way, but strong hands were holding him tight.

The heavy spike came down and hit the concrete with a resonating clang just a few inches from Ben's hip, sending concrete chips flying.

'I miss,' Gourko said with a smile. Another theatrical pause to flick a speck of dust off the end of the spike. Then he raised the pickaxe a second time.

This was the one. Ben watched helplessly as it rose up into the air. He had about three-quarters of a second to come up with a pretty damn good plan.

Chapter Sixty-Four

The pickaxe blade was just beginning its downward arc when a spattering halo of red erupted from the side of Spartak Gourko's head. He twisted away with a scream of pain and rage. The pickaxe dropped from his hands and hit the concrete with a clang that echoed through the empty building.

As Gourko clasped a hand to the fleshy tatters where his right ear had been, another silenced shot caught him in the chest, spun him and slammed him into the concrete pillar. His knees buckled and he collapsed into a heap.

The tall man called Maxim gaped down at his fallen leader, raised his gun and then was sent sprawling down on his back as a third shot punched through his body.

The men holding Ben down scattered. Ben twisted to see where the shots were coming from. He couldn't see anyone – but the hidden shooter could certainly see them. Switching from single shots to burst fire, the sniper took down another of Gourko's crew as the man went for his weapon. A triple burst hammered into the front of the parked Mitsubishi and blew out its lights and windscreen. Then another, and the bonnet lid popped open and water and coolant showered the concrete floor.

Gourko's body lay inert. As his men fled for the exit, one

of them spun round, returning fire – then jerked and fell back with a third eye-socket punched through the middle of his forehead.

Ben was up on his feet. Hearing soft footsteps behind him, he whirled around to see the shooter walking towards him across the factory floor, holding a large black assault rifle in gloved hands. The Heckler & Koch G36 rifle was a weapon Ben would have expected to see in a military battle-zone, not in the suburbs of Rome. It had a hundred-round drum magazine, laser sights and a folding bipod. A highly formidable tool – and it was pretty clear from what had just happened that the shooter knew exactly how to handle it.

The shooter approached a few more steps, the gun held tight to his shoulder, sweeping its muzzle cautiously from side to side. He was wearing a black motorcycle jacket, jeans and high-lace combat boots. The visor of his black baseball cap was pulled down low, obscuring his face. Then their eyes met, and the shooter gave a dry smile.

Ben blinked. It wasn't a he. It was Darcey Kane.

'Glad I stopped by?' she said, stepping over Gourko's body.

Ben hid his amazement. 'I had everything under control.'

'Oh, I could see you were right on top of things. Sorry for messing up your plans. Now, we're a little rushed, so if you'd like to come with me—'

'Where?' Ben said. 'Back to jail? No, thanks.'

She pointed the assault rifle at him. Her gloved finger was on the trigger. 'Let's move, Major.'

'You can call me Ben,' he said, looking down the barrel.

'That's nice, but maybe we can have this conversation in the car?'

'Hold on.' Ben stepped over to the plastic chair over which Gourko's jacket was draped. He fished in the side pocket, slowly drew out a phone and held it between forefinger and thumb so she could see it wasn't a gun or a grenade. He dropped it in the pocket of his blue prison overalls. 'Seeing as you chased them away before I could find out much.'

'They'll be back,' she said. 'Move it.'

With the weapon trained closely on him, Darcey led him quickly back across the factory space, past an old delivery lorry and out through a rear entrance. Hidden among a tangle of bushes and nettles at the other side of the building was a battered Ford saloon van. Darcey tossed Ben the keys. 'You drive. So I can keep an eye on you.'

'What, in my socks?'

'Just cope.'

Pistol shots rang out across the overgrown factory forecourt. A bullet whanged off the wall nearby. Gourko's remaining men had regrouped. They were moving from cover to cover, shooting as they advanced. Ben climbed in behind the wheel of the Ford and fired up the engine. Darcey swung her rifle towards the Russians and drove them into retreat with a long, rattling blast before diving into the back seat.

'Go!' she shouted, but Ben was already there. The van's wheels spun as it took off out of the bushes and went skidding across the cracked concrete. More pistol shots popped in their wake as Ben tore through the gates and sped away.

After a couple of kilometres, Darcey said, 'You can slow down now. Keep it at the limit.'

Ben glanced in the mirror. She was holding the HK steady. 'You're taking a chance,' he said. 'I could crash this thing.'

'Yeah, I've seen your driving. Maybe I'll just have to shoot you.'

'Funny,' Ben said. 'I was just thinking the same about you.'

'You had your chance. Fluffed it.'

'There's always a next time.'

'Dream on.'

'Where are we going?' he asked her.

'Somewhere we can get you out of those overalls. Anyone would think you were an escaped prisoner.'

She directed him for another few kilometres, then said, 'OK, turn in here.'

They were out of the city now, and coming into thickly wooded countryside. The track she was taking them onto led to a secluded picnic area, with a small car park and some wooden tables and benches. The place was empty. Ben parked up in the shade of the trees, turned off the engine and slowly got out of the van. Darcey climbed out with the rifle dangling loosely at her side.

'It's peaceful here,' Ben said, looking around him. 'My kind of place. Somehow I thought you were taking me somewhere with bars in the windows.'

Darcey nodded. 'I could have. But I thought we should consider other options.'

'Like what?'

Darcey jerked open the van's back door, reached inside and hauled out a military black canvas holdall. She tossed it down at his feet, motioned for him to open it.

'Boonzie sends his regards,' she said.

He said nothing, just stared at her for a moment; then dropped into a crouch and drew back the holdall's zipper.

The bag was empty apart from a spare hundred-round drum magazine for Darcey's G36 rifle and a military holster containing a well-worn, well-maintained and fully loaded 9mm Browning Hi-Power pistol. 'Take it,' she said.

Ben looked up at Darcey in confusion. 'What is this?' was all he could say.

'Peace of mind,' she said simply.

Ben thought back to the afternoon he'd spent with the

Scotsman, putting up the greenhouse. It seemed a lifetime ago. *I have my peace of mind, if you know what I mean*, Boonzie had said. Ben glanced at the assault rifle in Darcey's hands, and back down at the Browning. Peace of mind, indeed. He wasn't even going to ask where the Scotsman had got hold of a piece of front-line kit like the G36.

'Came in handy, didn't it?' Darcey said.

Ben picked up the pistol and stuffed it into the pocket of his prison overalls, at a loss for words.

'Confused?' She smiled, laid the rifle across the Ford's scuffed bonnet, leaned against the wing and took off her shooting gloves.

'Pretty much.'

'I wasn't always with SOCA. I used to be in CO19.'

Ben began to get it. 'That means you did some training in Hereford.'

'And Boonzie McCulloch was my instructor,' Darcey said. 'He was the best. I never forgot him. So imagine my surprise when it turned out he was the reason you were in Italy in the first place. I took a little trip out to his place in Campo Basso yesterday. When I told him I was assigned to bring you in, he nearly blew my head off. But then I told him some other things I'd found out more recently. After that, he couldn't do enough to help me.'

'Things like what?' Ben asked.

'Like the fact that I know you didn't shoot Urbano Tassoni.'

Chapter Sixty-Five

Ben looked hard at Darcey Kane, and could see nothing but sincerity in her eyes.

'I had my suspicions,' she said. 'Too many things didn't add up. Meanwhile, someone was working hard to keep key evidence out of my sight. The way Tassoni's surveillance DVDs seemed to go walkies, for instance.'

'They'd been taken right after the killing,' Ben said. 'I checked.'

'And the whole way it was carried out – I just didn't think you'd have been that sloppy.'

'I'll take that as a compliment. So who killed Tassoni?'

'The people I used to work for.'

'SOCA?'

She shook her head, pointed at the sky. 'The gods. The ones tugging on the puppet strings. The people who tell SOCA what to do, and set me up to catch you just the same way they set you up to take the fall for their dirty work.'

'Why me?' Ben asked.

'Because you killed Anatoly Shikov,' Darcey said. 'Son of Grigori Shikov, the world's most wanted and elusive Russian mobster, and Urbano Tassoni's buddy in crime. They were trying to work Tassoni to get to him. Thanks to Tassoni, they knew all about the gallery job in advance. When it went wrong, they decided to cut their ties with Tassoni and pin it on you, just so they could grab you and dangle you out there as bait. They knew Shikov would send someone after you for revenge. Once he'd taken you back home and had you tortured to death, they'd have something to charge him with.'

Ben suddenly remembered. 'There was a GPS tracker in my shoe.'

'There you go. They'll have planted it there after they arrested you. That's how they were planning to catch Shikov in the act. But I wanted to get to you first. I've been watching the hospital, waiting until they transferred you to jail. I had a feeling the Russians would make their move then.'

Ben thought long and hard. It all sounded ugly enough to be perfectly plausible. Just one vital piece was missing. 'How does a field agent become privy to this kind of information?'

'Three days ago, I met an informant in Paris. A young MI6 agent called Jamie Lister, who decided he still had some integrity left in him. I wasn't sure I believed him at first, but when someone tries to kill me to stop me finding out the truth, I know I'm onto something.'

'The informant's dead?'

'Along with the guy I was working with, Paolo Buitoni. And that pisses me off too. I don't like innocent people around me dying.'

'I can sympathise,' Ben said. 'But what do you want from me?'

'As of three days ago, I'm officially a rogue agent, right there at the top of the hit list. A fugitive, like you.'

'So?'

'So, I thought maybe we could help each other.'

'As in team up together? You and me?'

'You don't have to make it sound so terrible.'

'Haven't you fallen a little low, Agent Kane?'

She shrugged. 'You're somewhat rusty, maybe. Somewhat past your peak. But I've seen worse.'

'Flattery isn't going to change my mind, Darcey. Why should I trust you?'

'Because I'm a wonderful and sincere person and I'm completely on the level here. You have nothing to fear from me, I swear.'

'I've heard that line from you before.'

'Please.'

'I stayed in Italy so I could take care of certain business,' Ben said. 'My business, not yours.'

'You want payback for what happened at the gallery. You want to go after Grigori Shikov. I know that now.'

Ben nodded. 'He and Tassoni planned the robbery together. Now Tassoni's dead. I don't care who did it. All I know is that Shikov is next. And that's none of your concern.'

'Getting Shikov absolutely *is* my concern,' she said firmly.

'You want to catch the big fish? Reckon if you score enough little Brownie points your former employers will let you go back to your old life?'

Darcey's face tightened. 'You think I'm just a career girl?'

'You've been doing a good job of it so far, by the looks of things.'

'Well there might be more to me than you think, Ben Hope.'

'Surprise me,' he said. He could see a glow burning in her eyes, like a storm building.

'You know what the Black Shark is?' she asked him.

'The Russian Kamov Ka-50 attack helicopter,' Ben said. 'Probably the most sophisticated combat chopper ever built. It can run rings around our Mk1 Apache, and it carries enough weapons payload to destroy a city. But I don't see the connection.'

'Imagine those being deployed against our forces in Afghanistan.'

Ben could imagine it. It wasn't a pretty picture. 'So?'

'So maybe I feel I have a moral obligation to stop that from happening,' she said. 'And maybe there are things going on behind the scenes here that you don't know about. Like, for instance, the fact that Grigori Shikov is just about to sign a deal that would put two stolen Black Sharks into the hands of the Taliban. We've got to stop that deal from going through.'

Ben stared at her.

'Jamie Lister was willing to put everything on the line for something he believed in,' Darcey went on. 'To stop innocent people from dying and bad people from killing. And guess what – I feel I need to do the same. I want to do something good. You don't know what it feels like, being used as a pawn in someone's dirty little game. I'd never go back to that again.'

'Believe me, I know exactly what it feels like,' Ben said. 'It's why I left the army. But I don't think you came here to listen to my life story.'

'Will you help me, Ben?' she asked. He could see from the look in her eyes that she meant every word.

'And then what?' he said. 'When it's over? They'll keep coming after you. They won't stop until you're dead.'

In the distance, a car was approaching along the main road. They both watched as it neared the entrance to the picnic area, then passed by and carried on out of sight.

'I know they will,' Darcey said. 'And you, too. It's too late to go back.'

'You might be right,' he said.

'We're together in this, Ben, whether we choose it or not.' Darcey's face relaxed a little. 'Besides, you need me more than you think you do.'

He smiled. 'Really? I need you?'

'Look at you, for Christ's sake. You won't make it three kilometres looking like that. You don't even have any shoes.'

Ben glanced down at himself. The blue overalls were streaked with dirt and torn where he'd been struggling against the Russians. One of Darcey's bullet hits had left a conspicuous blood spatter across his chest and shoulder. His socks had worn through from running over the rough concrete forecourt earlier, and the grass was prickling his feet through the holes.

'Think you can find me something to wear without getting caught?' he said.

'Says the man who gets himself nicked for bar-room brawling. I'll manage. So is that a yes?'

'All right. But we do this my way. And you have to call me Sir.'

She grinned. 'Go fuck yourself.'

'Well, maybe that part's negotiable.' Ben picked up Boonzie's G36 rifle, stuffed it back in the holdall, zipped the bag shut and slung it in the van. 'Do you have any money?'

'Not much,' she admitted.

'Where'd you get the vehicle?'

'Stole it.'

'I have some cash,' he said. 'It's in my bag, in a locker.'

'At the airport. I know. I watched you put it there. Then let's go.' Darcey climbed in the driver's side. 'You'd better ride in the back.'

'We'll have to ditch this thing afterwards,' he said, climbing in next to the holdall and slamming the back doors shut behind him. 'We can take a train to Monaco.'

Darcey twisted the ignition. 'Tuxedos, roulette tables, superyachts. Wasn't quite what I had in mind.'

'Nor me,' Ben said. 'Not really my style. I was thinking about visiting an old lady there.'

'See, now, that's much more like it. An old lady.'

'Her name's Mimi Renzi,' Ben said. 'And I'm pretty certain she has something interesting to tell us.'

Chapter Sixty-Six

Ben waited, hidden in the back of the van and impatient to get out of his prison overalls, while Darcey did the rounds of a street market in one of Rome's many little squares. She came back a quarter of an hour later with a pair of white training shoes, jeans and a T-shirt, as well as the biggest pair of sunglasses she'd been able to find and a cheap designer version of a military fatigue hat in desert camo. Ben held out the T-shirt. Its glittery logo proclaimed 'Yeah, Baby!'.

'That's the last time I send you shopping for me,' he said. 'I'm going to look like an idiot in these things.'

She pointed at the crowds of tourists milling around the piazza. 'You want to blend in, don't you? Now hurry up and get changed. I won't look.'

She only took two little peeks as he peeled off the prison overalls and started pulling on the clothes she'd got him. 'Who is this Mimi Renzi?' she asked.

'The former maid and longtime companion of the artist Gabriella Giordani,' Ben said. 'Before all this happened with Tassoni, she tried to get in touch with me. Said she had something important to tell me. I don't know what, and I didn't care at the time, but now I want to find out.'

Darcey frowned. 'And this is relevant because . . .?'

As Ben finished dressing and laced up the training shoes, he ran quickly through what he knew about the counterfeit Goya. 'My bet is that the real artist was Gabriella Giordani herself. Back when she was a young countess, she had to paint in secret because her husband didn't allow it. I think she forged 'The Penitent Sinner' – maybe for money, maybe just for the hell of it. Pride in her skill or something. I don't know. The point is, Shikov sent his son to steal it even though he knew it was a fake. His man Gourko told me as much before you crashed the party.'

'Why would he do that?'

'Only one possible reason,' Ben said, tucking the Browning into the waistband of his new jeans. 'There's something about that sketch. Something that goes way beyond any inherent value it could have, even if it was genuine. When I talked to Pietro De Crescenzo in Salamanca, he couldn't come up with any ideas. But I have a feeling Mimi knows. And I have a feeling it's going to help lead us to Shikov.' He pulled the floppy rim of the fatigue hat down low over his face, and clambered into the front passenger seat.

'Very nice,' Darcey said, glancing him up and down. 'A definite improvement. Though I have to say, those overalls really brought out the colour of your eyes.'

'Please,' Ben said, and slipped the sunglasses over them.

They made it out of Rome and southwards to Fiumicino without an army of Carabinieri coming after them. Leaving the Ford on the far side of the car park, they merged with the crowds funnelling inside the airport building. A newspaper stand in the lobby was screaming with the latest reports of the dramatic shootout in the streets of Rome and the disappearance of Urbano Tassoni's killer as his armed gang sprung him from police custody.

'You just can't stay out of the news, can you?' Darcey said. Ben didn't reply. Security cameras watched them from all sides, and it felt as if every one of them was staring right at them as they crossed the busy lobby. Ben tried not to worry about them, and fretted instead that some resourceful cop going through his things after his arrest might have figured out what the little key tagged '187' was for. At the enquiries desk he did his best rendition of a hapless British tourist who'd lost his wallet with his luggage locker key inside. Darcey handed over the ten euro fine, the attendant went to fetch a duplicate key, and suddenly Ben had one less thing to worry about. Five minutes later he had his old green canvas bag slung over his shoulder, still containing his wallet and cash, and they were heading back towards the car.

Forty-seven minutes after that, shortly before midday, they parked the stolen Ford for the last time near Stazione Termini, Rome's main railway station. After pressing nervously through the crowds under the watchful eye of armed police, Ben bought tickets and they boarded a Trenitalia express heading for Milan and connecting to the Riviera train service to Monaco.

'First class,' Darcey noted as they found their seats, which faced across a table by the window. 'You wouldn't be trying to impress me, Ben Hope?'

Ben dumped his green bag on the seat next to his and shoved the holdall under the table. 'Don't flatter yourself. First's quieter. I'd prefer to stay away from crowds right now.'

After a few minutes, the train pulled away. Nobody else had boarded their carriage. Ben leaned back in his seat, watched the outskirts of Rome flash by through the window, and closed his eyes as the clatter of the tracks settled into that same steady, hypnotic rhythm that he'd found relaxing ever since childhood. His thoughts swam for a while.

Then some instinctual sense made him open his eyes suddenly, and he saw Darcey watching him across the table.

'I thought you were sleeping,' she said.

'I can't sleep with you staring at me. I can feel it.'

'I was thinking about you and Boonzie,' she said. 'He's been following the news and really worrying about you. If I hadn't threatened him with all manner of dire consequences, he'd have been out here like a flash to be with you in person.' She paused, and added, 'He loves you like a son, you know.'

Ben grimaced. 'First you disturb me, then you embarrass me. This is going to be a great journey.'

'A long lost son, from the sound of it,' Darcey went on. 'Seems you don't keep in touch with your old friends much. You're a bit of a rolling stone, aren't you, Major Hope?'

'I told you, don't call me Major Hope,' Ben said. 'He's ancient history. I'm just Ben, all right?'

'Tell me about Dr Marcel.'

'What do you know about Brooke?' Ben said. He felt his face flush as he said it.

'Jeff Dekker told me you were on your way to London to see your girlfriend. Brooke *is* your girlfriend, isn't she?'

Ben stared out of the window.

'She's very attractive,' Darcey said. 'I saw her photo on your website. Love that whole pre-Raphaelite look, with the curly red hair.'

'It's auburn,' Ben muttered without looking at her.

'How come she wasn't expecting you in London?' Darcey asked.

He glared at her. 'Jesus, you're like a pit bull with these questions.'

'Just that it seemed to me that if she'd known you were on your way to see her, she'd have stayed put. She appears to have gone off somewhere.'

'Portugal,' Ben said. As it came out, he heard the sigh in his voice and wished he'd kept his mouth shut.

'You don't want to talk about her, do you? Raw nerve?'

'That's very perceptive of you. So yes, I'd appreciate it if you could either change the subject or shut up.'

Darcey smiled. 'Ah. I think I get it now.'

He looked at her sharply. 'Get what?'

'The answer to a question I've been asking myself ever since I heard you'd been arrested. How a guy good enough to get away from me twice could have been stupid enough to get himself picked up for drunken brawling in some bar-room.'

'It's so unusual for people to get away from you?'

'Never happened before,' she said. 'Kind of got under my skin.'

'So what's your expert analysis, Commander Kane?' Ben snapped.

'You and she met up in Portugal. What happened between you? Lovers' tiff? That's why you got so boozed up. Next thing, picking fights with the local lads.'

Ben looked away. He gazed at a farm that was rolling by in the distance. The fields and orchards looked peaceful. He suddenly felt a great yearning to be there, strolling in the long, waving grass under the late summer sun.

'I'm sorry,' Darcey said, noticing his expression. 'I didn't mean to upset you.'

'She has a place there,' Ben said quietly after a long pause. 'Isolated, quiet. Somewhere to lie low, hide out. I didn't know she'd be there.'

Darcey watched him closely, reading his thoughts. 'She wasn't alone, was she? That's what this is about.'

Ben frowned. 'Can we stop talking about this now, please?' He leaned his head back and shut his eyes.

*　　*　　*

360

The train rumbled on. Darcey sat and watched Ben's body relax slowly and in stages, as if it was a struggle for him to give in to sleep. After a while he was completely still, breathing slowly, his head nestled against the patterned cloth of the seat, rolling gently with the movement of the train. She studied his face, the faint lines around the eyes, the way his thick fair hair fell across his brow. There was a serenity about him as he slept that almost made her want to reach out to him and stroke his cheek.

'Darcey, Darcey,' she muttered under her breath. She looked at her watch. They were still an hour out from Milan. She got up from her seat and wandered down the length of the train to stretch her legs and fetch a coffee from the buffet car. None of the carriages were packed. On the way back, she spotted a newspaper lying discarded on an empty seat. A British paper, she noticed – a copy of that day's *Daily Telegraph*. She picked it up.

Ben was still fast asleep when Darcey returned to her seat. She sipped her coffee and spread the paper out on the table. 'Tassoni killer still on the loose' was becoming old news now in the UK media, as they sought to divert their readers' attention to a breaking scandal of some ageing former pop idol who'd been caught allegedly grooming twelve-year-old girls for sex via the Internet. Darcey flipped overleaf.

And stopped, staring at the photo of the young man smiling up at her from the page.

It was Jamie Lister. The headline shouted: 'Civil Servant Slain in Paris Shooting'. Darcey's heartbeat picked up a step as she dived into the text. *'French police launched an official inquiry yesterday following the death of junior British civil servant, James Lister, 29, in a brutal attack in Paris earlier this week . . .'*

'Junior civil servant,' she muttered. She read on.

'. . . *speculation that Mr Lister's murder may have been a case of mistaken identity . . .*'

'Huh,' she said. 'Right.'

'. . . *body of a male passenger so far remains unidentified. Police are also searching for a woman seen leaving the car at the time of the incident. French Ministry of Justice official Philippe Roux is urging members of the public to come forward with information that . . .*'

Darcey thought about Paolo Buitoni and her throat tightened. She shifted her gaze to an adjoining article with the heading 'Tennis Club Mourns Loss'.

'"*We here are all devastated by this tragic news,*" said Edward Harrington, Secretary of London's prestigious Queen's Club, where James Lister had been a member for four years. "*Jamie was more than just a popular member and a talented tennis player. I counted him as a close personal friend. He will be sorely missed.*"'

Darcey looked up from the paper. 'Borg,' she muttered.

He hadn't chosen the name at random. Poor Jamie.

Darcey's brow furrowed as her mind went into overdrive. Then a second realisation hit her. 'Queen's,' she said out loud.

'What?' Ben said, waking up.

'The coin,' she told him. 'The Queen's head on the coin.'

'What are you talking about?'

'In the car. In Paris. It wasn't money he was talking about. He was trying to tell me the name of his tennis club.'

Ben looked confused. She ignored him, biting her lip, thinking hard. *Why? Why?*

As she racked her brains, she found herself staring at Ben's green army bag on the seat next to him.

'Oh my God,' she said. 'That's it. The locker. Every locker has a number, right?'

Ben was beginning to catch up. He'd flipped the newspaper

round and was scanning quickly through the text. 'Lister. The MI6 guy.'

'Just before he died, he was trying to tell me a number. On his fingers, like this. A number you can make on one hand.' Darcey struggled to remember, visualising the scene in her head. 'One-five-three,' she said. 'I'm sure of it.'

Ben pushed the newspaper back across the table. 'The man was dying,' he said. 'His brain was shutting down, neurons firing randomly all over the place. I've seen people do strange things in those last moments. You can't always take them at face value.'

Darcey shook her head adamantly. 'This wasn't just a brainstorm, some kind of neural meltdown. He looked right at me. He was trying to communicate, and he had a specific reason.'

'What reason?'

'I reckon Jamie Lister wanted me to see whatever it is that's inside locker 153 at the Queen's Club in West Kensington,' she said. 'And I know someone who can help us get to it.'

Chapter Sixty-Seven

Arriving in Milan, they bought a prepaid mobile phone at a stall in the crowded railway station. Darcey started keying in a number from memory.

'You'd better be able to trust this guy,' Ben said. His shoulder was hurting and he was feeling irritable. He set down the holdall at his feet.

'I'd trust Mick Walker with my life,' she retorted.

'That's very touching. But not with mine,' Ben warned her. 'Don't tell him where we are or where we're going.'

He hovered unhappily in the background as Darcey's contact answered the call. She spoke fast and clearly. From the way Walker kept interrupting her with questions, it sounded to Ben as if he was concerned.

'I'm all right,' Darcey assured him. 'Everything's under control. But I need a favour, Mick.' She ran quickly through the details.

Picking up the holdall, Ben moved a few steps away and leaned against a railing nearby where he could still listen to Darcey's call over the echoing noise of the station. According to the arrivals and departures noticeboard, their train to Monaco was dead on time and should be rolling into the station any minute. A cigarette would be nice around now, he thought. He missed his old Zippo lighter.

It had taken a bullet for him once, saving his life. Now it was probably buried in a box in an Italian prison service storeroom.

Darcey finished her call and looked pleased as she joined Ben at the railing. 'Sorted. He'll do it.'

'There's every chance they'll have already opened up the locker to pass Lister's stuff on to his next of kin,' Ben said. 'Could be a waste of time.'

'Mick knows he needs to move fast,' she said.

'Even if it's still there, you think this Mick of yours can just stroll into the place and ask them to open up a member's private locker?' He shook his head.

'A SOCA ID can open a lot of doors,' Darcey said.

'I don't see the point of it. You involving this guy, and for what exactly? You risk compromising us for nothing.'

'I have a feeling,' she insisted, with a look halfway between hurt and indignation. 'I always trust my feelings about things.' She paused. 'You resent me, don't you?'

'It's not so long ago you were trying to stick me in a jail cell. Maybe I'm not quite over it yet.'

'That's not what I'm talking about. You don't like it that I'm coming up with the ideas.'

'I have no problem with useful ideas,' he said.

'You know what I think? You're a little too used to working on your own, Ben Hope. Stubborn, grouchy, set in your ways.'

'I can be a team player,' Ben said. 'But I like to know who else is on my side. If I'd known you were going to start bringing every Tom, Dick and Harry on board I might not have let you tag along with me so easily.'

She stared at him, her hands on her hips. '*Tag along?* Maybe you'd have preferred it back in Rome, with that guy Gourko punching holes in you.'

'Forget it,' Ben said, picking up the holdall. 'We have a train to catch.'

It was just after six in the afternoon when they stepped down onto the platform at Monaco station. In the second smallest country in the world after Vatican City, its thirty-thousand-strong population crammed into just two square kilometres of intensely moneyed Riviera paradise, Ben was pretty sure Mimi Renzi wouldn't take a lot of finding. Five minutes later, he and Darcey grabbed an out-of-the-way table in the back of a cyber-café near the railway station, paid an extravagant amount for two tiny cups of espresso, and he started his search.

As he'd guessed, it didn't take him long. An online local business directory listed her as the managing director of a real estate company called Immobilier Renzi. A quick check of the company website confirmed that Signora Renzi had managed the firm since founding it in the seventies, running the operation from her villa in the Les Revoires district of the city. Immobilier Renzi seemed to have grown into quite a little empire over the years, with branches all up and down the Riviera catering for the rich and famous. Even Ben couldn't fail to recognise some of the movie star names on her client list.

'Now we'll find out if it was worth coming all this way,' Darcey said to nobody in particular as their taxi climbed the steep cliff road to the highest point of the tiny city, past verdant gardens and the glittering white homes overlooking the Rock of Monaco and the wide expanse of the Mediterranean. 'If this biddy we're going to see was the companion of Gabriella Giordani back when she was a countess, she must be a million years old.'

Ben kept his mouth shut. He wasn't inclined to argue with

her – partly because of the frosty distance that had come between them ever since Milan, and partly because Darcey's doubts only echoed his own. The worry that Mimi Renzi might have nothing of value to tell them had been growing in his mind with each passing mile. Plus, a lot of things had happened since she'd tried to make contact with him. He was the Tassoni killer now, and desperate criminals on the loose couldn't just wander into respectable elderly folks' homes and expect tea and biscuits.

The Renzi villa was perched high on a cliff overlooking Monaco harbour, set back a long way from the road. It was about four times the size of Pietro De Crescenzo's cosy little pad in Rome. White stone balustrades and columns glittered in the falling sun, and palm trees whispered in the early evening breeze. As they approached the house, a long-haired Pekingese dog barked furiously at them from a gated ornamental garden. A black limousine with smoked windows was parked outside the villa. Someone was obviously home. Ben laid down the holdall and knocked on the door.

The woman who answered couldn't have been much over sixty. Her hair was bottle-blond and she wore too much makeup and a well-tailored jacket with two pens sticking out of the breast pocket. Ben stared at her for a moment. 'Signora Renzi?'

The woman shook her head and informed them curtly in French that her aunt was not available. 'I am Madame Dupont.'

'We're here about a property,' Ben said. 'Signora Renzi is expecting us.'

'You have an appointment?' The woman flicked a disdainful up-and-down glance at him, from the floppy hat to the white training shoes. Evidently, prospective clients did not generally present themselves attired in T-shirts that said

'Yeah, Baby!'. Not unless they'd arrived in a chauffeur-driven Rolls.

Ben took out his wallet, slipped an old receipt from inside, reached out and plucked one of the pens from the woman's pocket before she could react. He scribbled something on the back of the receipt, folded it, then handed it to her.

'Madame Dupont, my name is Don Jarrett.' He motioned at Darcey. 'Mrs Jarrett and I have important business with Signora Renzi. *Private* business,' he added with emphasis. 'Please pass this note to her. We'll wait here.'

The woman stared icily at him for a moment, then disappeared back inside the villa.

'What did you write?' Darcey asked him when she was gone.

'I wrote, "*L'eroe della galleria is here.*"' If he couldn't shake it, he might as well make use of it.

Darcey frowned. 'Who the hell's Don Jarrett?'

'He's a Holocaust denier who lives in Bruges,' Ben said.

'Oh, and I'm Mrs Jarrett. Thanks so much.'

Minutes passed. Darcey paced up and down outside the villa, kicking loose gravel off the paving stones. Ben was beginning to think they'd have to find another way in when the surly Frenchwoman suddenly returned and invited them grudgingly inside. They followed her along endless marble-floored corridors, up a short flight of steps and then out through a set of double doors that led onto a broad balcony. Flowers spilled from pots everywhere. Beyond the elegant wrought-iron rail, the low sun cast a golden light on the sea.

Sitting in a high-backed wicker throne was the most ancient woman Ben had ever seen. She was tiny, dressed in a plain black dress and buckle shoes that barely reached the flagstones. Her hair was thin and white and drawn back under a headscarf. In one wizened hand she held a fan, which

368

she was waving slowly to cool herself. The other clutched a string of rosary beads. A walking stick was propped against the arm of the wicker seat. The old woman's body was withered and frail, as though every organ was on the verge of imminent shutdown – but behind the mass of wrinkles, her sharp blue eyes shone with alertness and strength of will. One look at her was enough to tell Ben this lady was a survivor.

Lying unfolded on Mimi Renzi's lap was Ben's scribbled note. As the French woman sullenly introduced them as Monsieur and Madame Jarrett, then left, the old woman's eyes never left his.

Ben took off his dark glasses and the floppy hat. 'Please don't be alarmed, Signora Renzi,' he said in Italian.

'I speak English, Mr Hope,' the old woman replied. Her voice was surprisingly strong. 'And I do not think you have come here to murder me. Please, sit.' She motioned at a pair of director's chairs.

'I didn't murder anybody,' Ben said.

'I did not think you had,' Mimi Renzi replied. 'The Dark Medusa has always been surrounded by death and pain.'

'The Dark Medusa?'

'She is the reason I wanted to speak to you, Mr Hope.' Mimi put down her fan on the white cast-iron table next to her, picked up a tiny golden bell and tinkled it. Almost instantly, a maid came running.

'Elise, my visitors are thirsty. Would you please bring some drinks?' Elise nodded, then scurried off.

'This is Darcey Kane,' Ben said. 'She's a friend.'

Darcey glanced at him, just a little surprised.

Mimi smiled. '*Enchantée.*' Turning back to Ben, she said, 'It makes me so happy to see you, Mr Hope. I was worried that my message had not reached you.'

'I've been a little waylaid,' Ben said, taking a seat with the holdall between his feet, very aware of the small military arsenal he'd brought into this little old lady's home. 'But now I'm here.'

'Can you spare an old woman a few minutes of your time?'

'I'm not going anywhere,' Ben said.

Mimi Renzi looked pleased. 'Good. Because I have a story to tell you.'

Chapter Sixty-Eight

'I was born Simonetta Renzi in 1912,' the old woman began. 'A very long time ago. I am in my hundredth year, but God has blessed me with a clear memory. Though at times,' she added darkly, 'I wish he had not.'

She gestured about her. 'I did not always live like this. My parents were peasant farm workers, both illiterate, who never left their village to the day they died. I had six brothers. All gone now.' She paused, as though remembering each of them in turn. 'Perhaps because I was the youngest, and the only girl, I knew from the start that the hardship of working on the land was not the life I wanted. At a young age, I taught myself to read and write, and I could sew and embroider beautifully. I was almost twelve when word came around that a local aristocrat was seeking a lady's maid for his new bride.'

'Count Rodingo De Crescenzo.' Ben said.

Mimi nodded. 'I was very mature for my age. Pretending to be fourteen, I presented myself to the count's head servants and somehow managed to persuade them that I was suitable for the position. That is how I first came to meet Gabriella, then the newly wed Contessa De Crescenzo. We quickly became friends. It was she who first called me "Mimi", after the seamstress heroine in Puccini's opera "La Bohème". The nickname has stuck with me all my life.' The old woman paused again as Elise returned with drinks. The maid placed a Campari soda on the table at Mimi's elbow, and a frosted bottle of white wine and a jug of iced lemon water on the side for Ben and Darcey. When she was gone, Mimi continued her story.

'In many ways, Gabriella's background reflected my own. She was born Gabriella Giordani in 1908, to an impoverished upper-middle-class Milanese family. By the time she was seventeen, her father had squandered much of his inherited wealth. All he had left to sell was his beautiful daughter. To help save her family from poverty she agreed to marry this Count De Crescenzo, twenty-five years her senior, and reluctantly went to live on his estate. I remember the house very well. It was a veritable palace, so huge that many parts of it were never used. And it was old, so old that some rooms and passages had even been forgotten. Gabriella took to wandering alone, exploring. One day she came on a hidden passage that led to a secret room which had been unused for many years. After she very discreetly asked the servants, she realised nobody knew it was even there.

'It became her refuge. You see, she was so miserable. Her husband was a cruel man, a weak man who lived in the shadow of his domineering mother and took out his frustrations on his poor wife. He did everything he could to destroy her confidence. He ordered his manservant Ugo, a terrible brute of a man whom we all dreaded, to spy on her; and meanwhile he and his mother would regularly go through her personal belongings, so that she had no privacy. Only her secret diary, the key to which she wore on a neck chain, remained safe from their prying eyes. And only I remained her friend. She and I spent many hours together, sharing stories and dreaming of a time when our lives would be different.'

The old woman sighed and was silent for a moment, deep in thought. Ben wondered what the look in her eyes was. Regret, certainly. Guilt, possibly, too.

'The one true solace in Gabriella's life at that time was her love of art,' Mimi continued. 'But again, the count put a stop to that. When Gabriella decided to apply to the art academy to study formally, she found herself rejected. She was told by the board that she had no talent. No eye either for form or composition, and no possible future as an artist.'

'Arseholes,' Darcey muttered, reaching for some wine. Ben shot her a look.

Mimi went on. 'She was suspicious, because she *knew* she had talent. She grew even more suspicious on discovering that the senior academy director who had most vociferously rejected her, and encouraged his colleagues to do the same, was a close acquaintance of her husband's. Gabriella realised then that Rodingo had conspired against her, to ruin any chance she had. It was not until three months later, when he announced that he was throwing a large dinner party and she saw the same art academic's name on the guest list, that she saw her opportunity for revenge. In the weeks leading up to the party, she devoted herself to recreating a lesser-known work by one of her most favourite artists. I think you may know what work I am referring to, Mr Hope?'

It wasn't a far stretch to guess. 'Goya's "The Penitent Sinner",' Ben said. 'Charcoal on laid paper.'

'Correct,' Mimi said.

'What was the idea?' Darcey asked, sipping wine. Ben could see she was getting drawn into the story.

'The idea was to expose the so-called art scholar who had humiliated her. When the work was finished, I helped her to frame it, as she had taught me. Then, an hour before the dinner was due to begin, while the count was too occupied to notice, Gabriella asked me to hang her sketch on the dining-room wall where it would be in plain view of the esteemed expert.' Mimi's face wrinkled into a smile. 'And the plan worked so beautifully. As the academy director took his place at the table, he suddenly leapt up and let out a roar of delight. "My God, De Crescenzo, you never told me you had a Goya!" Before Rodingo could speak, the academy director had rushed over to examine the sketch up close. "Magnificent," he exclaimed over and over. I was watching through a keyhole. I could see the triumph on Gabriella's face.'

'I like this woman,' Darcey said.

'At this moment, Gabriella stood up and addressed him. "I am pleased you admire it so greatly, sir. For it was not the great Goya who drew it, but one too lacking in talent to be worthy of a place at your illustrious academy." Rodingo was furious. When the guests had departed, he beat poor Gabriella and forbade her ever to paint again. He gave her one hour to destroy every piece of art she had ever produced, threatening that he would do so himself if she refused. As he watched from a window, Gabriella was forced to make a bonfire in the estate grounds. But she did not burn them all. Many she kept hidden in her secret room – including her perfect copy of "The Penitent Sinner".'

'The sketch that people have killed and died for, even to this day,' Ben said. 'What I want to know is why.'

Mimi smiled. 'And you will, Mr Hope. But in order to understand why I wished to speak to you, you must please bear with me.' She paused. 'How much do you know about Russian history?'

Ben was taken aback. 'A little,' he said. 'No more than most people do.'

'We must pause our story of Gabriella and Rodingo for a moment,' Mimi said, 'and return to the year 1903. Back to

374

the days of Imperial Russia, and an aristocrat named Alexander Borowsky. A distant cousin of the ruling Romanov dynasty, Borowsky was also the owner of the biggest gold mines in Siberia, and one of the richest men in the empire. He and his wife Sonja had three children: Natasha, Kitty and the youngest, Leo, born in 1895.' Mimi drew in a long breath. 'And now we come to it. For in that year of 1903, Alexander Borowsky came to be in possession of an object of terrible beauty and incredible value. It would become known as the Dark Medusa. And when I tell you what it was, you will begin to understand.'

Chapter Sixty-Nine

Ben waited for more. It was quiet on the balcony, just the roar of a speedboat cutting across the sea audible in the distance and the murmur of the palms. The sun was beginning to dip closer towards the sea, a shimmering gold disc burning the water.

'A painting?' Darcey asked.

Mimi shook her head. 'Not a painting. But a piece of art, yes. The Dark Medusa is one of the lost eggs created by Peter Carl Fabergé, jewellery-maker to the Russian Imperial court.'

From a forged Goya to a rich man's pointless trinket. Ben said nothing.

The old woman went on: 'Fabergé made thousands of wonderful ornate eggs, each with its own individual theme, and the one that Alexander Borowsky commissioned him to create was especially unique. The prince was an avid scholar of classical literature and mythology. He had read Ovid and Homer and Virgil in the original Greek and Latin, and the theme of the egg was intended to reflect this passion of his. It was so high,' – she spaced her thin hands vertically about eight inches apart – 'made of white gold, encrusted with diamonds, and around its outside were painted scenes from mythology. But the best part was inside. Each Fabergé egg contained a "surprise". Sometimes a fabulous jewel, sometimes a miniature portrait or icon. This one contained a tiny gemstone bust of one of classical literature's most infamous, terrible creations. The Medusa.'

'The lady with the snakes for hair,' Darcey said. 'Who could turn men to stone with just one look.'

Mimi nodded. 'And Fabergé's Medusa had eyes just as penetrating. They were crafted from alexandrite, a rare gem that was known as the national stone of Imperial Russia, named after Tsar Alexander II. It could change colour, from deep red to vivid green, depending on the light. The rest of the figurine was cut from a single bloodstone. Almost black, with flecks of red iron oxide that looked like spatters of blood. Fabergé intended the effect to be striking, even frightening. Little wonder that his creation quickly became known as the *Dark* Medusa.'

Ben was fighting to anticipate where this story was leading. What was the connection between a Russian piece of jewellery and a fake Goya forged by an Italian countess? 'You say this thing was lost. But the way you describe it, it sounds as if you've held it in your hand.'

Mimi gazed deeply at him, pursed her wrinkled lips, and went on. 'The egg was so magnificent that it rivalled even the finest of the so-called Imperial eggs that Fabergé had created for the ruling Romanov family. Completely captivated by its beauty while on a visit to the Borowsky estate, Tsar Nicholas II offered Alexander whatever price he wanted for it. Even in 1903, it was worth millions. But Borowsky was too proud of it, and he told the Tsar that it was not for sale.

'Tsar Nicholas was a greedy and unscrupulous man. Slighted, he sent a gang of thieves to steal the egg one night while the Borowskys were at the opera. Alexander was devastated at the loss. He strongly suspected who the culprit was, and that the egg was now in the Tsar's Winter Palace. But he knew better than to complain. The Tsar answered to nobody and the *Okhrana*, his secret police, had unlimited powers to make people, as well as valuable objects, disappear into the night, never to be seen again.

'So Alexander Borowsky wisely held his tongue. Years passed. Our story moves forward in time to the year 1917. By now, Alexander's wealth was greater than ever. His son Leo was now twenty-two, a handsome and charming young prince.'

Ben nodded to himself. *Of course.* Now he remembered why the name Leo had been tugging at his memory. It was the painting he'd seen in the gallery. Gabriella Giordani's portrait of the aristocratic-looking young man. So this was Leo.

'He was not like so many of these indulged young rich boys we see today.' Mimi gestured across the bay at the distant homes and palaces of Monaco. 'Leo had many accomplishments. He was a violin virtuoso, a published poet, an expert horseman. No doubt he would have distinguished himself at the military career he was considering, when everything suddenly changed.'

'The 1917 revolution,' Ben said.

Mimi nodded. 'Everyone is familiar with what happened next. Almost overnight, Tsar Nicholas was overthrown and imprisoned. After a short period of provisional government, the country fell to the rule of the revolutionary Bolsheviks, under Lenin. The country was plunged into turmoil, made worse by the fact that Russia was in the middle of fighting World War I at the same time. It was a time of brutal murder. The Bolsheviks executed the Tsar and his family. The new secret police rounded up the aristocracy, confiscated their property, their assets, everything. Sonja, Natasha and Kitty

Borowsky were taken and sent to a women's prison, never to be heard of again. Alexander Borowsky and his younger brother were incarcerated in Spalernaia prison, where in 1919 they were executed by firing squad on the orders of the Bolshevik committee. Only Leo managed to escape. Now he was a fugitive, virtually penniless. He fell in with a counter-revolutionary group angered at the duplicity and brutality of the Bolsheviks. One dictatorship had simply been replaced by another.'

'Tell us something new,' Ben said.

'Meanwhile, the Bolsheviks were loading their coffers with booty stripped from the aristocracy. Word reached Leo and some of his friends that the Dark Medusa had been among a hoard of treasures taken from the Winter Palace and stored in a warehouse together with piles of artwork, gold, silver and other valuables. They conspired to steal the egg back. Russia was flooded with weapons from the war, and so it was easy for them to procure rifles.

'The robbery was successful,' Mimi went on. 'And yet, at the same time it was disastrous. Leo and his friends were able to get inside the warehouse. But while they were searching for the egg, the revolutionary guards were alerted and the place was surrounded. They were compelled to shoot their way out. Many were killed. Leo was the only one who got away alive. But he had his egg.

'Now he set off to flee from Russia. He had just enough money salvaged to bribe his way across the border, but it was a dangerous journey. Russia was in a state of anarchy. Gangs of leaderless soldiers were roaming the country in those final days of the war, descending on villages, raping and murdering women and girls while their menfolk were hacked to pieces with bayonets to save ammunition. It was unsafe to travel the roads. Leo did not dare to attempt the journey with such a precious cargo. Too much blood had been shed to lose it to bandits. So he hid his treasure in a secret place and drew a map to mark its location, vowing that one day, when the madness was over, he would come back and get it.

'He was lucky. He managed to flee into exile in Europe, where he found haven among members of the nobility sympathetic to the plight of the Russian aristocracy. He was able to survive, playing on his charm and title and giving music lessons to the children of the wealthy. Then, in 1925, nearly eight years after fleeing his homeland, he came to stay as a guest in the home of an Italian count, near Rome.'

'Let me guess,' Ben said. 'Count Rodingo De Crescenzo.'

Chapter Seventy

The pieces were slowly coming together now. Ben could feel the first dawning rays of understanding poking through the darkness.

'Put a dashing prince into the mix with an unhappily married young woman and her prick of husband,' Darcey said. 'Pretty obvious what's going to happen.'

'Prince Leo could not have been more different from the cold, soulless philistine to whom Gabriella found herself enslaved,' Mimi agreed. 'And yes, inevitably, they became very close. He encouraged her passion for art, and she in turn confided in him that she had carried on painting in her secret room, behind the count's back. They were falling in love, though there was no . . .' Mimi frowned. 'What is the word?'

'Impropriety,' Ben said.

'That is it. There was no impropriety between them. Nothing of that sort. However, Count De Crescenzo did not see it that way. Crazed with jealousy at the growing bond between his wife and their guest, he accused her of infidelity, had Borowsky thrown out of the house and challenged him to an illegal duel.

'Gabriella knew that her husband was an expert marksman with a pistol. The night before the duel was to take place, she sneaked out of the house and went to Leo to beg him

381

not to fight. That was the night she stayed with him. Before dawn the following morning, she told him, "Now we really are lovers. There has been infidelity, and so there is no longer any honour to defend and no reason to fight him." It was senseless to stay and go through with the duel. They could run away together. She could paint, and he could teach music. They might never be rich, but money did not matter. They would have each other.'

'Leo didn't listen,' Ben said.

'His sense of honour was too strong,' Mimi said. 'But he cared deeply for what might happen to her. He told her that if he should die, he had something that would ensure her stability for ever. She would be free to leave her husband and be independent of him. She could pursue her dream, unfettered, for the rest of her life. This was when Leo confided in Gabriella the secret of the Dark Medusa. He gave her the map showing the location of its hiding place. He was convinced that the troubles that had descended on his country would soon pass, and that she would be able to travel there and retrieve the treasure with no danger to herself. After her tryst with the prince . . . this is the right word, "tryst"?'

Ben nodded. 'Go on.'

'Afterwards, she hurried home with the precious map hidden in her clothing. I let her into the house before the count could catch her. We ran together to her secret room, looking desperately for somewhere to hide the map. It was I who had the idea for a hiding place nobody would ever discover. We opened up the frame of her Goya copy. And we hid the map inside, between the picture and the back of the frame.'

'What happened to Borowsky?' Darcey asked.

'At dawn that day, he and the count met at the appointed place outside Rome. From forty paces, each fired a single shot. Leo's ball missed. Count De Crescenzo's struck the prince in the shoulder.' Mimi gave a shrug. 'Honour was done.'

'So Leo survived?'

'In the days before antibiotics, such a wound could turn fatal. He lasted three days. Gabriella was by his side until the end.' The old woman's voice was hoarse from talking. She took another long sip from her drink. 'When Gabriella returned from the hospital, heartbroken and weeping bitterly, clutching a dagger in the folds of her dress and vowing to use it to avenge her lover, she found the count gone and her trunk packed outside the gate. That terrible man Ugo had been ordered not to allow her into the house.

'And that was when I found her,' Mimi said sadly. 'Sitting alone in the gardens, inconsolable. She embraced me. We both wept when she told me she must leave, that she would never see me again. I replied that I would leave too, and come with her. She said to me, "Are you mad, girl? You have employment here. I can offer you little. The only money I will have are the few coins I can get by pawning this necklace and these rings." But I insisted I wanted to stay with her. "And the map," I said to her. "With the map, you could be rich again." Gabriella seemed uninterested. "I have lost my Leo," she said. "But Leo wanted you to have it," I replied. "Let me run to the secret room and fetch it."'

Mimi's voice drifted off. She turned her head slowly and gazed out at the darkening sea for a long moment. When she turned back to face Ben, he saw that her wrinkled old eyes had welled up with tears that spilled down her cheeks.

'I betrayed her,' she whispered.

Ben frowned, but said nothing.

'I went back to the secret room,' Mimi said. 'Gabriella's paintings were stacked against the wall. I found the Goya. I opened the back of the frame, the way I had learned. And then I did something that I have regretted for twenty years, since my Lord Jesus came into my life and I repented of my sins.'

'You took the map for yourself,' Ben said.

Mimi wiped her eyes. 'I was frightened. I was just a child. I suppose I could have simply taken it, hidden it and left. But I was terrified that somehow Gabriella would find out what I had done. There were papers and crayons on a table. I made a copy of the map before replacing the original inside the back of the frame. Then I ran back to Gabriella in the gardens, crying and telling her that Ugo had come and seen me before I could get to the secret room. It was a lie, but the next moment, we heard the dogs barking. Now Ugo really had spotted us. We had to run. We fled to the city.

'Pawning the few belongings that remained to her, Gabriella was able to rent cheap lodgings for us in a very poor quarter of Rome. We took work where we could find it. We cleaned. We mended clothes. By night, Gabriella would paint, driving herself to exhaustion in the hope that one day soon, she would find some small success as an artist. She never dreamed that she would become so successful – or that it would take so many years of hardship before she was able to sell her work. The art world was as ruthless and narrow-minded as it is today, and in Italy it was hard for a woman.'

Mimi gazed into space for a moment, as if reliving the memories. 'She did not find true success until the middle of the 1970s, when she was in her sixties. By that time, I had long since left her. We had lived together as friends for almost thirty years,' she added regretfully, hanging her head. 'And in all that time, I never told her that I had made a copy of Leo's map.'

'When did you go back for the Dark Medusa?' Ben said.

The old woman looked up at him sharply, then let out a long sigh. 'You have understood, Mr Hope.'

'All this didn't come from nowhere,' Ben said.

'I schemed for many years behind Gabriella's back. I learned much about Russia, its history and its politics, even studied some of the language. I knew that the country was impenetrable. Joseph Stalin held Russia in a ring of steel, making it too dangerous for a woman on her own to attempt to smuggle out such a treasure. I would certainly have been caught and sent to die in the Siberian labour camps. So I waited.

'Then, in 1953, I heard the news that Stalin had died. The same year, I took a job in a factory where I met Eduardo. He was three years older than me, a union representative and a member of the Italian Communist Party, which was very strong at that time and had particular links with Soviet Russia. I began to go to political meetings with him, and it was through those connections that the chance arose for the two of us to visit Russia on a special visa. My time had come at last. We travelled to the location shown on the map. In the graveyard of a ruined church near St Petersburg, inside the grave of a man called Andrei Bezukhov, just as Leo had said, it was there waiting for me. It was mine. It was beautiful.' Mimi's voice trailed away to a croak.

'You didn't keep it long, did you?' Ben said.

'We had to be careful. We found a dealer who valued the egg for us, and for a very high commission agreed to be discreet. This took many months. The man who eventually bought it was from Arabia, a sheikh who had made billions from oil. We met in a suite at the Ritz Hotel in Paris on 27 July, 1955, surrounded by his bodyguards and lawyers and the experts he had brought with him to verify the egg was genuine. I can still remember the sheikh's face as he held the Dark Medusa for the first time. The money was in two suitcases. Nine million US dollars in one, eight million dollars in the other. Ten minutes later it was ours.'

'I'm betting the Italian Communist Party never saw a penny in donations,' Darcey said.

Mimi ignored her. 'Eduardo and I never even returned to Italy. The possessions we had left behind were not worth going back for. Instead we moved here, to the Principality of Monaco where we knew our money would be safe from tax collectors.'

'And the two of you lived happily ever after,' Darcey said.

Mimi sighed. 'It seemed like a dream at first. We had been poor all our lives, and now this. Life became just one big party. We had no real friends, but we did not care, as we could buy all the false friends we needed to make ourselves feel contented. Eduardo began collecting fast cars, Ferraris, Bugattis. He bought a yacht.' She prodded her chest. 'By the time two years had gone by, this little Italian woman in her mid-forties was no longer enough to satisfy him. He began to stray. Then when he realised that these beautiful young French girls were only interested in him for his money – that they laughed about him behind his back and called him an old *connard* – he began to drink. One night, when he was very drunk, we fought bitterly. Eduardo stormed out of our villa, got into his racing car . . . and I never saw him alive again. The police found the wreck at the foot of the cliffs the next morning.'

There was silence on the balcony for a few moments. Darcey was sitting with her arms folded across her chest and little sympathy showing on her face. Mimi's eyes were down-cast as she clutched her rosary beads tightly in her frail, liver-spotted fists, rocking slightly in her chair. Ben looked at her and all he could see was a desperate old woman consumed with shame. Her conscience had caught up with her late in life, but it was hitting hard. It was eating her alive that she couldn't go back and repair the things she'd done wrong in her past.

And there was a part of Ben that understood that feeling very well.

'I betrayed the only true friend I ever had,' Mimi sobbed. 'When I had wealth and she had none, what did I do to help her? Nothing. And then, thanks to my deception, in 1986, those men came to her home. And they killed her to find the egg. It was my fault that she died alone and in fear. If we had gone to Russia together to find the Dark Medusa, if it had been sold openly as it should have been . . .' Mimi shook her head in sorrow.

'I believe the men who broke into Gabriella's home were the same that robbed the gallery,' Ben said. 'I think they found something in her house that night. Something containing clues that led them, all these years later, to the Goya when it finally resurfaced at the exhibition. I think it was her diary. Gabriella must have written in it that the map was in the frame.'

Mimi nodded sadly. 'This would explain why they knew to look for "The Penitent Sinner". She wrote everything in that diary.'

'Except where the hidden room was,' Ben said. 'That much remained a secret.' He paused. 'Mimi, I should tell you that the person behind this is a Russian gangster called Grigori Shikov.'

Mimi blinked. 'A Russian?'

'He's a very ruthless man and he clearly wants the Dark Medusa desperately enough that he won't hesitate to kill for it. In all these years, has anyone ever approached you; threatened you, or anyone around you?'

'No,' Mimi said. 'Never.'

Ben remembered what Pietro De Crescenzo had said about the mystery surrounding Gabriella Giordani's companion. Nobody had ever known her surname – and Gabriella had obviously never given away her identity in the diary, either. For a man of Shikov's power and influence, a Simonetta Renzi might have been traceable; but a 'Mimi' could vanish without a trace. Free to live a wealthy and contented life, while others had to suffer and die for what she'd taken.

Now Ben understood everything – all but one unresolved question.

'Why did you want to contact me, Mimi?' he asked quietly.

The old woman wiped a tear from her eye, then looked at him earnestly. 'Mr Hope, "The Penitent Sinner" is not a drawing. It is a real person, and she sits before you now. I cannot undo the crimes I have committed in my past, but now it is time for me to make amends as best I can. When I saw you on television, this good man who risked his life to save others – *l'eroe della galleria* – I knew that I wanted this man to help me repay my debt.'

Ben was silent.

'After Eduardo died, I started my business. I have worked hard, and been very successful. I am no less wealthy now than I was the day I sold the Dark Medusa to the oil sheikh. Mr Hope, I want you to take my money. All of it, save the small sum that will see me through to the end of my days. I want you to distribute the money among the families of those touched by the tragedy I have caused. I know I cannot bring back the loved ones they have lost. But it is all I can do.' She leaned forward in her chair and looked into Ben's eyes. 'Will you agree?'

Chapter Seventy-One

'She's a crazy, rotten, lying old bitch,' Darcey said through a mouthful of fillet steak. 'I don't like her.'

It was just after 9 p.m. and the night was still warm, a slight breeze wafting in from the sea. Their table for two had been set on the poolside patio of the guest annexe in the grounds of the Renzi villa, where Mimi had insisted they stay the night. The old woman had excused herself from dining with them, as she always retired early with just a cup of warm milk before bed. The food and wine she'd ordered in for them had come from one of Monaco's best restaurants. They were into their second bottle of Château Mouton Rothschild.

'She needed to confess to what she's done,' Ben said.

Darcey grunted. 'Talk to a priest, then.'

'She just wants to make amends. I can understand that. People make mistakes, Darcey.'

'Oh, sure.' Darcey didn't look convinced. 'People make mistakes. But they don't wait until they're about to cop it before they suddenly start coming on all repentant. So are you going to help her?'

'I told her I would think about it,' Ben said. 'And I am. But things are a little complicated at the moment.'

'You might say that.'

Ben pushed away his plate. He wasn't hungry any more. He got up and walked through the open patio doors into the luxurious two-bedroomed annexe, went over to the armchair where he'd dumped his bag and undid the straps. Inside, folded up next to his dwindling money supply, was the list of eight different mobile numbers he'd copied from the call records of Spartak Gourko's phone on the train journey from Milan. Out of the eight, three stood out as the ones Gourko had called most frequently and for longest. Ben had circled those three numbers so many times on the train that the paper was almost worn through.

And now he knew what to say. He perched on the edge of the armchair, turned on Gourko's phone and dialled the first number on the list. The call cut straight to a mobile answering service. Ben waited for the beep, then left his message. Short and simple, slow and clear.

'This is a message for Grigori Shikov. You know who I am. I have the Dark Medusa. Call me if you're interested.'

Getting no reply on either of the other two most-used numbers, he left the same message and then got started on the others. By the time he'd worked his way through to the bottom of the list, he'd had only two replies. The first sounded like a bar or nightclub, loud music booming in the background. He didn't leave a message. The second was an Italian guy who cut him off before he'd said three words.

Now all he could do was wait and hope that his message would hit its mark.

'You look tired,' Darcey said as he returned to the patio table. 'Maybe you should go to bed.'

'I'm fine,' he said.

'No, you're not.' Their glasses were empty. She grabbed the bottle, but there was no wine left. 'Shit. Is that all they gave us?'

'Maybe they thought a bottle of Mouton Rothschild each would be enough,' Ben said.

'There's got to be more booze around here somewhere.' Darcey jumped up and disappeared into the annexe. She returned five minutes later, wearing a grin and carrying a bottle and two crystal brandy glasses. '*Voilá*. Now we know what the little door at the end of the passage is. You need to check out that wine cellar. It's full of champagne. And look what *I* found. Armagnac, eighteen years old. Fancy a drop of the hard stuff?'

'You're a bad influence on me, Darcey Kane.'

'I will corrupt you yet,' she said, tearing the foil off the neck of the bottle. 'If I die trying.'

As she poured out two brimming glasses, Ben used a book of matches to light up one of the Gauloises he'd bought from a kiosk at Monaco station. Still missing that old Zippo of his. He offered the pack to Darcey.

She shook her head. 'No.' Then, after a moment's hesitation, 'Oh, fuck it, go on then.' She held the cigarette between her lips and Ben struck another match to light it for her. Inhaling too sharply, she gave a little cough. 'Who's a bad influence now?' she spluttered. 'What the hell are these things? They'll kill us.'

'Everyone says that,' Ben said. 'But if it's a choice between these, the Russian mafia and British Intelligence, I'll take the Gauloises.'

They sat and smoked and sipped the aged, rich brandy in silence for a while. From somewhere down below on the beach, there came laughter and the sound of someone plucking notes on a Spanish guitar – a soulful, melancholy melody that drifted up through the warm night air.

'Are you going to call her?' Darcey said.

Ben looked up from his thoughts. 'Brooke?'

'That's who you were thinking about just now, isn't it?'

It had been. 'I don't know what to do,' he said. 'Maybe there's nothing I *can* do. Maybe it's just over between us, and that's it.' He knocked back more brandy and decided he wanted to change the subject. 'Do you have anybody?' he asked her.

Darcey shook her head. 'I'm kind of in-between things right now.' She smiled ruefully. 'Well, that's putting it mildly. I'm *very* in-between things. Two years.'

'Long time,' Ben said.

'Long enough for the hurt to fade,' she said. 'His name was Sam.'

Ben looked at her.

'Oh, he's not dead or anything like that,' she said, catching his expression. 'Though he fucking well deserves to be. Now happily married to Angie, who *used* to be my best friend and now holds the number two spot on my personal shit list.' Her brow flickered with anger, and then she relaxed and smiled. 'So I do understand how you feel, Ben. I was pretty fucked up over it for a while. But then one morning I woke up there in my little flat and I just realised how free I was.'

Ben smiled. 'Thanks, Darcey.' He reached out and touched her hand. She didn't pull away from his touch.

'Free to do all kinds of wicked, wonderful things,' Darcey said. She laced her fingers into his, and moved a little closer.

Ben didn't pull away either.

Darcey stood up, leading him up to his feet. Her smile fell away and she looked seriously into his eyes. As he stood, her arms slipped around his neck and her lips came up to meet his.

Ben closed his eyes. He couldn't tell if it was tiredness making him dizzy, or the wine, or something else. He was standing on the edge of the cliff, everything happening in slow motion as part of him struggled to keep from tumbling head over heels into the warm, inviting waters below.

'Her loss, anyway,' Darcey murmured.

The first kiss was tentative, almost furtive. Then she pulled him in tight and crushed her lips hard against his. He felt her body pressing into him, and realised it was because he was holding her close. He could feel her heart beating fast against his own as the kissing turned more passionate.

She broke away, breathing hard, her face flushed. 'Come on.' Gripping his hand, she led him inside the annexe. Before they even got to the bedroom door she was kissing him again. She shoved open the door with her behind, then pulled him to the bed and swung him round with surprising strength. He flopped down on the soft duvet as she quickly stripped off her top and then clambered onto him, straddling him and smothering him with more kisses, giving him no time to think or to want to stop. She rolled over on her back, slipped one long leg out of her jeans, then the other, and kicked the jeans away and rolled back on top of him, giggling as she fumbled for his belt buckle.

Her phone rang inside the pocket of her jeans on the floor.

They both froze.

'There's only one person that could be,' Darcey said, her mouth an inch from Ben's. She tore herself off him, swung an arm down from the bed and scrabbled for her jeans. The phone was still ringing insistently. Fishing it out, she quickly put it into hands-free mode so Ben could hear, and hit reply.

'Darcey?' A man's voice Ben hadn't heard before.

'Mick?'

'You OK? You sound a little breathless.'

Darcey brushed a tangle of hair away from her eyes.

She couldn't stop smiling. 'I had to run for the phone. What's happening?'

'It was there in the locker,' Walker said. 'Just like you said. I got it, no problem.' He lowered his voice and sounded serious. 'It's a file, Darcey. And I think you need to see it immediately. Have you got a fax there?'

Ben pointed through the open bedroom door. There was a compact phone-fax on a stand in the front hallway of the annexe.

'Hold on, Mick,' Darcey said. She and Ben ran over to the fax machine, and she read the number out to Walker.

'Copy that,' Walker said. 'Sending it now. You might want to keep it safe, Darce. Original's going into a bank deposit box first thing tomorrow. You'll see why when you read it,' he added cryptically. 'Keep in touch, OK?'

Moments after Walker ended the call, the little fax machine whirred into life, sucked in the first sheet of paper and its printer went to work.

'What do you think it is?' Darcey asked as she hurriedly pulled her clothes back on.

Ben looked at the digital readout on the front of the machine. 'Whatever it is, there's twelve pages of it headed our way.'

The colour fax took less than two minutes to print. It was the entire intelligence file on Operation Jericho.

'Jamie Lister must have smuggled it out of his office when he went AWOL,' Darcey breathed. 'Holy shit. Look at this.'

The classified operation was described in fine detail. It was all there, every official stamp, every high-ranking signature. Some names, like Ferris, Blackmore and Yemm, came up over and over. The first two pages consisted of profiles of Grigori Shikov and his son, the latter shown in a couple of photos on the deck of a motor yacht with a pretty blonde in a bikini.

It wasn't until Ben got to the third page that the hairs on the back of his neck stood up. Here was irrefutable black-on-white proof that the senior intelligence chiefs heading up Lister's department had known about the gallery robbery well in advance from the reports they'd received from their informant Urbano Tassoni.

The next page showed a face Ben remembered from the robbery. Bruno Bellomo, one of the men he'd dangled from the window. His real name was Mario Belli, and he'd been an undercover agent with clear orders, signed and counter-signed by Lister's superiors.

'They didn't care if innocent people got killed,' Darcey said in disgust. 'Look at this line: "a degree of collateral damage may be deemed permissible in order to facilitate the operation". It's just like Lister said.'

On the following pages was a dry official summary of the Tassoni shakedown, incorporating a series of compromising photos of him with underage prostitutes, and a summary of the deal that he'd been offered. That information alone was enough to cause a major international incident.

And then, on the next page, came the money shot.

'Fuck me,' Darcey muttered.

Tassoni's picture, with the word 'ELIMINATED' stamped in official red across his face. Below it was the codename of the operative who'd carried out the job, with the signature of the chief who'd sanctioned it – Mason Ferris. The next page was a still from the suppressed security footage, showing the real assassin arriving at Tassoni's house several minutes before Ben.

The final printed sheets consisted of Ben's military record and some satellite images of him walking through the streets of Rome the night of the shooting. He was too dazed to even look at them.

'Waste of time, eh?' Darcey beamed.

That was when they heard the phone ring again. It was a different ringtone from before. The phone Ben had taken from Gourko. He laid the fax printout on a table, dug the phone out of his pocket and answered it. The voice on the other end was deep, gravelly, and hard as titanium.

'This is Grigori Shikov,' the voice said. 'You have something that I want.'

Chapter Seventy-Two

'You'd better believe it,' Ben said to Shikov.

A rasping chuckle down the phone. 'This is the problem. Why should I believe you have the Dark Medusa?'

'Because I'm sitting here looking at it,' Ben said. 'Let me see. I'd say the egg's about eight inches high, white gold, diamond-encrusted, with images from classical mythology around the outside.'

Shikov was silent for a moment. 'And on the inside?' he said suspiciously.

'The Medusa herself, you mean? The miniature bust is made of bloodstone, dark with little flecks of red. Scary-looking lady. What are those eyes made of? Alexandrite, isn't it?'

'Where did you find it?' Shikov said, audibly shaken and fighting to cover the tremor in his voice.

'In Bezukhov's grave,' Ben replied. 'Right where the map said. You were just a little too late, Shikov.' It was a wild bluff. The Russian had only to ask one hard question, and it was over. Ben knew he needed to steer the conversation away fast. 'So do you want it or not? I have other buyers interested.'

'How is this possible?' Shikov asked.

'It's possible because I'm smarter than you,' Ben said.

'I want it,' Shikov said. 'You must meet me. We will talk.'

'Right. And then you'll have your men kill me, for Anatoly.'

'My son was a worthless piece of shit,' Shikov said. 'So was Tassoni. The egg means much more. Trust me. I am a businessman. But I also must trust you to come alone.'

'You think I'd bring the cops?' Ben said. 'Think again. I'm a fugitive, wanted for murder. Tassoni might have been a shit, but he was an important shit.'

'Then we have a deal. You give me what I want, I give you what you want. The egg, for your life.'

'Not good enough. I need to disappear after this, Shikov. I want money.' As he talked, Ben carried the phone into the bedroom and shut the door behind him.

From outside the door, Darcey could hear him talking but couldn't make out the words. She paced, chewing her lip and wondering why he'd shut her out like that. After a minute or so, he'd gone quiet. The phone rang again, and she heard him answer it and talk a while longer. Almost twenty more minutes went by before he finally emerged from the bedroom and she attacked him with questions.

'Well?'

'We set up a meeting,' Ben said. 'We figured halfway house. Berlin.'

'What was all that about money?'

'To make it believable that I really have the egg. Nobody would let it go for free.'

'Who called you afterwards?'

'Shikov lost his signal for a minute. He called back.'

'This RV in Berlin. A precise location?'

Ben nodded.

'You're not thinking of going?'

Ben didn't reply.

'It'd be madness, Ben. Don't you see? This is perfect. I'll call Applewood. We'll spring the biggest trap in history and stick Shikov in a cage where he belongs. Anybody tries to fuck with us, we have *that*.' She pointed to the fax printout on the table. 'Our ticket to freedom. That information right there is all the bargaining power we need to buy us both our lives back.'

Ben grinned at her. 'You know, you're right.'

'Damn right I'm right.'

'Let's celebrate. Did you say there was champagne down in the cellar?'

'Enough bottles to knock out the whole of Monaco,' she said.

'You go and fetch one. I'll grab two glasses from the kitchen.'

'Now you're talking, Ben Hope.' Darcey trotted down the passage and unbolted the little door that led down to the wine cellar. She skipped down the concrete steps. The cellar was like a maze. Tall racks surrounded her, filled from floor to ceiling with row after row of dusty bottles. She drew one out, brushed away cobwebs. A vintage Moët. This would do just fine. As she ran her eyes over the label, she was thinking about when the bottle was empty and how she was going to haul Ben back in the bedroom and . . .

The cellar door banged shut. She heard the creak of the bolt sliding home.

'Ben!' she yelled. She flew up the steps, still clutching the bottle.

There was something on the top step that hadn't been there just a moment ago. A dinner plate, and on it a whole roast chicken, cellophane-wrapped, cold from the fridge. Next to that was a two-litre bottle of mineral water. Propped against the bottle was a scrawled note that said simply:

Sorry.

B

Darcey beat against the cellar door. 'Let me out, you bastard!'

But Ben was already gone.

Chapter Seventy-Three

Monaco's city lights glittered below as Ben ran down the winding cliff road with his bag on his shoulder. He hailed down a cab that took him the rest of the way to the harbour. Sitting on a low wall, he smoked a Gauloise, gazed out across the dark water and listened to the soft lap of the tide against the harbour wall and the jostle of the sailing yachts and catamarans in the marina. A party was in full swing on the lit-up deck of some trillion-dollar megayacht, a band playing, and women in long dresses parading up and down the jetty where it was moored. As he watched them from a distance, Ben thought about Darcey Kane. He'd had no option but to lie to her about meeting Shikov in Berlin, any more than he'd had a choice about shutting her in the cellar. She was too clever and tenacious. And his next move was one he needed to make alone, his way.

Then he thought about what had nearly happened between them. He'd had a choice there, all right.

He sighed and decided to try to stop thinking so much.

Far out to sea, a small aircraft was approaching. Ben watched as the seaplane's lights descended towards the horizon and it touched down a few kilometres away over the water. Dead on time. Shikov was definitely taking the bait.

Moments later, a fast outboard launch cut across the harbour, and Ben knew it was for him. He walked down the jetty to meet it and two guys ushered him aboard. One of them pointed a Smith & Wesson revolver at the pit of Ben's stomach as the other frisked him and checked his bag for any concealed weapons. Then the launch motored out of the harbour and out to sea, where the guy with the revolver waved him aboard the waiting Bombardier amphibious aircraft. More silent armed men flanked him as he buckled into a seat. The plane gathered speed, bounced once and then took off.

From the Côte d'Azur, the thrumming, vibrating Bombardier flew overland. Roughly northeast, Ben guessed by the stars, though he didn't ask, aware he'd get no reply. A long time passed before they finally touched down at a remote private airfield that could have been anywhere between Geneva, Milan or even Zürich. A Mercedes saloon took him and his armed escorts a few hundred metres up the runway as the Bombardier taxied away. A sleek white Gulfstream jet was on standby. Ben was hustled unceremoniously up the gangway and shown to a seat in the back. It was a little more luxurious than the flying boat. Ben spread himself out in the plush leather seat, ignoring his hosts, and closed his eyes.

He lost count of how many hours the jet stayed in the air – maybe six, maybe longer. By the time the Gulfstream dropped below the clouds, they'd passed through a couple of time zones and dawn was breaking over the wild landscape of mountain and pine forest that Ben could see from his porthole.

After a low pass through a wooded valley, the jet dropped suddenly and came down to land on a runway that looked as though it might have been hastily knocked together years before by military engineers. Ben noticed the rocket-pitted concrete and wondered what former European war zone they were in. Georgia, maybe.

As Ben stepped down from the jet, the Georgian plates of the black Humvee parked waiting at the foot of the strip told him his guess had been correct. The same pair of armed goons prodded him down towards the vehicle as its doors opened and another two men climbed out. Neither of them appeared to be Grigori Shikov. Ben guessed that honour would have to wait. The Humvee passenger was holding a stubby Kalashnikov rifle with a folding stock and a long, curved magazine. He barked an order, and one of Ben's escorts grinned and whipped a cloth hood from the pocket of his jacket. He stepped up to Ben and jerked it roughly over his head. Ben felt a big hand grab his arm, and he was shoved into the back seat of the Humvee.

Then it was more travelling, lurching and bouncing over rough roads as the vehicle headed east into the rising sun, whose glow Ben could see through the material of the hood. The drive lasted another twenty minutes or so; by the time the Humvee paused to pass through a set of gates and then lurched to a halt, Ben's eyes were tired from straining to make out his surroundings through the hood. He heard the doors opening, and the men hauled him out of the vehicle. They walked him across a stretch of paving, then shoved him through a door into a cool, airy building. Down a corridor, and into another room that smelled of antique leather and gun oil. He was thrust into a chair. Voices all around him. A whiff of foul breath as someone stepped up close to yank the hood off his head.

And Ben found himself sitting across a broad desk, face to face with Grigori Shikov.

The old man wore a light grey suit that was stretched too

tightly across the bulk of his shoulders and broad back. His large, rough hands, like a manual worker's hands, were curled into fists on the leather desktop. His eyes were set far apart, hooded underneath scowling brows and boring into Ben's. To Shikov's left stood a younger man, late forties, balding, wearing a suit, glasses and a nervous frown.

The big, broad, grizzled old man stared at Ben for a long time. Ben returned the stare, while in his peripheral vision he'd already counted the other men standing in the room in a loose semi-circle either side of him. In addition to the two heavies who'd accompanied him on the jet, there were the other two from the Humvee and another pair he was seeing for the first time. As far as he could tell, all the men were carrying concealed pistols. The Kalashnikov rifles were more obvious, and two of them were pointed right at Ben's head. He sat very still.

'You know who I am,' Shikov grated.

'I know who you are,' Ben answered.

Shikov motioned to the man at his side. 'This is my associate, Yuri Maisky.' Then he turned and cast a heavy glance at Ben's bag, which had been turned upside down and left sitting on a chair across the room. 'It seems you are travelling light, Mr Hope,' he rumbled.

'We'll do this the way we discussed on the phone,' Ben said. 'You give me half the money up front. Then I take you to where I left the egg and we exchange for the rest.'

Shikov let out a long breath, with the look of a patient teacher speaking to a slow-witted child. 'I could have these men extract whatever information I need from you.'

'I'm sure it wouldn't be the first time you've had a man tortured,' Ben said, glancing over at Maisky, whose frown had deepened as he stood listening. 'But if anything happens to me and I don't make a phone call sometime in the next

404

couple of hours, my colleague will know something's wrong. The only place you'll ever see that egg then is in your dreams.'

Shikov's eyes bored deeper into Ben, as if scanning the contents of his mind. Ben maintained eye contact. After a few seconds, Shikov nodded slowly. 'Very well. Show him, Yuri.'

Maisky motioned for Ben to get up. With the rifles still trained on his head, Ben followed the man across the room to a marble-topped sideboard, where an attaché case lay closed on its side. Ben stood facing Shikov while Maisky rolled the combination locks on the case.

'I counted it personally,' Maisky said. The latches flipped open. Ben pulled the case towards him. Slowly raised the lid. Ran his eye across the bound stacks of banknotes neatly arranged inside. He took out one of the bundles, then another, riffled them with his fingers.

'Well?' Shikov said, breaking the silence.

'This will do just fine,' Ben said. He nodded at Maisky.

Then reached into the hollow space among the stacks. His fingers brushed cool steel. His fist closed on the grip of the big Colt .45 automatic pistol hidden inside. It was cocked and locked and he was just going to have to trust there was a round in the chamber. He thrust the muzzle of the pistol against the inside of the attaché case lid and squeezed the trigger.

The gun jolted in his hand and the boom of the shot filled the room like an expanding wave. The heavy bullet ripped through the case and caught the nearest of Shikov's riflemen in the chest. By the time the man had gone pitching backwards across the study, Ben was already dropping into a crouch behind the antique sideboard and bringing the Colt to bear on the second rifleman.

A wonderful thing, the element of surprise. Even with his

Kalashnikov lined up and ready to go, the guy didn't have time to compute what was happening quickly enough to squeeze the trigger before Ben's second round punched through his skull and sent him sprawling to the rug. Two down. As the room erupted in chaos, pistols were being pulled and a lot of bullets were about to start flying.

But Ben wasn't alone. Yuri Maisky had reached into the pocket of his suit and brought out a compact handgun. He took wild aim and the little gun barked. The guy who'd driven the Humvee went down.

The Colt in Ben's hand boomed three times more in quick succession.

Maisky snapped off two more rounds of his own.

Then, in the space of a heartbeat, the room fell from deafening mayhem to dead silence. Shikov's six men were scattered lifelessly across the floor. The hole in the attaché case lid was still smoking.

Ben looked at Maisky. Until the moment he'd opened the case, he hadn't known whether he could really count on the Russian's help. The man stood uncertainly, the adrenalin tremor making the gun shake in his hand. Ben could see from the look in his eyes that he'd never shot a man before.

Shikov hadn't moved from his desk. His jaw hung open as he stared from Ben to Maisky and back again.

'I'll bet you're wondering what the hell just happened, Grigori,' Ben said.

Chapter Seventy-Four

The truth was that, back in Monaco the night before, Ben had lied to Darcey about Shikov calling him back after getting disconnected. Ben's conversation with the mafia boss hadn't lasted any longer than it had needed to, and had left him unsure whether he was doing the right thing.

When the phone had rung a second time moments later, it had been someone else responding to the message he'd left on the numbers from Gourko's mobile. Someone Ben hadn't been expecting to hear from.

In a tight, terse-sounding Russian accent, the man introduced himself as Yuri Maisky. 'Grigori Shikov is my uncle. I work for him.'

Ben had sat on the edge of the bed, cupping the phone, waiting for more.

'You say you have the Dark Medusa.'

'Right here in front of me,' Ben had said.

'You are crazy if you think my uncle will deal with you. He will have you tortured and killed.'

'I'm a careful guy.'

A hesitant silence. The sound of someone teetering on the brink of an irreversible decision. 'I can offer you another way. Split the Dark Medusa with me, and you can survive this.'

'What about Shikov?'

'I will convince him to let you go.'

'Just like that?'

'I have a lot of information. A lot of secrets.'

For the next couple of minutes, Ben had listened as Maisky described some of them. The things the man knew were enough to obliterate Shikov and his whole empire forever.

'And you'd threaten to spill this to the authorities, just to make him call the dogs off me? Why?'

'Because I want out,' Maisky had said. 'Out of this whole thing, before it is too late. I have a wife and a three-month-old daughter. I want the money to take them far away, somewhere safe. A new life for us all.'

Ben had stood up and started pacing the bedroom as he listened. The guy sounded genuine. More than that, he sounded desperate.

'Shikov's worth, what? Tens, hundreds of millions? Why wait for this opportunity to come along? You could have blackmailed him any time. Your freedom, in exchange for his.'

'You don't know him,' Maisky had insisted. 'He would never have given me the money. He would have found a way to fuck me.'

'I believe it. If it took him the rest of his life. Whichever way you do this, he's going to hunt you down. There'd be nowhere safe on this planet, for you or your family.'

Maisky had swallowed. 'It is the only way.'

'No, Yuri, it's the way that'll get your wife and baby butchered in front of you, and then Shikov's men will put a bullet in your brain. It's not going to work. But I can offer you a deal that will. Your uncle's going down, along with his whole organisation. I'm going to take him down.'

'I don't want to go to jail.'

'You won't. Not if you help me.'

There had been a long, wary silence on the line. Ben could sense the cogs turning furiously in the man's mind.

'You have no other options, Yuri. You said so yourself, and you wouldn't have called me if you did. Now listen carefully, and I'll tell you exactly why you need to trust me, and exactly what we're going to do.'

In the silence of the study, Grigori Shikov stared in disbelief at the scattered corpses of his men. He still didn't move from behind the desk. His face was as bloodless as a waxwork's. Yuri Maisky stood watching his uncle with an agonised expression.

Ben stepped around one of the dead bodies and faced Shikov across the desk. 'You weren't the only person to get my message,' he said to the old man. 'Yuri and I had a long talk. He's decided he doesn't want to work for you any more. He wants a life. Consider this his resignation.'

Maisky tossed down his gun. 'Uncle—'

Shikov's face turned from white to red as he glowered at his nephew. 'Yuri. This cannot be true.'

'Yuri wants to cut a deal with the authorities,' Ben said to Shikov. 'Nobody knows your organisation better than he does. He can deliver it to them on a plate. Names. Addresses. Deals. Contacts. Locations of dead bodies across Europe. Details of everything you've been doing for decades. Enough shit to lock everyone away for ever.'

'You will die for this, Yuri.'

'No, he won't,' Ben said. 'He's going to be just fine. He and his family will have a new identity and a new life far, far away, courtesy of a British government witness protection programme. All he needed was someone like me to help make it happen for him.'

Shikov stared at Ben in bewilderment. 'But—'

'I know what you're thinking,' Ben said. 'I'm not an agent, I'm not a cop. Yesterday I was an outlaw, wanted for murder. Where does a fugitive get the bargaining power to turn round and dictate terms to the law? Let's just say things are a little different now. Thanks partly to your pal Tassoni, I have a bit of an edge I didn't have before.'

A strange keening sound came from Shikov's throat. His whole face was trembling. His hands were splayed out flat and white against the leather desktop.

Ben kept the Colt pointed at him. 'As for you, Shikov, I promised myself I'd kill you for what you did to Donatella and Gianni Strada and all the other people who died at the Giordani exhibition that day. But now all I see is a weak, sick, sad old man who's going to spend the rest of his life in jail.'

Shikov suddenly drew in a gasp of air. His body seemed to convulse. He clawed at his jacket pocket, ripping the seam to get at the tube of pills inside. With a trembling hand he scattered the pills across the desk, grabbed two of them in his fist, shoved them in his mouth and swallowed them dry, choking and spluttering.

'The pills aren't working any more, uncle,' Maisky said. 'You need help. I can see to it that you are well looked after.'

Ben watched as the old man slowly recovered from his coughing fit. He flipped on the Colt's safety and let the gun dangle at his side. 'Yuri says you're dying of congestive heart failure. Says that, at best, you're looking at a year. If it was up to me, I'd leave you to rot in a dungeon. But I promised your nephew that you'll spend whatever time you've got left in reasonable comfort. That's part of the deal.'

'I promise this is all for the best,' Maisky said.

Shikov stared in hatred.

'And by the way, Shikov,' Ben said, 'I want you to know that your precious egg was dug up and sold on before you were even out of your teens. You've wasted your whole life looking for it. The Arab sheikh who paid millions for it in 1955 might not even have it any more. Who knows? And who cares? It's lost to you. Always was, always will be.'

Shikov seemed to subside internally as he heard the words, like a building rigged with demolition charges that were detonating in slow motion and collapsing it to the ground. He crumpled slowly to the desktop, sinking down in his chair, clutching his chest. His breath came in great gasps, drowning in the fluid on his lungs.

Then his hand darted to the desk drawer in front of him. Before Ben could react, the Russian's stubby fingers had hooked around the drawer handle and wrenched it open, dived inside and came out clutching an ancient Mauser pistol. Ben hit the floor at the same instant the shot went off. A display cabinet shattered behind him. Shikov swung the barrel of the Mauser towards Maisky—

And Ben shot him through the forehead.

Grigori Shikov's eyes and mouth opened wide in surprise. Blood coursed down his face from the hole in his skull. The Mauser tumbled from his big hand. A long, whistling, bubbling breath hissed from his lungs, and then his bulk went slack in the desk chair.

Yuri Maisky stared at the dead body of his uncle. Ben turned to him. 'You OK?'

Maisky ran his fingers down his cheek, nodded slowly. 'Yes, I'm OK.'

Then his head exploded.

Chapter Seventy-Five

Ben whirled around, his ears ringing from the huge gun blast that had come from just a few metres behind him. Spartak Gourko was standing in the study doorway. There was a thick dressing where his right ear had been, and a Russian military Saiga-12 shotgun in his fists. Its fat muzzle was pointing right at Ben's stomach.

Ben's hand tightened on the Colt, the muscles in his gun arm flexed ready to go into the rapid aim-fire motion that he'd practised a million times. Half a second was all he needed to hit his mark. But Gourko didn't need that long just to flick a trigger, and at this range the Saiga-12 would separate Ben's torso from his legs and smear him across the far wall. That would end things pretty quickly.

Ben let the Colt hang at his side. 'You're hard to kill,' he said.

Gourko's eyes flickered away from Ben to gaze at the corpse of his former employer. 'You did that?' he asked Ben, motioning with the shotgun. His hand had slackened on its pistol grip. Not much, but enough to make a difference.

Ben nodded.

'You do my job for me,' Gourko said. 'I should thank you. The old man was weak. It was time for me to take over. Now *I* will be the Tsar.'

'Do I get a prize?'

Gourko grinned. 'You are my prize.'

Ben saw the scarred knuckles tighten on the shotgun's grip. Saw the first joint of the index finger curl itself across the face of the trigger. The fingertip flattening and whitening around the nail as the pressure of the squeeze drove the blood from the tissues. A trigger break of maybe six pounds. Gourko had five and a half on it as Ben threw himself backwards over the broad desk with all the speed and strength he could muster. Knocking Shikov's chair over and spilling the corpse to the floor, he used his momentum to overturn the desk with a crash.

Gourko's shotgun roared, blasting a massive chunk out of the upturned desktop. Ben tumbled to the rug in a storm of flying splinters. His Colt whacked into Shikov's fallen chair as he scrambled for cover, and went tumbling out of his grip. Laughing, Gourko flipped a lever on the receiver of his shotgun. Ben knew what it meant. It meant the world was about to come apart at the seams.

In full-automatic mode with a high-capacity magazine loaded with solid slugs, the Saiga-12 was probably the most destructive thing in the world at close range, shy of a nuclear warhead. The room exploded into an orgy of devastation. Flying plaster and glass and wood and dust and deafening noise filled the air. Only the heavy mahogany desk saved Ben from being blasted into jelly. The shotgun ripped through its thirty-round mag in just over two seconds. Ben saw his chance. He grabbed a big ornamental globe and hurled it through the window. He dived after it through the shattered pane, numb to the glass spikes that lacerated his arms and sides and legs as he tumbled through and hit the ground outside rolling.

He was in the grounds of Shikov's home complex, a place

he'd never seen before. The building he'd just escaped from was some kind of boathouse, right on the shores of a glittering lake that stretched all the way to the distant mountain peaks. The main house was a hundred metres away, long and low and rambling with flower gardens and trees. Between the two buildings was a concreted yard.

The black Humvee was sitting there next to a jacked-up Jeep Wrangler, just fifty metres away from Ben. He broke into a sprint for it. As he reached the parked Humvee, Gourko came storming out of the broken window after him, yelling in rage, gripping the shotgun. Another massive ripping blast chewed up the concrete around Ben's feet and hammered the side of the vehicle, crumpling the gleaming steel panels as easily as stamping on a beer can.

But Ben had nowhere else to run. He ripped open the door of the Humvee and flattened himself across the front seats as the windscreen blew in and showered him with a hail of smashed glass. He groped for the ignition, praying his fingers wouldn't find an empty keyhole. His hand connected with the dangling fob of the ignition key. Twisted it. Threw the automatic transmission into drive and kicked down hard on the gas.

The Humvee bellowed into life and charged forward. Gourko fired again, blasting one of its door pillars almost in half and blowing in the side windows. Driving almost blind from below the level of the dashboard, Ben kept the pedal to the floor and twisted the steering wheel hard. The Humvee pulled a tight skidding U-turn, crossed the yard and ploughed through a perimeter fence with a shuddering crash that tore down a ten-foot-high wall of wire mesh supported by concrete pillars. The vehicle bucked and lurched over the top of the wrecked fence and kept going, speeding away over the rough ground towards the forest.

Ben could feel the blood cooling on his skin as the wind roared in through the broken screen. Not all of it was Yuri Maisky's. He ignored the pain from his cuts and drove faster. He had no idea where he was going. He just knew he needed to get away from Gourko.

In what was left of the wing mirror, he could see the man clambering in behind the wheel of the Wrangler and giving chase.

Ben powered the Humvee up a steep incline, unable to see anything but sky beyond its nose. Then the front of the truck dipped downward violently and he found himself speeding down a steep rocky valley into what seemed to be a huge stone quarry, a kilometre across from one steep wall to the other. It looked as though it had been put out of commission a long time ago and since put to other uses. In its centre, half-hidden behind tall wooden gates and barbed wire, a compound had been built consisting of a cluster of steel prefabricated buildings painted in military olive drab.

Seconds away and gaining fast, the Wrangler cleared the top of the rise and came jolting and bouncing down after Ben on its oversized tyres. Gourko had the windscreen down flat and the shotgun out over the bonnet, holding it with his left hand as he controlled the wheel with his right.

Ben heard the booming shots and felt the impact of the massive twelve-gauge slugs ripping through the body of the Humvee. The downward slope was steepening. Any faster, and the vehicle was going to start getting out of control. Ben jabbed the brakes – and felt no resistance from the pedal. It pressed flat to the floor, and he was still gaining speed. He guessed that one of Gourko's slugs must have taken out a brake line, reducing fluid pressure to zero.

With no way to stop, all Ben could do was wrestle the steering wheel and line up the harshly bucking vehicle with the wooden gates. The Humvee was doing over eighty kilometres an hour when it hit. Ben was thrown violently forward in the driver's seat as the Humvee burst through, ripped planks flying up over its roof.

The gates had barely even slowed the heavy truck down. It went speeding across the compound. Ben swerved to avoid one steel building, but the ground was loose and the vehicle went into a skid and smashed into the prefabricated hut next to it. Ben was hurled into the steering wheel and felt a rib crack.

A piece of buckled metal sheet fell to the floor as Ben opened the Humvee's door and stumbled painfully out into the wreckage of the shed. There were no windows, and the only light in the place was the hole he'd ripped coming through the wall. As his eyes quickly grew accustomed to the dim light, Ben saw the stacks of steel crates – hundreds of them, everywhere around him. The Humvee had knocked over a stack of oblong boxes stencilled in white Cyrillic lettering. Two had burst open, revealing rows of Kalashnikov AK47 assault rifles in their original Soviet armoury packing. The smell of gun oil was fresh and sharp. This had to be where Shikov had kept his little arms cache.

Ben heard Gourko's jeep screech to a halt outside.

He examined the fallen crates. Some ammunition for the AK rifles would have been handy at that moment, but it was probably stacked away in any one of the hundreds of other crates. He glanced around him, imagining Gourko striding his way with the Saiga shotgun in his hands. He kicked open another crate.

Inside, lying on its belly supported on a heavy-duty bipod, was a piece of equipment that was little more than a massive long steel tube with a crude stock at one end and a bulbous muzzle brake the size of a car exhaust silencer on the other.

Nestled in the crate beside it was a webbing ammunition belt that held a row of tapered brass shells six inches long, like cannon rounds.

It was a Russian bolt-action anti-materiel rifle. Something on the side for Shikov's Taliban friends, maybe. Accurate at fifteen hundred metres. Just the thing for taking out British army light armoured vehicles on patrol in Helmand Province.

Ben felt the strain on his lower back as he hoisted the heavy rifle out of its crate. He slung the ammunition bandolier over his shoulder. If Spartak Gourko wanted to play with big guns, let him get a dose of this.

There was no time to load the magazine. He opened the bolt and fed one of the enormous cartridges into the breech, closed the bolt and locked it. He lugged the huge weapon over to the ragged hole in the side of the shed and kicked through the buckled metal sheets.

The Jeep Wrangler was parked facing away from him between the buildings, eighty metres off. That was point-blank range for the AM rifle. Ben threw himself flat on the ground. Resting the gun on its bipod, he lined the Jeep up in the mil-dot reticule of the scope and squeezed the trigger. The rifle recoiled brutally into his shoulder with a sound like a thunderclap, sending a spasm of agony through his injured side. Almost simultaneously, the Jeep burst into a fireball that rolled up into a mushroom of flame and sent a column of black smoke rising into the sky.

Ben's ears were singing loudly from the shot. Enough to drown out the sound of his own whistle at the power of the rifle.

But not enough to mask the rapidly rising turbine roar that he could suddenly hear coming from a prefab construction hidden among the other buildings. Ben clambered to his feet, wincing at the pain in his ribs. Staring at the building, he realised that it had no roof. Bad news.

The noise was quickly building to a deafening howl. Ben worked the bolt of the rifle, and the empty casing the size of a small beer bottle fell to the ground.

Before Ben had time to insert another round, the Black Shark had risen clear of the roofless hangar walls, whipping up a blizzard of dust and debris with the blast from its twin concentric sets of rotors. The machine turned with terrifying agility. Nose down, tail up, scanning the ground like a huge mechanical predator seeking out its prey. The 30mm rotary machine cannon slung at its flank made Ben's sniper rifle look like a boy's airgun.

As the monster bore down on him, he drew a second shell out of the bandolier, slammed it into the breech and worked the bolt home. Firing at a steep upward angle into the air without the benefit of an anti-aircraft mount, the stunning recoil almost knocked him flat on his back.

In the movies, the helicopter would have exploded into a thousand spinning pieces of shrapnel and come crashing down to the ground.

This wasn't the movies. Ben's shell kicked sparks off the armoured fuselage and bounced off harmlessly.

And now it was Gourko's turn.

Ben sprinted for his life as the rotary cannon blazed into life. Its rate of fire was so high that the sound wasn't the regular staccato thunder of a heavy machine gun, but a continuous roar. The cannon excavated trenches deep enough to bury a car as Gourko chased Ben across the compound and into one of the buildings. Ben might as well have tried to take cover in a cardboard box. The strong steel walls and roof were torn into smoking shreds around him. A solid steel support girder snapped in half and its pieces crashed to the floor. He hurdled over them, almost dropping the rifle, and sprinted on through the destruction, half a step ahead of the pummelling 30mm shells. He dived out through the back of the building seconds before the whole thing folded in on itself with a screech of rending metal.

Ben could imagine Spartak Gourko laughing to himself as the helicopter roared overhead. He was sent sprawling on his face by the downdraught. Still clutching the rifle, he scrambled to his feet. The Black Shark was banking steeply for another pass, coming in faster and tighter than any combat chopper he'd ever seen before.

He desperately needed cover. There was none.

Unless . . .

It was crazy. Suicidal. But it might just work.

Ben took off towards the nearest wall of the quarry. A desperate, heart-pounding, breathless two-hundred metre sprint with the dead weight of the anti-materiel rifle in his arms. The Black Shark hovered in the distance, as if anticipating its prey's movements. Then its tail rose up and it came back in for the attack.

Gourko was having fun.

With a whooshing scream that froze Ben's blood in his veins as he kept on running, two rockets detached themselves from the Black Shark's bristling payload and snaked after him. Ben threw himself flat. The rockets roared overhead, scorching him with their jets, and impacted against the steep rock wall ahead of him. Stones and debris rained down. Ben looked up, coughing, half blinded by the massive dust cloud that was rising up all around him.

The dust cloud was just what he wanted. If it could cloak him for just long enough . . .

He dashed the rest of the way to the foot of the cliff and

started clambering wildly up the loose rocks, dragging the butt of the rifle behind him. As the dust cloud began to settle, he could make out the dark shape of the helicopter hovering ominously about three hundred metres away. He threw himself down in a hollow between two large rocks, planted the rifle bipod in the dirt and quickly loaded the last four of his shells into the magazine.

The Black Shark saw him and came roaring in for the kill, hard and fast, looming up like an express train. Except that express trains didn't come loaded with ordnance capable of flattening a mountain. There was nowhere to hide from it now, nowhere to run.

Stay calm. Breathing. Control. Ben fought the pounding of his heart and lined up the sights on the monster's nose and let rip with another harshly-recoiling round.

The Black Shark kept coming.

Ben ripped the bolt back, rammed it forward, fired again. *Boom.* The pain lashed through him once more.

Nothing. The machine was less than two hundred metres away now.

Two rounds left. Ben fired again. Saw the sparking flash of his impact on the armour plating just a hand's breadth away from the only weak point the impregnable machine had – the thick plate glass of the cockpit was resistant to normal small arms fire, but not to anti-materiel rounds.

One hundred and fifty metres and closing.

Ben ejected the hot casing and slammed shut the bolt for the last time. He sucked in a breath. The target was wobbling crazily in the crosshairs of the scope.

One shot, one kill.

He squeezed the trigger. Just before the recoil tore the sight picture away, he thought he saw a small black hole appear in the corner of the cockpit screen.

The Black Shark kept coming, undeterred. One hundred metres.

Ben ripped open the bolt and stared at the empty breech. That was it. He'd given it his best shot.

The readout on Gourko's console told him his missile systems were armed and ready to go. He had his thumb on the fire button, but he wanted to wait until the final instant. He wanted to see the last look in Ben Hope's eyes just before the rockets pulverised his body across a hundred metres of rocks. Who was this man who thought he could shoot him down with a puny little rifle?

Gourko watched the magnified figure in his viewfinder. *I have you now.* He hit the trigger.

Hit it again. Nothing happened.

The rockets didn't launch.

The quarry wall was looming up fast. Gourko yanked on the stick to peel off for another pass.

That was when he realised something was dreadfully wrong. The controls were no longer responding. For the first time in his life, Spartak Gourko experienced the cold tremor of fear. Twisting in his seat, he saw the smoke and flame pouring from the banks of electronics behind him, where he now realised the bullet had hit.

Malfunction. Systems meltdown.

The quarry wall was racing towards him.

Gourko had only one option. The Ka-50 was just about the only combat helicopter in the world with an ejector seat. He reached for the control, armed it, braced himself. His fingers closed on the lever. He yanked, hard.

And in that terrible fraction of a split instant of time that seemed to last forever before the rockets ignited under his seat and fired him to safety, he understood that the electronic safeguard that would blow out the rotor blades from the turret a flash before the ejector system kicked in . . .

Wasn't . . .

Working . . .

From where Ben was crouching among the rocks, clutching his empty rifle and unable to do anything but wait for death, he saw the pilot's overhead canopy burst open. In the next instant, Spartak Gourko was launched like a human cannonball from the cockpit.

Straight up into the concentric rotor blades.

There wasn't time to look away. From seventy-five metres, Ben could almost see the man's mouth opening in a scream – and then his body disintegrated into a red mist as he was minced into nothing by the spinning blades.

The Black Shark's nose, sprayed with blood and gore, dipped as the aircraft began its terminal descent.

Straight towards Ben's vantage point.

Ben let the rifle clatter away. He scrambled desperately up the quarry wall.

The aircraft impacted with the force of an earthquake. Its rotors shattered and its armoured fuselage crumpled and blew apart. Wreckage tumbled down the quarry face, flew a hundred metres in the air. Ben flattened himself against the rocks. For an instant he thought the fireball that engulfed the slope was going to roast him where he lay; then the hot breath of flames receded suddenly, and the next thing he was engulfed in choking, blinding black smoke. Racked with coughing, he kept climbing and climbing until finally he reached the top and stumbled over the lip.

He glanced back down at the quarry. The smoke was rising high into the sky from the burning helicopter.

'Maybe not so hard to kill, then,' he muttered.

He turned away.

He could see the lake in the distance, and Shikov's house, as peaceful as if nothing had ever happened there. He started walking towards it.

Chapter Seventy-Six

'You utter, absolute bastard.'

Ben smiled to hear the sound of her voice on the other end. 'Hello, Darcey.'

'It took me six hours to get out of that bloody cellar.'

'I knew you'd find a way out eventually,' he said. 'A resourceful lady like you. How was the champagne?' With his free hand he uncapped the bottle of old Bowmore single malt he'd been pleasantly surprised to find among the well-stocked drinks cabinet in Shikov's huge, luxurious kitchen. If there'd been any more of the Russian's men around, they'd long since scattered.

'Where are you? Where did you go?' Ben could hear the anxiety in Darcey's voice.

'I think I'm in Georgia,' he said. 'Not sure where exactly.' He poured a couple of fingers of the whisky into the crystal glass on the gleaming hardwood worktop. 'Shikov's dead,' he added. 'I'll tell you all about it.'

'Are you all right?'

Ben touched his side gingerly and narrowed his eyes from the pain of the cracked rib. 'You should see the nine other guys.'

Darcey paused. 'You did it to protect me, didn't you?'

'I had a feeling you'd want to come along. You're stubborn that way.'

'What a fine twosome,' she said. 'I'm stubborn. And you're crazy.'

'Maybe just a little,' he said.

Darcey sighed. 'Then it's over.'

'Not quite. Where are you?'

'I'm where you left me. In the old bag's place. Where else could I go?'

Ben smiled. 'Tell the old bag I'll do what she asked,' he said. 'On one condition.'

'What's the condition?'

'That she has her driver take you to Rome in the back of that limo of hers. I'll meet you there tomorrow at midday. Piazza del Campidoglio, in the Capitol.'

'I know it,' she said. 'Why Rome?'

'Because I could really use an ice cream,' he said. 'Oh, and Darcey? Bring that fax printout with you.'

When he'd finished talking to Darcey, Ben dialled the number for Le Val. Jeff wasn't around, so Ben left him a brief message to reassure him that things were OK and he'd be home soon.

After that, he poured himself another measure of whisky and stared at the phone for a long time. He saw Brooke's face in his mind.

He didn't even know where she was. Back in London, maybe, or still in Portugal with . . . it hurt to think about it. And the idea of talking to her confused and terrified him even more. He swallowed hard, grabbed the phone and stabbed out the digits of her mobile number. As he waited for it to ring, he downed an anxious gulp of whisky and tried to formulate what he wanted to say. Nothing came to him.

He caught his breath when a woman's voice answered – but then he realised it was the sugary tones of Brooke's answering service.

He hung up.

Piazza del Campidoglio, Rome

Ben's journey back from Georgia had been a long one, and a couple of times he'd thought he wouldn't make his rendezvous. In the end, he was there fifteen minutes early. The world passed him by as he stood in the middle of the square, licking a curly vanilla cone and gazing across at Michelangelo's facade of the Palazzo dei Conservatori. White statues gleamed against the blue sky. Pigeons flapped about the piazza, squabbling over the scraps left by the tourists.

At exactly twelve o'clock, Ben saw Darcey making her way through the crowd towards him. She was wearing new clothes and carrying a shoulder bag. He couldn't help but grin at the sight of her.

She trotted the last few steps towards him, put her hand on his shoulder and kissed him quickly. 'All this way, for an ice cream?'

'And a couple of other things,' he said.

'Am I one of them?' she asked with a smile.

Ben scanned up and down the broad square. 'She should be here in a minute. There she is.'

Darcey followed his gaze and saw a tall, attractive brunette in a dark trouser suit cutting across the square's geometric paving towards them. 'Looks glamorous. And familiar. Who is she?'

'She's someone we might be seeing an awful lot of on TV soon,' Ben said. 'Her name's Silvana Lucenzi. She's a reporter.'

Darcey raised an eyebrow. '*Might* be seeing an awful lot of?'

'That depends, Darcey. Depends on you. Did you bring the file?'

She nodded, dipped a hand in her shoulder bag and brought out a clear plastic folder.

'There are two ways we can go with this,' Ben said. 'One, we can call this guy Mason Ferris, tell him we have evidence that could sink him and his whole department for a thousand years and quietly blackmail him into dropping all the charges against both of us, as well as giving you your old job back. With promotion, of course.'

Darcey said nothing.

Ben nodded towards the approaching Silvana Lucenzi. 'Two, we give the file to Silvana and let her do her thing. Press the nuclear button on these people. The world will never be the same again. Neither will your career. It's your call.'

'You think I'd even hesitate?' she said. 'Fuck 'em. Let's do it.'

Silvana Lucenzi walked up to them, staring at Ben in astonishment. 'What are you doing here? You are wanted by the police.'

'Not any more,' Darcey said, handing her the folder. 'Not after this gets out.'

Silvana Lucenzi took it hesitantly. She flipped open the clear plastic cover, thumbed through a few of the pages and her eyes bugged. By the time she reached the last page, she was speechless.

'It's genuine,' Ben said.

'And if you want the original file,' Darcey added, 'you'll have to come to London for it. Just name the place and the time.'

The reporter's initial shock was already fading away rapidly. Ben could see the wheels turning. Possibilities spinning through her mind faster than news front pages through a printing press. Her eyes shone.

'You just got yourself the hottest scoop in media history, Silvana,' Ben said. 'Now go and do what you do best.'

'W-would the two of you like a coffee?' Silvana asked.

Ben and Darcey exchanged glances. 'Some other time,' Darcey told her.

They walked away through the crowds milling about the piazza, leaving Silvana rooted to the spot and still staring agape at the file in her hands.

'Bombs away.' Darcey laughed. She paused, looking at him as they walked. 'So what next, Ben? You heading back to France?'

'Thought I might stick around here for a couple of days,' he said. 'You?'

'I'm kind of at a loose end now, aren't I?'

'Let me buy you lunch,' he said.

She smiled at him. 'Lunch would be a start.'

Epilogue

London
Less than an hour later

Mason Ferris was at his desk going through some papers when his phone rang. He calmly reached out and picked up the receiver. 'Talk to me.'

The panicking, babbling voice on the other end was Brewster Blackmore's. As Ferris listened, his jaw fell slowly open and the blood chugged to a halt in his veins.

'They WHAT—!?'

Read on for an exclusive extract from Scott G. Mariani's
new VAMPIRE FEDERATION novel – *The Cross*,
coming in October 2011.

Prologue

The village of St Elowen
Southwest Cornwall

Where two quiet lanes crossed, just a stone's throw from the edge of the village, the grey stone church had stood more or less unchanged since not long after Henry V had ascended to the throne of England. The glow from its leaded windows haloed out into the frosty November night. From behind its ancient iron-studded, ivy-framed door, the sound of singing drifted on the wind.

Just another Thursday evening's choir practice.

Although that night would be remembered quite differently by those villagers who would survive the events soon to become infamous as 'The St Elowen Massacre'.

Inside the church, Reverend Keith Perry beamed with pride as the harmonies of his fourteen singers soared up to the vaulted ceiling. What many of them lacked in vocal ability, they more than made up for with their enthusiasm. Rick Souter, the village butcher, was the loudest, with a deep baritone voice that was only a little rough and almost in tune. Then there was young Lucy Maxwell, just turned seventeen, giving it all she had. The most naturally talented of them all was little Sam Drinkwater, who in a few weeks' time was set to audition for a place as boy soprano at King's College, Cambridge. Sam's parents, Liz and Brian, were there too, sharing a hymn book as they all belted out *All Things Bright and Beautiful* to the strains of the electronic organ played by Mrs Hudson, the local music teacher.

The only face missing was that of Charlie Fitch, the plumber. Charlie was normally punctual, but his elderly mother had been quite ill lately; Perry prayed that nothing awful had happened.

That was when the church door banged open behind them. A few heads turned to see the man standing there at the entrance, watching them all. Mrs Hudson's fingers faltered on the organ keys. Reverend Perry's smile froze on his lips.

The drifter had been sighted on the edge of the village a few days before. The first concerned whispers had been exchanged in the shop and post office, and it hadn't been long before most of St Elowen's population of three hundred or so had heard the talk. The general consensus was that the drifter's presence was somewhat worrying, somewhat discomfiting; and everyone's hope was that it would be temporary. He was unusually tall and broad, perhaps thirty years old. Nobody knew his name, or where he'd come from, or where he was staying. His appearance suggested that he might have been living rough, travelling on foot from place to place like an aimless vagrant. His boots were caked in dirt and the military-style greatcoat he wore was rumpled and torn. But he was no new-age traveler, the villagers agreed. His face was as clean-shaven as a soldier's, and his scalp gleamed from the razor. There were no visible tattoos. No rings in his nose or ears; just that look that anyone who saw him found deeply disconcerting. Cold. Indifferent. Somehow not quite right. Somehow – this was the account that had reached Reverend Perry's ears – somehow not quite *human*.

Mrs Hudson stopped playing altogether. The voices of the choir fell away to silence as all eyes turned towards the stranger.

For a drawn-out moment, the man returned their gaze. Then, without taking his eyes off the assembly, he reached behind him and turned the heavy iron key. The door locked with a clunk that echoed around the silent church. The man drew the key out of the lock and dropped it into the pocket of that long greatcoat of his.

Little Sam Drinkwater took his mother's hand. Lucy Maxwell's eyes were wide with worry as she glanced at the vicar.

Reverend Perry swallowed back his nervousness, forced the smile back onto his lips and walked up the centre aisle towards the man. 'Good evening,' he said as brightly as he could. 'Welcome to St Elowen's. It's always a pleasure to see—'

As the man slowly reached down and swept back the hem of his long coat, Reverend Perry's words died in his mouth. Around the man's waist was a broad leather belt. Dangling from the belt, at his left hip, was an enormous sword. Its basket hilt was lined with scarlet cloth. Its polished scabbard glinted in the church lights.

Reverend Perry was too shocked to utter a word more. The man said nothing either. In no hurry, he reached his right hand across his body. His fingers wrapped themselves around the sword's hilt and drew the weapon out with a metallic swishing sound. Its blade was long and straight and broad and had been crudely etched with strange symbols.

Reverend Perry gaped dumbly at the sight of the weapon in his church. He was only peripherally aware of the gasps and cries of horror that had started breaking out among the choir members.

The drifter smiled at Reverend Perry. And then, in a

smooth and rapid motion that was over before anyone could react, he swung the sword.

The chopping impact of the blade was drowned out by Mrs Hudson's scream. Keith Perry's severed head bounced up the aisle and came to a rest between the pews. And the choir exploded into screaming panic.

The drifter held the blade up lovingly in front of his face. He licked the running blood off the steel. Began walking slowly up the aisle towards the terrified parishioners.

'The vestry door!' Lucy Maxwell shrieked, pointing. Liz Drinkwater grabbed her son's arm tightly as she and her husband fled for the exit at the right of the altar. The others quickly followed, tripping over each other and their own feet in their desperation to get away. Rick Souter snatched up a heavy candlestick. With a scowl of rage he ran at the intruder and raised his makeshift weapon to strike.

The drifter swung the sword again. Rick Souter's amputated arm fell to the floor still clutching the candlestick. The blade whooshed down and back up, slitting the butcher from groin to chin so that his innards spilled across the flagstones even before he'd collapsed on his face.

The drifter crouched over the fallen body to dab his fingers into the pool of blood that was rapidly spreading over the church floor. With a look of passionate joy he smeared the blood over his lips, greedily sucked it from his fingers. Then he stood, raised his face to the vaulted ceiling and laughed out loud.

'You think you're safe in here? Think your *God* will protect you?'

The vestry door was bolted from the outside. Lucy Maxwell and the Drinkwaters were desperately trying to force it open, but even as the other choir members joined them, they knew the door wouldn't give. Little Sam howled as his mother clutched him to her. Brian Drinkwater was looking around him in panic for some other way out.

But there wasn't one. They were all trapped in here with the madman.

Charlie Fitch parked his van outside the little church. As he walked briskly down the stone path leading to the door, his mind was still full of his hospital visit to his mother earlier that evening. Thank God she was okay and would be home again soon.

Then Charlie heard the sounds that froze the blood inside his veins. It wasn't the singing of his friends in the choir he could hear from inside the church, nor the playing of the organ. They were screaming.

Screaming in horror and terror. In agony.

He rattled the door handle. The door was locked. He scrambled up the mossy bank behind him so he could peer in through the leaded panes of the stained-glass window.

What he saw inside was a sight that would remain with him until his dying day. The church floor littered with corpses and severed body parts. Blood spattered across the altar, on the pews, on everything.

In the middle of the nightmare stood a man in a long coat. Blood was spattered across his face, his shaven head, and the blade of the sword he was swinging wildly at the fleeing, screeching figure of Lucy Maxwell. It was surreal. Charlie watched as the girl's head was separated from her shoulders by the gore-streaked blade. Then the madman turned to little Sam Drinkwater, who was kneeling by the bloody bodies of his parents, too frightened to scream.

It wasn't until he witnessed what the man did to the boy that Charlie was able to break out of his trance of horror and run. He ran until his heart was about to burst, fell to his knees and ripped his phone out of his pocket.

Nineteen minutes later, the police armed response unit broke in the church door and burst onto the scene of the devastation. The first man inside nearly dropped his weapon when he took in the carnage in front of him.

Nothing remained of the Reverend Keith Perry or his choir members. Nothing except the horrific gobbets of diced human flesh that were scattered across the entire inside of the church.

The killer was still there. He stood calmly at the altar with his back to the door, stripped naked, bloodied from head to foot. His sword lay across the altar in front of him, gore still dripping from its blade. In his powerful hands he held a blood-filled chalice over his head.

The squad leader yelled 'Armed police! Step away from the weapon!'. The man ignored the command and the guns that were aimed at his back. Murmuring softly to himself in a language the officers had never heard before, he slowly turned his face upwards and tipped the bloody contents of the chalice over his head, drinking and slurping greedily.

'*Who the fuck is this person?*' The squad leader didn't even realize he'd spoken those words out loud.

Not until the man at the altar turned round to face him. And said: 'I am a vampire.'

Win an annual film pass with

APOLLO
CINEMAS

Avon are offering one lucky winner the chance to win an annual film pass.

Apollo Cinemas are the UK's largest independent cinema chain serving 2.8m customers a year across its 14 cinemas and 83 screens. Apollo is the market leader with an unrivalled 3D and digital offering through partnerships with global technology brands Sony, RealD and Arqiva. Apollo aims to continue to build the most advanced cinemas in Europe by adopting the latest cinematic technologies and platforms the industry has to offer. To find out more about Apollo Cinemas please visit www.apollocinemas.com.

To enter this free prize draw, simply visit www.harpercollins.co.uk/avon and watch the action-packed trailer for the new book *The Lost Relic* by Scott Mariani to give you the answer to the question below. The closing date for this competition is midday on May 31st 2011.

After watching the brand new trailer for *The Lost Relic* by Scott Mariani, what mode of transport is chasing the lone figure?

A.   A racecar
B   A train
C   A helicopter

4. All entries must be received by midday on 31st May 2011. No entries received after this date will be valid.
5. The prize is one annual film pass for the winner.
6. The prize is non-refundable, non-transferable and subject to availability. No guarantee is given as to the quality of the prize.
7. No cash or prize alternatives are available.
8. HarperCollins reserve the right in their reasonable discretion to substitute any prize with a prize of equal or greater value.
9. The winner of the competition will be drawn at random from all correct entries and notified by phone or post, no later than the 15th June 2011.
10. The prize will be delivered to the winner by 30th September 2011 by registered mail.
11. Any application containing incorrect, false or unreadable information will be rejected. Any applications made on behalf of or for another person or multiple entries will not be included in the competition.
12. HarperCollins' decision as to who has won the competition shall be final.
13. To obtain the name of the prize winner after the closing date, please write to Avon, Lost Relic Competition, HarperCollins Publishers, 77–85 Fulham Palace Road, Hammersmith, London, W6 8JB.
14. The entry instructions are part of the Terms and Conditions for this competition.
15. By entering the competition you are agreeing to accept these Terms and Conditions. Any breach of these Terms and Conditions by you will mean that your entry will not be valid, and you will not be allowed to enter this competition.
16. By entering this competition, you are agreeing that if you win your name and image may be used for the purpose of announcing the winner in any related publicity with HarperCollins, without additional payment or permission.
17. Any personal information you give us will be used solely for this competition and will not be passed on to any other parties without your agreement. HarperCollins' privacy policy can be found at: http://www.harpercollins.co.uk/legal/Pages/privacy-policy.aspx.
18. Under no circumstances will HarperCollins be responsible for any loss, damages, costs or expenses arising from or in any way connected with any errors, defects, interruptions, malfunctions or delays in the promotion of the competition or prize.
19. HarperCollins will not be responsible unless required by law, for any loss, changes, costs or expenses, which may arise in connection with this competition and HarperCollins can cancel or alter the competition at any stage.
20. Any dispute relating to the competition shall be governed by the laws of England and Wales and will be subject to the exclusive jurisdiction of the English courts.